BLACK NEON

BLACK NEON

Tony O'Neill

Bluemoose

Copyright © Tony O'Neill 2014

First published in 2014 by
Bluemoose Books Ltd
25 Sackville Street
Hebden Bridge
West Yorkshire
HX7 7DJ

www.bluemoosebooks.com

British Library Cataloguing-in-Publication data
A catalogue record for this book is available from the British Library

Paperback ISBN 978-1-910422-03-8

Printed and bound in the UK by Short Run Press

"Any movie, even the worst,
is better than real life."

Sebastian Horsley

"When the going gets weird,
the weird turn pro."

Dr. Hunter S. Thompson

ONE

Following an incident a couple of months ago where she almost ended up as the fifth victim of a serial killer who would later become infamous nationally as *The Reno Ripper*, Genesis Shania Neilson usually avoided making dates with guys she met on *Craigslist*. That time her sixth sense had kicked in as soon as she'd laid eyes on the guy. Genesis – who went by "Jenny" at work – had arranged to meet the guy at his apartment building. He lived in a skeezy dump nestled between an auto body shop and a 99¢ Store on the outskirts of town. She told the driver to keep the engine running. When the john answered the door a distinct odour hit her immediately – the heavy scent of bleach, with an undertone of something rotten that she couldn't quite place. There were other things that struck her as being *off* about this guy. His hepatitis-yellow eyes, for one. But it was what she saw behind him, on the corner of the unmade bed, that really sealed the deal. A leather-bound bible that was lying open as if he had just been reading it prior to her arrival. Even from where she was standing Genesis could see that this freak had made numerous neon highlights on the text. So many in fact that there were more words highlighted than not. Before he'd even said a word to her she mumbled something about forgetting her rubbers, then ran back to the cab, jumped in and told the driver to split. She looked back as they pulled out of the forecourt. He was still standing motionless in the doorway, as if somehow expecting the cab to circle around and bring her back to him.

The next time she saw that apartment complex was a few weeks later when she was watching the local news. Apparently the neighbours had complained about the smell coming from that same creep's room, and the Reno PD found the decomposing body parts of several hookers stuffed in a suitcase he kept underneath his bed.

This was the sort of thing, Genesis mused, that could only happen when you met a guy on *Craigslist*.

Sometimes though, the gig looked too easy to turn down. After all, that incident didn't scare her enough to remove her picture and ad from the Casual Encounters section. Now she found herself on another fucked-up *Craigslist* gig, arguing with three college-kid shitheads about how much a gangbang was gonna cost. Genesis had told those assholes that she didn't care whether or not it was the kid's birthday – for sixty bucks only one of them could fuck her. If his goony friends wanted to join in it was gonna cost extra.

"But it's his *birthday*!" one of the assholes protested again – the brawny blond one who looked like a reject from *The Real World,* fitted out in head to toe Ed Hardy crap. "Can't you cut us a deal? You only turn twenty-one *once* for Chrissakes..." When he said this he grinned at her and reached down, giving her ass a clumsy squeeze. She slapped his hand away and shot the kid a *Don't-fuckin-touch-me-before-you-pay-me* look.

"I don't do freebies. Sixty bucks, he gets to fuck me. If you wanna fuck –" she pointed at Ed Hardy, "or if this guy over here wants to fuck," she pointed at the other one, a scrawny Asian kid wearing a backwards baseball cap and American Apparel T-shirt, "then you gotta pay."

American Apparel looked up from his laptop, where he was tapping away distractedly. He sniffed and pushed his glasses further up his nose. "What if we want to watch?"

"Then call it an even hundred."

"Forty bucks to *watch*? What about if we, uh..." Ed Hardy made a jerking motion with his hand, "You know... *beat off*?"

Genesis shrugged, "No skin off my ass."

At this the birthday boy perked up a little. "Shit, this bitch is a real class act..." he slurred, "Where d'ya find her? Hanging around outside a fuckin' methadone clinic?"

"I found her on fuckin' *Craigslist*, Chad!" bellowed Ed Hardy, "Who'd you fuckin' expect was gonna show up? Anne Hathaway? Stop being such a fuckin' wuss."

The birthday boy was already stripped down to his boxer shorts, slumped across a couch in a corner of the suite. He had a goofy-looking paper hat on his head and a half empty can of Four Loko wedged between his legs.

Genesis had been in these college kids' suite at the Sands in Reno for only ten minutes, but she was already starting to get pissed off. For a start, Ed Hardy hadn't mentioned that there'd be a frat party going on when he'd called to make arrangements an hour ago. Second, these fucking kids were annoying the crap out of her. They were drunk as hell, and when the birthday boy – a smug little asswipe who looked like he got kicked off of an Army recruiting billboard – answered the door, he'd made some snide fucking comment about her looking like a crack whore. Not to say that Genesis hadn't been smoking crack before she came over, but she didn't appreciate the condescension in the snot-nosed bastard's voice. To top it all off, they didn't even have any decent drugs in the place.

"You want some of this?" American Apparel had asked when she'd first walked into the suite. He was holding a bong fashioned out of a two-litre Mountain Dew bottle, and a lighter. For an optimistic moment she'd thought that they were smoking rocks. "Whatcha got in there?" she asked. She took the bong from him with a coy smile. Although her preferred drugs were painkillers and crystal meth, Genesis still felt her stomach gurgle with anticipation at the very idea of smoking some cocaine.

"Salvia," the kid said with a shit-eating grin on his face. "Totally sweet stuff too."

Genesis's smile evaporated. She made a face and handed the bong back to him. What the fuck was this? An after school special or something?

After they'd finally negotiated the price, Genesis looked over to the birthday boy. He was nervously taking a slug from his booze. Eager to finish up and get out of here, Genesis tucked the bills in her purse and headed into the bathroom. She took a piss then gave herself a cursory wipe with a damp facecloth. She rummaged through her purse. Besides the money she had a bullet full of meth, a keychain with a miniature can of pepper spray attached, rubbers, a switchblade, and a tube of KY. She stared at her reflection in the bathroom mirror.

Genesis was in her mid-twenties, although you couldn't tell at first glance. She'd been a pretty girl when she was a teenager, but drugs and hard living had aged her dramatically. She still had the body though. She'd lived in Reno most of her life and had always planned on leaving as soon as she was old enough. A guy called Duane she'd met while working at Dairy Queen had introduced her to speed when she was sixteen. That particular relationship hadn't lasted more than a month or so, but her relationship with crank was a different story. Drugs made living in Reno seem bearable and when she was high life didn't seem so oppressive any more. By the time she was old enough to leave town the idea of getting out of Reno had receded, like the ache of a rotten tooth that you somehow learn to deal with over time. Meth made dull people seem interesting, crappy jobs more fun, ugly guys more attractive, and for once her brain seemed to finally catch up with her constantly racing mouth. No, for a while, meth had been the perfect solution.

It was only when she was coming down again that she remembered how badly she'd once wanted to get out of this lousy city for good. But while meth had made living in Reno more bearable, it made getting out of Reno almost impossible. The outside world was an unknown, a gamble, while drugs were her only certainty. The idea of heading to a strange city, one where she had no friends, no place to live and, worst of all, no drug connections filled her with foreboding. Nights like this reminded her of how she'd once promised herself that she would escape, for sure. Nights like this were enough to make her seriously consider just getting on a Greyhound and striking out for anyplace else. But she knew the horrors that awaited her if she ever went without drugs for long enough, so Genesis fell into a passive acceptance of her fate. For the time being, at least, she was stuck.

She pulled her shirt over her head and slipped her denim skirt off. She stepped out of her underwear and carefully folded her clothes in a pile by the sink. Naked, she reached into her purse, retrieved the bullet, and took a quick blast of meth in each nostril before she stepped out into the hotel suite to give the birthday boy his present.

The college kids were blasting a Kanye West album while Genesis got to work. The two goons were somewhere behind her while she tried to coax the birthday boy's pecker into life with her mouth. The birthday boy was complaining the whole time. "Aw Jesus, this is so skeezy. I feel like I'm in an episode of fuckin' *Intervention* or somethin'..."

Ignoring his comments, Genesis kept working his dick, determined to get this kid hard so she could finish him off as quickly as possible. When he was firm enough she reached down, ripped the packet open, and started rolling the rubber onto him. When it was in place she pushed him back onto the couch and straddled him backwards so she didn't have to look at his dumb fucking face. As she slid herself onto him she muttered, "Oh shit baby that feels so good," in her disinterested, practiced way. The other two assholes were leering at her. Ed Hardy had his pants around his ankles and was jerking off, red faced, his tongue hanging out of his mouth like a thirsty dog. American Apparel was sitting on the bed, half watching as he fucked around with his phone. She had just started to get into her rhythm when she noticed that the little fucker was holding

5

the phone up, watching her through the screen. She immediately stopped what she was doing and pointed an accusatory finger at the kid.

"Hey asshole!"

American Apparel ignored her, so she raised her voice further.

"You! Are you fucking *filming* me, you little prick?"

The kid looked up with a guilty look on his face. "Uh... uh... no... what, me?"

"Yeah you, fuck face! Are you fucking *filming me*?"

"No, I, uh." the kid put the phone down, "I wasn't doing nothing!"

Genesis got up, and felt the birthday boy's softening penis slide out of her as he groaned, "Aw Jesus!"

Ed Hardy leapt to his feet, and clipped American Apparel around the back of the head.

"What the fuck you stammering for, you chickenshit? Gimmie that thing!"

He grabbed the iPhone, and pointed it at Genesis and continued to film her as she stormed over to him. "Bitch, we paid you to fuck him, so fuck him!"

The birthday boy was on his feet now, pulling his shorts up. "Fuck this," he said, "I'm not in the mood any more."

Genesis tried to grab the phone from Ed Hardy. He was taller than her, and started making a game of dangling it just out of her reach. "We fuckin' paid you already," he laughed, "What's the problem?"

"You can't film me, asshole!"

"Says who?"

"Says ME!"

There was a *thump*, and suddenly everything went grey. It took Genesis a moment to realize that Ed Hardy had punched her in the face. Now she was sprawled on the carpet. Her entire head felt numb. Panic gripped her. She felt Ed Hardy's weight squeezing the air out of her as he straddled her chest. He smacked her again, open palm this time. She felt the coppery taste of blood in her mouth.

From somewhere far away she heard one of the others yelling at him to stop it. Screaming that he was hurting her.

Through her haze she heard Ed Hardy's mocking voice repeating 'Stop it! You're HURTING her!'

Then she was moving.

Genesis was being dragged toward the bed.

*

Later, Genesis was in the bathroom cleaning up. She felt tender, achy. She could hear them arguing in whispered voices outside.

– *The fuck is wrong with you, bro?*
– *I don't feel so good, that's all.*
– *Stop being such a pussy.*
– *I just feel bad. Leave it, okay?*

She looked at herself in the mirror.

Ed Hardy had raped her first.

He was pretty enthusiastic about the whole thing and it had had gone on for at least five or ten minutes. The others didn't want to do it, but Ed Hardy wasn't taking no for an answer. When he was done he yelled "boo-yah!" and gave the others high fives. The birthday boy was up next. He had been the worst, because he kept stopping every few minutes and asking if that was enough. Genesis was facedown on the bed, ears still ringing from that punch to the face, willing them to just get it over with quickly. Every time the birthday boy stopped thrusting Ed Hardy would clip him around the ear and demand that he finish the job. She heard the kid vomiting when he was done. American Apparel went next, but he couldn't stay hard. After a few unenthusiastic thrusts, punctuated by Ed Hardy guffawing and making racially tinged jokes about the size of his cock, the kid faked an orgasm and pulled out. Then she heard them opening more beer.

She got to her feet cautiously, before making it to the bathroom.

She locked the door after her.

She stared at her reflection. Her face was gonna bruise up, no doubt about it.

    –The fucking bitch loved it. She's a fucking crackwhore, Chad. You don't think she does worse than that to feed her habit like every fucking day? Wake up, dude.

    – I guess. It's just... you know. Rape, and all.

    – Don't use that fucking word! How the fuck can you RAPE a crackwhore, dude?

She insulated herself in two more blasts of meth. Fully dressed now, she opened the bathroom door and stepped out. She stared at them. American Apparel and the birthday boy were sitting on the bed looking like the sorriest assholes you'd ever seen. Ed Hardy was taking a slug of beer and parading up and down, his shaved chest glistening with sweat. He looked at Genesis. Smiled at her. Reached into his jeans and pulled out a fifty-dollar bill.

"Hey. Look, we're sorry if we got a little rough on you. No hard feelings, okay? Here's a tip."

    She stared at him like he had two heads. He sniggered a little. Added, "Go buy yourself some crack or somethin."

    Genesis looked the asshole up and down. "Go fuck yourself," she said.

She took the fifty anyway.

Ed Hardy walked her to the door. Genesis rummaged around in her purse as she went. He opened it for her. Playing the gentleman. As she went to step outside Genesis spun around and hit him in the face with a good blast of the pepper spray.

His hands went to his eyes reflexively.

As they did she brought her right hand up sharply.

Her blade missed his balls by a fraction. It sunk instead into his meaty thigh, tearing easily through the femoral artery.

Before the others knew what was happening Genesis was running along the corridors of the hotel, out through an emergency exit setting off a keening alarm, her high heels clattering wildly as she raced down the stairs leading toward the lobby. Ed Hardy was rolling around on the floor of the suite screaming. A powerful geyser of hot crimson pumped from his groin in time with the frenzied, rhythmic beating of his heart.

*

A few blocks away from the hotel she called Paco, a crazy Puerto Rican meth chemist she'd been seeing for the past few months. He sounded wired and antsy when he picked up. She told him she would stop by later. Paco never slept, at least not at night. Like most of the people Genesis could relate to, he was burning the candle at both ends. Even if she closed her eyes and tried real hard she couldn't imagine Paco as an old man. He was definitely more the 'die young, leave a good-looking corpse' type.

Paco was tweaked out and horny when Genesis's cab pulled up outside his place. He kicked Lilly – a strung-out Vietnamese chick who hung around from time to time – out the door as soon as he got a look at Genesis. *I sure as hell fucked a lotta hot bitches in my time,* Paco would tell Genesis when he was feeling romantic, *but there iz something about you that pushes my motherfuckin' buttons.* The girl was trashy and built like some centrefold wet dream: tiny waist, big silicone tits, a good-sized ass for a blanquita, and to top it all off she was a fiend for meth. The girl would do just about anything in exchange for a teenth. She was exactly the kind of girl that Paco loved: white, strung out, and all kinds of mixed up.

"You look like you had a shitty night," Paco said closed the door behind her.

"The worst."

"Come on, girl..." he said, "Let's take a blast and you can tell me all about that shit."

Paco's place was small and dismal, and stunk of the chemicals he used to cook up meth. The kitchen was a riot of test tubes, Bunsen burners, rubber hosing and funnels. Paco was a brutal, handsome bastard with mismatched blue and green eyes, long straight black hair down to his ass, and a taste for cheap wine and violence. He ran with some boys from Tijuana who moved the raw ingredients for methamphetamine over the border from crooked Mexican pharmaceutical outfits. He claimed to have killed four men. "Or seven," he would add laughing, "If you count *miyates.*" Tattooed round his neck was an incomplete chain of skulls, four white, three black.

He led her to the bedroom. Soon they were lying in bed naked, passing a 50oz jug of grape flavour Wild Irish Rose between them, smoking cigarettes and tweaking out. Genesis was running her hand over Paco's taut chest, admiring the definition of his muscles, and the prison tattoos that covered almost every inch of his mahogany skin. Paco had always been good to her, never made her beg for dope or gave her hassle when she asked for credit. Plus he was good in bed, with a thick cock and expert fingers. She supposed she would have gotten down with him even if he *hadn't* been a dealer.

"You know something?" Genesis said.

"Wassat, girl?"

"I'm thinking it's time for me to move on. Get out of Reno."

Paco snorted. "Where the fuck would *you* go?"

"Maybe to LA. Maybe up to Vegas, or San Francisco or something."

"Shit, sounds like a dumb idea to me. Why you gonna go fuck up a good thing, huh? You workin' for yourself, making good scratch. Why you wanna go fuck up a good thing?"

"You wouldn't miss me, baby. Would you?"

Paco rubbed Genesis's hair. "Sure I'd miss you."

Genesis lit a Capri menthol light, and exhaled a cloud of grey smoke. "It's not like you'd be lonely. You got plenty of bitches. You could call that chink bitch Lilly again."

"Fuck that bitch," Paco scowled. "That bitch is a pain in my ass. Always begging for free dope. Bitch is so skinny I get bruises when I fuck her."

"Doesn't stop you, though."

Paco sucked air through his teeth. "I'm a free agent, baby."

"Me too."

They lay there in silence for a while, smoking and listening to the sound of crickets.

"So you tellin' me you really gonna split this time? You always *sayin'* you gonna do it but ya never do."

"Sure. Why not? Ain't nothing doing here. I mean, I just get this feeling like life is just... it's passing me by, you know? I mean, there's gotta be something else, hasn't there?"

"Hold that thought."

Paco got up and stretched. "Gotta take a piss."

Paco swaggered out of the room. When he was out of sight Genesis sat up and looked around. She'd told Paco plenty of times that she was going to split. Pretty much every time she had a bad night she'd swear she was leaving Reno for good. This time felt different, though. It wasn't what happened tonight. It was as if her disgust with her life could no longer be kept at bay, not even by the pacifying effect of the drugs. There was nothing to stop her from just getting on a bus and getting the fuck out. If she had enough money and enough drugs to make it a couple of weeks, then she was sure she'd be able to find her feet.

A sudden thought occurred to Genesis, one that made her stomach woozy with the sudden lurch of vertigo. She knew damn well that under the bed was a box with ounce-baggies of meth all weighed out and ready to go. *Why not just grab one of those suckers and get the hell out?* The idea of helping herself to one had always been a temptation of course, but fear kept her from acting upon that impulse. Genesis had no doubt that if she ever stole from him Paco would snap her fucking neck without a second thought. No, if she was going to do something as dumb as that then she'd better be damn sure she never showed her face around here again.

But if she was *really* serious about splitting tonight...

She sat up, quickly. She couldn't hear Paco coming back. If she did it, she'd have to do it *now*. Do it before her nerve gave out. Quietly she rolled off the bed, dropping to the grimy rug on her knees. Reaching under the bed she felt the box – a black, faux-leather number she'd seen Paco reach for many times. She slid it out, and flipped the lid open. There were several large ounce baggies of meth inside, lying there like Jesus, like a million dollars. All she had to do was slip one in her purse quick. Like right fucking now.

Over the sound of the blood pounding in her ears, she didn't hear the quiet footsteps behind her.

Holding her breath she grabbed the baggie. Held it to her breast. Slid the box back under the bed and –

"Bitch! What the fuck you think you're doing?"

Before she could react, Paco had grabbed Genesis by the hair and stubbed his cigarette out against her forehead, making her flesh sizzle. She dropped the baggie and opened her mouth to beg forgiveness. Paco punched her. Everything went hazy for the second time that night. Cursing furiously in Spanish, Paco dragged her across the bedroom by the hair, and aimed several swift kicks at Genesis's behind along the way. She was on the floor, scrabbling around and yelping in pain, trying to grab her clothes while Paco booted her and screamed at her like a disobedient animal.

"All the free fuckin shit I give you, and you try an' fuckin *steal from* me, you cunt whore?"

In between her ragged cries of pain Genesis begged him to calm down, but Paco was too far-gone. He was shaking with rage. Eyes bloodshot and dangerous. Spittle flew out of his mouth as he cursed and screamed. He grabbed a pistol from the bedside cabinet and smashed the butt violently across her face, rattling her teeth. She tasted blood in back of her throat. She clambered up, half ran, half limped away from him, desperately trying to escape before he could set upon her again. Paco tucked the pistol into the waistband of his underwear and stalked after her. She'd almost made it to the screen door and when a brutal kick to the ass sent her sprawling out through it. She landed on the concrete driveway with a thump, followed moments later by her clothes as Paco tossed them out after her.

13

Genesis scrambled to her feet, blindly trying to escape Paco's fury. She suddenly stopped, finding her escape route blocked by a strange figure. In all of the chaos she hadn't noticed the black Eldorado that had pulled up outside of Paco's place.

The headlights beamed directly onto Genesis, blinding her momentarily.

She blinked and tried to focus her eyes.

She found herself looking into the face of an extremely beautiful, extremely pissed off Latin girl.

The woman that blocked her way was striking, short and lean, with the broad, powerful face of an Aztec earth goddess. Their eyes met. In that frozen moment of contact Genesis swore she saw red flames flickering inside of the irises. In less than a second the woman sized Genesis up and then roughly pushed her aside. Genesis sprawled on the sandy concrete with a yell. The woman yelled at Paco: "Nigga, you just burned the *wrong* bitch!"

Paco was standing in the doorway, his imposing frame silhouetted by the light from the hall.

"Who-zat?" he said cupping his hands to his eyes and peering out into the darkness. "Lupita? Izzat you, you crazy fuckin' bitch?"

"I ain't no bitch, an' I object strongly to you usin' such antiquated fucking sexist terms around me, *carbon*." Cowering on the ground, Genesis watched as Lupita raised her arm and aimed a pistol at Paco. "I want my goddamned money. Now, fuckin' *Maldito Bori!*"

As soon as he saw the gun, Paco shut the fuck up and stood very still. He was naked except for his tight, white shorts. He became very aware of the pressure of his own gun, pressing into the small of his back. His long hair hung down to his hips,

14

thick and shiny. His body was tough and wiry, not a spare inch of flesh on it. He was about to open his mouth and – very carefully – suggest that Lupita be reasonable and stop pointing that fucking gun at him so they could talk like civilized human beings, when Genesis – still lying semi-naked on the ground – suddenly screamed, "Look out – HE'S GOT A GUN!"

Paco raised his hand instinctively. He was going to yell at Genesis to shut the fuck up. Four loud pops cut him off. Paco flipped backwards. Both feet flew straight up into the air. He hit the ground with a heavy thump. When Genesis opened her eyes she couldn't see Paco anymore, just his bare feet poking out of the doorway. The doorframe had several dark splatters on it. Genesis looked up at Lupita. Lupita stared in Paco's direction for a moment before looking down at her. She smiled, cautiously.

"Thanks," Lupita said.

She tucked the gun away and held out her hand, helping Genesis to her feet. Genesis' knees were badly cut. She could feel the hot blood trickling down one leg. She stood there shivering in the chill air, wearing just her panties. Lupita looked her up and down slowly. There was a curious expression on her face.

"Was he your old man?" she asked.

Genesis shook her head.

"He's, uh, he was just my connection. We were just getting high. All of a sudden he bugged out, ripped my clothes off, started beating the shit out of me. I dunno what set him off..." Genesis's voice dropped to a hoarse whisper. "I think he woulda killed me if you hadn't come along."

Lupita put out her hand and lightly brushed Genesis's swollen face with her fingertips. "No kidding," she said.

Lupita and Genesis stared at each other. Genesis found her eyes fascinating. They were hazel, with pale yellow centres. Genesis felt something in the pit of her guts, a pleasant, woozy sensation, like taking painkillers on an empty stomach. It was then that she noticed for the first time that the girl's left arm ended abruptly at the elbow. How had she not noticed this before? She was wearing a white T-shirt, with a leather biker vest over it. The left arm tapered down to a point, ending in a smooth, unscarred stump that was the same caramel brown as the rest of her skin.

"Is – is he dead?" Genesis asked, nodding towards Paco.

"I dunno," Lupita said, shrugging. She casually rested her hand on the handle of the gun jutting out of her waistband. "You knew him better than I did. That motherfucker ever say anything to you about being bulletproof?"

"Bulletproof?" Genesis repeated in an unsure voice, "No, I guess not. Don't *think* so."

"Well then, I'd say the chances are he's dead. He caught two in the chest and one in the neck. That'd fuck up anyone's weekend, if ya ask me."

Lupita drew the gun again and cautiously walked over to the doorway, her heavy black motorcycle boots clumping against the concrete steps. Stepping into the doorway, she cautiously prodded Paco's body with her foot. Wedging one foot underneath him, she flipped him over with a grunt. She pulled the gun out of his shorts, checked the chamber, and pocketed it. She started looking around the hallway and found the fourth bullet lodged in a far wall, next to a holy water dispenser with an image of the Virgin of Guadalupe on it. She dipped her gun into the water and silently crossed herself with it.

16

Meanwhile Genesis scrabbled around trying to gather up her clothes. She managed to locate her T-shirt. She pulled it over her head, covering herself a little. From inside the hallway she heard Lupita say, "This asshole's gun wasn't even loaded."

"Huh?"

"The gun. It wasn't even loaded."

"Oh."

Genesis crept towards the house cautiously and peered down at Paco. There was a lot of blood. Those weird, mismatched eyes stared back at her, vacant and dull. She looked away again. "He pulled it on me. Hit me with it," she said, "I thought he was gonna shoot me."

In the light, Genesis got a better look at the woman who killed Paco. Her raven-black hair was styled in a pompadour, and her eyebrows had been shaved and meticulously painted back in place. She had a teardrop inked on one cheek and wore a studded biker vest with tight black jeans and steel-toe boots. Her lips were full and painted black, making her mouth seem even larger than it already was. She had a curious expression on her face. Genesis couldn't quite place it. Lupita tucked her gun away casually.

"Well, I guess that's just his tough shit. What kind of asshole runs around with an unloaded gun, anyway?"

Genesis shrugged.

"What's your name?"

"Genesis. Genesis Shania Neilson. But my friends call me... Jenny."

"Jenny?" Lupita snorted. "That's kinda weak, if you don't mind me saying, hun. I guess I'm just gonna call you by your proper name if that's all the same to you. Genesis, I'm Lupita Philadelphia Santos-Lucero Fatima de Garcia. Pleased to meet you."

Lupita looked out to where her car was parked and sighed, "I guess we'd better get the fuck out of here, before some fuckin' solid citizen calls the cops or something. You know where Paco kept his shit? Drugs, money, that kinda stuff?"

"The drugs are in a lock box under the bed. I don't know where the cash is."

Lupita nodded. "Why don't I grab everything, an' you can get dressed. You leave any of your stuff in here?"

"Don't think so."

"Wallet, ID, anything that can be traced back to you?"

Genesis shook her head.

"Okay. Good. Oh and Genesis, hun?"

"Yeah?"

"Don't go running off now. I'd really hate to shoot a pretty thing like you in the back, but I will do if I have to, you know what I mean?"

Genesis nodded, and Lupita headed into Paco's place. Genesis started hunting around for her clothes, pulling them on in a state of numb shock. Lupita emerged from the house a few moments later with a purse, a pair of stilettos and the drugs. "I guess the shoes are yours?" she said, "They don't look like they're his size."

"Oh shit, thanks."

Lupita tossed them over.

"You can walk in those things?"

Genesis shot a nervous grin. "Hell, I could tap dance in these babies."

"No shit? Maybe you can teach me that sometime." Lupita cleared her throat. "Genesis, I hope you wont think I'm being too forward but I'm hoping you don't got any plans?"

Genesis shrugged.

"Good. The thing is I'm not so inclined to just let you wander off after you saw me waste Paco like that. Doesn't seem smart. Now my first instinct would just be kill you, you know? I don't

18

much like leaving witnesses, never have. Thing is, this mother-fucker here was pretty connected, and I got the feeling I'm gonna have to leave town for a while and let things cool off. Until then… well, I can't have you talking to no-one."

Genesis nodded, but didn't say anything. Instead she watched Lupita with eyes that were a curious mix of fear and fascination.

"But we'll cross that bridge when we come to it. First things first – I'm kinda hungry, and I know a good diner about twenty minutes from here that should be open. I'd like to buy you breakfast, if you don't mind, maybe head back to my place later until I work out just what in the hell I'm gonna do with you. If you ain't okay with that… then I guess we've arrived at what the French call an *impasse*. What d'you say?"

Genesis managed to choke out the words, "Breakfast sounds good."

Lupita walked closer to Genesis and dropped her voice; "Look… I don't want you to think that I'm some sort of crazy killer because I plugged Paco here. This fucker burnt me on a dope deal and assumed he could get away with it because I'm a female. Even so, I was just planning on getting my money back when I came here tonight. I shot that motherfucker because I thought that he was gonna shoot me first. As you know."

Genesis nodded. Lupita brushed her swelling cheek with her finger and smiled, catching Genesis momentarily off guard. "So, now we got all the formalities out of the way Miss Genesis, would you like to join me for breakfast?"

Genesis looked over to Paco's corpse. "Sure," she said.

They walked to Lupita's car together. She was driving a black 1970 Cadillac Eldorado. Genesis could feel one of her eyes swelling shut already, and a portion of her face felt numb. She couldn't help but feel that Paco had gotten what he deserved as far as tonight went. Lupita opened the passenger door for Genesis and said, "Lemmie ask you a question."

"Shoot."

"You like biscuits and gravy?"

"Sure."

"Good. This is one of the only places in Reno were you can get biscuits and gravy as good as down south. It's a real find. C'mon. My treat."

Genesis got in the car. The dashboard clock read 4.15am. The sun was already creeping guiltily into the sky. Lupita walked around and got in, jamming the key into the ignition. The engine roared into life. Another strange day had begun.

TWO

Jacques Seltzer was a large man, tall and intimidating. He weighed an easy three hundred, and was swollen with money and good living. He was a man of insatiable appetites. He loved good food, fine wines, beautiful women and all kinds of extreme experiences. He pursued each and every one of his vices hungrily. At forty-three he remained a confirmed bachelor, and paid a handsome amount to each of the four children he had – up until this point – sired around the globe. He was balding, his remaining hair pulled back into a black, greasy ponytail. His left eye, which had been injured in a fencing accident when he was seventeen, hid behind an eye-patch that Jacques wore as a tribute to the director Nicholas Ray. Although he could not be called a handsome man by any means, his face carried the relaxed air of a man who had never had to deal with the daily shit of the real world.

His father was the notorious multi-billionaire shipping magnate Jean-Noel Seltzer II. Unlike his older brother Javier, he did not follow his father into the lucrative world of importing and exporting. The younger Seltzer had always been a dreamy child, artistic and temperamental, and easily his mother's favourite. Rootless and shiftless, he'd dabbled in oil painting, homosexuality, petty crime, poetry, drug use and the stock market with varying degrees of success. It was in the mid-nineteen-eighties, following a short-lived but intense love affair with the renowned fashion photographer Francoise Purcell, that Jacques Seltzer finally found his true calling: photography.

Jacques's success in this field was swift and lucrative. His first book was a collection of portraits of Dutch amputee prostitutes entitled *Wide Eyed and Legless*. It was a runaway success in Europe. Soon the infamy of the younger Seltzer surpassed even that of his well-connected and obscenely wealthy family. His images of Palestinian refugees – published in France as *An Auschwitz of Their Own* – won several awards and cemented his reputation as an *enfant terrible*, a provocateur and a lightning rod for controversy.

However it was Seltzer's lone foray into cinema, directing and writing the cult masterpiece *Dead Flowers* that briefly made him a household name. The film, made on a shoestring budget, was condemned and praised in equal measure. The New York Times declared it, "A masterpiece – brave, harrowing and repulsive, but at its core a truly groundbreaking piece of Art." In one of her final reviews, Pauline Kael – writing in the New Yorker – described *Dead Flowers* as, "Vile, scabrous, an assault on the senses that leaves the viewer feeling utterly violated." Soon after its release, *Dead Flowers* sat proudly alongside *The Birth Of A Nation* and *Pink Flamingos* as one of the highest grossing independent movies of all time.

Although it earned him millions, Jacques Seltzer never made another movie. Some blamed this on the car crash in St Tropez a few weeks after the release of *Dead Flowers*. His passenger was killed and Jacques spent a small fortune dodging drunk-driving charges. The resulting scandal forever tainted his reputation in Europe. The proposed follow up, which Jacques had talked of occasionally in the press, was known only by the title *Black Neon*. Apart from the title, little else seemed to exist of the movie outside of Jacques' mind. Obscenely wealthy, and disgusted by the notion that he should have to be *productive*, Seltzer was content to instead spend his days travelling, taking photographs, and consuming vast quantities of exotic drugs. As the months turned into years, and the years into over a decade, his agent's pleas for Jacques to come out of his "retirement" and start work on *Black Neon* grew more desperate. The answer was always the same: "The time is not *right* yet." With no actual *need* to make money, Jacques was content to pursue his photography and enjoy the lifestyle his wealth afforded him. He had no hunger for the kind of commitments and deadlines that another film would entail. As time went on his legend as a filmmaker – and the legend of *Black Neon* – continued to grow among hardcore movie aficionados. The title was bandied about endlessly on message boards and Internet forums, a subject of seemingly endless speculation. *Black Neon* often made the top ten "Most Legendary" lists of movie magazines and websites despite the fact that nobody – with the possible exception of Jacques – knew anything about it. All anybody had to go on was that vague, ambiguous title.

Unable to survive on fifteen per cent of the earnings of a legendary director who no longer made movies but preferred to occasionally produce photography books for three thousand dollar advances for obscure European publishing houses, Jacques' agent – Gibby Getnor – was pushed to the brink of penury. Today he was in Paris to make one final, desperate attempt to get his wayward client back into the directing chair.

Jacques was wearing a powder blue three-piece vintage suit by Dior, and custom-made snakeskin Chelsea boots. He was devouring a plate of Sevruga caviar, toast and sour cream, and was already on his second bottle of a fine vintage red at his usual table at Les Deux Magots, in Paris' Saint-Germain-des-Prés. Across from him, in a wrinkled Banana Republic suit, was Gibby Getnor. Getnor was hung over, pale and unshaven. He was bald and his once sparkling eyes now hid behind drooping lids. They had heavy, dark bags underneath them. He had once been considered a handsome man, but life had taken a heavy toll on his face. He was often mistaken for being a decade or more older than his forty-nine years. Neither the warm April sun that bathed Paris today, nor the sight of the countless beautiful French women strolling around the streets in their summer dresses, sleek and unobtainable as gold-plated Cadillacs, could improve Getnor's mood. He had drunk with his client until three this morning, ostensibly celebrating Seltzer's latest masterpiece, a dark collection of images showing the squalid lives of working class youths in stagnant Northern English mill towns. Now Getnor's bleary eyes hid painfully behind dark sunglasses. He waited patiently for Jacques to finish jabbering about his new book, so he could hit him with his latest proposal. He avoided looking directly at the man who had once been his highest earning client, as Seltzer hungrily heaped piles of slimy black fish eggs on his toast and talked incessantly through a mouthful of food.

"The kids in those little towns... they were *fucked*, Gibby. Nineteen, twenty years old and they looked like... the walking dead. Already two, three babies crawling around their council houses with runny noses and shitty asses. Pale, wrinkled, bloated, all the life sucked out of them!"

"I know the feeling," Gibby said, weakly.

"Oh for fuck's sake, Gibby. You rotten Americans cannot handle your drink. Now those kids in England – *they* know how to drink. Up there, in those little mill towns in Lancashire and Yorkshire, they stay solidly drunk from the age of twelve until the time comes that they inevitably die in a pool of their own urine. They smoke revolting low-grade hash, sniff glue and guzzle cheap lager from morning to night. On weekends, the girls stagger around these nowhere towns in miniskirts and high heels despite the fact that it is zero degrees outside, raining and snowing... and they puke, and piss, and fuck right there in the streets. They were *doomed* Gibby. Apathetic, bored, addled by alcohol, and totally *inspiring*. Imagine! I was with them for six weeks, drinking with them, observing them, and photographing them." Jacques lit an unfiltered Gitanes Brunes, took a long drag, and blew the smoke up into the cloudless blue sky. "What a trip!" he grinned.

Gibby's nose wrinkled at the smell of the strong French tobacco. One thing he could not get used to in this country was the smell of cigarette smoke wafting out from every fucking direction. Since smoking had been practically outlawed in public back in California, the sight of someone openly sucking on a cigarette at the lunch table was as disconcerting to Gibby as seeing someone injecting heroin while waiting for their croque-monsieur. Plus, ever since he'd quit smoking a decade ago the smell of tobacco revolted him. "It's an incredible set of images, Jacques." Gibby spluttered, "Undoubtedly your best work yet."

Jacques nodded, smiling broadly. He filled his glass again, topping off his agent's glass as well, and then took a thirsty gulp. He wiped his moist red lips with the back of his hand. Gibby took another sip from his own glass, hoping that by pouring more wine onto his hangover he might feel somewhat human in time for his flight back to LAX in a few hours. At this particular moment the very idea of getting onto an airplane was terrifying. He couldn't decide whether his most pressing urge was to vomit, shit, or pass out. Instead of doing any of those, he said: "Jacques, I have something I want to talk to you about."

"Ah-hah!" Jacques exclaimed, blowing a great cloud of grey smoke in Gibby's face, "Here it comes! Your ulterior motive, Gibby... as plain as the broken blood vessels on your nose!"

"Please Jacques, this is serious."

Gibby took a hard slug of his wine to steady himself.

"Are you going to ask me about this fucking movie *merde* again?" Jacques demanded, deflating Gibby expertly.

"Hear me out!" Gibby whined.

"Oh JESUS!"

"Wait! Just listen. An offer came through, I just wanna relate it to you, and that's it. No pressure from me, okay?"

Jacques rolled his eyes. Sullenly he shrugged and waved a dismissive hand toward Gibby as if to say *Go ahead*. Gibby cleared his throat.

"Have you heard of Kenny Azura?"

"*Non.*"

"He's the new head of Chainsaw Pictures, a brand new subdivision of Dreamscape Studios. This guy is the hottest shit in Hollywood right now. He's only twenty-eight fucking years old, but he's already got a résumé to die for. Everything this bastard touches turns to gold. Did you ever see *Endless Black*?"

"No."

"*The Piano Tuner*?"

"No."

"*The Seventeen Wives of Zachary Turner*?"

"No."

Gibby sighed and rubbed his throbbing temples dejectedly.

"Well Jacques, all of them are critically successful and high grossing movies with one thing in common. They were all produced by Kenny Azura. Hollywood Reporter calls him "The Boy King of Hollywood". Now he has his own production company the first thing he wants to do – the VERY first thing, Jacques – is to bankroll *Black Neon*, which he envisions as your triumphant return to cinema. *Dead Flowers* is his all-time, number one, favourite movie. He's offering deep pockets, the support of one of the biggest studios in the business, and complete artistic control. He's exact words to me were, "*Whatever Jacques wants to do with Black Neon, I want to make it possible.*" Jacques – nobody gets offered this kind of deal in Hollywood anymore. It's totally unheard of. And all you have to do... is say YES."

There was a frozen moment at the table, as Jacques seemed to actually consider Gibby's pitch. Then Seltzer sighed, reached under the table, and produced a manila envelope.

"Gibby," he said emphatically, "How can I do this movie when the time is still not *right* yet? Tell them thanks... but no thanks. Now, back to the book. Take a look at this. I have an idea for the title. Tell me what you think, okay? Imagine the cover."

Gibby choked back his disappointment as Jacques opened the envelope and slid out a glossy, black and white A4 image. He held it up to Gibby. Gibby had of course seen the image before. It was one of the standouts of the new collection. At first glance it looked like a simple enough nighttime shot of one of those typical featureless, suburban English chain pubs. However, soon the eye was drawn to the alleyway, next to the pub itself. A row of overflowing rubbish bins. A 'dead end' sign at the mouth of the alley. Illuminated by the harsh street light was a couple, fucking. The man had his back to the camera, pants around his ankles and a long white dress shirt covering his bare ass. He was thrusting into a girl, who was sitting on one of the bins. Her legs were wrapped around him. Her panties hung from one of her ankles like a flag of surrender. She had her hand on his ass, pushing him deeper into her. The other was holding a bottle of booze, which she sucked on as they screwed. The heart of the image – when you peered close enough – was the girl's face. She was bleached blonde, overweight, some indeterminate age between sixteen and forty, and heavily made-up. Her painted lips were wrapped round the neck of the bottle. Her eyes looked at the viewer – through the viewer, really – with a haunting expression that floated somewhere in between despair and utter boredom.

"*Teenage Hole*:" Jacques announced in a voice trembling with pride, "*Snapshots from the Void*."

Gibby sat in silence, regarding the picture intently. Then he removed his glasses, and rubbed his red eyes. He smiled and muttered weakly, "Yeah, I like it Jacques..." He replaced the sunglasses and muttered, "Sounds *great.*"

THREE

Jeffrey was snoring softly, oblivious to the rat-at-tat of air hammers and the whine of road drills outside of his room at the Gilbert Hotel in Hollywood. Agents of Progress were busy trying to raze this section of the city and replace it with something more palatable. Surrounding this seedy quadrant of flophouses, peepshows, grimy fast food restaurants and seedy bars were million-dollar condominiums, Zagat-rated eating establishments, boutique hotels and other signs of the steady encroachment of the young, the beautiful and the stupefyingly dull. With each passing day they displaced the population of this temporal, transient city-within-a-city inch by inch, a street corner at a time. But for now they hung on, like a stubborn rodent infestation.

Sitting up in the bed next to him was Rachel, Jeffrey's lover. Rachel was a concentration-camp-thin transvestite whose ebony-black skin was pressed tight against her bones, her face all angles and shadows. She silently smoked her first cigarette of the day, with unsteady hands. Thick, black stubble was pushing through last night's foundation, and her shaved skull was hidden underneath a black wig cap. Around the room were several Styrofoam heads with wigs of varying colours and lengths. Exhaling grey smoke, Rachel burped ominously and then leapt from the bed. She hustled naked across the floor and vomited violently into the toilet bowl, holding the cigarette aloft to keep it safe from splashing puke. When she was done she wiped her mouth with the back of her hand, pulled long and hard on the butt, then tossed it into the crapper with a hiss. Shuddering, she flushed the whole damn mess away.

She rinsed her mouth, crept back into the bedroom, and expertly pulled on a fire-engine-red bob wig. She crawled back into bed with Jeffrey. The thin mattress was damp and cool with sweat. She shook him gently, and he moaned. His pale skin felt rubbery, slick to the touch. She could tell from his shallow, fitful sleep that the sickness would be upon him soon.

"Jeffrey honey," she whispered in her husky, two-packs-a-day growl, "We'd better get moving. The clinic closes in an hour."

Jeffrey groaned, turned over, and buried his hollow face further into the stained, lumpy pillow. It was eight in the morning, and already the room felt like a furnace. The Gilbert did not boast air conditioners, although for $180 per week you got free HBO and all the adult movies you could consume. Outside of their third floor room sirens wailed, helicopters throbbed, and people honked their horns in futile anger. She ruffled Jeffrey's lank, greasy black hair.

"Come on. Rise and shine, handsome."

Later, Rachel was applying her lipstick and it was Jeffrey's turn to vomit in the bathroom. When he emerged she clicked her compact closed, and watched him admiringly as he slid his bare ass into a pair of black Levi's. He then pulled on a faded Iggy and the Stooges t-shirt. His hair was swept back from his face, hanging down around his shoulders. He was her beautiful, skinny, strung-out white boy. She lifted her arms and gave herself a curious sniff. Screwing her face up, she doused herself with a few generous squirts of *Charlie*. Her clothes and makeup fixed, Rachel stood and placed her hands on her hips, presenting herself to her man. She was wearing a red lumberjack shirt tied in a knot at the front exposing her tight, flat belly, and a pair of tiny denim shorts.

"How do I look?"

"Beautiful," Jeffrey deadpanned, "Like a black, cross-dressing Daisy Mae Duke. Now can we get the fuck outta here?"

Rachel pouted. "Mr. Grumpy today, huh?"

Jeffrey ran a trembling hand through his hair. "Honey, I'm sick as a fucking dog. Let's get dosed and I promise I'll be full of sunshine and flowers, okay?"

Rachel kissed Jeffrey lightly on the cheek.

"I'm gonna hold your white ass to that," she said.

Even in an area as low rent as Wilcox and Selma, Jeffrey and Rachel were a duo that attracted stares. The rail-thin six-foot-two black transvestite in size twelve platform boots walking arm-in-arm with the translucent Irish junkie with a greasy mop of black hair and weeping, inflamed needle marks festooning his extremities. They walked toward the Hollywood methadone clinic, where they had met a few months ago, hanging onto each other slowly and unsteadily all the while. Outside of the Check Cash joint on the corner of Hollywood and Cahuenga, already a smattering of junkies was congregating, shouting out for spit back methadone or sleepers. Inside the clinic you had to drink your dose on the spot, a practice that was intended to stamp out junkies reselling their government dope to other more desperate, bottom-feeding junkies. Some of the more entrepreneurial dope-fiends had perfected a method for regurgitating their methadone as soon as they walked outside of the clinic, to rebottle and sell. The process involved not eating the night before, and inducing vomiting to clean out the stomach immediately prior to showing up at the clinic. This puked-up methadone went for seven dollars a pop, the same price as a bag of shitty-quality heroin downtown. As they walked past this ramshackle bazaar, the assembled dope-fiends like The Doctor, Pop Gun Eddie, and Suzie Wong greeted them with the easy familiarity of old friends. Jeffrey and Rachel smiled pained smiles, and nodded without stopping. Then up the stairway and into the clinic, signing in at the front desk. They took their place at the back of the line.

The queue of dope-fiends crept painfully toward their dose. A few of the more chipper junkies bantered among themselves, cracking jokes and talking shop, but mostly the room was silent, full of sick, pensive addicts. The clinic had the grey, joyless air of a DMV or Social Security office. The staff hid behind thick Plexiglas windows, and smiles were rarely exchanged. No junkie is ever happy to be in a methadone clinic, and tempers often flared. Most street junkies considered the methadone clinics – "the old liquid handcuffs" as the expression went – to be just about as low as a dope-fiend could sink. But for those too old, too tired, or too beat up for the relentless hustle and grind of the streets, a stable dose of *any* opiate – even one as shitty as methadone – was a necessary evil.

In front of her Rachel recognized Nicky Forest, a skinny, longhaired hipster junkie who had once been the lead singer of a cult rock band called Popism, until his heroin habit had totally sidelined the band's career. Both of his arms were tied up in filthy looking slings. The word was that he'd muscled some dope infected with an aggressive flesh-eating bacteria. By the time he made it to the hospital it was all-but too late: the doctors had to cut away so much infected muscle from his arms and shoulders that it left him a virtual cripple. When the cup was passed to him, he bent over, gripped it with his teeth, and in one expert motion brought his head back and tipped the methadone down his throat without spilling a drop. Then he shuffled away, heading back to the Hollywood streets and whatever fresh horrors awaited him today.

When it was her turn Rachel slugged back her dose, swallowing it, topping up the paper cup with water to swish around and collect every last drop of the precious red liquid. She did this quickly, so as not to attract catcalls and threats from the other sick dope-fiends in line. If there was one thing guaranteed to antagonize a room full of sick junkies it was dragging your feet at the dosing window. Then it was Jeffrey's turn. He glared at the old Chinese woman behind the glass counter radiating icy-cold hostility. After he took his dose he pressed his middle finger against the glass, and left with a dramatic flourish.

"I dunno why you antagonize that bitch, baby..." Rachel said, as they made their way back downstairs. "You know she can have you kicked out of the program."

"Fuck her," Jeffrey said. "Would it fucking hurt to smile? To ask me how I'm doin'? I've been coming to her window for a fuckin' year now and that bitch ain't so much as acknowledged my existence."

"Maybe she don't like dope-fiends. Most people don't, honey."

"That's my point! Then why work with 'em? Go be a cop or some shit if you wanna *fuck* with me. But don't be giving me the stink eye at my own methadone clinic! That bitch is real lucky there's a couple inches of plastic between us."

"Shhh, honey. You're just sick. Be chill... You'll be feelin' better soon..."

Outside Jeffrey and Rachel found Pop Gun Eddie standing alone outside of the Check Cash place basking in the sunlight, eyes closed, face serene and immobile. Jeffrey slapped him playfully on the shoulder. "Eddie, what's happening man?"

Eddie opened one eye, looked at Jeffrey for a moment, and then closed it again.

"Very little, Jeffrey. Very little."

Pop Gun Eddie was an old-timer on the methadone maintenance program. He claimed to be a nephew of John

Agar – the one-time co-star of several John Wayne movies who ended up playing the lead in drive-in junk like *The Brain from Planet Arous* and *Curse of the Swamp People*. He wore a crumpled and cheap navy pinstripe blue suit, white shirt turned brown at the collar, and a pair of ancient white leather boots that had stained a dissolute charcoal colour over the years. His salt-and-pepper hair was cropped close to his skull, his nose broken and re-broken so many times over the years that it whistled softly every time he breathed. Eddie could be found on this corner most mornings trying to raise the cash for his first drink of the day.

"Whatcha doin', Pop Gun?"

"Meditating."

"Meditating?" Jeffrey looked around the busy street corner. "Here?"

"Yeah."

Jeffrey had known Pop Gun Eddie for a while, and the meditating thing was no shtick. Eddie could go to his happy place any time, without the need for downers. This, along with the whole John Agar thing, gave him something of an aura of mystique among his circle. After all, to survive in the dope game as long as Eddie had, you surely had *some* kind of secret knowledge.

"So everyone split already huh?" Jeffrey asked. With a sigh Eddie straightened up and rolled his head around, eliciting a series of sickening pops. He yawned.

"Yeah. The Doctor sold his shit and split to score rock with Chickenhawk Al. Suzy's off on the mooch down by Mann's Chinese. Busy morning. You showed pretty late, missed all the action..."

"Yeah, had a rough night. You holdin' anything?"

"Coupla Xanax bars, Lortabs, and a few Ambien."

Jeffrey took some of the Xanax, and motioned for Rachel to get the bread from out of her pockets. She handed him the money. Eddie pocketed the bills.

Jeffrey said, "I'm fucking starvin'. You wanna come grab a bite with us?"

"Nah. By the way, a fella came by here looking for you the other day. Fat sonvabitch, black as coal. He was givin' off some funky vibes. You know him?"

Jeffrey shrugged, trying to look non-committal. "Don't think so. What he want?"

"Just asking if I knew a Paddy junkie who comes by here. Figured he musta meant you."

"What you tell him?"

"Nuthin'."

"Good."

Eddie nodded. He closed his eyes again and resumed his previous position. Jeffrey waved a hand in front of Eddie's face, eliciting no response. Rachel giggled. The methadone was sitting easy in Jeffrey's stomach now, sending a warm, benevolent glow throughout his aching skeleton. Without dope to wrap him up in its velvet embrace, even the soft warm breeze that rattled the palm trees' dried out leaves had carried with it the taint of something ominous and ghastly. As the methadone warmed over his chill blood, all that was good and beautiful in the universe was slowly making itself apparent again, like some strange optical illusion hidden in plain sight all along. He grabbed Rachel by her hip, pulling her toward him. He kissed her.

"Oh, I get kisses now?" Rachel teased, "I take it you're feelin' better, huh baby?"

"Like a million bucks."

"Who you think Eddie was talkin' about? You owe money?"

"Not me. My old man used to say *neither a lender nor a borrower be.* Words to live by."

"Yeah right. Well, I hope it's nothing, Jeff."

"Don't worry. Come on, let's go enjoy the morning."

"That's my beautiful Irish boy. So, where you takin' me for breakfast?"

"How does a Denny's grand slam, followed by some strong-ass Mexican tar for dessert, sound?"

"Like heaven..."

Laughing, loose-limbed and free, they took off down Hollywood Boulevard, heading east. Jeffrey sang *The Days of Wine and Roses* in a joyful, tuneless voice. The morning was young and their spirits high; the smoggy air was tainted with the mildest threat of optimism.

FOUR

Lupita and Genesis had been laid up in room three-seventeen of the Double Down Motel, somewhere in the arid outskirts of Reno for close to 72 hours now. They were both naked, except for the rosary beads Lupita wore around her neck. Their skin was hot and beaded with sweat; Genesis' black hair plastered to her forehead, a ceiling fan futilely slicing through the sex-infused fug that hung above their bed. The sun was setting and the light in the room was growing dim. Genesis could taste Lupita in her mouth: an earthy, animal taste, blood and heat. On Lupita's small, battered boombox a cassette tape of old rhythm-and-blues songs was playing. Sonny Boy Williamson II was singing *Your Funeral and My Trial*. They lay in silence on the bed, naked, passing a crack-laced joint between them. Sonny Boy sang to his woman, warning her to knock off "that off the wall jive" before he put her in the ground. Lupita laughed, softly.

"You know, Genesis honey, if a man ever told me that he was gonna kill me if I cheated... straight up, I would cut that motherfucker's balls clean off. I wouldn't wait to see if he was joking or serious. Fuck that shit. To me, his even *thinking* about it is just as bad as if he actually *tried* it."

Genesis let her head flop against Lupita's shoulder. She passed the joint over to her.

"I don't doubt it, sweet thing. I mean, look what happened to... well, you know."

"Shit, it's okay. You can say his name; I ain't ashamed of what I did. Not one bit. The thing is, most of 'em *are* dumb, honey.

That's their problem. That's why I dig chicks, mostly." When she said this, she rubbed Genesis' hair affectionately.

Lupita had been prepared to dump this chick's corpse if necessary; in fact, up until they'd finished breakfast the other morning she'd been planning on it. But since they'd made it back to the Lupita's room Genesis had been acting like getting kidnapped by the woman who killed her meth connection was the most exciting thing that had ever happened to her. Thing was, her enthusiasm was oddly endearing.

"The point is though... this guy singing about killin' his woman, old Sonny Boy Williamson. When he sings it turns my fuckin' spine to jelly. What I can't figure is how come when Sonny Boy sings it I get hot, but if Joe Schmo who worked at the car wash said it his nuts'd be rollin' around on the floor?"

Lupita took a long drag of the joint and balanced it on the ashtray. She blew the smoke up into the ceiling fan in great billowing clouds, dreamily watching the strange patterns it made before dissipating in the air.

"Music..." Lupita said dreamily, "I dunno, it just *moves* me in a way that other stuff... y'know, stuff like books an' paintings an' the movies *don't*. I know for sure that if I'd have been around back when old Sonny Boy was alive and singing, I'd have probably fucked his brains out if I got the chance. So long as he sang like *that* to me, he could say whatever he damn well wanted."

Genesis stretched, and placed a protective arm across Lupita's chest.

"I guess I should be *glad* he's dead then," she pouted.

"Guess you should. But you know, if we're talkin' about doin' some time travelling for a lay, then we can't forget about Miss Billie Holiday. I hear she got down with females back in the day.

Least before they killed her." Lupita sighed. "I guess I just love those fucked up, tragic types."

"Is that why you got the Elvis tattoo?"

"Elvis? I don't got no damn Elvis tattoo!"

"Right there!"

The tattoos that covered Lupita's body fascinated Genesis. When they'd first got back to the motel room, Lupita had been obsessively checking the blinds as if expecting some of Paco's boys to storm in there guns blazing. Instead of being afraid, Genesis had felt a weird kind of excitement, an excitement she had never known before. She wondered to herself if this was what being alive was *meant* to feel like. She'd eventually convinced Lupita to stop worrying. She did this by opening up a baggie of Paco's stolen meth and loading a pipe for her. "Come on," she'd said, "It'll take the edge off."

"I guess."

After they'd smoked for a while the conversation was flowing free and easy, and Genesis had asked for a closer look at Lupita's tattoos. Without a word of prompting, Lupita started pulling her clothes off. When her underwear had been discarded Lupita placed her hand on her hip and said, "Knock yourself out, Genesis hun," with a crooked smile. She stood in front of Genesis, naked and brazen. Lupita's body was covered in ink. Fascinated, Genesis had carefully examined each tattoo in turn going from image to image like a starry-eyed visitor to the Louvre. Stoned and horny from the meth they'd been smoking, it wasn't long before Genesis' clothes joined Lupita's in a pile on the floor.

The portrait on the upper right arm that Genesis was referring to – with the lip-curling sneer and rockabilly haircut – was rendered in a religious, iconic style with the legend *Race With The Devil* underneath. When Lupita realized what Genesis was referring to, those weird hazel eyes with the blood-red flecks widened in mock outrage.

"*Ay Dios Mio*! Elvis, she says! Girl, you may be pretty good in the sack, but you got a ways to go when it comes to music. This," Lupita said proudly, "is Gene Vincent!"

Lupita got off the bed and started rummaging around in her pile of cassette tapes. She pulled the correct one out and swapped it with the blues cassette. Genesis watched her right hand as it went about this task with practiced dexterity. She found watching Lupita perform simple tasks like these fascinating. Instead of being impeded by her missing limb, the fingers of her right hand danced with the agility and grace of a concert pianist. She rewound the tape and said to Genesis, "Just check *this* shit out. *This* is Gene motherfuckin' Vincent."

When she said his name, Lupita stopped and closed her eyes, bowing her head as if in prayer. She turned the volume all the way up, the ambient hiss of the tape filling the room. She clambered back on the bed with Genesis and knelt down. She wrapped the rosary beads around her fist. She crossed herself, kissed the beads, then let them fall between her bare breasts again. The song began. Lupita closed her eyes. She performed along with it reverently. With a deadly serious expression on her face she mimed the words:

"*Blue jean baby... with your big blue eyes... Don't wantcha looking at other guys...*"

Her painted eyebrows were bunched together in concentration. She interpreted the song with the solemnity of a hymn. She performed the opening verse with her incomplete arms thrown out in a cruciform. Genesis watched her, studying the contours of her face and body in the dim evening light.

"Honey wontcha give me just one more chance..."

The song paused and Lupita leapt to her feet in one fluid movement. She clicked her fingers and her eyes snapped open as she sang along, "I CANT KEEP STILL SO BABY LET'S DANCE!"

She grabbed Genesis, and dragged her to her feet. They danced naked on the bed as Lupita serenaded Genesis with a frenzied rendition of *Blue Jean Bop*. When the song was done the bed was on fire. It was almost as if one of those strange red sparks had leapt from Lupita's eyes and ignited against the bed sheets.

In fact the joint had rolled off the ashtray in all of the commotion, and the cheap polyester duvet caught fire immediately. Little orange flames danced at their feet. Genesis let out a yell and jumped from the bed. Standing among the flames like some defiant amputee Joan of Arc, Lupita reached calmly for her bottle of Crazy Horse Malt Liquor and doused the fire with beer, extinguishing it with a loud hiss. In seconds, it was over.

Lupita hopped off the bed, grabbed Genesis by the hair, and pulled her face toward her roughly.

"*Gene Vincent was the greatest rock'n'roll singer of all time,*" she hissed. "*Santo Vincent!* He was a cripple, a drunk, and a *baaad* motherfucker!"

She crushed her lips violently against Genesis'. When she let go, Genesis was gasping for air.

"So get it straight," Lupita sneered, "That ain't Elvis. You gonna remember that next time, sweetheart?"

"Sure, I'll remember..." Genesis answered, slightly breathless.

"I remember the first time I ever heard Gene sing. This was out in LA. I was with a guy then. Adolpho." When Lupita said his name, she crossed herself quickly. "We were on our first job together, we was sitting in his car about to hit the place. This song came on. *Cat Man*. Adolpho was a big Gene Vincent fan, played his shit all the time, but it wasn't until I heard that song that I really... *got it*. That fuckin' voice... it made the hairs on the back of my neck stand up. It was a powerful feeling. I was sixteen years old. First time I'd ever pulled a job like that. It went real smooth, good haul, nobody tried to get stupid with us. I always kinda thought of Gene Vincent as good luck after that. A kind of patron saint, you know?"

Genesis laughed. "When you say *job*, I'm guessing you aren't talking about bagging groceries at K-Mart."

"You guess right. It was a pharmacy. Good haul too. You choose the right place and you can live off the proceeds of a pharmacy job for a good few months."

Genesis laughed. "Shit Lupe, aren't you fulla surprises? You robbed a pharmacy?"

"Not just *A* pharmacy. Pharmacies, plural. It beats flipping burgers, that's for damn sure. Cuts out the middleman, too. I mean, those places are packed full of money *and* drugs. Most of those pills get wasted on a bunch of assholes that don't even appreciate 'em. When you put a gun in someone's face and tell 'em you're willing to blow their fuckin' head off if they don't hand the shit over, they don't tend to argue, hun. If you ask me, I'd be crazy *not* to take what I want from those places..."

"I guess it sounds logical..."

Lupita sighed heavily as she looked at the still-steaming duvet.

"Fuck. Thing's ruined. We're gonna have to pay for that, and they'll probably want us to leave when they see what happened."

"Where will we go?"

"Who said anything about *we*?"

Genesis looked up at Lupita, down to the burnt duvet, and then back at Lupita with eyes starting to brim over.

"I don't understand," she said quietly.

42

"You know the deal, hun. I gotta get out of Reno, head on to new pastures. I just needed to make sure you didn't talk to no-one in the meantime, but I sure as hell ain't *staying...*"

Genesis looked around the small motel room and made a snap decision.

"Then take me with you," she said.

"You're crazy. You can't just up and leave with me. I *gotta* split. Paco's boys will be out for my skin. And anyway, I don't like to stay in one place for too long. I like to *drift*, you know?"

Genesis smiled, and grabbed Lupita's hand. "That sounds great. I've been dreaming about getting out of this place... *forever*, you know?"

Lupita looked away. "Thinking it and doing it are two different thing, hun. What about your family? What about your friends?"

"I don't got none," Genesis said quietly, "None to speak of at least."

Lupita came closer to Genesis and whispered to her, "This has been *fun*, Genesis hun. It really has. But it's not *reality*. You know how I make my living. I don't think you're cut out to live your life that way. You need to go *home*."

"*I don't got a home*," Genesis hissed, "And yeah, I know how you make your living. I dunno. It sounds better than making your living by having to fuck old men. Maybe I could *help you*."

Lupita kissed Genesis on the cheek. "You're *sweet* hun, you really are. But think about what you're saying. We're low on funds, first thing I gotta do before I hit the road is bring in some bread. You're honestly ready for that? It's a dangerous lifestyle, Genesis hun, you could get hurt."

"The night I met you three kids beat the shit out of me and raped me. That same night, Paco was about to pistol whip my face to a pulp when you showed up. That don't count as a *dangerous lifestyle*? Anyway, staying around here seems like it would be just as dangerous. There's at least one chick who knows I was the last person to see Paco alive."

Lupita's eyes narrowed to slits. "Whozat?"

"Bitch called Lilly. She was at Paco's place when I showed up."

Lupita cursed. "You *sure*?"

"Positive."

"Then that's a problem. They're gonna be looking for you, girl."

"So take me with you."

"Shit, I dunno."

"Look, if I slow you down, or it ain't working out, you can just leave me wherever I am. Go drift by yourself if you have to. All I'm asking for is a ride out of town, and a bit of company for as long as you want me. I can help *out*. Be a lookout, hell I don't mind handling a gun. My daddy taught me how to shoot when I was still in high school... Shit Lupe, when you showed up it was like... *God* talking to me, you know? 'Cos I'd been promising myself for years that this was the night I was gonna leave town and start over. Only I never had the nerve to do it before. Then you came along and..."

"I ain't nobody's guardian angel," Lupita said.

"No-one's saying you are. And I'm not saying I *expect* anything from you. But even if it's just to get me out of the way of Paco's goons... take me with you. *Please*."

There was a long silence, and then Lupita said, "Aw shit girl, whatever. You can come along, so long as you don't get in my way."

Genesis screamed, and threw her arms around Lupita's neck. The celebrations were interrupted by a loud banging. In the adjacent room a guy was hammering on the wall and yelling for them to quit screaming and turn the goddamned music down. Lupita shrugged Genesis away and stormed over to the connecting wall. She smashed her elbow against it a few times. "If you don' shut the fuck up, mister," she screamed, "I'm gonna come through this mutherfuckin' wall and break your fuckin' face! *Maricon!*"

The noise in the next room stopped immediately. Lupita turned up the stereo, which was still blasting Gene Vincent. Then she came back to Genesis, and put her incomplete arms around her neck. When she spoke, it was in the tone of someone imparting a great, cosmic secret.

"Genesis," she said, "Now that we're gonna be partners, or travelling companions, or whatever the hell you wanna call it, I'm gonna tell you something that someone told me a long time ago, and it's the truest thing I ever heard. Okay?"

"Okay."

"Honey. You can learn most things in life, but good taste is just something you're *born* with. You dig what I'm saying?"

"Sure thing, Lupe," Genesis breathed, holding on to Lupita like a shipwreck survivor clinging onto a piece of driftwood, "I understand..."

FIVE

Gibby Getnor was in the back of a taxi, speeding towards Charles De Gaulle airport. The young Moroccan driver was blasting some ferocious jungle music that featured a gruff-sounding DJ barking machine-gun lyrics in a thick Jamaican patois over a frantic, crackhead drumbeat. A nagging hangover still gnawed away at his skull and the blaring music wasn't helping any. Gibby was thinking about the inevitable long lines at customs he would have to endure, about having to strip off his shoes and belt, and about enduring a barrage of surly questions from some gun-toting mental subnormal in a polyester uniform. All this so he could enjoy eleven hours crammed in a flying sardine can, eating glorified dogfood, and breathing in other people's germs. Christ, he hated air travel.

An even more alarming thought was needling at him. After their disastrous meeting at Les Deux Magots, Gibby was coming to see that he could no longer represent Jacques Seltzer. For fifteen years Jacques' intransigence had reduced Gibby to a state of near penury. After Jacques' latest refusal, Gibby realized that waiting for his client to change his mind was an exercise in futility. He felt like a fool, like some pathetic cuckold who had watched his wife fuck the mailman, the gym instructor, the pool boy, the grocery bagger, their son's high school friends, all the while hoping that once she got it out of her system that she would come back to him. Gibby realized that Jacques Seltzer – like that irredeemable slut-wife – was never going to give Gibby what he needed. He had to get out now, before he was too old and tired to find someone else.

Gibby had come to this uncomfortable conclusion as he pondered how to tell Kenny Azura – one of the most powerful men in Hollywood – that the answer was a firm "no". In a flash Gibby realized that his life could no longer revolve around the abstract hope that one day Jacques might begin work on *Black Neon*. He had a daughter at Columbia for chrissakes, alimony payments, and a mortgage to pay on his Brentwood condo. A decade and a half of feigning interest in Jacques' shitty photographs was a decade and a half too long. If he dumped Jacques now, maybe it would provide him with the impetus to get out there and aggressively hunt down some higher-earning clients. Maybe. However it played out, something had to give.

Between his toxic thoughts, and the music blaring from the radio, the buzzing of Getnor's cell phone almost came as a welcome relief. He looked at it, glowing softly in the dim taxi. As if the phone had read his mind, it was Jacques on the line.

"Can you turn that down, *s'il vous plait*?" he grumbled, and then, clicking the phone open with a tone of forced joviality: "*Jacques*. I was just thinking about you... what's happening?"

"Gibby. I have a question."

"Shoot."

"But first you must understand something. I dropped acid an hour and a half ago."

"Oh. My God, Jacques, are you okay?"

"Of course I'm okay!" Jacques said, testily. "There hasn't been good quality lysergic acid available in France since the early seventies. However, I have also been smoking some top quality Moroccan hashish and this has given me an inspiration. Tell me Gibby, what do you know about street life in Hollywood? Whores, drug addicts, dealers, gangs, this kind of scene?"

"A little. It depends. What are you asking? You need me to... uh... hook you up with something?"

47

"Maybe. I have been actually thinking about our conversation this afternoon, yes? About this Boy King of Hollywood, and his offer to finance *Black Neon*."

"Really?" Gibby tried to subdue his new enthusiasm. "You really mean it, Jacques?"

"Putain! I want to do a film that will hold up a mirror to this disgusting pig whore that is Hollywood. I want to take this *boy king* and rub his nose in his own shit like a disobedient animal! If I am going to subject myself to this vile process again, then I want to make *Black Neon* the ultimate Hollywood movie. My magnum opus! This is my concept – a film about the *real* Hollywood. None of that red carpet, Angelina Jolie and Brad Pitt *merde*. I am looking for today's equivalent of the people that Bukowski or Fante were writing about. The beautiful losers. The fuck-ups. The junkies and the hustlers. No actors. Real people, living their real lives, must act out my movie. I do not want an actress who plays a whore. I want a whore who plays an actress playing a whore, *oui*?"

Gibby nodded, "Sure... I get you, Jacques."

"I will need a scriptwriter to flesh out these ideas... and of course, most importantly, I will need an *in* to this world. I will have to assimilate, *complètement*. In many ways this movie will be an undercover mission, yes?"

"I see." Gibby had no idea what Jacques was babbling about, but he knew better than to ask.

"Now, I warn you Gibby: I am very fucking high right now. So if I go off on an... how you say? Tan-*gent*, yes? Then you must stop me."

As the acid really started to take hold, twisting his brain in all kinds of frantic and fascinating ways, Jacques's grasp of English became increasingly flimsy. Gibby concentrated hard, trying to catch each twist and turn of his drug-mangled syntax.

"No, no, no. You're making perfect sense, Jacques. Really."

"So, you can help me, yes?"

"Of course!" Gibby beamed, "Of course I can! Kenny is gonna be thrilled, Jacques, I promise..."

"I do not give two *shits* about what Kenny thinks. What I care about is his *money*. I am an artiste, Gibby, and I want this whole business of complete artistic control in writing, *oui*?"

"Sure, sure." Gibby said in a placating manner, "You know something, I might just have the guy for you..."

Recently, Gibby had been taking note of an interesting character who attended his Thursday Alcoholics Anonymous meeting at The Viper Room. Even though he regularly attended AA meetings in and around Hollywood, Gibby did not think of himself as an alcoholic. In fact he enjoyed alcohol immensely, and had no more intention of quitting booze than he had of giving up eating avocados. Gibby Getnor attended AA meetings for the same reason that half of the agents and producers in Hollywood attended AA meetings: to make connections.

The meetings themselves, for all their talk of humility, anonymity and "all addicts being the same," worshipped at the altar of fame and celebrity just as much as anywhere else in America. Whenever an A-list actor was rumored to have started attending a particular AA meeting, the church or recreation centre which held it would have to move the weekly sessions from a small circle of metal chairs in a chilly rec room, to the long rows of tables in the cafeteria in order to handle the inevitable overflow. Suddenly the place would be packed with the same girls you would see staggering out of Château Marmont on a Saturday night, with the conspicuous addition of *The Big Book of Alcoholics Anonymous* tucked under their arm. Dozens of opportunistic hustlers would converge there each week trying to sell their latest script or at least talk 'recovery' – and maybe a little business – with the fresh meat. Sometimes the celebrity would simply read the Twelve Traditions of Alcoholics

Anonymous at the beginning of the meeting and then split, as if making a reluctant cameo in an otherwise lacklustre movie.

Despite the fact he wasn't a celebrity, Gibby still found this character – whose name was Randal – utterly fascinating. Gibby felt that the stories he shared about his own insane drug use would have made a great movie. One time Randal let slip that he worked for Chainsaw, the hot new boutique studio at Dreamscape, and then it took all of Gibby two minutes on his iPad at IMDB Pro to figure out Randal was none other than Randal P. Earnest, son of Donald Earnest – founder of Mercantile Studios – and brother of Harvey Earnest, the founder and CEO of Dreamscape. A Hollywood insider with a working knowledge of the street drug scene, Gibby reasoned, could be the perfect tour guide for Jacques.

In his thirty-thousand-dollar-a-month apartment overlooking the Church of Saint Germain, Jacques began to absently rub his forearm with his hand. The skin began to get warm, then hot, and then he watched in silent horror as the flesh started to bubble and melt away altogether...

"Hey – you still with me, big guy?" Gibby said, after listening to Jacques distractedly muttering to himself in French for a few moments.

Jacques shook his head, and realized that the arm looked perfectly normal again. "Oh, uh, yes. Sorry. Well, it seems we are in business. Speak to this fellow and email me when you arrive home. You must remind me in case I do not remember this conversation, *oui* Gibby?"

"You got it. Take it easy, baby."

Gibby clicked the phone shut. He closed his eyes for a moment and listened contentedly to the soft rumble of the taxi's engine. He felt dizzied by his sudden and unexpected change of fortune.

After a decade of being nothing more than an elusive industry rumor, *Black Neon* was suddenly and unexpectedly alive. The driver cranked the music up to a brutal volume again, jolting Gibby out of his thoughts.

"S'il vous plait!" snapped Gibby, but when he opened his eyes he saw that the driver had pulled off the motorway and they were already in the airport itself. He started rummaging in his pockets, looking for his wallet. He silently hoped that he had enough Ambien to keep himself knocked out for the entire journey back to LAX.

SIX

Randal P. Earnest, thirty-eight-year-old black sheep of the Earnest film dynasty, six months clean and holding onto sobriety with slipping fingers, was sitting in the doctor's office waiting to hear the results of his test. The Doctor was an old, fat Russian called Titov. The test itself had been surprisingly quick, and so far the doctor had spent more time reading Randal's answers than Randal had spent filling out the questionnaire. Titov studied the paperwork in front of him for several minutes, his grey, bushy eyebrows furling and unfurling in concentration, before he leaned across the table and told Randal that – *regretfully* – the results were positive.

There was a frozen moment in the room as the two men regarded each other. Randal's receding bleach-blond hair had almost totally grown out to its natural black, and his pale, watery eyes hid shivering in his skull like a couple of paranoid crackheads holed up in a thirty-dollar-a-night motel room. He had once been handsome, for sure, but the steady accumulation of self-loathing and sobriety weight had made the face in the mirror almost unrecognizable to itself. Although he had been expecting a positive diagnosis from Titov, Randal still felt a palpable sense of relief. He felt the urge to reach across the desk and kiss the old fucker right on the lips. Instead he just nodded sagely, his face a mask of acceptance and regret.

"The positive result is the bad news," the Doctor said in his thick Russian accent. "However, the good news is that there are many options open to us, and I am to suggest that we begin treatment immediately."

At this late stage in his life, Randal P. Earnest had just been informed that he suffered from Attention Deficit Disorder – a cognitive defect that made concentrating on many everyday tasks incredibly difficult. For the past few months he had been working at the behest of his older brother at a new subsidiary of Dreamscape Studios, called Chainsaw Pictures. Randal thought of all of the meetings he had suffered through these past few months with Chainsaw Pictures' head honcho Kenny Azura. The wunderkind at the helm of Chainsaw was an insufferable little shit-sucker with a carefully barbered goatee and the manner of an overprivileged child. Azura's reputation was built upon his uncanny ability to attach himself to projects that ultimately hit big at the box office. The word was that he had nearly destroyed several of these movies in the process, throwing production into chaos with his megalomaniacal demands and his legendary mistreatment of writers. In fact, among Hollywood screenwriters Kenny was *particularly* loathed. He had a tendency to fire anyone who disagreed with him and was even rumoured to have personally re-written scripts himself, in flagrant violation of Screenwriters Guild rules. The word on the lot was that Azura often had to be worked around, and the many films he took a producers credit on had succeeded *despite* his involvement, not because of it. Still, when the films were released Kenny Azura was sure to be seen on the red carpet performing a victory lap, and giving interviews to all the major networks about bringing "his movie" to the big screen. At best Azura was an astute motherfucker who had an uncanny knack for predicting when a movie would be a hit. At worst – and this was certainly Randal's perception – he was nothing more than a ruthless self-promoter who'd had the outrageous good fortune to stumble upon several projects so good that not even an idiot like Kenny Azura could fuck them up. Either way he had a notable track record of success, and in the movie industry box office receipts were one thing that could not be argued with.

Randal thought of himself shifting from buttock to buttock while the stupid bastards who bankrolled the crap that Chainsaw was working on rambled endlessly about test audiences, demographics, viral campaigns and script re-writes. He'd sit there day after day, week after week, staring out of the window and wishing he was holed up in a sleazy motel with a couple of Filipino whores and an eight-ball of crystal meth. It was a comfort to have it confirmed by a medical professional that this wasn't some kind of moral defect on Randal's part, but instead a medical disorder that could easily be treated with liberal doses of amphetamine salts. After all, for poor, unfortunate souls like Randal P. Earnest, without amphetamines in their system it was almost impossible to concentrate on *anything*.

After providing the diagnosis, the Doctor proceeded to ramble at length about the philosopher Emmanuel Kant, at which point Randal again found himself zoning out, merely nodding and *uh-humming* at the appropriate moments. Since his last stint in rehab Randal had been sequestered in a small apartment in West Hollywood. His access to the family money had been severely curtailed by his older brother, who now controlled the Earnest estate. He was given a weekly allowance and a leased car, and was expected to show up at Chainsaw Pictures' offices in Century City a minimum of three days a week to "help out". This translated to Randal being forced into the role of a glorified flunky for an overgrown USC frat boy who drove a canary yellow Lamborghini Reventon and had a private doctor who came to the office twice weekly to shoot him up with B-12. Randal could tell that Azura despised him – his smile was as fake as his Orange-Glo tan – but knew that the head of Chainsaw Pictures tolerated him out of deference to Randal's older brother, and

Kenny's boss, Harvey Earnest. The agreement was that if Randal could make it for twelve months drug free, regularly working at Dreamscape and attending 12-step meetings, he would finally be allowed unrestricted access to the family's money again. His weekly "touch base" meetings with his brother were a drag, a glorified pep talk from a man who thought that Tony Robbins was the pinnacle of western intellectual thought. Since getting sober back in '89 Harvey had read nothing but self-help and recovery books and had a maddening habit of peppering his day-to-day conversation with bullshit phrases like "self actualization", "personal mission statement" and "it is what it is".

As much as Randal resented performing intern level work for his brother's heir apparent, he did find working with people who were at least a decade his junior to be a bleakly fascinating experience. Sober, he began to notice his age and the cultural shifts that had happened while he had been locked away in the blissful embrace of the speed pipe. This sudden disconnect terrified him. All of the bands that his coworkers talked about were completely alien to him. He saw one kid wearing a Ramones T-shirt by the copy machines his first week on the job, and Randal tried to use it as an excuse to make conversation.

"Cool shirt. So you're into the Ramones? I love their shit, too."

"Oh, uh, I dunno." The kid looked down at his shirt with a puzzled expression. "They're, like, a *band*?"

He also started to wonder if everybody who worked there was completely straight. Cocaine no longer seemed to be the drug of choice amongst the gophers and social climbers in the studio scene. Randal had not touched drugs since getting out of the treatment centre, although he had started secretly drinking again. He had pissed in a cup daily at his brother's behest since leaving rehab and always come up clean. The day his brother told him he would no longer be enforcing the piss tests to prove his sobriety, Randal stopped at his local Ralphs and bought a bottle of cheap bourbon and a litre of Coca-Cola to celebrate. When it came to drug talk though, his ears were still particularly attuned to even the slightest narcotic-influenced vibration. For months he detected nothing. He could not fathom these fucking kids. It seemed to Randal that they would be the first generation to come up who were actually more dull and conservative than their forebears.

Then, during a late night meeting to discuss the possibility of a hip-hop remake of Xanadu starring Beyonce in the Olivia Newton John role, he had spotted Kenny Azura's new PA popping a pill. When he pulled the kid aside later to question him, the assistant admitted that it was Adderall. A hushed conversation later, and Randal P. Earnest found himself in the office of Dr Titov, the newest member of the estimated 4.4% of American adults who are diagnosed with ADD each year.

The doctor prescribed Randal thirty 20mg Adderall, and set an appointment for two weeks time to have his dose adjusted.
   "We will start you off small," Dr Titov had said, "and then after a few weeks, once the body has adjusted to the medication, we can start to move the dosage upwards."

Randal did not tell Dr Titov that as a lifelong user of crystal meth, his body was already well used to the effects of amphetamines. It was crystal meth that had landed him in the treatment centre again, after a near-fatal speed and sex bender in Las Vegas. The Vegas debacle had culminated in a drug-fuelled robbery where he and his accomplice Jeffrey ended up getting ripped off by their co-conspirator. Jeffrey was an Irish dope-fiend he had roomed with in a treatment centre called *Clean and Serene*. He'd roped Randal into this scheme as a last, desperate throw of the dice. Their partner – a self-proclaimed "artist" named Damien – had provided the target and the pass codes for the safe, but fled for Europe with the loot in the aftermath of the heist, leaving them both up shit creek. The last he heard, Jeffrey was heavily strung out and living in a motel somewhere in the shitty end of Hollywood. Out of drugs, and cut out of his family's money by his pissed-off older brother, Randal had checked into drug rehab for the twelfth time. He promised Harvey and himself to take the programme seriously this time around.

As he watched Titov hastily scribble out the prescription, Randal felt relief flood him. Life without amphetamines had proved to be almost impossible. It was as if he could only truly be himself when he was on uppers. It had been so long since he had existed without meth in his system, that he no longer recognized himself without it. This dull, tired, slow, self-hating lump he saw in the mirror disgusted him. His mind felt weak, as if his skull was wadded full of cotton wool. He was suddenly aware of how charmless and awkward he was, as if he had regressed into some dreadful, tongue-tied pubescent boy. His wit had left without so much as a note. Without speed, Randal found himself to be at the mercy of several other vices, mainly booze, food, and masturbation. He had halfheartedly hoped that his frantic masturbation schedule – four times a day if he had things to do, up to seven if not, would at least help to keep some weight off of him, but even jerking his bloody penis like a deranged monkey to his sizeable collection of porno DVDs could not ward off the fattening effects of the sugary drinks, pastries, booze and heavy Mexican food that Randal now craved as much as he had once craved crank. He felt like some foul, lumpen Igor, a weak-brained moron who did not even have the decency to just die.

His brother, of course, had been less than sympathetic to his plight. He'd advised him to visit the gym when Randal had complained that sobriety was turning him into a blimp. He'd reluctantly showed up there once, pale and uncomfortable in a brand new gym outfit. He took a long look at the rows of exercise equipment and the ludicrous, sweaty dudes hopping around on running machines to the relentless beat of Lady Gaga and Rihanna. Was *this* his only other option? He immediately bolted. His head was spinning and a lump formed in his throat. He found himself in a nearby Pocito Mas, inhaling four chorizo tacos with a side order of yellow rice and black beans, all topped off with a litre bottle of Coca-Cola that he slugged down in his car, hands shaking like a desperate alcoholic. Then he burst into tears of frustration. He felt bloated, ragged and pathetic. As Dr Titov handed him the prescription Randal felt certain that things were about to change for the better.

"Thank you doctor."

"See me in two weeks," the Doctor said, "We can discuss your progress and make any adjustments then. Now, listen to me. Take one pill a day to start with. Have a hearty breakfast before taking your medication. This drug will reduce your appetite dramatically. You will also feel more focused, and alert. Do not take it in the evenings, as it will certainly disrupt your sleep. If you have any questions or concerns... any at all – you call me. Yes?"

"Sure."

"Do you have any questions?"

"I don't think so."

The prescription cost fifty dollars to fill at a nearby CVS. On his way over there it was as if his peripheral vision had disappeared altogether. He stalked down the street with a sense of purpose he had forgotten he possessed. Even before he handed the slip to the pharmacist, in a strange way Randal realized he was already high. When he paid for the pills, he momentarily thought about how much meth he could buy with fifty dollars. He pushed the idea out of his head. If he started up on meth again, everything would fall apart. He was sure of that. However, with a steady prescription from a legit doctor, and with careful monitoring of his dose, he figured that he could definitely keep his use of these pills to a manageable level. He had another six months to endure before Harvey would be forced to back off and let Randal live his life without interference. Six more months of dealing with that snot-nosed little weasel Kenny Azura. In six months he would walk out of there and never look back, but until then a little prescription to help him through the bad days was just what the doctor ordered.

When the pharmacist handed him the pills, Randal smiled broadly and thanked her. Then, noting the time, he cursed under his breath. He was late for his AA meeting.

SEVEN

Jeffrey was hustling down Hollywood Boulevard, trying to make it to the Frolic Room by two. His gym bag was slung over his shoulder. The bag, which was lined with aluminum foil, contained around twenty books all stolen from the Borders at Hollywood and Vine. The selection weighed heavily toward the drunks and the junkies: Kerouac, Burroughs, Thompson, Bukowski, Fante, those kinds of guys. Jeffrey's fence, a Chinese Cuban called Doug, had told him those authors had the highest resale value. The rest of the haul was graphic novels and a handful of CDs.

The first time Jeffrey had stolen for Doug he'd shown up with a bunch of shit from the bestseller lists: vampire novels, ghost written celebrity memoirs, bloodless Serious Novels about The Way We Live Now with endorsement stickers from Oprah Winfrey, the latest tract by Jeffrey's one-time mentor and reality television star Dr Mike, addiction memoirs by New York Times journalists, and three-hundred-page rants by Fox News pundits. Thinking he had a good score, Jeffrey was dismayed when Doug threw out three quarters of the books and declared them to be unsaleable.

"I can't *move* these types of books," Doug had whined, "There's three types of books I can really sell. Books about getting loaded, books about fucking, and comic books. The rest of it... nobody gives a shit, Jeffrey, hate to break it to you."

"All these books are on the bestseller list, Doug! How the fuck can they *not* sell, man?"

Doug shrugged. "Well, that's the conundrum. I guess maybe the kind of person who buys stolen books off the street is just more interested in the raunchy shit than whatever crap is in the bestseller lists. Alls I know is that I'll have a bitch of a time tryin' to unload some crapola by Tori Spelling. It don't got shelf life! Next week some other piece-of-shit celebrity book is gonna be out, and nobody is gonna care about this one no more."

Security had been a little heavier than usual and Jeffrey had not had enough dope this morning to thoroughly coat his nerves against the strain of having to go on a stealing spree, so the score was lighter than usual. Jeffrey liked to think that his shoplifting was keeping him and Rachel afloat, but he knew deep down that it amounted to no more than pocket change. With habits like theirs to feed and the cost of Rachel's black market hormones, they needed a constant inflow of cash. The lion's share of their money came from Rachel's prostitution.

He was meant to meet Rachel at two and he was already running late. Rachel was due to return from a date with one of her regular johns, a music video director who worked out of an office on near Sunset and La Brea. His deal was that he'd pick her up on his weekday lunch breaks for a suck-job in his SUV. She'd blow him as he'd drive around Hollywood, the guy gulping his Starbucks and talking frantically the whole time. He would regale her with stories about his clients and their on-set antics. Listening to Rachel talk about this guy, Jeffrey started to suspect that he was really paying for someone to listen to his crap without interrupting. The blowjob seemed like an afterthought.

He was a block away when Jeffrey heard a car door open next to him and before he knew what was happening he had been grabbed by the collar and dragged into the backseat of a filthy-smelling Dodge Charger. The door slammed shut.

Jeffrey felt something cold and sharp pressing against his cheek.

Carefully he allowed his eyes to travel to the right. A young, light skinned black kid was holding a switchblade to his face. The kid was trembling, and snot was running down his nose. He sniffed it back in, making an awful bubbling sound.

"I'll cut you the fuck open," the kid warned in a high-pitched voice that betrayed his tender years. "No sudden movements."

"Okay." Jeffrey breathed.

He looked toward the front seat. The back of the head was fat and bald. In the rear view mirror he saw a pair of puffy, beady eyes staring at him.

Jeffrey felt his bowels churn.

Smooth, the coke dealer he'd recently burnt for two hundred bucks, smiled coldly at his reflection.

"*Jeffrey*," Smooth gloated, rummaging around in his nose with an enormous pinky finger. Smooth's smell filled the car – unwashed skin and pungent sweat. "*Jeffrey, Jeffrey, Jeffrey.*"

"Smooth man, I'm –"

Smooth removed his pinky from his nostril and held it to his mushy lips. "*Shhh*," he cooed. "It's my turn to talk now. I wuz jus' sayin' to youngblood here, how junkies and dogs is a lot alike. Ain't that right, youngblood?"

"That's right," the kid said.

"They're both dumb as fuck. They both stink. They're both... uh... what the phrase I'm looking for?"

"Creatures of habit," the kid said.

"That's right. They both creatures of habit. It's like... a dog takes a piss, you know, and for the next three months that fucking dog will go right back to where he pissed and take a good sniff of that shit." Smooth inhaled deeply through his nose. "Woo-eee. He can't get enough of that stale ol' piss. You can fuckin' grab that dog off the streets, drive it someplace else, dump it out in some fuckin' strange alleyway, and that mutt'll find his way back to that stale patch of piss so he can go stick his fuckin' nose in it again. Ain't that right, youngblood?"

"That's right."

Smooth's eyes narrowed to dangerous slits. "And look at *you*, you stupid Irish cocksucker. You fuckin' burnt me for an 8-ball of coke, and you're fucking stupid enough to be wandering around Hollywood Boulevard like you own the fuckin' place. Jeffrey, king of the dope-fiends. You didn't even bother to change your routine, not even a little bit. Coulda give me a *modicum* of challenge, or some shit."

Smooth enunciated the word *modicum* like a man speaking in an unfamiliar language. He reached into a *Del Taco* bag in the passenger seat, removed a paper napkin, and patted his glistening dome dry with it. "Lemmie ask you something," Smooth said. "You think all niggers are lazy or somethin'?"

Jeffrey gulped.

"Youngblood," Smooth said, addressing the kid with the knife, "If I ask this fuckin' faggot a question and he don't answer me, you feel free to cut him, okay?"

"Can I cut his eye?" the kid asked.

"You can cut anywhere you like so long as you don't kill him. Not yet. We're not killing him unless I don't get my money. If I know this broke-ass motherfucker the way I think I do, then he won't be carrying the bread on him. He's gotta stay alive so he can settle his debt. But as far as you hurtin' him, or disfiguring him... blinding him, shit like that? You can get creative."

Jeffrey stiffened as the kid brought the tip of the blade up to his right eye-socket. The blade began to press against the bottom lid. With one application of pressure Jeffrey knew the kid could easily gouge the eye right out of his head.

"Now wait a second, youngblood..." Smooth said, his voice dripping with honey. He smiled, exposing a row of filmy yellow teeth. "Now, you can call me a lot of fuckin' things. But one thing you can't call Smooth is unfair. Let's hit the reset, 'cos this fruit didn't know the *consequences* of his actions yet."

The kid looked visibly disappointed, but kept the knife against Jeffrey's eye. "Now I think of it, you know, that's another reason why junkies remind me of dogs. They'll go right on pissing on your couch until you fuckin' *discipline* them. I mean, you can *ask* a dog not to piss on your couch, for sure. I mean, you can do that shit till you blue in the fuckin' face. But it seems to me you always gotta kick a fucking mutt a few times before it *really* gets the message."

The kid reluctantly lowered the knife and put it against Jeffrey's throat. Jeffrey opened his eyes fully again.

"So now you know that's up, lemmie ask you again. Do you think all niggers is lazy or some shit?"

Aware of the blade that pressed against his skin, Jeffrey carefully shook his head. "No," he whispered, "No I don't think all niggers are lazy."

"Hm. I was thinking that's what it *must* be. You know, like you figured I'd be too busy eating some fucking watermelon or playing basketball to come looking for you. Especially since you know damn well that I know where you hang out. I mean, are seriously telling me you was just too fucking *stupid* to even run? I mean, is all that shit they say about you Irish motherfuckers being stupid actually *true*? 'Cos I just figured that was just some racist bullshit, you know? Like how they say all niggers can dance, or all Jews are good with money, or whatever."

"Or how the chinks can't drive," the kid interjected.

Smooth shrugged. "Tell you the fuckin' truth that one got more than a ring of truth to it. I never met a chink that could drive worth a shit, as God is my witness. Funny, isn't it? I mean the motherfuckers are so good at math and shit, but when it comes to drivin' a car..."

Smooth drifted off, seemingly lost in thought for a moment. Then, as if remembering where he was, he turned his enormous head and glared at Jeffrey. "All I know is if *I* owed a crazy nigger like me money, you bet your white ass I woulda left town with the fear of God in me. I'd be workin' in some diner in the fuckin' Midwest under an assumed name, cooking up home fries an' shit and lookin' over my goddamn shoulder every time the door opened. But *you*? I watched you the past week, wandering up and down around here, not a care in the fuckin' world. I watched you come and go at that fuckin' methadone clinic. All I had to do was wait until you didn't have that fucking *shim* in tow so I could pick your dumb ass up." Smooth looked at the kid holding the knife and said in a conspiratorial tone, "I been to prison, youngblood. Those fucking tranny bitches can be crazy and I ain't fucking with that. Don't need one of those freaks takin' my eye out with a fuckin' stiletto heel or somethin'."

Smooth returned his gaze to Jeffrey. "Shit. You truly are a dumb motherfucking Irish cocksucker."

Jeffrey blinked the sweat out of his eyes. It was hot in here. No A/C, just the steamy heat rising from Smooth's massive, stinking bulk.

"So what was it, dummy? How the fuck you think you was gonna get away with that shit? You think I was gonna *forget*? I told you – I don't mind fronting a little stuff if you one of my regulars. But if you don't have that fuckin' money for me when you say you're gonna have it, you got a big fucking problem. Ignoring my *calls*. Wasting my *time*. I don't got patience for your trifling *shit*, homeboy. Where is it? Where's my money, bitch?"

"The bag," Jeffrey croaked.

Smooth looked at the gym bag at Jeffrey's feet.

"*She-it*. You got a bag fulla money? An' there's me thinking you just got done workin' out. Pass that shit over, blood."

Without taking the blade from Jeffrey's throat, the kid reached down and passed the bag to Smooth. Smooth dropped the bag on the passenger seat and unzipped it. He rummaged around inside for a moment.

"The fuck is this shit?"

"Books."

"Nigga, I can SEE it's fucking books. What I *mean*, faggot, is where is the fucking *money*?"

"I – I'm on my way to see my fence. He's gonna pay me for these..."

Smooth sucked the air through his teeth. The kid raised the blade slightly, and pressed it against Jeffrey's eye again.

"Can I cut this fuckin' cracker now?"

Smooth sighed and rubbed the bridge of his nose, dejectedly. "I guess you gonna have to. Motherfucker owes me money. Instead of coming to me like a man, he fuckin' tries to avoid me. Then, when I'm finally forced to snatch his stupid ass off the sidewalk he tries to pass off a bag of fuckin' *books* to me? Jeffrey, do I *look* like the kind of motherfucker who takes books in exchange for coke?"

"Smooth!" Jeffrey stammered, "Listen man... Rachel... Rachel will have dough. If you just drive me up to the Frolic Room she'll be in there. I'll get you the bread, I swear man. Just tell this kid to get the knife outta my face. *Please.*"

Smooth looked over to the kid, and nodded at him. The kid lowered the knife. He kept staring at Jeffrey with mad dog eyes. Smooth turned around, and stuck the car into drive. Then, almost as an afterthought he said, "I'll tell you straight up, motherfucker. If that fucking ladyboy of yours don't have the bread, I'm gonna kill you *and* it. You fuckin' hear me, cuz?"

"Yeah," Jeffrey croaked. "I hear you..."

It was half past two in the afternoon at the Frolic Room on Hollywood Boulevard. The barmaid, a tall thin Russian lady called Rita peered over her pearl-rimmed spectacles and asked Rachel, "You want another, honey?"

"Sure. Gimmie a Canadian Club and ginger."

The place was deserted. The only other customer, a grey bearded fellow who'd drunk a few beers while intently watching General Hospital, had cleared out a half hour ago. Rachel was wearing white hot pants and a neon purple wig. She took her heels off, sat then on the stool next to her and she rubbed her aching feet.

"Psst!"

Rachel saw Jeffrey poking his head around the doorway. She waved him over, but he just stood there with a strange look on his face. "Uh, baby..." he stage-whispered, "Can you come out here for a second?"

"Shit, my dogs are barkin' Jeff. I been walking for the past half hour in these goddamn heels. Why dontcha come in here!"

Just then, from behind Jeffrey, a young, skinny black kid shuffled into view. He was holding a glinting blade to Jeffrey's neck.

"Bitch," he said in a slow, even voice, "You'd better do what your boyfriend says before I cut his fuckin' head clean off."

With that the kid disappeared back behind Jeffrey again. Jeffrey looked at Rachel with pleading eyes. Rita appeared with the glass and slid it over. "Everything okay?"

"Sure," Rachel said, slipping her shoes back on. "I got some business to take care of. Be right back."

*

A few minutes later Smooth's Dodge charger pulled away with a squeal of brakes. Giving the car the finger as it tore away, Rachel screamed, "You better pray you don't see me coming first, you fat motherfucka!"

Jeffrey staggered over to the Frolic Room, dragging the gym bag full of books behind him. He collapsed onto the sidewalk next to the door. He clutched his stomach and groaned. Rachel clip-clopped over to him and folded her arms.

"Four hundred fucking bucks that fat motherfucker stole from me! Four hundred fucking bucks for an 8-ball of coke!"

"He said it was interest."

"Interest my ass! That motherfucker ain't Wells Fargo, he ain't got no right to be charging me no interest. More to the fuckin' point, when did you get this motherfuckin' coke from Smooth? Huh?"

Jeffrey looked shame-faced.

"Three weeks ago. When we had that fight, you know? Over at Joe's place."

"Uh-huh. And?"

"And I was pissed off, and I had no dough, and I called Smooth and got him to front me an 8-ball."

"Jeffrey. We made up the next fuckin' day. How come you didn't tell me you had coke?"

"You know how it is when you start up shooting that fuckin' stuff. It was gone in a few hours. I didn't want you to be pissed off at me..."

"So you wuz lying to me when Eddie was sayin' that fat fuck was looking for you? Giving me bullshit about how you didn't know what he wuz talkin' about! Well I just sucked someone's dick to pay off your fuckin' shady coke, asshole, so now I'm doubly pissed."

"Fuck," Jeffrey hissed, "that little fucker almost broke my ribs."

"You lookin' for sympathy, Jeffrey? Way I'm feelin' right now I might just finish the fuckin job off myself. How the fuck did it work out that I'm the fool suckin' dick and shit to pay for our drugs? How the fuck did you end up being a kept man, you wanna explain that to me, you fuckin' shit?"

"Rach... I'm sorry."

"I'm a princess, Jeffrey!" Rachel yelled, wagging her finger in his face, "And don't you *ever* fucking forget that, motherfucker. I'm a goddamned princess and you better start treating me like one. Because you turning into one of those freeloading type motherfuckers, and I ain't down with being nobody's sugar momma. I'm too fuckin' young and pretty for that shit, Jeff! You better sort your fuckin shit out and start making some bread."

"I'm goin' to see Doug now. I was just gonna meet up with you, grab a beer..."

"Fuck grabbing a beer! We can't even pay for the drink I got sittin' on the bar right now. You'd better get your sorry ass over to that short-ass motherfucker and get your bread, because we're gonna need it. And while you're doin' that, you better be ruminating on how the fuck you iz gonna start contributing to this fuckin' relationship like a fucking *man*, instead of collecting the dough like you're my motherfucking pimp or some shit."

"Rach," Jeffrey said, getting gingerly to his feet, "That's not fair. Don't say that I treat you like a pimp, I love you..."

"Nobody *said* you treated me like a pimp, Jeff." Rachel said coldly, "At least if you treated me like a pimp I wouldn't have to rescue *your* ass from no fat fuckin' coke dealers and their snot-nosed nephews. At least if you was a *pimp* you'd have kicked both their asses instead of asking me to bail you out. And can it with the *love* shit! You only ever start in with that foolishness when you *know* you're in the wrong. Now go get that *money* motherfucker."

Jeffrey looked up at Rachel with puppy dog eyes.

"*Git!*" she spat.

"Okay, okay. Jesus. What you gonna do while I'm gone?"

"I'm gonna sit my ass down at this bar, take off these fuckin' heels, and finish this fuckin drink that I can no longer afford. Okay with you?"

Rachel crossed her arms, and watched as Jeffrey trudged east, heading toward Doug's place. When he was out of sight she cursed under her breath and walked back into the dim cool of the Frolic Room. Rita was cleaning glasses with a rag, and peering at a copy of the LA Times spread out over the counter. Rachel sat down and went back to her drink. Rita looked over and smiled. "Everything okay, hun?"

Rachel shook her head. "You don't wanna know."

"Men trouble?"

She took a long sip from her straw and smiled weakly at Rita.

"Ain't it *always* fuckin' men trouble?" she said, "Men trouble, money trouble. It's always one or the other, Rita..."

EIGHT

The "Happy Hour Group" Alcoholics Anonymous meeting at the Hollywood Lutheran Church was taking a cigarette break. Randal made his way to the back of the room to fill a Styrofoam cup full of weak coffee. He stared at the distorted reflection that he saw in the silver urn: the bleached blond hair with dark roots, thinning on top, the face which seemed to be expanding around the jowls at an alarming rate, the once emaciated body which now sagged at the tits and the gut in an unpleasant way. He shivered. He cleared his nose, and more sweet-tasting goop from the Adderall he had crushed and snorted on his way over here dripped down the back of his throat. His guts fluttered in a pleasant way. He might look like a fat piece of shit but at least Randal could honestly say that he felt good for the first time in months. As soon as he had snorted the first of these miracle pills it was as if he had never been away. The pills welcomed him back, told him they missed him, reminded him of how *good* they used to be together. All of the enthusiasm and excitement that had drained out of him these past months suddenly came rushing back with the intensity of a spontaneous orgasm. Even the AA meeting he had just sat through seemed radically more interesting and helpful now that his brain had been jolted out of its long hibernation. It was the sudden revelation of feeling *alive* again. A couple of months on these pills and Randal even anticipated that he might make it back to something approximating his old physique.

"Are you gonna get a coffee, or just stand around staring at the fuckin' urn?"

Randal turned. He found himself face to face with Gibby Getnor. He and Gibby shared a passing familiarity with on the AA scene. Randal smiled apologetically, got himself together and filled his cup.

"What's happening, Gibby?" he asked, "Don't usually see you at this meeting."

"I was down at the Viper Room meeting the other day. Didn't see you around..."

"Nah," Randal said, "That scene is getting on my nerves. If I have to listen to that Robert Downey Jr. share for forty minutes about his bullshit one more fucking time, I'm gonna have a breakdown."

"He *is* a long winded bastard," Gibby agreed.

"Hard to believe a multi-fucking-millionaire could have so many problems. They need to start playing music over him, like they do with those rambling Oscar speeches."

Randal gulped his coffee, and Gibby pointed his thumb in the direction of the guest speaker, the long-haired ex-lead singer of the hugely successful 1970s soft rock act The Emotions.

"What did you make of that guy?"

"Pretty intense. I liked the story he told about trying to pawn his own gold records for dope money. That was kinda wild."

"Uh-huh. I'd have never had that guy pegged for a junkie back when The Emotions were still around. They always seemed so clean cut."

"It's the quiet ones you gotta look out for, Gibby."

"I guess that's true..."

Gibby and Randal sipped their coffee. It was weak, but it was all most people in this place had anymore.

"So, was there any particular reason?" Randal asked.

"For what?"

"That you were looking for me at the Viper Room? I don't think I owe you money, do I?"

"Actually... it's just that... well, I have a business proposition for you. Turns out I'm gonna be working with an associate of yours. Kenny Azura. You know, I was kinda surprised to see you were working underneath anybody over at Chainsaw, to be honest. With you being Harvey Earnest's brother..."

Randal raised an eyebrow, and Gibby shrugged. "IMDB," he said with a hint of apology in his voice.

A month or so earlier Gibby and Randal had been talking idly over coffee, and Randal had mentioned – in a casual way – that he was working over at Chainsaw. Almost as soon as he'd opened his mouth he'd had the feeling that he might regret mentioning it.

"So you're gonna be working with Kenny, eh?" Randal said dryly, "Lucky you."

"Yeah, I've had quite a few conversations with Mr. Azura already. He's quite a piece of work, isn't he?"

"He's a piece of *something*, all right. Listen Gibby, before you gimmie the spiel I gotta be straight with you. I think you might be talkin' to me under false pretenses. Just because you looked me up on fucking IMDB and you got some skewed impression of who I am, you gotta understand something. I got no interest in this industry. Zero. Just because I was born into it, it doesn't mean that I give a shit about it. In fact I'd go as far as saying that I *hate* it, and I've spent most of my adult life trying to get away from it."

"So how come you work for Chainsaw Pictures?"

Randal took a mouthful of coffee. "I got no choice. The last time I bottomed out, Harvey was threatening to cut me off altogether. Right now I'm at his mercy. Part of the deal for me even bein' able to speak to the family and keep a roof over my head is that I work for Harvey for a year, stick to the programme, and all of that shit. It's his way of keeping me outta trouble, I guess. So he stuck me over at fucking Chainsaw with Kenny.

Believe me, this isn't a career choice for me. Once my time is up I'm gone, baby."

"Okay Randal, I hear you. Still, I have something that I think might interest you. Will you at least hear me out?" Gibby looked around, lowered his voice and said, "You wanna split so we can go talk?"

Randal shrugged. "Sure, why not? I think we saw the main attraction already."

"Great! I'm fucking ravenous. How about you?"

"For the first time in about six months I can honestly say no, I'm not. But I do know a good Mexican place near here..."

*

"*Play and party?*"

"No," Gibby said through a mouthful of tortilla chips, "Party and play. You seriously never heard of it? I thought you were into all kinds of degenerate shit."

Randal and Gibby were huddled at a table in El Chavo, a dark cave-like Mexican place on Sunset. The ceiling was adorned with dayglo sombreros, and over by the bar was a glow-in-the-dark portrait of Dolly Parton. The place looked like a Mexican homosexual's acid freak-out.

"I guess I'm a little behind the times. So what is it?"

"It's an internet phenomenon. It's, like, a gay subculture thing. A bunch of guys – speed freaks mostly – they meet up on message boards and chat sites... places like Manhunt, or Hot4Cox... and they arrange these orgies, right? A bunch of strangers get together so they can get high on crank and fuck. There's all this coded language an' shit, that's where the 'party and play' thing came from. It's real covert. Websites started cracking down on it. But it's still out there...

"Anyway, Jacques was, like, knee deep in that scene for six months. He said it was some of the craziest, darkest shit he'd ever seen. These guys... they would just get high and fuck for days on end. Just jacking up more and more speed and fucking like... like *machines*. Jacques used to call them *Fuck Robots*."

"Sounds pretty crazy."

Randal absently recalled how it felt to fuck on crystal meth. The superhuman focus, the weird sensation that your entire being – your soul itself – was about to explode out through your cock with nuclear propulsion. He missed sex feeling that intense. He sniffed, and reflexively reached for a chip before remembering that he wasn't hungry.

"You should have *heard* some of the stories Jacques told me. There was this one guy, he was a retired schoolteacher and his whole deal was that he liked to be wrapped up – mummified really – in Saran Wrap. It would take a couple of rolls to get him really snug. He'd have a straw sticking out of his mouth, y'know, to breathe through. The only other thing he'd have sticking out of this Saran cocoon was his dick."

"Figures."

"Uh-huh. Just before they wrapped him up they'd shoot him up with a huge fucking hit of crystal meth..."

Randal took a gulp of his water.

"...and they'd just lay him out in the middle of the room. There's be a bunch of these guys all hanging out, fucking, shooting up, whatever – and this guy is tweaking his balls off in the middle of it all, with a raging hard on, and he can't even move a muscle."

"They'd just leave him there?"

"For hours, man. HOURS! Like once in a while one of the dudes would go over and do something with his pecker or whatever, but mostly this guy's whole trip was just watching all this kinky shit go down, totally helpless."

"Takes all sorts, I guess."

"Uh-huh. And then there'd be parties called "conversion parties" for guys who wanted to get the virus. Like AIDS, you know? They call those guys "bug chasers". They'd show up specifically so they could get fucked bareback by a bunch of HIV positive dudes. It's a fetish thing, you know? They said they got the same kinda kick out of it that someone might get out of playing Russian Roulette, or whatever. I mean, it was this whole other fucking world, Randal. Try as I might, I couldn't find a publisher with the balls to take on the pictures. We had a good run exhibiting them around Europe though. The cops raided a gallery in Munich; Jacques spent a night in the cells."

"And these guys, they were cool with your pal... Jacques... photographing all of this stuff going on?"

"Oh they were wary at first, believe me. It's a pretty secretive scene. But you gotta understand, Jacques has a hell of a reputation as a filmmaker. He's a pretty big deal. You *really* never saw *Dead Flowers*?"

"Nah. I remember when everybody freaked out about it. I don't really dig cinema, Gibby. I grew up surrounded by those people: actors, screenwriters, producers, the whole fuckin' circus. The idea of actually paying money to sit through a movie... it's just weird to me. You know, my favourite movie of all time is *Abbott and Costello Meets Frankenstein*. You ever seen it?"

"Sure, they used to show it on Saturday morning TV all the time."

Randal nodded. "Yeah. You know that was the only other time that Bela Lugosi played Dracula in a movie? I mean he played plenty of vampires, obviously, but besides the original movie that was the only time he was actually cast as Dracula himself. Anyway, that's what I call a *movie*, ya know? I like the classics. The new stuff doesn't do it for me..."

Randal took a gulp of his water and fixed Gibby with a serious look. "So anyway, your pal Jacques, he directs one hit movie and then spends the next fifteen years snapping pictures of guy-on-guy gangbangs. Is he a fruit?"

Gibby laughed, "Nah. He's just into bizarre shit, you know? The extreme."

"Uh-huh."

The waitress arrived, bringing Gibby's margarita and grande carnitas burrito along with Randal's coffee. Randal watched the waitress go, and then said, "Margarita huh? So you're one of those guys just who show up to network?"

"Hell, I gotta eat," Gibby said, with an apologetic shrug.

Randal started pouring sugar into his coffee. "I hear ya," he said.

Gibby started laying into his burrito with gusto.

"He said the worst thing was the smell," he carried on through a mouthful of food, "After eight hours of fucking and getting high, Jacques said the place just reeked. He said they'd give off this distinctive, chemical smell... compared it to a mix between body odour, ammonia and the stink of a well-used peep show booth."

"Delightful. So why you telling me all of this? Your client has finally dragged his ass outta retirement to direct a movie for Kenny 'douchebag' Azura. So what?"

"So... he wants to hire you."

Randal put his coffee down. "Come again?"

Gibby leaned in close.

"Listen Randal, this is on the down low, okay? Azura has given my client the go ahead to direct his dream project, a movie called *Black Neon* that he's been working on the past fifteen years. He's offering him fat pockets and total artistic control. Jacques needs a tour guide... someone who knows the drug scene over here. All of that shit you've shared about in the meetings. The street scene. The hookers. The dealers, the scuzzball motels. Hollywood, man... *your* Hollywood. He wants *Black Neon* to be set entirely in the LA drug scene with a cast made up of actual dope-fiends. It's gonna have a script, but none of the on-screen action is gonna be faked. You ever hear of James Stein?"

"Yeah. Isn't he the guy who wrote *Point of No Return*?"

"That's him. We just got him on board to write the script."

From what Randal could remember, Stein wrote his bestselling book *Point of No Return* when he was a twenty-year-old Columbia student. It was a novel about the adventures of a group of rich, nihilistic, sex-crazed, coke-zombie Columbia students that was hailed as one of the defining books of its era. It sold millions, was adapted badly to the big screen, and made the author instantly famous. After that his career had mostly been one of diminishing returns and these days he was better known for his legendary cocaine habit and the string of young actresses and models he had been linked to in the pages of TMZ.

"Jesus, so your dream team consists of a guy who hasn't directed a movie in fifteen years and a writer who hasn't written anything decent since the nineteen-eighties? This sounds like it's gonna be *great*."

"I'd can the sarcasm if I were you. Azura is betting the house on *Black Neon*. He's giving Jacques a blank check to make the movie, no interference from the studio. That's why we can't talk about what Jacques is actually planning... it might rock the boat with Chainsaw... but Jacques is offering you twenty thousand dollars for an inside track on the drug scene."

Randal was quiet for a moment.

"He'll pay *twenty grand* to see some Hollywood sleaze?"

Gibby shook his head. "No. He don't wanna SEE it Randal. He wants to LIVE it. He wants to smell it, touch it. Most of all... he wants to film it."

Randal nodded his head slowly, considering this. With his brother's weekly allowance barely keeping Randal in groceries and gas money, twenty thousand had a nice ring to it. An especially nice ring when Randal considered the fact that it would actually be Harvey's money, pissed away by that arrogant little fuckwad Kenny on a movie that sounded like it would sink like a stone. Randal absently fantasized about Kenny Azura leaving Dreamscape in disgrace, his career in tatters, after producing one of the most expensive flops since Paramount lost 130 million on *Sahara*.

"One question. What's the movie *about*? I mean, okay, he wants to set it in Hollywood. And he wants a bunch of junkies and whores starring in it. But what's the film *about*?"

Gibby laughed sourly and shrugged. "I haven't got a fucking clue. I don't really understand what the hell goes on in Jacques' mind most of the time. The thing is, there's no doubting that Jacques is... or was, at least... a really talented guy. I saw him change right after *Dead Flowers* came out. He was dating an actress, Isabella Simonelli. Beautiful woman, talented too. She was on the verge of an incredible career. At least she was until she fell in with Jacques. They used to call them "beauty and the beast" in the European press. Nobody could figure out what this woman saw in Jacques – he isn't exactly what you'd call a *handsome* guy, you know? But I saw them together. They really *were* in love. She adored him. Jacques? He was fucking *smitten*. He'd *glow* when he was around her. The press followed them everywhere, people just... I don't know. It was sad. How it all turned out."

"What happened?"

"Car crash. They'd been at some party in St Tropez, both of them drinking, having a good time. It was around four in the morning. Jacques was flooring this obnoxious sports car he used to drive, and he told me they were passing a bottle of champagne back and forth... suddenly, *boom*. I guess he lost control. There was a terrible crash. She was flung through the fucking windshield and impaled on an iron railing."

"Jesus Christ."

"Jacques emerged without so much as a fucking scratch on him. He told me even the bottle of champagne they'd been drinking survived intact. The capper was that when they did the autopsy, they discovered she'd been pregnant. Neither of them knew, according to Jacques. Well, the press... they fucking *pilloried* him. Called him a murderer, baby killer, monster, the works. I know he had to throw a lot of money at it to make it all go away, as far as the law was concerned. In the court of public opinion though he was found guilty as hell. He only ever talked to me about it once. He told me that she was the only woman he would ever love. He never said it to me in so many words, but I got the sense that he kinda gave up after that. When the media called him a pig, a degenerate, drug addict, fiend... I guess he just shrugged his shoulders and decided to give them what they wanted. If you ask me, that was the point that Jacques the *persona* took over. He also told me that the crash convinced him that he was *immortal*, if you can believe that. *How could she die, Gibby, and I survive? How can all of my contemporaries OD or crack up or admit defeat and get clean, yet I keep going? It's because I'm special, that's why.* Those where his exact words to me. *Because I'm SPECIAL.*"

"He sounds pretty fucked up. You think he can hold it together long enough to finish this movie?"

"I don't know. All I know is that some people – Kenny included – seem to think he's a fucking genius, and that's enough for me. You wanna know what *Black Neon* means to *me*? It means fifteen fucking percent. That's what it means."

Randal smiled, and gestured towards Gibby's margarita glass. "May I?" Without waiting for a reply Randal slid the drink over, brought it to his lips and guzzled it hungrily. He waved the empty glass toward the waitress and said, "Two more, por favor!"

He turned back to Gibby, shivered, and said, "Goddamn, that was a good margarita. If you want my opinion, they got the best in the city."

"Fucking hell, Randal. Are you sure you should be drinking? You've been clean for *months*. Should I, like, call your sponsor or something?"

Randal laughed. "My sponsor? You're a fucking crack-up, man. Of course I still *drink*. How in the hell do you think I've made it this far without killing someone? Shit, Gibby, I'll do it. Sounds like it'll be interesting, to say the least."

"Great! I'm real happy to hear that, Randal. I'll give Jacques your details, and he'll be in touch to arrange things..."

Gibby looked down at his empty glass, still looking unsure. "Seriously though... aren't you worried about your, y'know, *clean time*?"

Two more drinks were brought to the table. Randal picked up his glass.

"Clean time is a state of mind," he declared, "So long as I'm not strung out on crank, then as far as I'm concerned, I'm clean."

"Well, you're the boss," Gibby said cautiously, as they clinked their glasses together. "*Cheers!*"

NINE

O n the car's tape deck Sunnyland Slim was singing, *"I'm gonna buy me a Johnson Machine Gun... and a carload of explosion balls... I'm gonna be a walking cyclone from Saginaw to Niagara Falls..."*

"Where in the hell is Saginaw, anyway?" Genesis asked, tossing her smoldering Virginia Slim out of the window.

"Someplace in Michigan," Lupita said. "Never been, but I don't imagine it's anyplace special. You know something Genesis? You gotta stop smoking those bitch-ass Slim cigarettes. They don't suit a tough girl like you. You ever smoked a cigar?"

Genesis shook her head. "Nah. My daddy used to smoke 'em and I always hated the stink. He smoked a pipe for a while too, and I didn't mind that so much 'cept that I always thought he looked pretty ridiculous puffing on it. Made him look like a college professor, which is ironic considering he didn't even finish high school. And anyway, I ain't tough Lupe, I'm just resilient. There's a big difference."

They were sat in Lupita's idling Eldorado, watching the comings and goings at *The Friendly Drugstore*. It was almost six thirty, and the place was due to close any minute. *Friendly's* was a tiny little place tucked away in an anonymous strip-mall. It was sandwiched between a Thai take-out and a liquor store. Lupita had been keeping an eye on this drugstore for a while, paying special attention to *Friendly's* clientele. It was a mom and pop operation, still limping along despite competition from a CVS five minutes away.

Lupita had paid several visits to *Friendly's* over the past few weeks, buying gum, cigarettes and Band-Aids. The pharmacist was an elderly Asian man, bald and rail-thin with prominent ears and wispy white eyebrows that looked like they were made of cotton candy. Both girls she had seen working in there were young and disinterested. They looked like they wouldn't cause any trouble. She'd hoped for a little more time to case the joint, but Paco's murder made the need for money, drugs and a quick exit from Reno all the more pressing.

"So, you ready or what?" Lupita asked.

"As I'll ever be, s'pose."

"You getting nervous? It's okay if you are. Only natural, it being your first time. If you don't wanna do this... you don't have to. You could wait out here, I don't mind going in alone."

"No. I'm not *nervous* I guess. Just want everything to go okay. And anyway, if I'm gonna come with you then I want to *contribute*."

Lupita smiled. "That's cool. And it'll be fine, girl. The pharmacist is as old as Confucius, and those bitches he has working there ain't gonna do shit. Not when they get an eyeful of the ladies..."

On their laps were the "ladies". A Heckler and Koch P7 self-loading pistol for Genesis, and a SIG-Sauer P-225 police issue pistol for Lupita. Lupita had a real fetish for the power and efficiency of German handguns. Each gun was fitted with a silencer.

"I got a good feelin' about the haul. They got a pain clinic just down the ways there, next to the business park. Plus, there's been a ton of old fucks hobbling in and out of this place on walkers an' shit, picking up all kinds of pain medication. The oldsters got the key to the candy shop man, least as far as prescription meds are concerned. Not to mention the middle school two blocks away."

"What's the middle school have to do with it?"

One of Lupita's painted-on eyebrows arched extravagantly. "*Adderall*, girl. Or Ritalin. Dexedrine. You know most of those little fuckers are doped up on *something*. Nah, Genesis, I got the feeling that this place could be a gold-mine."

Genesis took a deep breath. "I'm ready," she said. "I'm fuckin' ready, let's do it."

It hadn't been too tough to convince Genesis that knocking off this pharmacy would be a breeze. After all, Lupita told her she'd robbed dozens in her time, never getting caught once. The staff in those places are trained not to interfere with a robbery, Lupita explained, they were supposed to just hand the shit over without trying to be a hero. After all, they're all insured up the wazoo.

"So long as you're prepared, organized, and you don't go in there dope-sick and desperate," Lupita insisted, "there's not a lot that can go wrong."

Still, Lupita had half expected Genesis to cop out at the last minute. After all, it's one thing firing guns at a paper target down at the shooting range, it's another to walk into a drug store and point it at another human being. But so far Genesis' desire to get out of Reno and hit the road with Lupita seemed to be keeping her nerves in check. Lupita would never have ordinarily considered roping in an amateur on a pharmacy job, but the girl was strong-willed and serious. Lupita had a strong gut feeling that Genesis would have what it takes, so long as she did what she was told and didn't lose her nerve at the last minute.

"Okay. Let's go through it one more time. First step is we go in, and you lock the door and put up the closed sign."

"Yeah."

"I head straight to the back of the store. It's a tiny place, four or five aisles of crap, pharmacy at the back. I show 'em the gun and the bag, and tell 'em to hand over the dope and the money. You cover me from the back. If you don't wanna say shit, you don't have to. Just listen to how I do it, what I say, and how I say it. Just keep that fuckin' gun pointed at them. And Genesis, if anyone tries any bullshit – they won't, but just *supposin'* they do – let me take care of it. I don't want you panicking and accidentally hitting me with a fuckin' bullet, okay? In a place that size, a bullet could ricochet and hit you or me in the face."

"Goddit. I just keep it pointed at them."

"That's right. We'll be in and out in five minutes, tops. When we've got the shit we need we use the handcuffs to slow 'em down, give us time to split. We leave the engine running, and get the fuck outta here. And that's all she wrote."

Genesis nodded. Lupita reached out, and caressed her earlobe. "The first one's the hardest. Once you get this one over with, the next time'll be a breeze."

They pulled the red bandannas over their faces and their baseball caps low over their eyes. Lupita had insisted on red bandanas, muttering cryptically about red being a protection against the evil eye. In their new motel room in Carson City she had already constructed a miniature altar out of religious artefacts, votive candles, and figurines of Catholic saints. *What the hell*, Genesis had figured, *everybody's got their quirks.* The fact that she suspected Lupita was some kind of religious nut was small potatoes. Lupita was smart, beautiful, and her ticket out of Reno.

They pulled the car around and drew up in the empty space in front of the drugstore. They were confident that the place was empty of customers. The last one – a black man wearing a hard hat and overalls covered in concrete dust – left over ten minutes ago. The guns were cocked and loaded. They looked at each other one more time and then hustled toward *The Friendly Drugstore*, slamming the car doors after them.

They strode inside purposefully, a tinkling bell over the door announcing their arrival. Genesis closed the door roughly, snapping the lock in place. She flipped the "Closed" sign over. Lupita headed to the back of the store, gun drawn, stopping when she got to the counter.

She pointed the SIG-Sauer P225 at the pharmacist's chest.

The old man just stood there, his mouth flapping open, paperwork fluttering from his hand to the floor. He was wearing a colourful sweater and bow tie underneath his white lab coat.

"Drugs and money," Lupita said, tossing the empty bag onto the counter, "Don't make me repeat myself."

Without a word, the pharmacist walked over to the counter and picked up the bag. Lupita noticed with satisfaction that his hand was trembling.

"Don't shoot," he said.

"Drugs and money," Lupita repeated.

Genesis was standing next to her now. She kept her gun on the pharmacist, too.

"Where's the girl?" Lupita asked.

The old man stood there gawping at the guns.

"You can fill the bag while you're talking, granddad. The girl who works here. Where is she?"

Meekly, the old man pointed toward the back of the pharmacy. "Bathroom," he said cautiously.

Lupita sucked on her teeth, scowling.

"Stay on him," she said to Genesis, gesturing toward the pharmacist. "Make sure he doesn't try any shit. Keep him filling the bag. I'll go check on the girl."

Encouraged by the expression of terror on the pharmacists face, Genesis told the old man to move it. She led the pharmacist at gunpoint to the narcotics drawer, while Lupita walked back through a tiny corridor cluttered with boxes, until she came to the bathroom. She placed her ear to the door. She could hear someone humming softly to themselves while they pissed. The girl obviously hadn't heard what was going on. Off in the distance she could hear Genesis saying in a monotone, "Hurry up, old man. We'll take whatever you got." Lupita smiled to herself, a feeling of pride filling her chest. Then she kicked the bathroom door solidly, busting it wide open.

Inside the tiny bathroom a young woman with frizzy red hair and acne scars was sitting on the toilet. She was wearing a white lab coat and sneakers. Her tights and panties were around her ankles. Her purse was on the floor, and she was reading a copy of *In Touch* magazine. She looked up at Lupita, her mouth frozen in a silent "oh". She dropped the magazine.

"Glad to see you're not on your cell-phone, Annie," Lupita deadpanned, "I'da really hated to have to kill someone while they're sitting on the can."

The girl, whose nametag read "Sienna", just sat there stunned. There was no colour in her face. Another weak trickle of pee hit the toilet bowl.

"Come on, bitch, this is a *robbery*! Get your ass out there. Piss break's over!"

Cautiously, the girl went to reach for the toilet roll at her side.

"You can wipe later, okay honey?" Lupita cocked the gun. "Right now you got some work to do. Pull your fuckin' pants up and move it."

The girl stood, pulling her underwear and tights up quickly. She said, "I got a kid at home, please don't shoot me."

"Then do exactly what I fuckin' say. Move it, and keep your damn mouth closed."

When they made it back to the counter, the old man was done emptying the drugs into the bag. Genesis handed the bag to Lupita. Lupita glanced inside and whistled. Then she shoved the bag into the girl's hand and said, "Empty the fucking register."

Lupita and the girl went over to the cash register. Genesis sat the pharmacist down on a swivel chair, keeping the gun on him. "Don't look at me," she said. He averted his eyes.

"Okay, we're done here," Lupita yelled. The bag was zipped up, slung over her shoulder.

She led the girl over to the pharmacist and told her to lie down on the floor at his feet, face down with her hands behind her back. She knelt on the girl's back, making her grunt a little in protest, and cuffed her, tight. Genesis cuffed the old man to the chair. Lupita ripped the phone from the wall, and stomped on it until it broke into pieces. "Okay, let's go." They both headed towards the exit. "You count to fifty Mississippi before you get up," Lupita yelled back at them. "If I hear that you fuckers got smart and tried to follow us out I promise I will come back and waste the pair of you, goddit?"

They were by the door when Lupita said, "Stop." She reached out and placed her hand on Genesis's shoulder, with an expression calculated to give the impression that she'd just remembered something vitally important.

"What is it?"

"Peek through the door. We still clear outside?"

Genesis put her face up to the glass. "It's deserted. Let's go."

"No. There's something... somethin' I gotta do."

Lupita looked back toward where the pharmacist and the girl were tied up.

"What?" Genesis whispered, "What's wrong?"

"Look, don't panic, okay? There's just something I've got to do, and I need to you keep watch for me, okay?"

"What do you have to do? What's goin' on?"

"Wait here, okay? If you see anything outside, holler."

Genesis watched Lupita walk to the back of the store and make her way behind the counter. Cursing to herself Genesis peeked out of the door again, anxiously watching the street. Lupita stood over the pharmacist and the girl. She felt her breathing get deeper, infusing her whole body with a terrible power. The pharmacist had his eyes closed tight, muttering to himself, his forehead a mass of wrinkles. The girl, however, was staring up at Lupita with eyes that seemed ready to pop out of her head. Her mouth was pursed and she silently shook her head back and forth. Lupita raised the gun and put it to her lips in a *shushing* motion. She tucked the gun in her waistband and knelt down, leaning in so their faces were only inches apart. She could feet the girl's jagged breath fluttering against the bandana that covered her face. Lupita whispered, "How old is your kid?"

The girl didn't answer. Instead she let out a small, terrified moan.

Off at the front of the store Genesis looked back. Now that Lupita was crouched down, she was out of sight completely. Swallowing hard, Genesis hissed, "Come *on*! Lets get the fuck *outta* here!"

Lupita turned her head and in a low voice – the kind of low, guttural voice that Genesis recognized from when they made love, a voice that dripped with desire and heat – she said, "I'm *coming*, hun. Gimmie one second." Then, turning back to the girl, "How old?"

"F-four," the girl whispered. "My daughter... is four years old."

Lupita smiled. She reached up to her face and pulled the bandana off. Exposed, she smiled benignly at the girl and whispered, "Kiss me, mami."

The girl just lay there, trembling. Lupita leaned in further and forced her lips against the girl's mouth. The mouth was hot, feverish. As she crushed her lips against the girl's she grabbed a handful of that tangled, red hair and wrenched some out of the scalp. The girl let out a muffled squeal, and Lupita felt her jaw trembling underneath those soft, furnace-like lips. They broke apart. Lupita stood and tucked the handful of hair into the pocket of her jeans, before drawing the gun.

"*Gracias...*" Lupita whispered. She winked at the girl and then casually shot the pharmacist twice in the chest. The girl opened her mouth to scream.

Before she could make a sound Lupita shot her in the face. The bullet blasted the steaming contents of her skull all over the floor.

At the sound of the muffled gunshots, Genesis came running. She saw the pharmacist and the girl dead, blood splattered all over the floor. She clamped her hand to her mouth to keep herself from screaming. Lupita looked at Genesis blankly and said, "What the hell's the matter with *you*? You look like you seen a ghost."

"*Th-they're dead!*"

"Uh-huh." Lupita seemed oddly calm. "I was talkin' to the girl, making sure that she knew what the consequences would be if she talked. All of a sudden the bitch tries to bite me. She didn't get me, but she pulled the bandana off my damn face with her teeth. Once they'd seen my face, hun, I had no fuckin' choice. It was them or us."

Genesis just stood there, looking at the bloody corpses. Lupita tucked the gun away, fixed the bandana over her face again. She grabbed Genesis by the shoulder. They locked eyes.

"Listen to me. I had *no choice*, okay? That's the goddamned truth. I had to kill the both of them. It was out of my hands. They saw my face."

Genesis nodded quickly.

"You understand?" Lupita hissed, "Because if this is a problem we can go our separate ways right now. I had to do it."

"I understand," Genesis whispered.

"Enough talking, then. Let's get the fuck out of here before we have to explain it to a judge."

*

When they made it back to the motel, Lupita headed straight for the altar. She lit a votive candle and sat cross-legged in front of it. She held the long strands of red hair she had taken from the dead girl over the flame. They sizzled, sending a distinctive smell and wisps of black smoke into the air as Lupita dreamily recited a prayer in Spanish.

Genesis watched all this from the bed, a sick, heavy feeling in her gut. Observing this odd ritual the thought had occurred to her that Lupita might be insane. She had killed three people in the short time they had known each other, and in Genesis's experience anyone this obsessed with religion was usually using it as a cover for some kind of darkness inside. But, Genesis mused, when Lupita wasn't killing people or praying to plastic statues of the Virgin Mary... she seemed so *normal.*

Lupita caught Genesis's gaze on her and asked, "You okay?"

Genesis nodded quickly.

Lupita gazed at the candle's flickering flame. A pained expression came over her.

"I don't *like* to kill, Genesis hun. Taking someone's life... it's not something I do easily. But it was them or us. If she'd have just listened to me and acted cool...."

There was an awkward silence. Then Genesis spoke cautiously.

"What were you doing there? I mean, with the hair."

"Praying for her. She didn't die a happy death, hun. I was just praying that she'd find some peace. You know, on the other side. That's all."

Genesis nodded slowly. She looked at the bag on the bed, and tried to force the ugly thoughts out of her head. Now that they were away from the drug store, and away from Reno, Lupita seemed more like her old self again. And there were all the drugs to consider...

Lupita stood, and as if reading Genesis's mind asked, "You wanna check out the haul?"

Genesis's face brightened. "Damn straight."

They counted the stash – both of them kneeling on the floor, with the haul spread out on the bed. It added up to almost eight hundred dollars and a literal pile of controlled substances. Chunky white Vicodin, chalky to the touch. Perfectly round Oxycontin, in a variety of enticing colours: white, pale pink, yellow and best of all the 80mg in lime green. At least ninety 8mg Dilaudid that were triangular with rounded corners. Blister packs of perfectly formed little Ritalin pills. And the Adderall: two hundred or so two-toned capsules full of tiny orange balls that tasted sickly-sweet in the back of your throat when crushed and snorted. Not to two mention dozen morphine ampoules and a couple of boxes of Fentanyl patches.

"Oh my God," Genesis said as they went through it all, separating out the drugs and counting the money, "all of these pills are making me horny. I never seen so many in one place before. I just – I just wish we didn't have to... you know. Kill those people."

Lupita playfully grabbed Genesis's hair, and nuzzled her neck.

"It's a dog eat dog world out there, hun. You need to stop worrying about other people and start worrying about covering your own ass. You think that either of those motherfuckers would give a shit if the cops blew us away, or tossed our asses in jail? Honestly?"

"No," Genesis conceded.

"Fucking right. It's okay to feel bad, Genesis hun. Only human. But you just gotta pray on it for a while, and then move the fuck on. Otherwise that shit'll eat away at you, either send you crazy or make you fuck up so bad you end up in jail or the morgue. Baby, you did *good* today. You made me proud. You were cool as a fucking cucumber, and you didn't take any shit. It kinda turned me on."

"Thanks, baby," Genesis said, smiling a little. "Still, you gotta make me a promise. I know you didn't have a choice today, but you gotta swear to me – *swear to me Lupita* – no more killing. I just couldn't bear to have another thing like that on my conscience."

"If it makes you feel any better, it ain't on *your* conscience. It's on *mine*. You had no part of what went on in there after we took the drugs. None. I had to make an... *executive decision* is all."

"I *understand* that, Lupe. But I still need you to promise me. No more killing, okay? I mean it."

"Okay, hun. I promise. I'll do my fuckin' best, okay? If that's what makes you happy."

Genesis nodded eagerly. "It is. That'll make me real happy. Okay, enough of that shit. We got more drugs than I ever seen in one place in my whole life before."

"Beautiful, ain't it?"

"Sure is. So what do you wanna do first? You ever shot Ritalin and Dilaudid together? It's pretty wild."

"Oh yeah? Sounds good to me. You got something you gotta do for me first, though."

Lupita stood up and unbuttoned her skinny black jeans. She tugged them down, and stepped out of them. She wasn't wearing any underwear. She picked up the SIG-Saer P-225 from the bed, and pointed it at her black, curly pubic patch. Genesis looked up at her, laughed softly and said, "Oh God, baby! What *do* you got in mind?"

"Time for your lesson," Lupita said. "You're a natural at robbin' drugstores, girl, but your technique down here still needs a little work. It's time for schooling, and I gotta tell you... I'm as hot as hell right now."

"You mind if I get a little high first?" Genesis said, fake pouting.

"Okay by me, Genesis hun, just do it quickly 'cause I'm about liable to explode right now. And remember, this ain't no porno flick. Don't eat me like you're trying to impress a guy." She tapped the barrel of the gun against her crotch lightly. "You got to make *me* happy. No acting. You gotta really show the pussy some affection. Show it who the boss is."

"Yes m'am," Genesis said, kissing her belly lightly, and rubbing her face against Lupita's pubic hair like a cat. She could feel the animal heat rising from her lover's cunt in waves. She turned her attention back to the bed and started hungrily separating out pills.

TEN

Under most circumstances Kinder Eggs would have held very little appeal for Jacques Seltzer. He found the cheap, mass produced chocolate to be utterly abhorrent, preferring the craft and workmanship of Parisian master chocolatiers like Michel Chaudun. The simple children's novelties hidden inside the eggs – the miniature Smurfs, plastic toy cars, or what have you – likewise were of no interest to him. In fact, if it wasn't for the hard yellow plastic shell inside the chocolate egg that the novelties came hidden in, Seltzer might easily have gone his whole life without ever having bought one.

However, when Seltzer was crossing international borders those yellow plastic shells were an essential part of his travel kit. Each one could reasonably hold a significant amount of contraband. On top of this they were also a perfect size and shape for rectal insertion. It had taken some practice, but in time he was able to fit up to four of them inside his ass without causing himself serious discomfort.

Jacques had arrived in Los Angeles an hour earlier to meet Randal. Over the phone Randal had intrigued Jacques. He felt that this wealthy, aimless decadent was someone he could relate to. Jacques was particularly fascinated by two types of people: the extremely rich and the extremely poor. Jacques knew that the extremely rich lived their lives without any rules because their money convinced them – rightly, in most cases – that the traditional norms of society did not apply to them. They had been brought up to believe that they were *special*. Barring murder, there were few transgressions that could not be smoothed over if you had enough money. Even murder was, Jacques felt in some deep, locked away part of himself, negotiable.

The poor interested Jacques because they lived their lives without rules as well, although their rationale was different. They had no investment in society, no illusions of mobility or respectability to protect. Although there were plenty of cosmetic differences between the extremely rich and the extremely poor Jacques found their moment-to-moment attitude to life very similar. After speaking with Randal for just an hour, Jacques was convinced that he had found his man. Inspired, he booked a flight to Los Angeles and arranged to meet Randal on his home turf.

While Randal sat at the bar of Encounter, Los Angeles International Airport's premier Sixties sci-fi themed restaurant, poking unenthusiastically at an ahi tuna salad, Jacques Seltzer was in the men's room squeezing one 8 ball of cocaine, one eighth of an ounce of hash, fourteen ecstasy tablets and an 8 ball of heroin out of his anus. They landed in the toilet bowl one after the other, *plop! Plop! Plop! Plop!* Another good thing about those Kinder Egg shells was that they were completely waterproof.

After having four shells stuffed up there for over fourteen hours it felt particularly satisfying to hear the last one splash down in the bowl. He allowed himself a moment to relish the feeling of relief. He closed his eyes and sat contentedly, listening to the wailing theremin music that they piped into the bathrooms. Then he stood and turned around to retrieve his bounty.

The moment Jacques stood a terrible noise filled the stall, a violent *whooshing* sound, like an airplane passing low overhead. Jacques stood frozen in horror as his drugs were instantly sucked away by the toilet's super-powered automatic flush. Too late Jacques noticed the infrared detector that had caused the toilet to flush the moment his considerable bulk had shifted from the toilet bowl. In a fraction of a second his entire stash had been vacuumed away into the Los Angeles sewer system via this vile, space-age crapper.

At the bar a disinterested barmaid dressed like a 99¢ store Judy Jetson filled Randal's glass with soda. The dispenser was shaped like a Ray Gun and made a zapping sound when it sprayed. A sudden burst of indecipherable obscenities, a garbled hodge-podge of French and bastardized English erupted from the bathroom. It was loud enough to cause the entire restaurant to fall into a startled hush for a moment. When Jacques Seltzer emerged from the men's room a minute or two later and took his seat next to Randal, he looked manic. His eyes were blazing and his face seemed even more flushed and sweaty than before.

"Everything okay?"

Ignoring Randal's question Jacques barked at the barmaid, "Martini, s'il vous plait!"

Jacques stared at the ceiling for a moment, and then looked around his kitschy surroundings. The restaurant itself was housed in a circular building that looked something like an Ed Wood-style flying saucer. The decor was a riot of lava lamps, white plastic pop art furniture, and acid-flashback colour schemes, pitched somewhere in between a Seventies bachelor pad and a high school production of *Star Trek*. He shook his head and looked at Randal.

"Forgive my rudeness Randal, but I just had a very disturbing experience."

"More disturbing than the decor in here?"

Jacques did not laugh. Randal wondered what could constitute a disturbing experience to man who had watched an ex-schoolteacher mummified in Saran Wrap getting meth injected into his cock. The barmaid brought over Jacques' drink, and he rested his hand on the stem of the glass.

"I suppose we should get to the matter at hand," Jacques said.

"Sure. So how you wanna play this, Jacques?"

"Randal, my intention is to stay in the city for two weeks. Get to know the scene, meet some people, yes?"

"Sounds good, Jacques. Where are you gonna be staying?"

"Wherever you put me, Randal! Where else? The motels you mentioned, the transient places, this is where I need to be. I must soak up and capture as much of the authentic city as is humanly possible in my short time here. I cannot do that if I am drinking champagne in the Four Seasons, no?"

"I guess not."

"I will be shooting some footage on this trip. Making plans, documenting the early stages of the project. The most important thing is that I can assimilate, oui? Pass unnoticed in this world. I do not want to be treated any different from the average junkie on the street."

"Well, if that's the way you want to play it. I gotta tell you Jacques, I've met the average junkie on the street, and he's usually a real asshole."

Randal thought of the cold, desperate rooms he had stayed in when he was on one of his serious meth runs. Even when he had his own place, he preferred to check into a cheap motel when he was indulging in a sex and speed bender. For a start, it lowered the chances that whatever desperate meth whore he had convinced to sleep with him would be able to steal anything too valuable. Also he preferred the anonymity. There were no worries that his family would barge in trying to pull one of their periodic surprise interventions. These were ugly, desperate rooms – perfect for committing ugly, desperate acts in. In a weird way, the sleazy motel rooms had been as much of a part of his drug ritual as the drugs themselves.

Randal had little doubt that setting foot in one of those hell-motels that he had once frequented regularly would be a difficult experience. He imagined himself laying on one of those typical half-collapsed twin beds, the black and white TV bolted to the wall, the busted drawers, scuttling cockroaches and threadbare carpets... and to top it off, this strange Frenchman demanding an audience with junkies, drug dealers, hookers... Randal reflexively felt for the bottle of Adderall in his pocket. He was seeing Dr Titov tomorrow to up his dose. Focusing his attention on the twenty thousand dollars at hand he hoped that an adequate dose of pharmaceutical amphetamine would provide enough of a cushion to help him survive the next two weeks without relapsing.

Jacques looked at Randal, very seriously, and said, "Randal. I have a question for you."

"Shoot."

"Have you ever taken a two-thousand dollar shit?"

"I can't say I have..."

Jacques shook his head, and took a long, thirsty gulp of his cocktail.

"Well I just did, and I am not too happy about it. It necessitates a slight change of plan. We must score drugs, Randal. Heavy drugs, yes? Immediately! The whole project depends upon it..."

Jacques grinned maniacally at Randal. "Oh Jesus," Randal said, thinking about his twenty thousand dollars, "Look Jacques, I'm not one to be giving lectures about drugs, but..."

"Everything that follows *but* is meaningless, Randal. If you are not one to be giving lectures about drugs, then spare me. I need drugs. You know where to get them, yes?"

"Yes Jacques. Of course I know where to get them."

"Perfect!" Jacques suddenly relaxed, and gave Randal a friendly slap on the back that nearly knocked him off his seat. He bellowed, "Drink with me!"

He ordered another martini for Randal, and proposed a toast: "To that vile, demanding bitch – art!" For the first time – but not the last – that day, Randal had the suspicion that maybe, just maybe, this whole deal might not have been as good an idea as he'd first supposed.

ELEVEN

" It was the only time I'd ever lived outside of Reno. I was in LA
for a year and a bit. I was working at *Jumbo's Clown Room*...
I'd just turned twenty. This musta been... what, eight years ago?"

Genesis lit a Virginia Slim and tossed the smoldering match
out of the window. Lupita's 1970 Cadillac Eldorado tore through
the desert somewhere between Yerington and Shurz. The dry
heat gushed in through the open window for a moment, like
the scorching blast of a hair dryer. She rolled the glass up again
quickly.

Genesis and Lupita had been talking for two hours straight,
snorting meth out of a small plastic bullet as they sped toward
their destination of Laughlin, Nevada. They were due to meet
a connection of Lupita's who had agreed to buy the excess pills
from the *Friendly's* job. Plus, Lupita said, the bigger the distance
between themselves and Reno the better. For the first time in
years Genesis felt truly *free*. For once there was no need to
worry about money, no tricks to turn, no drug dealers or irate
landlords to pay off. Lupita was her protector, her teacher, and
her liberator. Ever since they had met there seemed to be an
abundance of *everything*: of drugs, of time, and best of all there
was an abundance of Her. This sense of liberation – sudden,
total liberation – made Genesis euphoric. For once in her rotten
life she was actually living in the moment, and the limitless
possibilities of the road turned her on. She didn't know where
they would head after Laughlin, but Genesis was excited to find
out.

"I had a boyfriend back then," she carried on, "his name was Jack. He was real handsome. Square jaw, dark hair. Looked like he mighta played football back in high school, you know? Like he'd walked straight out of a J Crew catalogue."

Lupita laughed. "He sounds like a real cocksucker," she said, turning down Amos Milburn singing "Bad, Bad Whiskey". They had a bottle of Wild Turkey stowed under the passenger seat, which Lupita would occasionally take a long slug from while she drove. When Lupita held the bottle, Genesis would reach across and hold the wheel steady. The booze, speed and painkillers made them feel invulnerable and holy, and their conversation weaved and danced along with the thunderous roar of the Eldorado's engine.

"No... no, he was a nice guy. Totally polite and respectful. Treated me good. Didn't drink, didn't do drugs or any of that stuff around me."

"What were you with him for?"

Genesis shrugged. "He liked me. He had some good payin' job that he tried to explain to me once... he was in mergers and acquisitions, he said. He'd come over to my place most nights in his suit and tie, carrying that silly briefcase of his. You know, he was the first guy I ever knew who owned a *briefcase*. I actually met him at Jumbo's; it was a party for one of the guys at his office. He seemed kinda shy, but he asked me for my number and... and he called. We just kinda hit it off. It was real secretive because of his wife... so we had this little routine worked out. He'd be done with work around seven. He'd come over most nights so we could fuck, or talk or whatever. Then he'd go back to his wife's place. Sometimes he'd bring take out, and we'd have dinner together. Maybe a bottle of wine, but he wouldn't drink. Went on like that for six months, or more."

"He sounds like a real sweetheart. How was the sex?"

"Good. I know you don't like dick none, but it *was* good. He was a little... *predictable*, I guess is the word."

"Honey, it's not that I don't like dick, I just don't like what they come attached to. Anyway, so you said it was predictable?"

"Yeah, not bad or nuthin'... it was good I suppose, just nuthin' mind blowing. I mean, I wasn't complaining. I was getting off three, four times a week. It was just..."

"Dull."

"Right. When we were done we'd lay around talking about this and that, just lay there bullshitting y'know? He didn't have too much to say for himself, tell the truth, and that's why I was already getting itchy feet. I was still seeing other people, but it was getting to be a *commitment* with him. I didn't see any future there. I was thinking about cutting it off when it happened."

"When *what* happened?"

"Well that's what I'm getting' to. Hey, you want some of this?"

Genesis pulled the bottle out from under the seat, pulled out the cork, and took a long hit. It burned like hell, but somehow with the crank burning in her nostrils and head it seemed bearable. She was drunk but alert. She smiled at Lupita. Lupita looked beautiful today, Genesis thought. Smiling and carefree, the desert sun made her profile look like a faded Polaroid of some long-ago summer love. She passed it over.

"Thanks hun," Lupita said, taking a hit and passing it back without dipping below 80mph. "So go on, I'm intrigued – what happened between you and Mr. J. Crew?"

"Well, that's the funny part. One night he comes over as usual, and he's got a present for me. All wrapped up in pretty paper, with a bow, the whole bit. I figured it was clothes, from the way it felt, you know? It felt kinda soft, and bulky. I went to open it and he tells me no, he wants to take me out to dinner first. This is weird, because like I told you if we ate together he would

103

always bring the food. He was too weirded out about getting seen out with me, what with his wife and all. Apparently she was some big hotshot bitch in the movie industry, a producer, or an agent, or some shit like that. Everybody in town knew her an' she knew everyone. But this night, he wants to take me out. I could tell it was a big deal for him, because he was acting as sketchy as hell the whole time. But whatever, right? I understood. I thought it was sweet that he was even gonna take the risk.

"So he takes me out to some fancy-ass French place in Venice, and I notice that he's drinking wine. When I saw that I started to figure that maybe he's trying to work up the nerve to tell me that it's over, or something."

"Hmm. What did you do? Were you upset?"

"Nah. Like I said, I was thinkin' about calling it off myself, so I wasn't too bothered. I just made sure that I ordered the most expensive shit on the menu, you know?"

"Thatta girl."

"I ain't no fool. You ever eaten steak tartare?"

"No, can't say I have."

"Well don't bother, unless the idea of eating a plate fulla raw chuck with a side salad appeals to ya. The snooty little bastard waiting the table didn't tell me that they don't even cook that shit."

"Girl! You actually ate raw meat?"

"I could only manage a coupla bites. After that I started hitting the wine, hard. Jack didn't even notice. He was too preoccupied. He was hitting the wine pretty hard himself. We got through three bottles in all. After that we split back for my place. He didn't say a word to me the whole way over. Just kept looking at me with these moony eyes, like some dopey teenage kid with a hard-on.

"When we get back to my place, we're barely inside the door when he jumps me. Grabs hold of me, spins me round, and starts kissing me. Really kissing me, like he was trying to eat me alive. I gotta say, it was pretty nice. I'd never seem him that... *passionate* before. He was normally one of those *reserved* types, you know? He practically drags me into the bedroom, and then he tells me – in a real serious voice – he tells me that he wants me to tie him up."

There was silence in the car for a moment.

"That's it?" Lupita finally said, "All that buildup, and he just wants you to tie him up? Damn, even this motherfucker's kinks were boring."

"Shhh! I'm not done, baby. I had this bed back then, a real nice one. Solid oak, four-poster, the whole bit. It was the first expensive thing I bought when I started making serious money stripping. When I was a kid I slept on this shitty, thin mattress and I always promised myself that when I made some decent scratch, I'd buy myself a real nice bed."

"Okay. So Mister Wonderful drinks a coupla bottles of wine and tells you he wants you to tie him up. Did you do it?"

"Well, that's the thing. It was no big deal, right? Seemed like a lot of fuss over nothing. I told him that I figured I had some scarves or something around the place that we could use. That's when he starts looking real sheepish, you know? Shakes his head and says – real businesslike – *That won't be necessary.* So he goes and gets his briefcase, puts it on the bed. It's one of those nice leather ones, with a combination lock, the whole bit. He puts in the combination and pops it open. Lupita, I ain't kidding, my jaw just about hit the floor."

Lupita grinned. "Oh yeah? What was in there?"

"Okay, dig this. He'd had this briefcase along with him every time he'd come over for the past six months, yeah? 'Cos he'd always come over after work. I'd never really thought too hard about it, but I guess I'd figured it would be full of a bunch of shit like papers, and fuckin' rolodexes or whatever people put in those things normally. Planners, shit like that? I'd never been interested enough to ask, to be honest. It was a fuckin' briefcase, you know? Hold on."

Genesis took another long snort from the bullet. "God," she said, "That's some good ice. Feel like I'm snorting broken glass."

"Uh-huh. Top-notch shit. At least old Paco was good for something. So, go on..."

"Okay. The inside of the case was a custom job. Red velvet, with, like, sections cut into it. All the right size and shape, so nothing moves around in there. And he's got all of this shit laid out there. Handcuffs. A gag, one of those ones with a rubber ball that fits in your mouth. A bottle of lube. And to top it all off: dildos."

Lupita laughed her deep, throaty laugh. She motioned to the bullet. Genesis held it to Lupita's nostril. She inhaled deeply as they flew through the remorseless desert, the methamphetamine burning its way up her nostril and deep into her brain, sending her head buzzing with a delicious jolt of electricity.

"You say *dildos*? Plural?"

"Uh-huh. Four of them. Each one bigger than the last. The biggest one was this brutal-looking black rubber number that looked like you could beat someone half to death with it."

"Shit. So what *was* his deal?"

"Well. He sees the look on my face. So he tells me to open my present. And god damn it, instead of some nice underwear or a dress or something, it's a fucking belt, a harness thing with an attachment for the dildos. Like a strap-on thing. I got the picture real quick after that, what he was working his nerve up to ask me to do. Jack wanted me to cuff him to the bed, gag him, and fuck him in the ass with the strap-on. And when he starts talking, suddenly he's real calm and businesslike. He's telling me, *First you're gonna use Ringo, you gotta start with Ringo, 'cos that's the smallest one and then you can work your way up to George. If things are going okay, we can go all the way up past Paul to John, but we gotta be careful with that one 'cos if you force it in I won't be able to walk straight tomorrow.* That's what he called them, John, Paul, George and Ringo... I gotta tell ya, I wasn't expecting that."

"I'll say! Fuckin' hell, so old Jack liked it in the ass, huh?"

"Sure did."

"Did you do it?"

"Yeah! Of course. I'd never got to fuck a guy in the ass before, so I was all into it..."

"So wait – what happened with Jack after all of that? So you fucked him in the ass. Did you still cut him loose?"

"Actually, no. After he laid that whole trip on me, I started to get interested in him again. Made him seem more... I dunno, interesting, or alive or something. I started to figure that maybe Jack had some other hidden depths to him, and he wasn't as plain and boring as I'd figured before he pulled out the cuffs and the strap-on, you know?"

"I can see that. So what *did* happen with you two?"

"Ugh." Genesis rolled her eyes, and lit another cigarette. "Two months later, it's my birthday. I made the fuckin' mistake of telling him. He stops over the day before with a present for me. Says he told his wife that he's gonna be away on a business trip over the weekend. So he can spend some real time with me, you know? He says he has something planned for us, and hands me an envelope. You know what that cocksucker gave me?"

"Nah, what?"

Genesis exhaled a cloud of cigarette smoke and rolled her eyes.

"Tickets to see the fuckin' Dave Matthews Band. Backstage passes, the whole bit. Says he spent hundreds of dollars getting them, the show was sold out or some shit. Apparently, some people actually *pay* to see them."

"Fucking hell."

"I know, right? I mean, I went along with him. To be polite. But after that... I dunno, I just didn't look at him the same way no more. He went down in my estimation so much, I just couldn't even find him *attractive* after that."

Lupita nodded, smiling sadly. "Well, I can understand that Genesis, hun. It'd be a deal breaker for me, too."

They drove in silence for a while after this, lost in their own thoughts. Lupita scanned the arid landscape, looking for a place to pull off. Genesis reached under her seat, and had another long pull on the bottle.

"I mean, *the Dave Matthews Band*?" she said again, mostly to herself, "What was that motherfucker *thinking?*"

Lupita pressed harder on the accelerator, and they tore down Highway 95, kicking up a storm of sand and gasoline fumes in their wake.

TWELVE

" So this your first time in LA?" Randal asked, as they crawled down the 110 toward Los Angeles. The traffic was bumper to bumper, a sea of gleaming chrome stretching off further than the eye could see. The cars crept toward the city like an army of asthmatic turtles reluctantly dragging themselves toward the grave.

"Unfortunately no," Jacques said, flicking through the channels on the digital radio. He settled on an oldies station playing *Surfing Bird* by The Trashmen. "They dragged me out here when *Dead Flowers* was released. It was dreadful. A bunch of boring parties with slow-witted movie executives and their wives with the face like this..." Jacques placed his meaty hands on either side of his face and pulled the skin back. It gave his face an obscene, leering effect. The sight of Jacques' fat, wet lips pulled tight over his skull reminded Randal of some bottom-feeding undersea creature. "And the movie stars! What a lousy lot! Dull and stupid, all of them talking to each other and craning their necks in case someone more important entered the room..." Jacques shook his head. "*Putain.*"

"Not a fan of the city of angels, huh?"

"Los Angeles is the end of civilization." Jacques said. "I am fascinated and repulsed by it in about equal measure."

Randal smiled a little. "That sounds about right. Goddamn, this is a *great* tune." He turned the radio up, nodding his head slowly to the beat of the music. "Okay Jacques, well I guess we'd better get the formalities out of the way. I'd better tell you upfront that I'm in recovery. I've been clean for six months.

That's the most clean time I've had in as long as I can remember. And I aim to keep it that way."

"Totally clean?" Jacques raised an eyebrow, theatrically. "No drugs at all?"

"Nope. Nothing except the medication my doctor prescribes, that's it."

"Ah, oui. God bless *doctors*. They have all the best shit, anyway. And, uh, what about alcohol? I seem to remember that you took a drink with me, did you not?"

"Well, yeah. I mean, I might have a glass socially or some shit... I don't really see booze as a problem. I was a speed freak, you know? Booze was never my vice."

"I see. So when you say you are clean, you mean that you only avoid doing the things you truly *enjoy*." Jacques smiled as he said it, but the comment still made Randal bristle with indignation.

"No. That's not it. I was an *addict*, Jacques. I didn't *enjoy* meth. I hadn't enjoyed it for many years. I just couldn't stop doing it. Big fuckin' difference."

Jacques continued to grin, but said nothing. Randal considered just letting it go but instead, already antagonized by the heat, and the traffic, and Jacques' condescending tone of voice, he bit.

"You find something about that statement... *amusing*?"

"No. Not at all, Randal. You must forgive me. Maybe it is the language barrier, or just my sense of humor. I meant no offense."

"Yeah? Then what you smiling about?"

"It's just that you seem to be slightly.... How I say? *Disingenuous* when you speak."

Randal stared at Jacques long enough that he almost rear-ended an idling SUV in front of them before hitting the brakes.

"You're calling me a fucking *liar*?" he spat.

Jacques shook his head. "Putain! Always you Americans think that you are starring in some dopey Dirty Harry type of a movie! Everybody is a tough guy in America, no? Randal, I do not say

110

that you are a *fucking liar*. Okay? Just that I feel you are being a little dishonest with yourself."

"For example?"

"Well, for example, your assertion that you did not *enjoy* using drugs for many years, but instead you were *compelled* to use them. I find this hard to believe."

"How so? If you knew the first thing about addiction..."

"I have used drugs for literally *decades* Randal. If there is something about drugs I have yet to discover, then please enlighten me, *Monsieur Americain...*"

Randal spluttered in indignation. "Are you telling me you are an *addict*, Jacques? Or just a drug user?"

"This is the conundrum is it not? How do you make this distinction? I use drugs when I want them, and I want them most of the time. Some drugs I have become physically dependent on and I have even needed to visit the hospital to... how you say... clean out the blood, yes? But do I think of myself as some helpless slave to my compulsions? Not at all, Randal. No more than I consider myself a helpless slave to anything else I enjoy. So no, I do not think of myself as an *addict*. I suspect you feel the same way, yet you patronize me by using these generic recovery phrases. About how you are an *addict*, and you didn't *enjoy* using that speed, and all this other *shit*. I'm sure you did enjoy using those drugs, Randal." Jacques looked at Randal, who was gripping the steering wheel with white knuckles. "In fact, I'm sure you *loved it*. And now you have quit, which is an admirable feat, don't get me wrong. But this revisionism, this rewriting of you own history. '*Oh I hated it!*' I find it a little... strange, that is all."

They drove in silence as they headed east. It was a disconcerting experience for Randal to have the very same arguments he had once employed against zealous drug counselors and even his own family thrown back in his face by this drug-hungry director. The worst thing about it was that those arguments had not become any less persuasive over time. Randal gripped the steering wheel hard and found himself grinding his teeth. Jacques was cutting through the flimsy cocoon the pills had constructed around him, and he found himself getting agitated and anxious. They made the turn off at the Santa Monica exit toward Pico Boulevard. Once they were in Westlake Randal finally broke his silence. He looked at Jacques and muttered, in a barely audible voice, "Jesus *Christ*, Jacques. Can't you at least consider the possibility that I might need to believe that bullshit to keep myself *sane*?"

Jacques pondered this for a few minutes, stroking his chin thoughtfully. "Of course," he conceded, "I can understand that."

Randal sniffed. "Anyway, fuck it, all I was saying was that I won't be joining in this little bacchanal you have planned, so please don't offer me any shit, okay? I'm operating on willpower here, and one fuck-up could royally screw things up for me. This isn't a joke, Jacques. I'm doing this for one reason only – I really need the cash that Gibby promised. A year ago, twenty thousand dollars wouldn't have been a big enough incentive to drag my ass out of bed. *Now* it's a big fucking deal, and that's all thanks to the mess I got into when I was using. You understand where I'm coming from?"

"Oui, Randal. I do. And I promise, you will have full co-operation. There is nothing sadder to me than the idea of wasting perfectly good drugs on someone who will not appreciate them."

At this, Jacques' cell phone rang. He picked it up and said, "Oui? Ah, yes. No problems, no not at all. Uh-huh, I am with Mr. Earnest as I speak…." Jacques looked over to Randal and rolled his eyes, "Oui. We are getting to know each other, yes. Yes… bonding… Right now? We are picking up… uh, *souvenirs*. Oui. Okay. Oui. Goodbye."

Jacques clicked the phone closed.

"Gibby?"

"Yes. Apparently I have my first meeting with Kenny Azura tomorrow evening. Tell me honestly, Randal – is he as despicable as I suspect he is?"

Randal shrugged. "I don't wanna prejudice you. You should see for yourself... But yeah, he ain't my favourite person in the fuckin' world. So look man, what you want? I know a place near here we can get you a room, and you're gonna be right in the heart of all the drug shit. I can get you crack, heroin, speed, whatever... I mean, it's pretty much all on offer in this neighbourhood if you know where to look. What do you want?"

"Everything, Randal!" Jacques declared with a look of absolute certainty in his eyes, "I want *everything*."

Randal took them toward 7th Street and muttered, "Somehow I knew you were gonna say that."

THIRTEEN

On Sunday morning the methadone clinic was closed. Jeffrey and Rachel woke leisurely around noon and shuffled over to the bathroom to prepare their first fix of the day. The brown medicine bottles containing their take-home doses of methadone were kept aside for later. After all, it would be a waste to start the morning with that shit when they had some actual honest-to-god dope to wake up on.

Jeffrey smoked two Pall Malls down to the filter before he found a decent vein. His arms were swollen and smeared with blood by the time he finally got his hit. When it was done he sat back, ripped the tourniquet away from his arm, and sucked up some of the excess blood from his wrist with a dreamy expression on his face.

"Goddamn," he said, "my veins are a fuckin' mess."

"Your veins ain't the problem. It's your blood pressure," Rachel said in the sleepy voice of the satiated junkie, "It's always lower in the morning. I told you before – soak your arms in hot water before you fix, it'll help."

Rachel, who had good, thick veins and never had much of a problem fixing, was lounging around on the bed in her underwear.

"I ain't got time for running the hot water or soakin' my fuckin' arms," Jeffrey muttered, allowing his head to flop back a little "I'm too impatient for that shit. I need to get my *fix*, y'know?"

"It took you twenty minutes of poking around to get it, too. It'd jus' take you five minutes to soak your arms."

"Suppose."

They sat like that for a while, silently regarding each other from across the room, suspended in that blissful netherworld between consciousness and death. Then Rachel said, "I had some crazy-ass dreams last night, baby."

Jeffrey opened his eyes to slits. "Oh yeah?"

He lit his third cigarette and joined Rachel on the bed. Rachel was a vivid dreamer and often attached profound significance to the content of her dreams. Over the past six months they had developed a routine of discussing Rachel's dreams on Sundays as they lazed around, happily stoned.

"Well," Rachel said, "The first one was another one of those crazy-ass things where I wake up but I can't speak, or move, or blink or shit. Like I'm trapped in my own body. Only this time, in the dark, I can hear people moving around in the room. Cops. Whisperin' in their radios an' shit. My eyes are closed an' I can't open them but I can see the light from their torches... flashing like crazy against my eyelids as I'm laying there. An' I can make out every word they're sayin'... *We got a burnt spoon here... used syringe... oh shit, check it out, here's their dope stash... These junkie motherfuckers are goin' away for a loooong time...* I was freaking out."

"Jesus baby," Jeffrey cooed lightly rubbing her taut belly, "I'm sorry. That's some freaky shit."

"Uh-huh. It went on for... man... it felt like a long-ass time. Eventually I managed to, like, shake myself awake. Of course, the room is empty and I realize I was fucking dreaming. Still, I was too scared to go back to sleep for a while. Smoked a cigarette, watched a buncha shitty infomercials on the TV. You slept right through..."

"You know me. I could sleep through a fuckin' earthquake."

"Ain't that the truth? I got back asleep around four, I guess. But as I was layin' there, just driftin' off... Something happened. I heard a voice. Calling me. Calling my name. It was as clear as day... calling my *old* name."

"Raquel?"

"No! My name *before* that. The name I was *borned* with. *Reggie*. I knew the minute I heard it, it was Nay Nay speaking. My grandmother. She passed back in ninety-two."

"Did you see her?"

"No. But as I lay there, the room got kinda... bathed with light. Twinkling light, like when a spotlight hits a mirror ball, you know? It was shimmerin' all around the room. It wasn't *scary*, though. I felt very calm, and peaceful. Jeff, I *felt* her here. She was in the room; it was my Nay Nay all right, as real as you are. She... she came to warn me, honey."

"Warn you?" Jeffrey laughed, "Warn you about what?"

He kissed Rachel lightly on the cheek. Rachel's face was sombre, her eyes somewhere far away.

"She told me that I gotta stop tricking. She told me that if I didn't stop tricking and living my life this way that something bad was gonna happen. Something *real bad*. She told me that she had come from the other side to try and save me."

Jeffrey sighed softly and said, "It was just a dream, Rachel. That's all."

"No," she said firmly, "It wasn't a dream. Nay Nay was *here*, Jeffrey. She was warning me."

"You're just freaked out 'cos of the papers. Remember we were reading the paper in Greco's pizza the other day? And there was that story, the one about the Marine who picked up the transgender prostitute in Hollywood, and after she blew him he shot her like ten times and stuffed the body in a dumpster on Melrose? Told his friends that he did it because he didn't realize she was a guy? And then the cops ended up shooting the crazy bastard to death in a McDonalds' parking lot?"

"Yeah. Of course I *remember*, Jeff."

"Well, there you go. It was probably just some kinda... subconscious recollection...."

Rachel shook her head firmly. "No, Jeff. It wasn't no damn subconscious anythin'. It was *real*. It was Nay Nay. She really spoke to me. You know, I'm not tellin' you this shit so you can start psychoanalysing me, motherfucker..."

Rachel's voice was getting louder, more strident. It seemed like the prelude to screaming fit. Backing off, Jeffrey said, "Shhh. Okay, I'm sorry. It was your grandmother. I believe you. Okay?"

"Okay."

They lay there for a while, nodding quietly. Time seemed to slow down to the pace of the specks of dust that floated lazily in the humid air. Eventually Jeffrey said, "So what do you think it all means? The warning, I mean?"

"It means I can't turn tricks no more," Rachel said quietly and determinedly. "I'm sorry, honey. But I can't. Not after Nay Nay came to me. Something bad'll happen, I can *feel* it."

Jeffrey face was frozen. "For how long?"

"Until Nay Nay tells me otherwise."

"Shit. Okay. Shit."

Jeffrey blinked his eyes open and stared at the cracked plaster ceiling.

"Well, this is the situation. We got maybe three hundred bucks left. We're paid up until Wednesday here. Rent is one eighty for the week. Plus seven dollars each per day for the methadone clinic. We gotta figure at least eighty a day for dope. And that's if we cut back. Plus food, cigarettes..."

He fell into a pensive silence.

"Don't forget my hormones. I ain't plannin' on growing no damn beard or losin' my titties, Jeff."

"Shit. Forgot about that."

"So what you sayin', Jeffrey?"

"Well, I'm sayin' that we'd better figure a way to make some decent scratch, and do it soon. I can only make so much from boosting. If we don't figure out another revenue stream, we're gonna be some homeless, dope-sick, hungry bitches, you know?"

"I know. But I'm telling you I just can't *do it* no more. I guess this is the time for you to step up and be the *man*, Jeffrey. Pass me a cigarette."

"We're out."

"Shit."

"I know. Look, I hear you, and it's gonna be okay Rachel. I gotta think is all." Jeffrey stared at the ceiling.

"I just gotta think."

FOURTEEN

They checked into the Motel De Ville on 7th Street in downtown Los Angeles, a run-down dump that Randal had often haunted when he was desperately in need of a place to hide from the world. He thought of the last time he had stayed there, furiously smoking meth with a beautiful seventeen-year-old Ukrainian whore called Rani. He'd spent three or four days in there with her, huddled away with the blinds drawn, supposing in some overheated part of his brain that maybe he'd fallen in love. He remembered how it ended too: an ice-pick wielding Russian pimp kicking the door in while they were lying naked in bed, taking hits off the pipe and watching coverage of the Phil Spector trial on CNN. The furious pimp was only pacified when Randal offered him two and half thousand dollars cash for Rani's time. The last time he saw Rani that greasy-haired Russian bastard was beating the shit out of her in the parking lot, before she was shoved into a beaten-up Toyota Corolla and driven away forever.

The Motel De Ville was a magnet for the broke and the desperate. 63 rooms in all, the most expensive of them running at 50 dollars a night. For a motel in walking distance from the Los Angeles Convention Center, these kinds of rates were almost totally unheard of. Occasionally the odd optimistic tourist would show up there, lured in by the price and the kitschy 1950s signage that had all but disintegrated over the years, assuming they had found some quaint hidden gem. Often those same tourists would be seen hustling out of there under cover of darkness, dragging their cases behind them. It was usually right around the time a meth-crazed whore had started loudly threatening her pimp with a stiletto heel in the next room, or some washed-up alcoholic screenwriter had collapsed on the walkway outside their door having some kind of awful benzo-induced seizure.

When they entered the room, Jacques looked around disdainfully and said, "It is a dump, Randal. You have exceeded yourself. I feel like I'm walking into a Diane Arbus photograph."

"No worries Jacques. I aim to please. And we're a stone's throw from Macarthur Park, where the boys of 18th Street will be happy to serve all of your narcotic needs. In other words aesthetics *and* convenience."

"Good. I will always take aesthetics over convenience, Randal, but both together is *tres bon*."

Although Randal made the effort to delete all of his drug connections' numbers from his cell phone when he went into rehab, it really didn't matter. Each dealer's number was ingrained upon his psyche as indelibly as his birth date, social security number, or the name of the first girl he ever laid. He decided to try Carlos first, who was one of his more reliable downtown connections. Although most of what Carlos sold was of negligible quality, he at least dealt in a variety of drugs. Most dealers stuck to a narrow selection. That's why the whole "gateway theory" of drug addiction always amused Randal. The very idea that someone who bought pot on the black market would be unwittingly exposed to harder drugs was totally unrealistic. A pot dealer would never fuck with heroin, as they tended to be slightly superior, self-righteous types who looked down on straights, drinkers and users of all other drugs with equal distaste. Heroin and crack were usually sold together, since they were as natural a pairing as coffee and cream, but the typical heroin dealer would not deign to deal with speed freaks, for example. In a way, drug users and dealers were not so different from the rest of society: all of them bunched together in their own exclusive cliques, looking down their noses at everybody else. During free time in rehab, Randal would often notice that the crackheads would invariably sit off on one table, the speed freaks at another, and the junkies somewhere else. In fact, the only thing that united them was a near-universal distaste for the alcoholics who – they all agreed – were fat, slow, red-nosed motherfuckers who didn't even have the good sense to get hooked on *decent* drugs. Randal's recent embrace of the bottle caused him more secret embarrassment than a lifetime of humiliations brought about by his meth use. Since Carlos was one of those rare cats who dealt in a variety of substances, low quality though they were, Randal hoped they could at least be in and out of Macarthur Park without having to see too many old faces.

As he pulled his cell phone out to make the call, an unexpected stomach cramp hit him. He needed to use the bathroom right away. He locked himself in there while Jacques flicked on the TV. He doubled over and took a long, watery shit. As he wiped himself he shook his head in wonder at this powerful psycho-logical reaction to the very *idea* of scoring drugs. No sooner had he held the phone in his hand and considered dialing Carlos's number, than his body had thrown itself into paroxysms of psychosomatic drug-need. His intention was to introduce Jacques to Carlos so that Randal could remove himself from any more direct interaction with his old drug connections. He knew that even this one encounter was a big risk. This was exactly what his brother had referred to – in his typically lecturing tone – as "slippery places and slippery faces". "A relapse is like the flu, Randal," Harvey would often warn him. "It doesn't matter whether or not you *intend* on using drugs. If you're in those places long enough, if you are around those people long enough, you'll catch their sickness as sure as night follows day."

Randal flushed, and splashed cold water on his face. He looked at himself in the bathroom mirror. In a corner of it he saw a splash of something dry and brown that looked suspiciously like a blood splatter.

"You are *not* going to relapse, motherfucker," he told himself. His voice sounded weak and unsure. He popped another Adderall, chewed up the extended release beads, and swallowed the resulting goop.

He walked out and found Jacques lying on the bed transfixed by some Latin soap opera with a dumb grin on his face.

"Okay man, I'm gonna make the call. You want speed. What else?"

"Heroin."

"Okay."

"Hashish?"

"Hash?" Randal looked thoughtful. "That shit is practically legal in California. The gangs don't bother with it. Anyone who wants it can just get a legit script from a doctor. There's no black market for that shit anymore."

Jacques screwed up his face. "Disgusting," he muttered, "Who the fuck wants to use *legal* drugs? Where is the excitement in that? Soon this city will be as dull and uninspired as Amsterdam..."

"You want cocaine?"

"Oui, of course."

"The best I'll be able to do is rock. Not powder. There's not much powder coke in this neighbourhood."

"That's okay."

"Good."

Randal made the call, his fingers instinctively punching out the correct pattern on the keypad. Carlos was one of the last dealers he knew to still use a pager. He punched in his number, and waited. A minute later, the cell buzzed into life. Randal, although he was not intending on getting high, felt his guts lurch in Pavlovian anticipation as soon as the phone rang. There was no small talk when Randal picked up.

"I thought you wuz dead, homie!"

"Nah," Randal said, "Worse. I've been clean."

He hated it, but this admission made him feel a prickle of shame. As if he had sold out.

"Whatchoo need?"

"I need to go uptown *and* downtown. Actually, I'll take whatever you got, and bring quantity. I got a friend here from out of town and he's stocking up."

"Okay, homie. Beep me 555 when you close by. Peace."

Randal clicked the phone closed. Jacques was already on his feet, stretching like a cat.

"Come on, big guy," Randal said, "Time for you to get acquainted with the city..."

*

They drove slowly down Bonnie Brae, looking out for Carlos. A couple of shadowy figures regarded their car, occasionally calling out for rock or heroin as they crawled down the street, but Randal did not stop until he saw Carlos' familiar figure step out of the shadows on the corner of 5th Street. They pulled over and Randal cranked the window down. Carlos, a young smooth-skinned Mexican with a goatee and a Lakers cap pulled low over his face, stuck his head inside.

"'Sup, homie?"

"Carlos, long time no see, man! This is my friend, Jacques..."

Carlos looked at Jacques blankly, and nodded. "'Sup, Jack?"

"Hello."

Jacques looked stiff, a little intimidated by the young drug dealer. Although Carlos was basically harmless, Randal had painted him as a gun-toting psychopath with a hair-trigger temper in an attempt to scare the Frenchman into behaving. The last thing he needed was Jacques embarrassing him in front of the only man who had ever called him "homie", a title that Randal was oddly proud of. Jacques stared hard at the young gang-banger, as if trying to commit every detail of him to memory. Randal had already warned him to keep his damn camera hidden, unless he wanted to get his ass shot.

"So whatchoo need? Go fast?"

"Uh huh. Give us an 8-ball of chiva, a G-rock, and an 8-ball of go-fast."

Carlos put his hand to his mouth, and started spitting out bundles of drugs. The heroin was wrapped in black balloons, the crack – which was pressed flat in neat rectangles – wrapped in aluminum foil. The speed was in blue balloons. The amount of drugs Carlos could hold in his mouth almost defied physics. Randal handed over the bills, and Carlos glanced cautiously over his shoulder as he counted them.

"Yo, I got some pills, too. Xanax, Oxy, benzos, and a coupla Es if you want 'em."

Randal looked over to Jacques, who was already nodding eagerly.

"You want that shit?"

"Of course!"

"We'll take it," Randal said, turning back to Carlos. "All of it."

"If you wanna take everything I got..." Carlos whistled and did some instantaneous calculations in his head, "I can do the pills for an even two-hundred. An' that's a good fuckin' deal, homie."

Randal counted out more bills from Jacques' roll. Carlos handed over a battered pack of Camels, filled with black-market medication.

"Yo," Carlos whispered to Randal as Jacques checked out the merchandise, "Check it. I gotta bindle of angel dust. Good shit, if that's your bag. You about cleaned me out, so you might as well take this as well. On the house."

Carlos reached into the vehicle and slipped the bindle in the breast pocket of Randal's jacket. Although the powerful hallucinogenic had never really been his bag, Randal nodded his thanks.

"I'll be seeing you around man. My friend over here, Jacques, he's a good guy. Is it okay if I pass on your digits to him?"

"So long as the nigga ain't a cop." Carlos peered a little closer at Jacques. Jacques smiled at Carlos ingratiatingly. "Motherfucka looks a little too fat, even for the LAPD. Sure, tell him to call me, whatever. Peace."

With that, Carlos was gone, cutting back into the shadows of 5th Street, heading toward Bonnie Brae. Randal said, "Stash that shit until we get back to the hotel. Cops are all over this damn scene. If you see flashing lights, dump it out the window..."

FIFTEEN

" Okay, check this shit out. Homie of mine got all hopped up
on Angel Dust two weeks ago, went on a fuckin' rampage.
Dude went straight up *loco*. Wuz running around the streets
naked and shit, terrorizing people. I hear all of this screaming
and yelling out the front of the apartments and there's Mike
buck-naked tryin' to hold off the cops with a fuckin' pool cue.
Man, half the fuckin' neighbourhood was out watching. Mike has
bugged the fuck *out*. He's waving the pool cue around screaming
STAND BACK THIS MOTHERFUCKA IS LOADED! Fool
thought he was holding a shotgun, or some shit. I mean, even
the cops are busting up at this stupid bastard. So the pigs try
and calm him down for a while, but Mike ain't giving the shit
up, so they decide *fuck it*. They fucking tazered the *shit* outta
him. They musta zapped him, like, twelve, thirteen times. He
wuz just down there on the concrete flopping around like a big,
dumb fuckin' fish.

"Best part is I filmed that shit. On my iPhone, yeah? That
fucking shit went *viral*. Got over ten *thousand* views on YouTube
already. Someone even did their own version of it, added some
beats, fed his voice through some kinda computer an' called it
the "This Motherfucker Is Loaded Song". Funny shit. I told Mike
that when he gets out he's gonna freak, 'cos he's kinda famous
now..." D-Low sniffed, looked around, and then whispered, "I've
got a hook up for some dope-ass crystal right now, but I'm
having trouble moving it. Still, I don't mind having it sittin'
around, ya know? Nice to know it's there when I want it."

Without waiting for anyone else to speak, D-Low carried on, warming to his new theme.

"I'm tellin' ya it's the weirdest thing. I can have the fuckin' best meth in the world and it don't matter. When those little college niggas are buying off of me, all they want is this pharmacy goop – Adderall, Ritalin, all of that shit. They fuckin' look down on speedfreaks, like they're the *real* dope-fiends or some shit, but all the while these little bastards are gobbling up this milk-sugar pharmacy speed like it's fuckin candy."

D-Low, although you wouldn't know it from listening to him, was a skinny white drug dealer who dealt mostly in speed and pharmaceuticals. He was severely tweaked out, talking fast, his eyes popping out of his skull. His blond hair was braided into tight cornrows, and his platinum grills twinkled in the dim light as he spoke. "I'm tellin' ya," he continued, taking a gulp of his Incredible Hulk, a bright green cocktail made of Hennessy and Hpnotiq, "I'm fucked if I understand young niggas these days. They all seem whack as shit, yo."

"The poor bastards were raised on it," Lupita said, "They don't know any better. I can't believe this stuff has a higher street value than the real deal."

"Oh yeah. Same with junk. These niggas'll turn their nose up if ya offer 'em some smack, but if you got Vicodin or any of that other crap they're all over it..."

They were drinking in Casanova's, a run-down down little hole in the wall across from the Starlight Motel, where D-Low and his crew operated out of. The bar was dark and cool, with wood panelled walls and a sticky black floor. The only light was coming from the neon Budweiser and Pabst signs on the walls, and the cathode glow of the TV set. Maury was on, with the sound turned down. On the jukebox James Brown was singing *Living*

In America. A fat man wearing denim overalls and a cowboy hat was the only other customer, sitting at the bar nursing a beer and reading the newspaper. The barmaid, an elderly American Indian woman, was sitting behind the bar, breathing softly with her eyes closed.

"The game's changing man. It's all fucked up. But you gotta adapt or die, right?"

"You got that right, D-Low. Adapt or die. Well, I guess we'd better get down to business."

Lupita nudged Genesis. Genesis slid a McDonalds bag across the table to D-Low. The bag contained a couple of hundred pills, mostly amphetamine-based ADD medication, and some milder painkillers like Norco and Tylenol 3s. Without peeking inside, D-Low took the bag and placed it on his lap. He reached into his racing jacket, which was emblazoned with an image of Al Pacino as Tony Montana, and took out a sealed envelope. The envelope was fat with cash. He slid it over to Lupita, who pocketed it. They sat there for a few moments, contemplating their drinks.

Genesis looked at Lupita, and then at D-Low. D-Low was tall and skinny. Besides the Scarface jacket, he wore a pristine white wife-beater and a thick rope-like gold chain. On one wrist was a watch encrusted with diamantes. D-Low caught Genesis's gaze on him and smiled at her. When he exposed his teeth, he looked like a shark.

"So, uh, how you ladies meet?"

Genesis shrugged. "We had a friend in common."

D-Low sucked his teeth thoughtfully and nodded. "You gonna stay in town for a while?"

Lupita shook her head. "We're just moving around. Been thinking of heading to San Francisco. Got some buddies out there I've been meaning to look up."

"Hear it's a nice place. Lotta faggots, though."

Noticing the dark look that came over Lupita's face, D-Low smiled apologetically and said, "Not that there's nuthin' wrong with that, yo..." He held up his palms. "I mean I don't got nuthin' against it. 'Specially when it comes to chicks. I mean, yeah the idea of a guy, you know, putting his dick in another guys ass... it kinda skeeves me out, yo, but *chicks*? That's a different story... yuh know what I mean?"

Lupita looked at D-Low and imagined putting her gun against his forehead and blowing a hole clean through his skull. She imagined the surprised look that would cross his ridiculous face the moment he realized he'd just talked himself into an early grave. Her hand fluttered, ready to appear above the table again holding the piece... but somehow she controlled herself. After staring through D-Low for a couple of beats, Lupita smiled coldly and said in a low, dangerous voice, "Stop stuttering, buttercup. You don't gotta convince us."

Genesis laughed, and the situation was – for the moment at least – defused. The fear in D-Low's eyes was perfectly obvious. Genesis had intended to ask Lupita why the fuck she hadn't checked the envelope to make sure that D-Low hadn't burned them. After all, he looked like the type who'd pull the morphine suppository out of his dying mother's ass if he thought he could make a buck off of it. But when Lupita called him "buttercup" D-Low didn't do shit. He just laughed awkwardly along with Genesis, and pretty soon after he went back to jabbering nonsense again. Now he was being careful to avoid saying anything that might set Lupita off. Genesis saw that D-Low was *scared* of Lupita, so scared that he wouldn't dare try to fuck her on the deal.

On the jukebox, *Juicy*, by Notorious BIG came up. "Oh shit!" D-Low laughed, "That's my fuckin' jam!" He looked to be pleased to have an opportunity to change the subject.

"You like rap?" he asked Genesis.

Genesis shrugged. "Some."

"You know a rapper called Trina? She did one of my favourite tracks – *Nann Nigga* with Trick Daddy. You know it?"

"No." Genesis did not crack a smile or feign interest. D-Low didn't seem to notice.

"That bitch was pure fire on that track," D-Low rambled on, "That bitch could spit like crazy..."

Lupita leaned across the table and said in a low, clear voice: "*Motherfucker*. I think you must be feeling a bit too comfortable around me these days or something, because you're dropping the B-word a hell of a lot, and to be perfectly honest you're starting to piss me off. You got me? I don't dig rap. I don't dig all this fuckin' talk about faggots. And I sure as hell don't dig all of this bitch talk. You got your fuckin' pills, so why don't you go take your fake-ass honky self back to that fuckin' motel you live at before I shoot off your little Caucasian cock? Okay *homie*?"

They watched D-Low scurry out of there moments later. Genesis leaned over and kissed Lupita on the neck.

"I love you, baby," she said.

Lupita turned to Genesis, and raised an eyebrow.

"Now what on god's earth brought *that* on? That's a pretty heavy thing to say to someone, Genesis hun. I don't take that shit lightly."

"Me neither," Genesis whispered, kissing Lupita on the neck again. "Thanks for keeping your cool around that big mouth motherfucker. I thought for a moment you was gonna blow that little prick away right here at the table."

Lupita grabbed her drink and finished it with a flourish. She looked around the bar one last time and said, "Honey, what do you think I am? As much of an asshole as D-Low is... I mean, killing someone in a bar full of witnesses over an *insult*? Genesis hun, you'd have to be crazy to even *consider* doing some shit like that."

Genesis laughed a little, "Yeah, I guess you're right."

"I know I'm right. D-Low may be a little prick but his money's still green. Come on, let's get the fuck outta this dump. I feel like blowin' off some steam. You up for dancing?"

"Always."

"Ok sweetie. Come on. Let's go see if we can find some fun in this shit-hole town."

SIXTEEN

B ack at his apartment, Randal was planning a quiet night in. Cocktail in hand he examined his bookshelves, browsing through his collection of porno DVDs. He was reading the blurb of *Raiders of the Lost Ass* (Winner of the 2003 AVN Award for best group anal scene) when the phone went off. He checked the caller ID – Gibby. He had been putting off a call to Gibby all day after enduring a particularly difficult evening with Jacques. With a sigh he decided to get it over with now.

"Gibby, man," Randal said, "What's up?"

Across town Gibby was in the back of a taxi with the windows rolled down. Next to him Jacques was passed out cold, a long trail of drool hanging from his chin.

"Oh nothing, Randal." Gibby said coldly. "I just managed to crawl out from underneath a three-hundred-pound naked Frenchman, but apart from that things are just *dandy*. What's new with you?"

"Gibby, what the fuck are you talking about? Didn't you have a meeting with Kenny tonight?"

"Oh sure. The meeting was over at *Le Poisson Cru*. You know it?"

"Nah."

"It's this hot-shit new French-Sushi fusion joint in Beverly Hills. Been getting all kind of rave reviews. I guess Kenny was trying to impress Jacques."

"Was it any good?"

"I dunno. If paying a hundred and fifty bucks for two thin slices of raw yellowtail garnished with peppercorn sauce is your idea of *good* then sure, I guess it was. You seriously never been to that place? It was like eating in a fucking operating room – white on white. All that was missing was waiters in scrubs. I guess they were going for that whole ultra-minimalist thing, you know? Lindsay Lohan was having dinner with some chick at the table behind us."

"Musta been her lawyer."

"Maybe. But apart from the fact the place was pretentious as fuck, dinner went pretty good. In fact up until a certain point I'd say it went *better* than good. It went *great*. Kenny was putty in our fucking hands, Randal. I didn't realize just how in *awe* of Jacques he is. He wasn't kidding when he said that *Dead Flowers* was his favourite movie. He acted like a fucking pre-pubescent girl at a Justin Beiber concert."

Randal took a slug of his drink, clanking the ice cubes together. "Who the *fuck* is Justin Bieber?"

"Ah, never mind. I forget, you don't got teenage kids, do you?"

Randal looked at the DVD in his hand. *Co-Ed Contortionists.* "Not exactly," he said.

"Yeah, well, all I'm sayin' is that instead of the arrogant prick I've had to deal with on the phone the past few weeks, tonight I got to meet Kenny Azura the fan boy. Talk about cognitive dissonance! He was *fawning* over Jacques. Randal, I gotta tell you it was kinda pathetic."

Sliding the DVD back, Randal plucked another from the shelf. It was still in the shrink-wrap. A hardcore zombie spoof called *Dawn of the Spread.* "And how about Jacques? Did he behave?"

"He was okay... once he got there. He showed up a half hour late, looking like he'd slept in his suit. But once we actually made it to the table he was fine. They got the full-on Jacques experience – he wouldn't take his sunglasses off, and he sat there glaring at all of these Chainsaw bigwigs looking all Gallic and intellectual. Kenny was with this real hard-faced bitch. Sharon something-or-other?"

"Lindenbaum. She's a tough lady. Smart as hell."

"Uh-huh. Well, you know Jacques. He keeps making these obscure statements, a bunch of arty farty old shit really. He drops this one like about his art being an enormous cock that he wants to fuck infinity with or something, and old Sharon looked like she was gonna shit a brick. The best part was that Kenny was swallowing it all, hook line and sinker. He asks Jacques what the movie is about, and Jacques gives him some bullshit about how he wants to break down the third wall and make the audience complicit in his crimes... I mean, old Sharon looked like she wanted to call bullshit on all of this, but I got the distinct impression that everyone there was kinda scared to contradict Kenny."

Randal was perusing the box of an all black porno flick called *Screw The Right Thing*. "Kenny's the *man* right now. Nothing happens at Chainsaw without his say so, and everybody knows it. Until he fucks up... nobody can say *shit* to him."

"Well, I got the distinct impression that quite a few people at the table were getting a little freaked out by Jacques. But Kenny was just eating it up. I mean he'd push here and there, but we basically got the deal we wanted – complete artistic control, full support of the studio, a free hand when it came to casting. He didn't even ask to see the script, which is fucking great because there *isn't* one. All we gotta do is sign on the dotted line, and we're golden. I was just about to hustle Jacques outta there when everything went to shit."

"Howdja mean?"

"It was fuckin' *Jacques*. When was the last time you saw him, anyway?"

Randal laughed dryly. "It was at the motel... around eight, I guess? He was all cracked out. Fuckin' asshole was blasting that Stones track, *Fool To Cry*, so fucking loud. Every time it finished, he'd start it up again. Ranting on and on about how it's the most beautiful song ever recorded. He was hitting that crackpipe like a maniac. Kept offering it to me too, the fucking asshole. I told him I had to leave, right? I mean, I'm in *recovery* Gibby; I can't be around that kind of shit any more. He was being a real dick about it too, goading me, you know? Calling me a pussy, a fucking hypocrite. He's going through the back of the *LA Weekly* calling up whores, trying to get them to come over. But he sounded so crazy on the phone, even the *whores* were avoiding him. I mean it was getting real messed up there, and if I had to hear that fucking song one more time I was gonna lose it. So I split, left him to it."

"Yeah, well looks like he stayed up all night. Maybe it was a good thing he kept the shades on, 'cos who the fuck knows what his eyes looked like. But anyway, right as the meeting is wrapping up he goes to take a leak. I'm sat there making small talk with Kenny and his cronies. Five minutes later he's still not back. Kenny's going on and on about some fucking yacht he's got in the fuckin' Virgin Islands or some shit. Ten minutes pass. I mean, the check has come and gone, Kenny's signed for it and all of that, and everybody's waiting for Jacques to come back so we can get the fuck out of there. Now they're all giving me funny looks. So what can I do? I gotta go and check it out. You've never been to this place before, huh?"

"Nah. I hate those fucking pretentious Beverly Hills places."

"Well, the bathrooms in there are fucking massive. Like, cavernous. Their gimmick is that they tiled the floor with thousands of silver dollars. They're like set into the floor or something, so it just looks like a sea of silver when you go in, and when you look closely you realize that they made the floor out of fucking money. Place looks empty, right? No sign of Jacques. I call for him. Nuthin. I'm just about to leave when I hear this noise coming out of one of the stalls. Like a *whimpering*. Sounded like a dog that just got kicked or something. So I walk

135

over to check it out. I'm like, *Jacques? Jacques is that you?* And I hear it again. I give the door a little push and it swings open. Okay, get this. In the stall, like, cowering up on the fucking toilet, there's Jacques. He's completely fucking naked, and he's *crying*. I mean literally *sobbing*. His clothes are in a pile by the toilet. And as soon as I opened the door the *smell* just hits me. I see something, you know, I don't wanna look too close, but it looks like Jacques smeared *shit* all over himself. He's got this brown stuff caked all over his legs, right? So I'm like, *Jacques? The fuck is going on, man?* Then he looks at me. His fucking *eyes*, Randal. When I saw his eyes that's when I knew something serious had gone down. He wasn't *there* no more. Jacques had gone insane, Randal. He'd flipped his lid."

By now, Randal had lost interest in the DVD's. "Jesus. What was going on?"

"That's what I asked! I'm, like, *Jacques? What's going on, buddy?* I ain't kidding you, the motherfucker *leapt* at me. Fucking sprang out of there like a jack-in-the-box and landed right on top of me. Tackled me! The smell was overpowering. I mean, just think about that! I got all of Chainsaw Pictures' top brass upstairs waiting for us to get back, and I'm lying on the floor of the john with my naked, shit-stained client lying on top of me. Not a good look."

Randal started laughing. He was just about to ask Gibby what the hell had provoked this, when Gibby cut him off. "You'd better hold that thought, Randal. We're pulling up at the hotel. I'll call you back in a minute, okay?"

Randal hung up the phone, and smiled to himself. He walked into the kitchen and poured the last of the whisky into his tumbler. He decided to call Pink Dot to have some more delivered before Gibby called back and tied up the line again.

SEVENTEEN

After cutting the deal with D-Low, Genesis and Lupita checked into a room at the Casa Soledad Motel, a forty-buck-a-night dive off of the shady end of Laughlin's downtown strip. They pulled into the lot and killed the engine. The sign outside read VACANCIES – $40 ROOM – WEEKLY RATES – HBO – ADULT MOVIES. The Casa Soledad's lonesome forecourt was bathed in the sickly orange glow of cathode lights. An RC Cola machine outside of the office had long since rusted into obsolescence.

"This place is a dump," Genesis said, as they got out of the car.

"Yup. But it's got one thing going in its favour."

"What's that?"

"It's forty bucks a night. And I'd rather waste my cash on the casinos than some fancy-ass hotel I'm barely gonna spend any time in. And no-one's gonna be pryin' into our business here."

Above the door to the front office was a colourful Virgin Mary wind-chime that tinkled softly as they entered. The office was dim and smelled of an uneasy mix of mildew and Bengay. The walls were wood-panelled and the old sagging couch in the reception area had worn thin in several places. The only decoration in the office was a vase of dusty plastic flowers on the front desk. It seemed as though the room had long since begun a steady slide into decay.

Off in the back a Spanish language soap opera was blaring. Lupita walked up to the desk and rang the bell. After a few moments a dark skinned old woman shuffled out eyeing them both suspiciously. To Lupita's eyes she looked to be Dominican, Puerto Rican or possibly Brazilian. She had Indian blood for sure. Noting the hostile look on the woman's face, Lupita did her best to pacify her by addressing her in Spanish.

"*Buenos noches, deseamos una habitación?*" Lupita said. She smiled broadly at the old woman. The woman's face remained stoic. She was ancient and frail, with shocking green eyes set deep into the parchment thin folds of her face. A thick white afro framed her shrivelled head.

"A room?" she replied in stiff English, refusing to play along with Lupita by speaking in her native tongue. "One room only?"

"Yes."

"Two twin beds?"

"No. One double bed will be sufficient."

The woman glanced at Genesis then back at Lupita. Puckered her lips.

"For the *both* of you?"

"That's correct." Lupita's voice hardened a little. The old woman stared at them for what felt like a very long time. She looked like she had just caught a whiff of something rotten. Looking closer Lupita noticed that the old woman had a smudge of grey ash on her forehead. In the dim space back where the TV was blaring Lupita saw a flickering Sacred Heart candle that was the centrepiece of a dim shrine of knick-knacks and religious statues.

Genesis pushed past Lupita and leaned across the desk so her face was only inches from the tiny woman on the other side.

"Excuse me? M'am? We'd like a room with one bed only. I hear it gets real cold around here at night. I'm countin' on this lady here to keep me warm... ya know what I'm saying?"

The old woman muttered something in Spanish, and made her way slowly back into the other room. Genesis looked at Lupita and frowned.

"What she *say*, Lupe?"

"You don't wanna know, hun."

"She can't treat us like that. They have *laws* about that sort of stuff, don't they?"

Lupita shrugged.

"Anyway, I don't like this place. The old woman gives me the *creeps*. Maybe we should just find another place..."

"It's cheap and it's low profile," Lupita said, "It'll be fine. Just let me do the talkin' okay?"

The old lady returned. Without making eye contact with either of them she went through a rehearsed spiel, in an inflectionless monotone.

"Room is forty per night, two-fifty per week, pets are extra, no visitors, no drugs, no loud noise after ten pm, one parking space per room. Ice machine's round the back of the office, TV's got regular channels and pay-per-view. How many nights you..." her voice wobbled slightly, "you... *women* planning on staying?"

"Just a couple." Lupita said.

"There's a ten-dollar deposit per key. You pay up front. Check out is at noon. Cash or credit card?"

"Cash," Genesis said pulling a C-note out of the stuffed envelope. She slapped it on the counter with a flourish. "Hope big bills aren't a problem."

The old woman examined the hundred-dollar bill for a good two minutes, holding it up to the light and peering at it doubtfully, before reluctantly giving them their change and key. The cash register was the old fashioned kind, and it *pinged* loudly and rattled when the drawer popped open.

"Thank you," Genesis cooed as they went to get their bags.

On the way to their room on the second floor balcony Lupita grumbled, "Girl, why the fuck you waving that money around, drawin' attention to us an' shit? I told you to let me do the talking…"

"I just wanted to put that old bitch in her place, Lupe. I don't like her attitude."

"Shit sweetie, I don't like it either, but who gives a fuck about her? She's just some uptight *veija*. Seen a million like that cunt. Probably thinks we're heading straight to hell. You give her any more agita she's liable to toss your dyke ass outta here. You know how those old-school country-ass bitches are…"

Genesis stuck the key in the lock and pushed the door open. She clicked on the light.

"Who you callin' a dyke, anyway?" she asked. "Just 'cos I dig *you*. Don't be casting no aspersions."

"*Aspersions*? Damn girl, you go an' swallow a dictionary after you got done eatin' my pussy or something?"

Giggling, they stepped inside and took in the room. It was dismal and small. A queen size bed with a puke splatter duvet on it, red velvet flocked wallpaper, and 1970s brown deep-pile carpet that now resembled the fur of a mangy dog. The décor consisted of an ancient television set bolted to the wall, a chest of drawers with most of the handles missing, and a black velvet portrait of the Sacred Heart above the bed.

"Looks like the set of the world's creepiest stag movie," Genesis said.

Lupita skipped past her and sat on the edge of the bed, bouncing up and down, causing it to emit a series of disconcerting squeaks and clangs. "Well," she said, "the good news is that we won't be here so much. We'll go hang out in the casinos, play a little blackjack, get into some trouble… We just need a place to crash. It might be a dump, but it's close and it's *cheap*."

"I'm just fucking with you Lupe. I like it fine. 'Cept for the creepy fucking picture on the wall."

Lupita looked up at the image of Jesus that stared down at them with eyes full of pain and compassion. She pulled her wife-beater up over her head, exposing her breasts. She tossed it aside and beckoned for Genesis to join her on the bed.

"Come over here beautiful," she said as Genesis locked the door behind them. "Whaddya say we give old *Jesus* here somethin' to look at?"

EIGHTEEN

Pink Dot still hadn't shown with the booze, and Gibby had resumed chewing Randal's ear off about Jacques' little episode at the Chainsaw meeting. Randal had resigned himself to putting the porn on the back burner for the time being.

"Jesus, Gibby," he said, cradling the phone in his neck as he used a spoon to crush the contents of two 60mg Adderall capsules up into fine snortable lines, "He was lying on you covered in *SHIT*? What didja do?"

"Do? Randal, Jacques weighs, like, three, three-twenty at least. Whaddya THINK I did? I fuckin' lay there trying to *breathe*! I couldn't move a muscle!"

"I guess I should be shocked, Gibby. But I gotta tell you... even in the brief time I've been around him, I definitely got the feeling that Jacques was... *unstable*. What the hell set him off, anyway?"

"You did, Randal!" Gibby snapped. Then, fighting to get his voice back under control he added, *"Don't play innocent with me. Jacques told me about how you poisoned him!"*

"Gibby, I have no fuckin' idea what you're talkin' about. Hold on a second, okay?"

Randal pressed the 'hold' button, and put the phone down on the table. He snorted the Adderall and snuffled, rubbing his nose with a trembling hand. It was a cheap, shitty high but it was better that nothing. Disturbed by the hollow sound of the pill bottle, Randal poured out the rest of his two-week supply and was astonished to find that he had only eight pills left. A desolate feeling came over him. *Surely I must have more pills left than this?*

His mind started doing instantaneous calculations. Dr Titov had regularly upped his dose over the past few weeks. Every time his dosage was upped he received another full month's supply of pills. That – by Randal's calculations – should have left him with a significant reserve of Adderall capsules of various strengths. *But* – some awful, needling part of his mind interjected – he *had* been taking a minimum of two pills a day. And that didn't include the 'special occasions' when he would take two in the morning and two in the afternoon. Special occasions like the days he had to work, or the days when he felt particularly tired, the days when his regular AA meetings had irritated him, or the days when his brother, or his boss, or any of the other people he interacted with regularly had pissed him off.

The *other* special occasions were the days when none of these things happened. Then, Randal would snort a few extra pills to celebrate making it through the day without someone making him feel murderous. With mounting dread, he realized the short supply of pills made perfect sense. He guessed he was lucky to even have *eight* left. Randal shuddered. He would have to make an appointment to see Dr. Titov as soon as possible. It was a pain in the ass, but he was sure that Russian quack wouldn't bat even an eyelid... not considering the exorbitant amount of money he was creaming from Randal's health insurance and co-pay.

Fingering the near empty pill capsule caused a sudden cold shock to his veins. Although he did not think about the pills as being *drugs* – not really – the idea that he might have to do without them filled him with a nauseous terror. He recognized it as the same black fear that used to well up inside of him at the end of a meth binge, when the dirty sun was creeping into the sky and he realized that the comedown was already beginning. Although the stakes were smaller this time around, the routine was the same – he was back on the dizzying on-and-off carousel of *need*. Still feeling the vertigo of this realization, Randal suddenly felt very old and very tired. He ran a hand through his thinning hair and clicked Gibby back on line. "Hey man, I'm back. Sorry about that. I just... lost something. Okay, so... what the hell where you sayin' about it being *me* that set him off?"

Gibby cleared his throat. "Yeah. So what I was *telling you*, is that Jacques said he went to the bathroom to take a bump of the coke that you'd helped him procure last night."

"Coke? Like powder coke? I didn't help him score any coke... oh, man. The *bindle*, that's right!" Randal shook his head as he started glancing around the room, wondering if he'd absent-mindedly stuffed stashed some pill-stuffed medicine bottles around the place. "I know what happened.... There *was* no powder coke in the shit we scored last night. After we cut the deal for the rocks and the rest of it, my guy stuck a bindle in my pocket, you know? A freebie. When we got back to Jacques' place I must have left it on the dresser. I was gonna tell him what it was but then with all of the craziness, and him trying to get me to smoke with him, and the hookers, and that fucking song playing over and over again, I just kinda ran out of there before I had chance. That shit wasn't *coke*, Gibby, it was fuckin' PCP."

"PCP? What is this? Nineteen fucking seventy-two? What the hell are you doin' with a bindle of angel dust, man?"

"I told you, Gibby. It was a freebie! The guy just gave it to me, what was I *supposed* to do... say NO? My name ain't Nancy Reagan. Look, I told him there was no powder coke in any of that stuff. Maybe he shoulda checked with me about what it was before he went and stuck it all up his nose during an important business meeting."

"Oh well thanks for the advice, Randal," Gibby deadpanned, "But it doesn't really help at this point, does it? All I know is that Jacques *thought* he was doing coke and the next thing he knows he's out of his mind, naked and smeared in his own shit. When I barged into the stall he totally freaked out. After he pinned me to the floor, I couldn't get him to budge. I finally managed to talk him down, but it wasn't easy."

As Gibby droned on, Randal's mind was preoccupied.

Of course, he realized, it would be just as easy to call up Carlos and pick up some speed from him now that they were back in contact. Then Dr Titov wouldn't have to know that Randal was burning through his Adderall prescriptions at a rate of 240mg-plus a day. It would be a hell of a lot *cheaper*, too.

"So, uh, what did you do about Kenny and those guys?"

"I did the only thing I could think of. After I got Jacques offa me, I locked him up in a stall, cleaned myself off in the sink and I had to go up there with my filthy, wet suit and explain that Jacques was feeling a little *unwell*, and could they excuse us? I blamed it on jetlag."

"That's the best you could come up with?" Randal snorted, "Fuckin' *jetlag*?"

"Yeah well, pardon me Randal but I'd just crawled out from underneath a naked, shitty Frenchman. I was kinda thrown off my game, you know? But that's the thing – the *looks* those bastards gave me! I wouldn't be surprised if they canned the whole frigging project! They *knew* something was up. That goddamned assistant of Kenny's was giving me the total stink-eye. Thing is I'm starting to come to the conclusion that Jacques might be burnt out. Maybe he couldn't handle the success of *Dead Flowers* and all of the bullshit that came along with it. But if that's the case, I sure as hell can't let Kenny figure that out. Not until we've signed the contract at least. He must suspect that *something's* up, though. Azura can't be *that* fuckin dumb, can he? He's one of the richest and most powerful men in Hollywood, for Chrissakes!"

"Of *course* he can be that fucking dumb! If money and power was a sign of intelligence, then Britney Spears would be one of the smartest bitches on the planet, ya know? It'll be fine, I'm sure. Don't freak out."

"I guess."

No, Randal decided, *there's no fucking way I'm gonna call Carlos.* He was infuriated with himself for even considering it. He was just months away from being out of his brother's clutches and getting his hands on his rightful inheritance. Months away from being a free man again, beholden to nobody but himself.

How could he risk throwing that all away, so close to the finish line?

"By the way Randal, what kind of a fucking place have you got Jacques booked into here?"

"Huh?"

Gibby looked around the squalid room he was standing in, and frowned. "It's a fucking *dump.*"

"It's exactly the kind of place that Jacques *wanted.* It has *flavour.* So how's Jacques doing now?"

"He's passed out. I had to dress the bastard myself and sneak him out the back door and into a cab. He *stank.* I had to slip the cabbie an extra fifty up front just to let us in the car. I forced three Ambien down his throat and made him wash it down with a beer, so he's gonna be out for a while. But get this: right before he conked out completely I told him I was gonna call you up and chew you out for poisoning him with that bogus coke, and you know what that crazy frog bastard said to me?"

"Go on."

Gibby adoped a ridiculous fake-French accent. "*Ask 'im if 'e 'as any more of zat shit.* Jesus Christ!" Gibby shook his head dejectedly, "I hope you can see the kinda bullshit I'm up against here."

Randal knew well what dealing with Jacques entailed. Even here and now, as he fretted about running out of Adderall , Randal knew that his problem was not the pills, nor even his mounting desire to call up Carlos and score some meth.

These things were merely *symptoms*.

His problem was *Jacques*. Until Jacques turned up on the scene, things had been okay. Not great by any stretch of the imagination, but at least *okay*. After only a day and a bit in the drug-addled director's company, Randal felt sure that he was on the verge of a relapse. Being around Jacques while he played the role of the unrepentant hedonist was forcing Randal into a position that he felt utterly unsuited for – the nagging voice of reason. He knew there was no way in hell that he could keep up *that* charade for long. The only other option left open to him would be to say *fuck it*, and join in with the madness. But even if Randal was about to relapse, he had no desire to do it with a moron like Jacques. The more he hung around Jacques, the more all those laughably trite AA slogans started to seem prescient. *People, Places and Things*. Jacques brought along the baggage of all three: the People being his old drug connections, the Places being all of the old motels and alleys where he once scored or crashed, and the Thing was Jacques Seltzer himself, a narcotic-crazed mountain of a man, seemingly on a kamikaze mission of total self-obliteration.

Randal realized he had been struck by what the old-timers in the program called "a moment of clarity". He knew with absolute certainty that he could no longer be around Jacques Seltzer. In fact, his very life *depended* upon it.

"Look man, it'll be fine," Randal said soothingly, "Azura is as dumb as shit. If anything, he probably thinks this kinda bullshit gives Jacques *cachet*, or something. If it'll make you feel any better I'm heading into Chainsaw tomorrow and I can sound him out about how it all went. You know, on the down low."

"Okay, Randal… That would be great…"

Randal cut him off. "Hold that thought, Gibby. I need to talk to you about something really fucking important." Randal took a deep breath. "The thing is, this whole Jacques deal… it's just not working out. I'm sorry, but I'm done. I can't baby-sit Jacques no more. It's fucking me up."

"*What?*"

"I'm serious. I'm about one step away from a relapse here and the more I hang out with Jacques the quicker that relapse is coming. I feel like I'm standing on the tracks and that crazy bastard is driving the train that's bearing down on me. I gotta move out of the way, or I'm toast."

Careful not to wake his sleeping client, Gibby hissed: "*Randal! Jesus Christ, you've only had to put up with his stupid ass for 48 hours! I've had to deal with this bastard for over a fucking decade! And you're gonna BAIL on me ALREADY?*"

"I don't have a choice, Gibby. I gotta think about my *health* here. I'm too old for this shit. If I fuck up this time I'm *done*. My last name won't mean shit, because for all intents and purposes I'll no longer be a member of the Earnest family. I'll just be another schmo. And I'm *telling* you man, I've been in schmo-ville for, like, six months now and it just ain't me. Sorry."

There was a long silence on the other end. Then in a small, pleading voice Gibby begged, "Can't you do this *one thing* for me? If Jacques doesn't get the material he needs in LA, we're all fucked. I know him, I know what he's like! As soon as this starts to seem too difficult he'll bail on the movie and fuck off back to Paris. He'll go straight back into that drug and supermodel cocoon he's been wrapped up in the past decade. This is my last fucking shot at this, Randal. If *Black Neon* doesn't get made *now*, it'll *never* get made. Where will that leave *me*? I've invested years of my life into Jacques' career... Think about the *money*. You said it yourself, your brother has you on a tight leash. You're really gonna turn *twenty grand* down?"

Randal sniffed. "It's twenty thousand now, versus twenty million in six months. I may not be Albert fucking Einstein, Gibby, but I'm not *that* dumb."

"You gotta help me!" Gibby whined, "I have a daughter at *Columbia!*"

"Look..." Randal said, regretting the words almost as soon as they had escaped his lips, "What about if I get someone to take my place? I'm too out of the loop, Gibby. Even if I don't quit right now I've got the feeling that Jacques is gonna tell me to fuck off before too long anyway. The fact that I don't get high anymore obviously annoys the crap outta him. He wants someone to *join in* with all of his bullshit. He doesn't want a tour guide, Gibby, he wants a partner in crime. I can't BE that, and he and I both know it."

There was a long pause on the line as Gibby paced Jacques' motel room.

"Yeah, but even if you're right about that... *who?* Where the fuck can we find a junkie scumbag I'd be willing to trust my client with? Jacques may be a prick, Randal, but he's no use to me if some fucking dope-fiend slits his throat and takes his wallet. I mean, lets face it... he's not exactly street smart."

"To tell the truth," Randal said, "I only ever met one trustworthy dope-fiend in my whole fucking life."

"Who?"

"He was a good friend of mine. I've had to keep away from him ever since I got sober. He's still out there using, and being around that kind of stuff is just too much of a trigger for me. But... I know how to find him. Last I heard he was staying at a hotel in Hollywood. I have a number for him, somewhere."

"You can really vouch for him?"

Randal gnawed anxiously on a hangnail. "Look Gibby, straight up, I can vouch for him. That isn't the issue here. The thing is he's a real good friend of mine, and I need to know whether *you* can vouch for Jacques. I don't want to see this guy being taken advantage of. There'd be conditions. He needs to be paid some up front money. Plus, I know that Jacques is very free and fucking easy with that camera of his, so if you use any images or video of this guy I want it guaranteed *in writing* that he'll be fairly compensated. I don't just mean those bullshit, hundred dollar model fees that Jacques palmed off of on those Party and Play freaks. I need a guarantee that my friend will have a stake in the ownership of his own image and he'll get paid *every fucking time* it's used. I don't wanna see this guy's face plastered all over the walls of some pretentious gallery in Soho while he's scuffling around trying to raise enough money to buy a bag of crappy dope. If you can't agree to that, no deal."

Taking Gibby's silence as a sign he might actually be considering this proposition, Randal pressed home his advantage. "Plus I want a finder's fee for putting you guys in touch."

There was an even longer silence on the other end of the line.

"What you're asking me for is insane," Gibby said finally. "I mean, it's frankly *ludicrous*."

"This whole THING is ludicrous, Gibby. Why the fuck should you and Jacques be the only ones who profit from it? He's a good guy, Gibby, one of the only straight shooters I ever met in the dope game. He just... he just *can't* stay clean and it's killing him. But he's no fool, and he doesn't deserve to be treated like one. Anyway, this guy can get Jacques inside that world way better than I can. Maybe some kind of... *financial security* might make the difference in his life, who the hell knows."

"Or maybe it'll kill him quicker," Gibby sneered.

"That's a possibility. But it's not as if he's making it now. I don't think compensating him fairly for his time and experience will make his situation any *worse.*"

Gibby looked at Jacques' still form, snoring softly on the motel bed. *Well Jesus*, he reasoned, *why the fuck start acting rational at this late stage in the game*?

"Okay Randal, I'll talk to Jacques. See if we can set it up. But I promise you, if this junkie friend of yours hurts or endangers my client in any way I will hold you personally responsible. This isn't just about Jacques, Randal. My family's financial future depends upon *Black Neon* getting made. I don't have any more chances either, you understand?"

"I got you. I'll still be *involved*, Gibby. I can keep an eye on Kenny for you; maybe even try to use some of my influence over him. He hates my guts but he's not too dumb to realize that I'm Harvey's brother and he's gotta take me seriously."

"Okay. Okay. Jesus Christ, this is some fucked up shit Randal. I can't believe I'm agreeing to this. Lemmie get off the phone. Look, tell me what Kenny says about our meeting, and we can rap about this some more *mañana.*"

"Sounds good, Gibby. Just take it easy. Make sure that fat fuck doesn't choke on his own puke in the meantime, okay?"

Randal hung up the phone. He hoped to hell that he was making the right decision. The only thing he was one hundred percent sure of anymore was that he couldn't spend another minute babysitting Jacques-fucking-Seltzer. He went to the kitchen, poured himself a generous whisky and coke, and then began a long, futile evening hunting around his apartment, desperately trying to find some leftover pills.

NINETEEN

The next morning Genesis made it about half a block away from the motel before she doubled over and vomited into a trashcan. Lupita held her hair tenderly until she got it all up. It wasn't even noon but the desert air was hot and muggy already. When she was done Genesis straightened up and croaked, "I gotta go back. I'm too hung over for this."

They had planned on getting some food at the Nugget Diner on Virginia Street, but the oceans of booze she had consumed last night had taken too heavy a toll. Two casinos, at least three bars, and more shots than either of them could recall... She couldn't remember how much she drank, nor even making it back to the room, but the ominous taste in the pit of her gut informed her that cheap tequila had definitely been involved. There was a hazy recollection of Lupita cracking a bottle over the head of some hick who tried to grab Genesis' ass. Genesis was pale and unsteady. She looked like she was about to faint. Lupita smiled indulgently and ruffled her hair.

"Okay hun. Go back to the room. I'll go grab some food to go and come right back. You need me to get you anythin'?"

"Alka Seltzer."

"Alright. Can you make it back okay?"

"Uh-huh. I'm sorry baby. I feel like such a lightweight."

"You ain't a lightweight, far from it. Now go lie down, I'll be back in ten."

Lupita made it back to their room a half hour later. She slid the key in the lock and opened the door. Genesis had been sitting on the edge of the bed. She jumped anxiously to her feet when she heard the door open. "Oh, it's *you*..." she said.

"Who the fuck else would it be? I got your Alka Seltzer..."

She tossed the pack over and Genesis caught it. "How you feelin'?"

"Lousy. I'm kinda freaked out... you didn't see some crazy looking bitch hanging around outside, did you?"

Lupita stopped. She cocked her head to the side, like a dog picking up on some inaudible high-pitched frequency. "Whaddya mean, *crazy looking bitch*?"

Genesis took a deep breath.

"When I got back here... there was someone in the room. Some *girl*. She was snooping around."

Lupita frowned. "Like a cleaning lady?"

"In this place? Don't think so. I figure she musta been the old bag's grandkid or something. She was too young to be working here otherwise. She musta been like thirteen or fourteen, tops. She wasn't cleaning *shit*, that bitch was here to *snoop*. She was real freaky looking, too. She had all of this... *powder* all over her damn face."

Lupita started pacing the room.

"Whaddya mean, powder? Like make-up?"

"No. It was... it looked like the bitch just sneezed into a bag of coke or somehin'."

"And she was sneakin' around in here?"

"Uh-huh."

Lupita started furiously checking their bags.

"Wait, wait! It's okay. I already checked. She didn't take anything. Everything's still here. I think I musta disturbed her before she had time to really take a good look, ya know?"

Unconvinced Lupita started checking around the room, as if looking for bugs or hidden cameras. "What did she do when you came in?" Lupita demanded.

"She just *froze*. Like a deer in the fucking headlights. She was kinda... leaning over the bed, like she was looking at the pillow or somethin'. When I walked in she straightens up and just... *stares* at me. That's when I saw she had all of that weird powder shit all over her face. She had this crazy expression.... Like she'd been smoking sherm or something. I dunno, something about this chick really freaked me out, Lupe. There was something real weird about her. We just stood there lookin' at each other for a minute."

"And then?"

Genesis came over to Lupita. She draped her arm over her neck. Lupita's body was coiled, like a cobra about to strike.

"Chill baby," Genesis said, "I just told that snooping little cunt to get the fuck outta our room, before I kicked her skinny ass. She practically ran out of here. Never said a word to me."

"Fuck," Lupita said. She shrugged Genesis's arm away and started pacing again. "We gotta get outta here. Last fucking thing we need is people snooping around in our shit!"

Genesis sat on the bed and ran her trembling hand through her hair. It was the first time she had ever seen Lupita lose her cool like this. It was strange because the incident seemed so *trivial*. After all, this place wasn't exactly high end. The kid was probably just looking for cash or jewellery.

"Tell me about that powder again. Was it like... ashes? Like the stuff that was on the old lady's forehead when we checked in?"

"Ashes? I guess, maybe. I dunno. Why?"

"No reason."

"Look sweetie..." Genesis sat next to Lupita and pulled her close. She kissed her lightly on the neck. "I ain't feeling up to much anyway. There's no way I could make the drive today, I feel lousy. We already paid up for two nights... Maybe we could just stay in tonight and split tomorrow morning? We'll be in here. Nobody'll try to come in again..."

Genesis felt Lupita's body relax slightly. "You really told her you was gonna beat her ass?"

"Uh-huh."

Lupita smiled a little. "She got lucky. If I'd have walked in here and caught her I'd have shot that cunt in the face. Still, I guess grandma down there ain't gonna be amused when the kid tells her what you said."

"Fuck that old bitch! I'll bet she put her up to it. Thinkin' we're throwing some crazy lesbian dope parties up here, or some shit."

Lupita laughed. "Well, she wouldn't be too far off in that case, would she? Still, I guess it wouldn't hurt to take a night off." Lupita looked around their room and smiled. "Stay in and enjoy the surroundings, you know?"

They fixed some Dilaudid, which helped with Genesis's hangover and Lupita's anxiety. Lupita's paranoid reaction had disturbed Genesis, reminded her of the hair-burning and prayer routine that had gone down after the massacre at the pharmacy. An uncomfortable hint that all might not be quite *right* with Lupita. As if she had caught a glimpse of some madness that was lurking under the surface of her lover's public face. But after she fixed Lupita seemed to relax, and after a while so did Genesis. The night unfolded with the quiet hum of an opiate haze. They lay on the bed idly watching re-runs of *To Catch A Predator with Chris Hansen* on CBS. On an ad break Lupita looked dreamily at Genesis and said, "Genesis hun, you shoulda seen the pharmacy I picked your stuff up at."

"Oh yeah?"

"Yeah. They got one old lady working in there. Place is like something out of *Leave It To Beaver*. I had a good look around. They don't even have cameras... It was one of those places that looked too good to be true, ya know?"

"Sounds... great..." Genesis slurred through heavy, slack lips.

Sensing that Genesis was too far into her nod to listen, Lupita said, "Shhhhh. We'll talk about it later..."

Later that evening Genesis was sleeping while Lupita lay next to her, staring at the ceiling. The TV droned away in the background but Lupita was lost in her own thoughts. She was thinking about many things: about the old woman at the front desk, and the intruder Genesis had caught. About the road that lay ahead of them. About a man who looked a little like Charles Bronson who had once said to her *"The shit has to flow, yes?"* But mostly she was thinking about the pharmacy three blocks away: the one with the elderly pharmacist, minimal security, and a pile of controlled substances just there for the taking.

A strange sound jerked Lupita out of her thoughts. A faint scratching noise, like mice in the walls. She wondered if she had imagined it at first. But no, there it was again.

It seemed to be coming from the door.

Careful not to wake Genesis, Lupita reached under the pillow for her gun and crept out of bed. She clicked on the outside light and put her eye to the peephole. She saw nothing, just the deserted walkway and the bugs that swarmed around the bulb above the door. She opened the door a crack. She peered around. Nothing.

She was about to close the door again when she saw something out of the corner of her eye. Something black was lying on the walkway, just off to one side. It was maybe ten inches long, thick, and it seemed to be *squirming*. Lupita felt her heart's steady tattoo in her throat. She opened the door further and peered at the alien thing, still unable to determine what it actually *was*. She cautiously crouched down, and gave it a solid shove with the nose of the gun. The air suddenly came alive as a swarm of bugs erupted from the object as the gun made contact with it. Lupita jumped back in disgust. She could see now that underneath the mass of insects the thing was reddish-pink. Lupita's stomach turned as she realized what the glistening, meaty thing was: a cow's tongue, already swarming with parasites. Sickened, Lupita immediately understood what this meant. She closed the door, pulled the bolt across, and began frenziedly packing their bags. Genesis slept through it all.

When she was done Lupita lay next to her in the bed, wide awake. She clutched the gun to her chest all night. Every time she heard a noise her eyes shot over to the door, as if she expected the devil to come bursting through it. Like the onset of a bad acid trip, all the latent evil and darkness in the universe came seeping out of the shadows. The very air she breathed seemed thick as molasses, infused with the stench of the grave. She occasionally glanced over at Genesis, who lay dozing next to her, oblivious in the pre-dawn gloom.

As soon as the sun was up, Lupita told herself, they were both getting the fuck out of this place. She thought of the pharmacy she had been casing. How easy it seemed. Ripe for the picking. With omens like this in the air, maybe it would be smart to go underground for a while. Hide out. Draw the curtains and withdraw from the world until the winds changed. There were bad vibes in the air, gathering storm clouds.

She thought of the pharmacy again.

One job, a quick hit and run on their way out of town... that would buy them some time. Give them some room to breathe. Lupita ran her thumb lovingly over the smooth contours of the handgun. One more job and they could hide out. Keep their heads down in anticipation of the coming deluge. She listened to the wind, and the steady rise and fall of Genesis's soft snores.

TWENTY

G hosting the streets of Hollywood in a pair of skinny black jeans and scuffed leather Chelsea boots, Jeffrey cursed and sniffed, the dark wind of heroin withdrawal gusting steadily from some unseen future point, relentlessly rolling toward his present, invisible, unstoppable and grimly smothering everything in its way. It was shaping to up to be a shitty day.

Rachel was back at the Gilbert, dope-sick and pissed off. She was still refusing to turn tricks and Jeffrey had begun to suspect that the prophetic dream Rachel claimed to have had was nothing more than a passive-aggressive ploy to get back at him for the incident with Smooth. Over the past few days Rachel had withdrawn from him almost completely. She spent her days lying in bed chain-smoking anxiously, occasionally looking at him with eyes that radiated disgust. Jeffrey knew that unless he found a way to start bringing in some bread, he was going to come back to their room one day to find she had cleared out for good. There was no doubt in his mind that without money and without drugs it was inevitable that Rachel would split for greener pastures.

In some ways he knew that this would make his life easier. He would be able to come and go as he pleased. He'd never have to share his dope. But in most other senses it would be a disaster. It was always better to have a partner in the dope game, someone to rely on to help you get fixed when your luck and your dope ran out, as they inevitably did from time to time. More than that, Jeffrey remembered how it was to face up to the nights alone, with only his drugs and his self-loathing for company. The despair that had threatened to choke him so many times.

What they had wasn't what most people would call *love*, but it was something deeper than mere co-dependence. It was junkie love, a kind of *ménage a trois* were both partners tolerate each other's faults because of a shared romance with the needle. A trade off, where the one thing that causes all your problems also smooths them out completely. Jeffrey wondered how anybody could tolerate the messy complication of human relations *without* dope. He resolved to make one last-ditch effort to fix the situation. He hit the streets with fourteen bucks and change in his pocket hoping to somehow transform this – like Jesus with that old water into wine routine – into enough dope to warm over both their bones.

Jeffrey wandered Hollywood's starved streets, his mind squirming, desperately trying to figure out another way to make some decent scratch. His fence, Doug, had recently dropped the bombshell that he was getting out of the book hustle altogether. "It's a dying business," he had whined. "The fucking publishers have been hammering the public with crap so long that people have stopped caring. I'm thinking of getting into pimping again. At least there's always a market for pussy." The book thing had been Jeffrey's most reliable way of making money. Although he had no real stomach for overt acquisitive crime, he took to the streets anyway hoping that some kind of miracle opportunity would present itself. Jeffrey knew damn well that magical thinking was an essential part of making it in the dope game.

He hopped the Metro at Hollywood and Vine and rode the train downtown, trying not to make eye contact with the crazies and commuters onboard. He got off at Union Station, unsure of why he chose this stop, drawn to downtown by some kind of diviner's instinct. Just knowing that dope was nearby made him at least feel that he was at least headed in the right direction.

He found himself in the main hall of Union Station, retracing the steps he had taken many times in the past as he'd cruised for young Latin trade to bring home to his late boyfriend, Bill. Bill had liked to watch Jeffrey screwing these young guys, staring with bulging eyes as the action went down on his king-sized bed, one hand holding a bottle of amyl nitrate to his nose, another frenziedly working his pecker. Those had been happier days, easier days, when money and drugs were both plentiful. Now Bill – and the security that his money had provided – was long gone. Today there was barely enough money for dope, and not even enough *time* for a luxury like cruising for sex. Jeffrey was certainly too long in the tooth to try and make a few dollars by turning tricks the way he had when he was a teenager. What with an abundance of younger, prettier guys cruising for fun, Jeffrey suspected that he probably couldn't even *give* it away at the moment. He had lost his latest tooth – bringing the running tally up to seven – biting into the crust of a stale slice of pizza. He knew he wasn't exactly a hot commodity these days.

He entered the station's bathroom, experiencing a weird feeling of nostalgia. Inside, the familiar smell of bleach and the undertone of stale piss. Jeffrey noted that it was unusually quiet in there for the time of day. A bald man wearing a charcoal grey trench coat was off to one side, taking a suspiciously long time at one of the urinals. The place was quiet. Even though the bald man in the trench coat was standing with his dick in his hand, there was no accompanying sound of urine against porcelain. He just lingered there with an absent look on his face, with the resigned air of someone waiting for a bus. A faucet dripped, slowly and steadily. The row of stalls against the far wall was empty, except for one. The stall on the furthest right, the larger stall that allowed for wheelchair access, was definitely occupied. The door was closed and Jeffrey could see a pair of expensive-looking leather shoes underneath. There was a slow, steady sniffing noise emanating from inside the stall. Jeffrey looked at the positioning of the feet, indicating that the person was sitting on the toilet, twisted around to the left, and obviously snorting coke or some other drug from the top of the toilet roll dispenser. Next to the feet, propped against the door, was a black laptop case.

Interesting.

Jeffrey calculated in an instant the odds of getting away with the laptop. It seemed quite possible. If he got on his knees he could slip his hand under the wall of the stall – there was a good two-inch gap – turn the laptop on its side and slide it out easily. He figured he could make his escape before the guy inside had even got the rolled-up bill out of his nose. Hopefully. It would take a couple of seconds before the guy would be able to give chase, which would be just enough time for Jeffrey to get the fuck out of there.

But he had to act fast. The guy inside would finish up any moment. Jeffrey was suddenly convinced that Bill had a hand in this, that it had been some kind of supernatural nudge from his dead ex-boyfriend that had guided him down here to this bizarrely easy score. Jeffrey walked purposefully toward the stall. The bald man half turned, pecker still in his hand, and stared at Jeffrey with a smile playing on his wet, rubbery lips. Jeffrey shot back a look so poisonous that the bald man immediately turned away, and went back to looking intently at his dick in his hand, waiting silently for someone else to pass by. In one swift movement Jeffrey hunched down, grabbed the laptop and slid it out of the stall. He was already heading toward the exit when he heard the guy in the stall yell, "What the FUCK? HEY! COME BACK!"

Holding the laptop to his chest Jeffrey ran, easing up when he was well away from the bathrooms and safely surrounded by commuters. He was pretty sure that the guy in the stall wouldn't be able to catch up with him. Besides, he didn't want to draw attention to himself by running through the station in such a conspicuous manner. There were so many people that Jeffrey felt he could make it back onto the metro without being spotted. He didn't fully relax until he was back on the red line, heading toward Pershing Square. He finally allowed himself to breathe easy as the train trundled away from Union Station, allowing himself to open up the case and peek inside.

There was a white laptop inside. It looked like a brand new MacBook, definitely worth a few dollars to the right person. *Goddamn!* When they pulled into Pershing Square Jeffrey hopped out, smiling inanely at the people he made eye contact with. Everything was suddenly all right with the world again. He made his way up to the street, virtually skipping past a gaggle of homeless men loitering at the top of the escalators. By the Angel's Flight train, in the neighbourhood that was once known as Bunker Hill, Jeffrey found a payphone and called a fence he knew who operated out of downtown. They arranged to meet at the Grand Central Market, at a taco joint called *Tacos Tumbras a Tomas*. He walked over there, found an empty table, and opened up the laptop while he waited. He turned it on and stared at the peaceful blue screen as it loaded up, wondering exactly how much he could get for his haul.

*

"Man," Jeffrey said, "and you people say that us faggots are sick in the head? This is some twisted shit, Whitey."

Jeffrey and his fence, a hulking six-foot-two African-American albino called Whitey – real name Winston Edward Delacroix – had been huddled over their table for half an hour now.

Whitey's carne asada taco was forgotten and long since gone cold. Mute, they flicked through the hundreds of images on the stolen MacBook of a portly, grey haired man in a variety of sexual positions with a gaggle of blank-eyed, emaciated Cambodian child-prostitutes.

"Shit, jus' 'cos they females, don't make this motherfucka *straight*. This homeboy iz sick in the head, Jeffrey. This cocksucker's a fuckin' *pedophile*, cuz. That's a whole other kettle o'fish."

"Okay man," Jeffrey said with a wince, slamming the laptop screen closed, "that's enough pre-teen poontang for one lifetime. Let's talk green. Although, I gotta say having seen that shit I don't feel so bad about ripping this bastard off."

Whitey pulled the computer over to him and opened up the screen again. Looking over his shoulder to make sure that nobody else was looking at the disturbing images on the screen, he started frantically tapping at the keys with a look of intense concentration. Jeffrey sniffed and looked away. "Jesus Whitey, you ain't seen enough already?"

"I'm looking for somethin'. Like I said when I saw the first fuckin' pic, this bastard looks *familiar*."

Whitey tapped away, his brow furrowed in concentration. Losing interest, Jeffrey watched a down-at-heel man in a dirty blue polyester suit buy a short dog of Wild Irish Rose over at the liquor counter. He meticulously counted out the balance in greasy change, much to the annoyance of the old hunched-over Latin man behind the counter.

"I fuckin *knew* it," Whitey said.

"Knew what?"

"That I *recognized* this prick. It's Kevin Macmillan. I just found the motherfucker's tax returns on here."

"Oh." Jeffrey tore his eyes away from the man in the blue suit as he staggered out onto Broadway with the booze. "So who the fuck is Kevin Macmillan?"

Whitey raised an eyebrow. "You heard of *Californians for Family Values*, right?"

Jeffrey shrugged, non-committal.

"You remember all those ads that were running about Proposition 8? The ones that said if gay marriage was legalized then the homos iz gonna start adopting kids so they can diddle 'em? And about how gay teachers'll be diddling their pupils and the school won't be able to fire 'em? They were all over TV back when the vote was goin' down."

"I don't watch TV."

"Or the Prop 19 commercials?" Whitey carried on, ignoring him, "The ones that went *Don't Let California Go To Pot!* All about how a yes on 19 would mean your kids could buy weed at the grocery store and pretty soon the entire state would be strung out on meth and heroin? And about how weed causes cancer and insanity? It was some real *Reefer Madness* shit... You never saw those?"

Jeffrey shook his head.

"You said he was gettin' high when you snatched the laptop?"

"Uh-huh. Either that or he had the worst case of allergies I ever heard in my fuckin' life."

Whitey shook his head. "Figures. Most of these cats are motherfuckin' hypocrites..."

"So how much, Whitey? I'm kinda hurtin' here, man. If you're gonna blackmail this guy I guess it's gotta be worth some decent scratch..."

Whitey seemed to consider Jeffrey's blackmail suggestion for a moment. "Well," he said, "Could do that, fo sure, fo sure... Then again this motherfucka's *connected*, cuz. I hear he's bankrolling Tea Partiers, eatin' lunch with mayors and police chiefs. Donating money to the Church of the Latter Day Saints...

sonvabitch could be a damn Scientologist for all I know. I'm jus' a buyin' and sellin' type of a guy. Small time motherfucka like me could have an unfortunate... *accident* tangling with the likes of this prick. Happens all the time. Besides..."

Whitey powered the laptop down, closed it up, and slipped it back in the case.

"Be-*sides*... it might give me more personal satisfaction jus' to send these pictures to every major news source in the fuckin' country. Jus' bring down that playa-hating, baby-fuckin', tea-baggin' piece of shit for kicks, ya know?"

"So how much, Whitey?"

Whitey sucked air through his teeth and raised four fingers. "Howzat sound?"

"Shitty. Six."

"Five. Final fuckin offer."

"Five fifty?"

"You'd better get back on that fuckin' Lucky Charms box, motherfucka and ask those damn kids if they wanna buy this thing for five-fifty. Cuz I'm offerin' five-even."

Jeffrey ran a hand through his greasy hair. Five hundred dollars was probably a fraction of what this thing was worth, but Whitey was offering straight up cash, immediate payment. Whitey pulled out his wallet, and flashed the bills. Jeffrey nodded weakly. Whitey counted out the notes, and Jeffrey pocketed them. The fence grabbed the case, nodded his thanks to the shivering Irish dope-fiend, and headed out to the street. He pulled his cheap plastic sunglasses down over his face on his way out. Jeffrey watched him go. He was already yammering into his cell phone, making plans, brow furrowed, gesturing with his free hand.

Moments later, Jeffrey's cell phone – a pre-paid piece of junk he'd bought in a 7-11 for the sole purpose of communicating with his drug dealers – started ringing, pulling him out of his thoughts. For almost a year now the only calls he'd received on this thing were calls from irate dealers complaining that he still owed them money from the various small time buys that he'd showed up twenty dollars light to. He didn't recognize the number, but answered anyway. His experience with Smooth still fresh in his memory, he picked up the phone with the intention of pacifying whoever was on the other end.

"Yeah?"

"Jeffrey, is that you?" said a crackly voice.

"Yeah. Who's this?"

"It's Randal, man."

There was a long silence. Jeffrey's dry lips cracked a smile.

"*Randal?* That's really *you?*"

"Uh-huh."

"Jesus *Christ* Randal, how you doin' man? It's good to hear your voice! Shit, what's goin' on? You making it?"

"Barely. You?"

"Not at all. So what brings you outta the woodwork?"

"Don't laugh," Randal said, "But I got a business proposition for you. Some easy money, if you're looking for a gig."

"Man, you don't know the half of it. Lemmie grab a pen..."

After he hung up, Jeffrey grabbed Whitey's uneaten taco. He smiled to himself imagining the look on Rachel's face when he showed up not only with money and dope, but Mexican food as well. If this deal Randal had proposed was for real, then maybe – just maybe – they'd be able to dig themselves out of the pit they were currently in. All of a sudden, life had thrown him a bone. Jeffrey headed out to the street. He shot an easy smile at the old drunk in the polyester suit. He was sitting on a dolphin-shaped kiddy ride outside of the market. Jeffrey rummaged around in his pockets and found a quarter. He popped it in the slot and the machine announced *"Attention parents! Please do not leave your child unattended while riding the ride. Have fun kids!"* before jerking into life, bleating out a creaky rendition of *Old MacDonald Had A Farm*. The drunk rode the dolphin unsteadily, raising his paper bag and toasting Jeffrey as he headed back toward the Metro.

TWENTY-ONE

Genesis was screaming.

Tears were streaming down her face as she waved her mutilated hand around. Lupita floored the accelerator. They were tearing away from the pharmacy empty-handed. Genesis held up her bloody left hand and wailed, "My fucking finger! That bitch shot off my damn finger!"

"It's gonna be okay," Lupita said as they headed toward the freeway, careful to stay 5mph below the speed limit. "Just shut up and stop waving that fucking hand around! If the cops notice you screamin' and bleedin' all over the damn place we're dead meat."

"But it HURTS!"

Lupita looked over to Genesis' mutilated appendage. She nodded curtly. "I *know* it does baby. But we gotta get the fuck away from here without being spotted, otherwise we're lookin' at some serious jail time. That pharmacist is dead, no doubt about it. That's murder one, for starters. Just wrap your hand up in the gauze I grabbed... It's right there, the box by your feet." Lupita glanced over as Genesis clumsily tended to her wound, "Uh-huh, that's it. Wrap it tight. Keep the hand elevated, above the heart. There you go..."

As she drove, Lupita silently dissected what had just gone down. The place had seemed like such a breeze. They kept watch for a few moments after the old lady opened up. Nobody was around. They pulled their bandanas over their faces and stormed the place, guns at the ready. "Cash and drugs!" As they burst in there, the old dear behind the counter looked like she was about to shit. The whole thing was too fucking easy.

*

"I'm bleeding like a stuck pig!"

The car stereo blasted an old rock'n'roll number called *Bad Boy*. Lupita hummed along with it grimly, as Genesis moaned and continued to mummify her bloody hand with the gauze. Irritated by Lupita's seeming indifference to her pain Genesis snapped, "Can you turn the fuckin' music down? It's ruinin' my concentration. I'm trying to patch myself up here! I'm not in a Little Richard mood right now, you know?"

"This ain't Little Richard," Lupita shot back, "it's Larry Williams. He's *another* rock'n'roll guy... he was the guy who threatened to *shoot* Little Richard. Over a coke deal, I think. What I know for sure is he scared Little Richard so bad he quit rock'n'roll for a while and went off to be a born-again Christian. Funny thing is, Larry ended up getting shot himself justa few years later."

"That's real fascinating," Genesis said through gritted teeth as she continued to wrap layers of gauze around her bloody hand, "But I'm bleeding to fucking death here, and the music's too FUCKING LOUD!"

With a grunt, Genesis turned the volume down herself, smearing the tape deck with blood. They tore on, Lupita driving in silence while Genesis whimpered and groaned, holding her freshly bandaged hand up to her chest. After a few tense moments of watching an agitated Lupita mutter angrily to herself, Genesis snapped. "You got nerve, Lupe, I'll give you that."

"Huh?" Lupita glanced into the rear view mirror, obsessively checking for black-and-whites. "Nerve? Whaddya mean?"

"Pouting 'cos I turned that fuckin' radio down. That takes some balls, especially after what you did!"

"What I *did*? What the fuck did I do?"

Genesis snorted. "You mind telling me what the fuck that was all that about?"

"What, Genesis hun?"

"Don't *hun* me, Lupe. You know damn well what I'm fucking talkin' about! Why'd you insist on knocking off that place like that? I fuckin' wake up and you're rushing me out of the damn motel while I'm still half asleep... you shove me into the car and tear off, and the next thing I know we're pulling up in front of that fucking drugstore and tell me we're gonna *rob* the fucking place? Jesus Lupe, I hadn't even had breakfast!"

"What the fuck's breakfast got to do with anything?"

"You know what I'm talking about, don't play dumb. What was the fucking hurry? You just had us run into that place with no fucking plan, no *thought*... I mean we was just *asking* for something to go wrong! I told you it was a stupid idea. Why didn't you *listen* to me?"

"Genesis hun... you just don't *understand*. I had my reasons...."

"If that was all then maybe I *could* understand. But *no*, that wasn't even the *worst* of it. On top of everything, you fuckin' LIED to me, Lupe! You fucking lied straight to my face..."

Genesis was sobbing now, tears of pain and anger streaming down her face as the blood seeped steadily through the bandage. Lupita looked over to her lover, her face a mixture of hurt and concern.

Softly now, "Lied to you, Genesis hun? I don't follow..."

"You made me a *promise*, Lupe! No more killing. You fucking *swore* to me."

"Oh Jesus Christ!"

With a screech of rubber against asphalt Lupita made a risky cut across lanes to avoid slow-moving traffic. "You have *got* to be kidding me! In case it escaped your notice Genesis, that bitch *shot you* back there! What the fuck did you want me to do? Write a letter of *complaint*?"

"*I don't need your fucking sarcasm!*" Genesis wailed. "I'm in PAIN! I'm BLEEDING!"

Lupita momentarily considered kicking Genesis's ass out of the vehicle without stopping. Genesis was sobbing, big fat tears streaking her face. Feeling her rage deflate a little, Lupita smiled faintly at her lover.

"I know you're in pain, Genesis hun," she said in a half-whisper, "But you're gonna be okay. It's all going to be okay, sweetheart. I promise you. I just need you to keep calm until we get away from here. Look hun, I know I promised you… and I meant it… but that was a clear case of self-defence. I did it to save your life."

Lupita took a deep breath and then said something she hadn't said in many, many years. "I … I love you Genesis. That's why I did it. Because I *love you.*"

Genesis smiled painfully through her tears. Pacified, she blubbered, "I love you, too, but I just don't *understand…*"

*

Just before they'd turned their guns on the pharmacist, they'd locked the door after them, put up the CLOSED sign and pulled the shade down. "Cash and drugs!" Lupita spat, "Don't make me kill you over some goddamned pills…" However, as the old woman stood there with her mouth hanging open, shit started to unravel fast.

Moments after they'd burst in, someone started trying the door.

The bell rattled, as someone frantically tried to force it open. Instead of paying attention to the CLOSED sign, the dumb fuck kept rattling the damn door. That was their first mistake, Lupita realized. They both took their eyes off the old woman for a moment. They turned instead to watch the silhouette of this dumb-fuck as he rattled the door incessantly. He eventually gave up and split. They turned their attentions back to the pharmacist.

Lupita had a fraction of a second to process the sight of the gun in her hand before it went off with a loud crack. Genesis hit the ground screaming. Her gun skittered across the floor.

The next shot came from Lupita.

The bullet hit the pharmacist in the chest, knocking her over in a spray of crimson. Cursing, Lupita checked Genesis out. Her left hand was a bloody mess. The bullet had hit her pinky finger, blowing it clean off. She looked back to the dead pharmacist, lying there in a slowly expanding pool of blood. She dragged Genesis to her feet. Told her that they needed to get the fuck out of here. Right. Fucking. Now. They stopped on the way out to retrieve Genesis' weapon and grab a box of bandages from the shelves. That was the sum total of their haul, Lupita thought grimly. A few dollars worth of fucking bandages.

*

As they drove Lupita said, "Look, I know this is kinda hard for you to understand... and it might sound a little, I dunno, *crazy* or somethin'... but that fucking bitch... she put a fucking *hex* on us!"

Genesis was wincing, looking at the bandaged hand. The bandages were fat and heavy with blood. "I need to get to a hospital..." she groaned.

"Keep that shit elevated! And don't worry, hun. I got us covered. Mama Z is gonna fix you up, Genesis. Just hang on."

"Who the fuck is Mama Z?"

Lupita looked over to Genesis and then back at the road. "Mama Z is about the only one who can help us right now," she said through clenched teeth, "I hate to break it to you, but we been *cursed*, girl. Getting to a doctor is the least of our fuckin' worries right now, believe me."

Genesis held the bloody, bandaged hand to her chest desperately hoping for relief. The pain was intense, an unbearable fire spreading up the whole arm. She groaned. "Whaddya mean *cursed*? Whaddya mean we don't need a doctor? I need someone to sew me up! I could bleed to death here..."

Lupita shook her head. "You ain't gonna bleed to death, hun. You could lose a couple of pints and not even notice. Wrap the bandage tighter, and you won't bleed out. Not by a long shot. Mama Z's no joke. She'll fix you up. You just gotta hold on 'til we get to Los Angeles."

"*Los Angeles*? Oh my GOD Lupe, I'm in fucking PAIN here! That's gonna take hours..."

"It's gonna take eight hours to be specific, a little less if I don't hit traffic. Like I said, you ain't gonna bleed to death. You just gotta sit tight and deal until we make it to Mama Z's place. Take a fuckin' Dilaudid. Take two." Lupita nodded toward the glove compartment, "Go crazy. I can get more pills in LA. This is no joke, Genesis. And what I mean by cursed is what that old bitch did to us back at the motel. *Santeria*."

"Huh?" Genesis squirmed around, pulling at the glove compartment with her good hand, "What you *talking* about, Lupe?"

"Santeria. Magic! I got a weird vibe from the old bitch that ran the motel. And then you caught that bitch in our room? Suddenly we hit this kinda luck? That's no coincidence. That bitch you found snooping, she was probably looking for some of our hair, or nail clippings, or blood or something. To help the old lady make the curse with. The fuckin' powder on her face was a dead giveaway that she practiced that stuff. GODDAMNIT. I shoulda figured! Shitty luck like that don't just fall from the damn sky. Now look at us! You got a missing finger, we didn't score no dope, and there's a dead fuckin' pharmacist back there. This is FUCKED UP, Genesis hun."

Genesis swallowed a couple of Dilaudid, and washed them back with a slug from the half-empty bottle of Wild Turkey that was rolling around under her seat. She put the bottle between her legs, and shoved the cork back in with her good hand. The pain was receding a little now, but her head was foggy. Lupita's crazy talk about magic and curses definitely wasn't helping matters. Suddenly too tired to argue, Genesis changed tack and tried to reason with Lupita.

"Lupita, honey, I don't believe in any of that stuff. Black magic, curses, all of that horseshit. I'm sorry, but I just don't."

"It don't matter whether you believe in it or not," Lupita said evenly, "It'll still bite you in the ass just the same. I don't wanna freak you out but... I *found* something last night. Outside of our room. A tongue, y'know, from a cow?"

A hysterical whine crept into Genesis's voice. "What the fuck are *talking* about? I don't under*stand*..."

"Shh. It's okay. It's just... you *wouldn't* understand. I don't *expect* you to. All I know is that we gotta get to Mama Z's place, and we gotta get there fast."

"Honey, I need to get to a doctor. I get that you're a bit fucking... freaked out right now, but what about my *hand*? I can't wait eight hours, no way! I can't TAKE it..."

"Oh yeah? Genesis honey, believe me, you can. You lost a finger. I know it looks bad, and I don't doubt it hurts like hell, but what you got there is a non-life-threatening injury. You gotta trust me on that. If we stop around here to look for a doctor, we're toast. It would be madness to stop anywhere near here to get that injury loked at. We might as well go turn ourselves into the cops. Once we get to Mama Z's we can get you fixed up nice and quietly, nobody needs to know."

Despite the fact that Genesis thought all of Lupita's talk of curses and hexes was crazy talk, she couldn't argue with her logic here. She closed her eyes and started to whimper like a kicked dog.

"...we could get a fuckin' lethal injection for what just went down back there, Genesis hun. You gotta trust me girl, I'm the only one thinking straight right now. Just keep the rag wrapped tight around the wound. Once the Dilaudid hits, you ain't gonna feel shit. You're gonna feel like a million fucking bucks, okay?"

Genesis groaned.

"Okay?"

"Okay!" Genesis snapped. Then she muttered, "Talk to me, Lupe. Talk to me about something else. Distract me..."

"Talk? Talk about *what*?"

Genesis closed her eyes. "Tell me how you lost your arm."

They drove in silence for a while. With a resigned sigh Lupita said, "Shit, Genesis hun. It's a long story..."

"So I guess it's the perfect time then, isn't it? You just told me I'm gonna be sitting around *bleeding* for the next eight hours..."

"Yeah, I guess you got a point."

Genesis stared at the horizon as they whizzed on down the I-80 West towards California. The pain in her hand was almost unbearable, but she knew that the pills would soon dull most of the edge from it.

"Come on then," Genesis said through gritted teeth, "Start talkin."

PART TWO

TWENTY-TWO

Gibby had just made it back to his apartment when the phone rang. AZURA, KENNY the Caller ID announced. He considered ignoring it and then, realizing the futility of such a gesture, picked up the phone.

"Hi Kenny."

"Gibby. One second, okay?"

There was a click as Kenny hit the hold button. Gibby found himself stuck, listening to some hideous digital musak.

In his Beverly Hills home, Kenny looked over to the bed. A nineteen-year old Russian whore called Kristina was lolling around on there, fully dressed, tapping lethargically on her Blackberry. He bent over and snorted a huge rail of cocaine from the case of a Michael Bublé CD. He sprung upright again, red-faced and sniffling. He barked at the girl, "Hey sugar tits!" She looked up. "Yeah, you!"

"Yes Mister Azura – is... *problem*?" Kristina pouted.

"Too right there's a fuckin' problem. You're on the goddamned clock here! I'm not payin' you to check your fuckin Facebook status! Why don't you make yourself fuckin' useful and take your fuckin' clothes off or somethin'? The bathroom's over there – don't you bitches usually like to go clean up first?"

Looking slightly shocked by Kenny's outburst, Kristina quickly composed herself like the professional she was and simpered, "I just had *shower*, Mister Azura. Before *coming*."

"Yeah? Well I'm taking a guess that you don't live in this fuckin' neighbourhood, right? I mean, I doubt you make *that* much sucking dick, right honey?"

Kristina looked confused.

"Lemmie guess? Santa Monica between Fairfax and La Brea, somewhere down there in fuckin' borscht land, right? So that's at least forty minutes you've been sitting in a cab getting all stale and funky. Why don't you stop sitting there looking useless and go freshen up for me, okay? Despite what Al Pacino mighta led you to believe there ain't nuthin' enticing to *me* about the fuckin' scent of a woman, okay? *Chop chop!*"

The girl just stared at him, as if not understanding a word of Kenny's coke-garbled insults, so he simply resorted to pointing the bathroom and yelling "GO CLEAN YOUR SNATCH!" Kristina had a pretty ropey grasp of English, having just arrived in the US two months ago from a small town outside of Moscow, but she did understand his agitated tone of voice well enough. She'd had it drilled into her by her new bosses at *Angel LA Escorts* that Mr. Azura was a rich, valued customer who must be obeyed, so she trotted toward the bathroom as ordered with a submissive, simpering smile on her face.

"And hurry it up!" Kenny called after her, muttering darkly to himself as he clicked over to Gibby again.

"Gibby!" He cleared his throat. "So where's the goddamned *script*?"

Gibby, momentarily caught unawares, stammered, "Wh-wh-what?"

"Fuck is wrong with you? You having a fuckin' seizure over there? The *SCRIPT* Gibby, where the fuck is it?"

"You didn't say that you... needed to see it!"

"Gibby. I am about to sign off on a contract that will make you and Jacques a hell of a lot of money. Or, I should say, that will put a hell of a lot of MY money – and Chainsaw's money for that matter – in your hands so you can deliver *Black Neon*, yes? Now tell me, Gibby. Do I look like a pretty Korean cocktail waitress to you?"

"I'm sorry Kenny, I don't follow."

"A pretty. Korean. Cocktail waitress. Do I look like one to you? It's a simple fucking question Gibby, so stop stuttering and start answering…"

"No Kenny," Gibby answered evenly, "you do not look like a pretty Korean cocktail waitress."

"Fuckin' goddamn straight I don't. So why are you trying to stick your fucking DICK in me? You expect me to sign off on this shit without even a script? I know that Jacques is a talented motherfucker, but as for *you* Gibby, I don't know. If I can't even count on you to get me a few scenes of this script he's working on, then a part of me has to wonder exactly what fucking value *you* add to all of this? I know what *I'm* bringing to the table, Gibby. You do know what I'm bringing, right?"

"Yes," Gibby croaked, mindful not to set Kenny off again, "you're bringing the money."

"Correct. Correct-a-fuckin-mundo. And lets be clear on this point – I'm bringing a *lot* of money. That's not to mention my vast expertise in the movie game, plus my contacts. I am fucking untouchable in this town, Gibby, and you should be feeling pretty fucking lucky that you are getting the benefit of my experience and my extraordinary fucking *brain* if you ask me." Kenny snorted loudly, dislodging a chunk of cocaine that proceeded to drip down the back of his throat throughout the rest of the conversation. "Now, I know what Jacques is bringing to the table. I've admired Jacques for a long fucking time, Gibby, you know that. Truth is, I don't think that Fellini is worthy of rolling the used condoms off of Jacques' dick. But *you*, Gibby? You are a fuckin' *enigma* to me. What exactly *do* you do, except lurk down there with the rest of the trolls and the parasites leeching off a percentange of Jacques' genius, and stuttering like a fuckin' retard when I ask you when I can see a *simple* fucking *script?*"

Gibby gripped the phone so hard that the plastic casing started to groan and creak ominously. He took a deep breath and said, "When will you need it by?"

"Hold on."

The line clicked again, and Gibby found himself listening to that awful musak one more time.

Kristina had emerged from the bathroom naked, one of Kenny's monogrammed towels wrapped around her lithe body. Kenny gestured wildly at her to come over to him.

"Drop the towel," he hissed.

Kristina did as she was told. Kenny cast an appraising eye over her pale, thin body. He twirled his finger, gesturing for her to turn around. "Slowly," he warned. When her back was turned to him he said, "Bend over. Touch your toes."

The girl did as instructed. Kenny squatted down so his face was level with her buttocks. He put his face between her ass cheeks and inhaled deeply, his nostrils nicely cleared out by the coke. He filled his lungs with the bouquet of her freshly soaped asshole. Standing, Kenny snapped his fingers and pointed her toward the bed. She went over there and lay down, waiting for him obediently. He clicked over to Gibby again.

"Gibby."

"I'm here, Kenny."

"Good. In the meeting you mentioned that he is working with James Stein on the script, yes?"

"That's correct."

"I've heard Stein is washed up. My assistant has informed me that he has written seven books since *Point of No Return*. Shitty reviews, dwindling sales, and I haven't even heard of any of them. This *worries* me, Gibby. So I want to see some of what they've come up with. Just to put my mind at rest, yes?"

"Well..." Gibby lied, "I believe that they're pretty much done, but Jacques is being quite secretive about it. It's part of his... process, you know? You know how artists can be."

"Gibby, I will accept the artist defense from Jacques, because he *is* undoubtedly a fucking artist. From you, however, that shit will not fly. I want to see something, and I don't care if you have to sneak it from his fucking laptop while he is taking a nap. I want to see something, do you understand me?"

"Yes. I understand you *completely*, Kenny."

"Good."

Kenny's eyes drifted over to Kristina, who was watching the small, agitated man who had paid for her time with wide, doe-like eyes. Kenny cleared his throat.

"Well then, I have some business I gotta take care of now. Let's touch base at the end of the week, okay? You know where to find me in the meantime."

Before Gibby could say another word the line went dead.

Dropping his pants and stepping out of them, Kenny advanced on Kristina. He clicked a remote control that caused music to swell from his $94,000 *Avant-Garde Trio Classico* speaker system. It was the German Symphony Orchestra and Sting performing *If I Ever Lose My Faith In You* from the *Live In Berlin* album (which Kenny considered to be one of the Police front man's finest recorded efforts). With speakers this good, Kenny often told his guests, it was better than sitting in the front row of the concert itself. As he advanced on the young hooker, Kenny mimed conducting the music, and sang along with what was undoubtedly one of his favourite songs of all time. He climbed on the bed, straddled her chest and said "Lie flat, face up with your mouth open. Do you gag easily?"

Kristina shook her head. She got into position without question. "Hope you don't," Kenny muttered, "The last bitch puked all over my designer Egyptian cotton sheets..." Then he straddled her head and rammed his cock into her gullet without so much as a warning. He proceeded to roughly fuck her face with all of the detached aggression of a man using a plunger to fix a badly blocked toilet.

Back at his place, Gibby slumped on his couch, unbuttoned his shirt and sat there cradling his head in his hands for a while. He knew for a fact that there would be no script. He felt that they had dodged a bullet in the original meeting when Jacques had managed to steer the conversation away from scripts altogether, but now Gibby was faced with the unenviable task of producing material from a script that did not exist in an attempt to pacify a rampaging, coke-crazed dwarf with the power of life and death over his career.

He thought back to how he had left Jacques at that awful, fleabag hotel, fat, sweaty and drooling over himself in the aftermath of his accidental PCP freak-out. He wondered absently what kind of degenerate shit Jacques was currently up to, while he should be working on the script of *Black Neon*. He thought about a lifetime spent catering to no-talent, ill-tempered, self-aggrandizing assholes like Jacques so he could lap up his meagre cut, the fifteen per cent backwash from the sewage his clients foisted upon the great, consuming maw that was the general population. Jesus Christ. Gibby realized he truly was a man out of time. What the fuck did someone who actually *cared* about creating something vital, lasting and timely have to offer this air-conditioned cesspool?

Even Jacques – who had certainly at one point been possessed by the zeal to create something pure – had either grown out of such naïveté, or had the urge beaten out of him by a decade of drugs, relationships gone bad, and relentless media vilification. Sure, he had recently climbed back into the ring but more and more Gibby could see that Jacques was a mere shadow of the man who had once created *Dead Flowers*. Now he was staggering around Hollywood like a weakened bull with colourful *banderillas* sticking out of its back, making some final, instinctual charge toward a target it could barely comprehend anymore.

Hoping to find some kind of a distraction from his thoughts he turned on the news. The top story was about some freak called Rupert something-or-other who'd just paid nine thousand dollars for a pair of Queen Elizabeth II's used panties. He flicked the TV off with a shudder, concluding that the world had gone quite mad. He went to pour himself a stiff drink.

TWENTY-THREE

"My folks were immigrants, my mom was Haitian, my pop Ecuadorian. They settled in Houston, that's were I was born and raised. We lived in a trailer park. Place called the Lone Pines, in North Houston. It was a tiny fucking place, but it was okay. We were happy, I guess. We were happiest when my pop was out working and it was just mom and me."

"Wait – you're half Haitian? You never told me."

"You never asked. But yeah, I don't look it I know. Anyhow, my pop he was a super over at a housing complex called the Dayton Plaza, fixing toilets, leaky ceilings, all that kinda shit. He also did a bit of work on the side for a guy called Angel Caribe. Angel was a *coyote*, had a network of guys smuggling people across the desert from Mexico, Guatemala, all over the damn place."

"Damn, so this Caribe guy was some kinda gangster, huh?"

"He was some kinda *something* all right. He was pretty well known in Houston back then. He put a lot of money back into the community, building immigration advice centres, donating to schools, community centres, political campaigns, all that kinda shit. Some people considered him to be something of a Robin Hood type. That was just romantic bullshit though. Truth was he was just a businessman, pure and simple. I actually met him once, long time after the fact. Handsome older guy with silver hair and one of those George Hamilton tans that scream money. But back when this all went down – I was fifteen at the time – I'd never even laid eyes on him. I didn't even know my pop was involved with him. The only place I'd heard Caribe's name was on the local news." Lupita looked over to Genesis

186

who had her eyes closed. The gauze was red and moist. "How's the hand feeling? Those pills helping any?"

"I guess. I still feel pretty shitty, Lupe. Keep talking, it stops me thinking about how much it hurts. So what did your pop do for him? Was he like a hit man or some shit?"

Lupita laughed. "No, hun. Not even close. My pop was strictly small time. The only person my pop was comfortable hitting was me. He'd get home after a day of unblocking white folks' toilets, and he'd take it out on mom and me. If I looked at him funny, I'd get it. If I didn't eat enough – or I ate too much for that matter – I'd be liable to get my ass kicked. You never knew what was gonna set him off. My pop was basically a coward, an angry, dumbshit fucking *nobody*. Everybody treated him like shit. They walked all over him. Outside of our trailer he was the weakest, most powerless motherfucker you could possibly meet. I guess that's why he acted like such a fuckin' tyrant when he got home. Made him feel like a *man* or some shit. Pass me a cigarette, will ya? Here... you got a lighter? Great. Thanks hun." Lupita exhaled through her nose, and her eyes looked kind of dreamy as she said, "No... my pop working for a local gangster? Well, let's just say that the thought never entered my fucking head. As it goes, he worked as a go-between for Caribe. When people arrived this side of the border, my pop would act as a broker, hooking them up with off-the-books work, or maybe with guys who dealt with phony paperwork, birth certificates, work permits and that kinda shit. Strictly small time, coupla hundred bucks here and there at most. Mom didn't even know, 'cos any extra money that pop made doing that shit went on the horses."

"So your pop liked to gamble, huh?"

"He liked to gamble, he liked to drink, he liked to do every damn thing. Anyway, the first I know anything about my pop and Angel Caribe happens this particular afternoon. My mom is in the kitchen cooking, and she's singing along to the radio. Remember it real clear. She was singing along to *Emotional*

Rescue, you know the Rolling Stones? It was funny, 'cos my mom had a pretty shaky grasp on the English language and she'd just make up the words she didn't understand. And let's just say she didn't have much of a singing voice. Anyway, I was in the next room watching TV, and mom was singing, and a van pulls up outside... There's a knock at the door. I heard my mom answer it, and then screaming, banging around. I figured it was maybe pop, drunk again. But then I hear other people yelling and all kinds of shit, and all of a sudden my mom is shoved into the room at fucking gunpoint. This little bastard, tubby guy with a pencil moustache is with her. Looked a bit like a shorter, fatter version of Charles Bronson. He's got my mom's hair in his fist, and a gun pointed at her forehead."

"Jesus Christ. What did you do?"

"What do you think I did? I was fifteen years old. I stood there about to piss my pants. Behind this Charles Bronson-lookin' motherfucker there are two other goons. Chollo types, you know? The bastard with the gun says, in Spanish, *We're looking for Jesus Garcia, girl. Where is he?*"

"That's your pop?"

"One and the same. Now I'm just standing there, gawping. All I can think is *Someone is pointing a gun at my mom's head.* It's like my fucking brain has disconnected from my mouth altogether. Now my mom she doesn't speak much Spanish, but I guess she figured out what they wanted. She starts trying to tell them that pop ain't around, but she's freaking out, and her English is real bad, and it's all coming out garbled. The guy, he just raises the gun a little, and smashes the butt of it down on my mom's nose. *Crack!* My mom screams and there's a lot of blood. Like my mom's face is *covered* in it. Her knees buckle, but this fucker's got her good by the hair and he keeps her on her feet. I'm about to run over there to help her, but I see the other two guys have got guns too, and they're pointed right at me. So I stand real fucking still."

"Jesus Christ, Lupe. That's horrible. What the fuck was going on?"

"Well, my mom is crying and mumbling in French, you know? She's just hysterical at this point. So I kinda snap out of it, and I start talking real fast. I tell the guy that my pop is at work, he's not around. I ask 'em what they want, tell 'em we didn't do anything. Anything I can think of to get these assholes out of our home, you know? That's when the guys says, *Your father works for Angel Caribe, yes?* Now this makes no sense to me. My pop – that stupid, broke-ass motherfucking slob – working for a gangster? There's no fucking way. I tell him, no, he fixes toilets for a living. The guy laughs at that. He puts the gun back against mom's head. He says to me, *Ah, of course he does. The shit has to flow, yes?*

"So then his two goons come into the room and start turning the place over. I mean really *trashing* the joint. Ripping drawers out, overturning the tables. One of them pulls the TV over, busts the screen open. Soon they're just walking around on our broken stuff and I can hear it all crunching underneath their boots. Then one of them, a tall guy with a wart on his nose, starts yelling, *Where does he keep the money? Where does he keep the money he makes working for Caribe?*

"I want to tell these crazy bastards that if we had any *real* money, then why the fuck would we be living in a trailer park? But the words won't come out. All I can think about is my mom, with all of that blood dripping down her face and a gun pointed at her head. They're surrounding me. Then all of a sudden, everything goes black. One of the guys pulled a plastic bag or somethin' over my face. I can feel the gun pointing in my back. One of them says to me, *If you try to run, you'll be dead before you make it two steps. Now move.*"

"Jesus Christ, Lupe. You musta been freaking the fuck out. So they took you?"

189

"Marched me out to their van, broad fucking daylight. I couldn't see shit, but they musta had like a false bottom in the van because the next thing I know I'm tossed into this little space, felt like a fucking coffin or something. I can't even stretch my legs out; I'm all pretzeled up in there. And it's *hot*. I'm trapped. When I heard the lid come down on me I started struggling, but I couldn't move a muscle. I tried to push it up, but the lid – or whatever it was – was on tight. I hear the doors slam, then the engine starting. I could feel it, smell it. The whole place filled up with this rotten gasoline smell. Then I feel us driving away. That's when I really started freaking out. I realized just what kind of a fucked-up position I was in. These crazy bastards had me in a van, my mom – well, I didn't know what had happened to her, but I figured she was back at the trailer all fucked up. The scariest thing is that *nobody* knows where I am. *I* didn't even know where I was. I just lay there, and all I could think was *I'm gonna die. These crazy bastards are gonna kill me and there isn't jack shit I can do about it.*" Lupita had a dreamy, faraway look in her eyes when she said this.

"I mean, I realized that I was totally helpless and at the mercy of these people... Maybe they were gonna rape me first. Hurt me. It wasn't a matter of whether I was gonna die, it was more a matter of *when* I was gonna die, and how fucking painful it was gonna be."

"Jesus Christ, Lupe. I mean, I been some dark places in my life honey. I ain't even told you all of it... But I can't even imagine what was going through your head right then. So what was it? I guess your father owed these guys money or something?"

Lupita laughed coldly. "Not even. That's the fucked up thing. Of course, I didn't know this at the time, but I managed to piece it together later. Like I said, years after the fact I managed to meet Angel Caribe. I actually met him at pop's funeral. You couldn't miss him. He was tall. Really fucking tall, shoulder length grey hair, cheekbones and lips. He looked like an actor on one of those awful fucking *telenovelas* I useta watch. I had most of the story down by then, but he filled in the holes. Basically, the guys who took me were *bajadores*. That means they were freelancers – bandits basically – who specialized in ripping off the bigger guys. Now in and of itself that should tell you a little about how insane these motherfuckers were. Any place these assholes hit was *guaranteed* to be full of gangsters... real gun-toting fuckin' psychopaths who weren't afraid to kill to protect their patch. We're talkin' houses full of drugs, weapons, or in Caribe's case the *pollos* they were holding hostage..."

"Whaddya mean, *pollos*?"

"That's what they'd call the people they'd smuggle over the border. Most of the time it would go down that they'd pay say a thousand or so US dollars to get over the border, and then the *coyotes* – the guys who would smuggle them across – would bring them to a safe house. But instead of just letting them go free, most of the time they'd hold them to ransom. So unless they could come up with even more money – or their family could – the first thing that would happen to 'em north of the border was that they'd get offed by a bunch of pissed-off people smugglers, or sold into prostitution or whatever."

"Jesus, that's cold blooded."

"Uh-huh. Happens all the time though. This wasn't just Angel Caribe's guys who did this shit. It was pretty much standard practice with most of the smuggling operations. The pollos might pass through two or three sets of hands before being turned loose, getting re-ransomed and abused every step along the way. Crazy bastards like the guys who took me would burst in on a safe house, kill the guards, and kidnap the pollos. Then they'd re-ransom them to their families. It was just like they were property or something."

"So how does this involve your pop?"

"Well it turns out that these guys had been pretty busy doing hit-and-runs on Caribe's patch. They'd just hit one of Angel's houses. They'd kidnapped a few people, killed the rest. One of the guys they took was an associate of Caribe's called Lucky Marcelino. The Charles Bronson look-a-like was the boss man, a fuckin' psycho who went by the name El Cortador. It means *the cutter*, which should tell you somethin' about the kinda shit he was into. Well, El Cortador tortured Lucky Marcelino until he gave up some names... other associates of Angel's, you know?"

"Man," Genesis said, "I guess he wasn't so lucky after all."

"Damn straight. He wasn't the only one with shitty luck though. Apparently Lucky managed to hold out for a few hours. Thing is, he knew that if he talked he was a dead man anyway. Caribe would have had his head. When he couldn't take it anymore he cracked and gave up a name in an effort to save his own ass... just some low-level operator that he had dealt with from time to time. He started talking about my father, Jesus Garcia, painting him as some major player in Angel Caribe's organization. I guess he figured that if he gave up someone who was of little consequence to the organization, then on the off-chance that he'd somehow got out of El Cortador's clutches the punishment for talking might not be so severe. So he convinced these assholes that my pop was some big time player and that's why they decided to hold me to ransom."

"What happened to this Lucky guy? Did they let him go?"

Lupita shook her head. "I asked the same thing when I met Caribe. I figured if this motherfucker got away, then maybe I'd wanna pay him a fucking visit, you know, and say *hello*. But it was too late; the *bajadores* beat me to it. Apparently they found Lucky's head two days later. It was stuffed into a backpack that had been dropped off outside of a local police precinct. The body never showed up.

"Of course I didn't know any of this at the time. When the van pulls up, and I'm dragged out of that fucking crawlspace in the back, I don't have a clue what the fuck is going on or who these people are. All I know is I can barely stand because my legs are cramping up so bad, and I'm about to piss my pants. I mean, I was still dressed in my fucking pajamas, and here I am in some fucking garage with a bunch of crazies. We must have driven for twenty minutes, half an hour maybe. I had no idea where the fuck we were. Charlie Bronson – you know, El Cortador – he pulls the bag off of my face and waves the gun at me. *Get up the stairs,* he tells me, *it's picture time.* Here, Genesis. Let me get a drink of that will ya? How you feeling?"

"Little better. The pills are takin' the edge off, a little. Here." Genesis reached down for the Wild Turkey with her good hand, "Let me hold the wheel steady... Go for it."

As they cruised down the I-15, heading toward Las Vegas, Lupita tipped the bottle back and took a slug. She coughed, and said, "Thanks." She took the wheel again.

"So anyway. They take me into the living room. It looks like one of those showroom houses. You know, beige on beige. Plastic flowers, marble counter tops, the kind of place that looks like nobody really lives there. They tell me to get upstairs. When I get upstairs it's a different scene altogether. There's, like, a landing with three doors shut tight with padlocks, kinda crudely fitted on there. There's one open door. They tell me to get in. Inside the room..." Lupita shuddered at the recollection, "It was horrible. Really horrible. It smelled like a fucking abattoir. Newspapers covering the floors. The only light is a bare light bulb hanging from the ceiling. The walls are unfinished, and it looks like they got blood splattered all over them. There's a radiator in there, the only window is boarded up, and the only other furniture is a plastic bucket and a bloodstained wooden chair. When I saw the room I felt like I was gonna puke. No shit Genesis, the place reminded me of those newspaper reports

193

about those crazy fucks over in Belgium or Utah... you know, the ones who kidnap girls and keep 'em in dungeons for years? That's *exactly* what it looked like, hun. A fucking *dungeon*. So they shove me in there, and by now I'm about ready to faint, you know? And then El Cortador, says, *Strip.*"

There was a long pause. Lupita kept her eyes firmly fixed on the dusty desert horizon.

"I'm looking at the guy like he's got two heads. I'm hoping I maybe misheard, because I know that if these bastards get me undressed, that's it. The best that can happen – the very *best thing* that can happen – is that I'm getting gang raped. And I don't even wanna think about what the worst thing is. So I'm standing there, playing dumb, and he says it again to me. *Strip.* I hesitate and he points the gun at me and says with this real malicious look on his face, *Take it all off bitch, or you're dead fucking meat.*"

"Oh, Lupe. What the fuck did you *do*?"
Lupita looked at Genesis, and smiled sadly. "Girl, I wasn't looking forward to getting raped, but as far as it goes that possibility sounded a hell of a lot more appealing than getting myself shot in the face. What do you *think* I did? I fucking stripped and I kept my goddamned mouth shut. Hey wait. Let's pull over here. I gotta get high."

TWENTY-FOUR

J acques Seltzer was at Denny's on Sunset with a streetwalker
called Peggy. Peggy was black – not just *black* as in "African
American" but truly, literally *black*. Her skin was deep ebony,
the colour of space, beautifully, undeniably black. Her tattoos –
and she had plenty – were almost totally camouflaged against
the inky pigmentation of her corpulent flesh.

Her skin colour was the first thing that drew Jacques to Peggy
when he encountered her last night, loitering outside of a
taco stand on La Brea. The image of her smoking a cigarette,
standing under a flickering cathode light captivated Jacques. She
wore a platinum blonde wig and weighed at least two hundred
and fifty pounds. She was big all over: big tits, big lips, big ass,
big thighs, all squeezed into a lime green PVC corset and flesh-
hugging white hot pants. The whole ensemble was finished off
with thigh-high, spike-heeled white patent-leather go-go boots.
Jacques circled around the block to check her out, and then
pulled the rental BMW over. She negotiated a generous price
for pictures and sex. Peggy smiled, flashing her hot pink gums,
and got him to throw in breakfast as well.

"Not some cheap-ass joint like this. Somewhere *decent*."

After an evening of debauchery in his room at the DeVille,
Jacques and Peggy drove to the Denny's on Sunset and Gower,
close to the 101 on-ramp. When they walked in there even the
hardened nighthawk denizens of Denny's on Sunset did double
takes and gawped as Jacques – wearing his red sharkskin
Alexander McQueen suit and cowboy boots – walked in with

Peggy, still dressed up in her dime store hooker outfit. They strode inside arm in arm, Jacques beaming like a proud groom.

Ravenous after a night of crack, anal sex and posing for Jacques' hungry lens, Peggy was wolfing down a Grand Slam Breakfast. Jacques was on his third cup of black coffee. He watched, smiling indulgently, as she poured blackberry syrup on her remaining bacon and hash browns.

"So, uh, Jack," Peggy said, through a mouthful of syrupy eggs, "What exactly you gonna *do* with those pictures? I mean, you got me in some pretty... uh, *compromising* positions."

Jacques reached into his pocket and produced a blurry, photocopied sheet with the header MODEL RELEASE. He flattened it out on the table.

"Peggy my love," he said, "If you sign here your pictures will hang in the finest galleries in Paris."

"Galleries?" Peggy snorted, "What you mean, Jack?"

"*Art galleries*. The most highly respected galleries in the cultural heart of Europe."

Peggy's mind drifted back to some of the positions she had found herself in last night, while Jacques snapped away with his camera.

"Honey," she said, "I ain't really one for art. But I kinda find it hard to believe that any *gallery* – in Paris or anywhere else – is gonna hang that picture you took of me taking a leak while I was hittin' that crack pipe."

"You would be surprised, Peggy. Prurience *is* art, my sweet. Here's a pen."

Peggy signed the release form without glancing at it. Then she frowned at Jacques. "You *sure* this shit ain't gonna end up on that damn Internet? I got two young boys in a foster home, an' I don't want them finding a picture of their birth momma on some kinda porn site..."

196

Jacques leaned across the table. "However the pictures will be used, I assure you that it will be... tasteful. Credible. I am an *artiste*, not a pornographer."

Peggy's plate was clean, and she mopped up the last of the syrup with a slice of buttered white toast. Then she gulped down the remains of her root beer float. Wiping her mouth with a napkin, she said, "An artist? Maybe I shoulda charged ya more."

Jacques laughed, and said, "Pah, Peggy – you must know that all artists are starving, no?"

Peggy raised a painted-on eyebrow and gave Jacques a playful prod on the belly. "No offense, Jack, but ya don't look like you're starvin' to me. Can I ask *YOU* a question?"

"Oui, of course."

"Well, I ain't done much travelling Jack, but I heard that Paris is a beautiful city. Is that right?"

"Oh, oui, it is. It is one of the cultural centres of Europe... it has some of the most breathtaking galleries and museums in the world. Our cuisine and our artistic achievements are the envy of Europe."

"Uh-huh. So tell me somethin'. What the fuck iz you doin' hanging around roach-infested motels smoking ghetto crack and taking pictures of *me* for? I mean, I know I got me some fine-ass titties, Jack, but I'm figuring bitches got *those* over in Paris too. I mean – what in the hell are you thinkin'?"

Jacques laughed, and reached across the table. He gave her meaty arm a squeeze.

"Peggy, my love," he said, his coke-numbed tongue fumbling with the words, "I came here to find America. The *real* America. I came to find her soul, yes? And the only way to get to her soul is to crawl up... through her *guts*. To confront America on her own terms."

"Come again?"

The waitress brought the check over. Jacques rummaged around in his pockets and dumped a pair of crumpled twenties on the table.

"Peggy, it is as simple – and as complex – as this. I am here to find the American Dream. And when I find it, I am going to make love to it... with my *camera*, yes?"

Peggy looked at Jacques, incredulously.

"The American dream?"

"Oui."

"And you're gonna make love to it?"

"Oui."

"With your camera?"

"Oui. *Exactement!*"

Peggy looked around the diner thoughtfully before fixing Jacques in a quizzical stare. "An' you think you're gonna find the American Dream in a room at the De Ville motel?"

Jacques nodded. "Why not? It is as good a place as any, no? But you are right about something, my dear. You have *magnificent* tits. They remind me of my mother's. You make me want to be an *enfant* once more."

"You smooth-talkin' bastard. Look Jack, this has been fun and all, but I gotta get some shuteye. You wanna call me a cab?"

"Of course. But first, tell me something, Peggy. Why is it that I can buy the finest Columbian cocaine on the market, straight from the Amazon rain forest, one-hundred percent pure and uncut... the kind of cocaine reserved for Presidents, movie stars and European Royalty... yet it does not *thrill* me the way that a twenty dollar rock of crack smoked in a sleazy motel room does?"

Peggy laughed. "You wanna know what I think, Jack?"

"Of course! You are *inspiring* me, Peggy. Speak your mind..."

"Well, seems to me that you're one of those *hard to please*-type motherfuckas. You know what I'm saying?"

Jacques nodded sagely. He waited a few beats, as if fully digesting the enormity of her words.

"You should become a therapist, Peggy," he said at last. "You could make a lot of money. Well... I think we are done here. Thank you, Peggy. You are not only a beautiful woman, you are a philosopher and an original mind. You will make some man very happy one day."

Peggy sucked in her gut a little, and reached into her purse for her pack of Kools. "Shit. If you hurry up and call me that cab so I can rest up for a few hours, I can prolly make a whole buncha men happy later tonight."

TWENTY-FIVE

" We're almost outta crank," Lupita said, holding the bullet up to her nostril and inhaling sharply. "You want some?"

Genesis shook her head. "I'm gonna take more painkillers. If I can, I wanna sleep later. Hand still hurts like a motherfucker."

Lupita put the bullet away, and ruffled Genesis's hair. "Cheer up hun," she said. Genesis pouted. "Come on, lemmie see a smile."

Genesis smiled unenthusiastically. They pulled away from the rest stop and got back on the freeway. Lupita turned the music on again. They were listening to one-hit wonder '60s group Mouse and the Traps doing a Dylan-esque number called *Sometimes You Just Can't Win*.

"So what happened after they made you undress?" Genesis asked. "They raped you?"

Lupita shook her head. "No, actually."

Genesis shook herself out of her painkiller and booze addled haze. "Really? So why did they make you strip?"

"To take pictures. That was part of their M.O. They'd take a buncha humiliating pictures and send 'em back to the family. It was a way of pressuring 'em to pay up, I guess. The head guy keeps a gun pointed at me, and the other guy – the bastard with the wart on his nose – he pulls a balaclava over his head. He comes over and pulls his dick out. He stands next to me, and they tell me to hold it. The third guy is snapping pictures on a Polaroid instamatic. They took four or five pictures like that, with me posing with this motherfucker in all kinds of positions. You know... *sexual* positions. The guy snapping the pictures says to me, *Nice big smile for daddy!* I couldn't stop crying the whole time, Genesis hun, but these motherfuckers thought this shit was real funny. I remember just closing my eyes and praying, you know, praying to Our Lady that they wouldn't rape me. Just praying for it all to end. When they were done the bastard with the gun, El Cortador, he says *You guys wanna fuck her?* Real casual, like. Just like they was talkin' about running out to pick up some drive-thru. *You guys wanna fuck her?*" Lupita shook her head, "So that's when I tell 'em I'm on the rag."

"Were you really?"

"Uh huh. Only just though. It was, like, my last day, but I still had a tampon in. I showed 'em the string, and after that – thank God – they wouldn't go near me. Typical machismo Latin guys. You'da thought I had fuckin' AIDS or some shit. Instead of raping me they kicked me about a bit and handcuffed me to the radiator. Left me to stew overnight."

"Goddamn."

"Uh-huh. Only I've ever been happy to be on the rag in my whole damn life I'll tell ya. But now I'm chained up like a fucking dog. If I gotta piss, I gotta do it in the bucket. And don't let the fact I was chained to a fuckin' radiator fool ya – it was fucking *freezing* in there, like a damn meat locker. I didn't sleep a wink. The worst thing was I could hear all kinds of screams and noises and shit coming from next room. It was El Cortador and his goons torturing some poor bastard with a fucking electric drill. I can hear it as it's going on, this horrible, high-pitched whining sound... And this guy *screaming*... I never heard anything like it, Genesis. I guess maybe they got this guy's family on the phone or something, because the whole time this is going on I can hear El Cortador yelling that they'd better pay up or they'd fuck this poor bastard up beyond all recognition. It went on for hours. Then... I dunno. Maybe the guy died or passed out, but it all quieted down. Can you imagine? There I am, chained to a fucking radiator listening to all of this shit go down, and all I can think is, *It's my turn next!*

"So the next morning, they unlock the handcuffs and drag me downstairs. Put me on speakerphone with my pop. As much as I hated my father, I was so fucking excited to speak to the old bastard that day. I needed to know if mom was okay. I figured that for sure my pop would be able to help me out, you know? Pay 'em off if he had to, or get the cops involved. *Something*, you know? But right away I can tell that something's wrong. For a start, from the moment he picked up he's being real *weird* with me. I mean, not just the kind of weird you'd expect when your kid calls up telling you that if you don't pay a ransom someone's gonna kill her... I mean... it was like he was mad at *me* or something. He doesn't get excited, or ask me how I am, ask me *where* I am, or anything. He's just... *cold*. It was like I was calling home after breaking my fucking curfew or something. They gave me a piece of paper to read, saying that unless he paid twenty thousand they were gonna kill me. And he's like, *Uh-huh. Okay. Yeah.* Like I was telling him the football scores or somethin' – no emotion. So after a minute of this shit, I can't take it no more. I stop reading and I ask him straight out. I mean, I'm fucking crying and shit. I'm like, *Pop! Why are you being like this with me? Why do you sound so WEIRD?*

Lupita choked a little. It felt like there was a ball of fire lodged in her throat. She swallowed hard.

"Of course my pop denies he's being weird, tells me I'm hysterical. But I just *knew it*. I knew that the motherfucker wasn't gonna pay. "

"He wasn't? That's fucking crazy! What the fuck was his problem?" Genesis shook her head. "You're his *kid*..."

"Well, I guess he knew there was no way he could come up with the money for a start. And he sure as hell wasn't gonna risk jail by getting the pigs involved. Basically, I realized at that point that my pop was acting weird because he'd already written me off as dead. So the guys holding me realized that this call wasn't going according to plan, and El Cortador grabs the phone and starts in with his whole routine about how if they don't pay within twenty four hours, he's gonna start mailing me back to them, piece by piece. I don't remember much after that. I was in shock, I guess... They just dragged me back to the room and locked me up again."

They whizzed past mile after mile of featureless freeway. Genesis stretched, totally numbed by the booze and the Dilaudid.

"So what happened?" she asked sleepily, "Your father *really* didn't pay?"

"Nope. He didn't have the money because he'd pissed it all away on the horses. Apparently when he went to Angel to tell him what was up, Angel told him that even if they paid the twenty grand El Cortador's boys would just keep the money and kill me anyway. That was their style – no survivors, no witnesses. Instead of offering money he tells my father that he's on the trail of the safe house, and that they'd find me. You gotta remember that Caribe was still on the warpath over what happened with Lucky, so he wanted El Cortador and his guys dead anyway. It wasn't that he gave a shit about *me*, you know? I was just a side issue. If they caught up with those guys in time to save me, great. If not, well who gives a fuck anyway?"

Genesis looked at Lupita with heavy-lidded eyes. She saw a solitary tear roll down Lupita's cheek. Genesis reached out with her good hand, and touched Lupita's face lightly. "It's okay, Lupe. I love you baby," she whispered.

Lupita looked over, and smiled sadly. "I know you do, hun. It's just that I put all of this shit behind me a long time ago... but it's still tough to talk about it. I don't make a habit of telling people this stuff. I haven't told this story in years, and it hasn't got any easier in the meantime."

They drove in silence for a while. Lupita gathered her thoughts.

"They kept me in the room for... well, I dunno how long. There was no natural light in there. Just that fucking light bulb, which was on twenty-four-seven. A couple of times one of the guys would come in and give me a piece of bread, or some instant ramen. I didn't eat. I couldn't. Sometimes they'd start up torturing the poor fucker in the next room again. I never heard screams like that before or since. Like they came right up from that fucker's *soul*, you know? Eventually, I guess they killed the guy. I heard... I heard him screaming. And I heard what I figured out later was one of those big fuckin' electric power saws. Sounded like a motorbike or somethin'. And then... nothing. Just some talking... laughing... the sound of shit being dragged away. I lay there, knowing I was going to die.

"You know, my mom raised me to believe that there was some kind of logic to all of this... that everything happens for a reason and all of that bullshit. But lying there, chained to a radiator, waiting for my turn with the drills and the saws, disowned by my fucking *father* even... it suddenly became real clear to me that there was no logic to any of it. None at all. Shitty things happen to good people, good things happen to shitty people. What a sick fuckin' joke, right? Everything that you think is real, and true, and important... you could wake up tomorrow and all of that shit will be just swept away. Irrelevant. Suddenly, instead of worrying about your homework, or whether your pop is gonna beat you today or whatever, you're lying there wondering how long it will take you to die once they start cutting you with those power tools." Lupita laughed a sour laugh. "It kinda puts shit into perspective, you know?

"When the time came that they opened the door up... I dunno. It's weird. When I try to think about it, I just see it in flashes. It's like one of those horrible dreams... the ones that make you almost jump outta bed, but when you try to remember the details it all starts to fragment, and you're trying to grab hold of it but the harder you think the further away it gets. I remember screaming. I didn't stop screaming the whole time. Two of them came in and un-cuffed me. I struggled, so one of them punched me in the mouth. Everything went hazy. I could see that fucker El Cortador standing in the doorway. I saw the power saw in his hands. I was thrashing around, screaming myself raw. They were holding me down. I saw him plugging into the wall. One of them was holding a cordless phone right up to my face. Maybe they had my folks on the line so they could hear what they were about to do to me. I dunno. All I can remember is screaming, screaming, screaming. Then one of them knelt on my chest and I couldn't breathe properly, but I was still screaming inside my head, y'know? They held the arm out. I remember El Cortador leaning over and holding my head still. He kissed me on the forehead, real gentle. I still remember the feel of his lips on my forehead. And then him talking, but I couldn't hear what he said, I just remember his lips moving. I remember the sound of the saw when he turned it on. I could feel it in my *bones*. I remember looking at the saw, at fucking blade as it crept closer and closer to me, and then I closed my eyes and everything was black… I could feel the pressure on my chest, and I couldn't move and eventually I stopped struggling. I just went… *limp*. I felt the guys moving around, shifting their weight, moving out of the way of the blade. And then… that's it."

Lupita's face was streaked with silent tears. She shook her head. When she started up again, it was in a small, hesitant voice.

"I woke up in the back of a car. That's the next thing I remember. I didn't know whose car it was. I was in the backseat. I felt… numb. Like I wasn't in my body at all. Before I passed out again, I remember wondering where all of the blood came from. Everything was covered in blood."

"What happened? Caribe's men found you?"

Lupita nodded.

"They tracked down the house through some ex-associate of theirs. Caribe's men stormed the place, kicked the door open right as they were cutting me. I don't remember any of this, I only heard later. Caribe's men showed up at the house, killed every motherfucker inside, grabbed me, and torched the place. Well, when I say that they killed everyone, that's not exactly true. Caribe wanted El Cortador alive. They shot him alright, but didn't kill him. While the house burned El Cortador was taken off in the trunk of one car, and I was rushed off in another. The next thing I remember is being laid on out a kitchen table. Some old guy in a while coat and a mask was shooting me full of morphine."

"Did they try an' re-attach the arm?"

Lupita shook her head. "In all of the fuss, nobody thought to pick it up. I guess it burnt up when they torched the house. You know, the thing is I found out later that El Cortador did me something of a favour because he at least cut the arm *cleanly*. If you cut the artery cleanly it kinda... curls over itself and you don't bleed out as quickly. I lost a lot of blood, but they were able to patch me up without getting the authorities involved. They took me to the house of some retired surgeon who was on Caribe's payroll. Lived up in some fancy-ass place in River Oakes."

"Jesus. I can't believe you survived."

"It's not so strange. Did you ever hear about Mary Bell Vincent?"

"No. Who's that?"

"It was a big story back in the seventies. She was a fifteen years old hitchhiker? Got picked up by a crazy bastard called Larry Singleton? He took her up into some damn canyon somewhere, raped her, and cut off both of her arms with an axe. Then he dumped her in an underground drain, just left her there to die. Well, she managed to walk out of there, she got help, and survived. Managed to get Larry convicted too."

"That's incredible. She just walked outta there with both of her arms chopped off like that?"

"Uh-huh. The shitty thing is he only did eight years for it. When he got out – he was, like, seventy or somethin' – he went an' stabbed a prostitute to death. Died of cancer on death row in Florida. But the thing is, that just goes to show you. The human body is pretty fucking resilient. Compared to poor old Mary Bell Vincent, I had it pretty easy I guess."

"Eight years for raping and mutilating some poor kid?" Genesis shook her head, "If he'd have been selling dope you'd bet he'd a got more time than that. This country is *fucked*."

"True that."

"So what happened afterwards?"

"Well, it's all kinda hazy. I was on so many fucking painkillers after they patched up my arm, everything seems a bit like a dream. But the guy who took me over to the doctor's place was one of Angel Caribe's men. Guy called Adolfo Alarcon. He was a big guy, chubby you know? So they all called him *El Puerco*."

"Whassat mean?"

"Like... pork. Like they were calling him "The Pig". It doesn't seem as rude in Spanish, I guess. He was sweet. He stayed with me the whole time I was recovering. Nobody could know where I was, Caribe's orders. Not until I was well enough to go home. They had to make sure that the wound didn't get infected, the old guy – the surgeon – he was on hand to make sure everything was okay. But it was lonely up there, so El Puerco stayed with me. Read to me. We got to talking. About silly stuff at first. Music. Movies. Anything to distract me. But as the days went on he started to *really* talk to me. Turns out he was a hit man. But he was a real sweet guy. Very religious, in a weird way. I could tell he didn't feel good about how he made his living. Talked about going to hell a lot. He kept me company while I recovered. After a few days I was well enough to call home. Pop didn't even get on the phone with me. My mom was a mess. Hysterical.

She said something about how those guys had *"ruined me"*. Not exactly what I wanted to hear right then, you know?

"Pretty soon it was time for me to leave, and Adolfo was supposed to bring me home. As soon as we were in the car I told him, *I don't wanna go home. I can't go home no more.* So Adolfo, he says, *Here. Lemmie show you something that might make you feel better.* So we drive out to this industrial-looking place, out by the airport. There are all these warehouses. We pull up into one, and Adolfo tells me that this is where they have El Cortador locked up. He asked me if I wanted to see him. *Don't worry,* he tells me, *he can't hurt you no more.* They had him stashed away in this fuckin' warehouse, apparently they'd been keeping him alive for shits and giggles. And there he is, locked away in a storeroom. He was barely recognizable any more. He'd been burnt, drilled, shocked, the whole bit. By the time I got there he looked like a fuckin' Halloween costume. I'm just standing there, staring at him. I don't think he even recognized me anymore. One of his eyes is missing, just a hole covered up with a bloody bandage. The other one is just kinda rolling around in his skull, like his brain don't work so good anymore. Adolfo asks me if I wanna do the honors. Hands me a gun, and asks me if I know how to use it. He walks me through it, takes off the safety and all of that shit, and helps me raise my hand so I'm pointing the gun right at this fucker's head. He doesn't even move. You'da thought he was already dead, if he wasn't breathing so heavy. Sounded like a thirsty dog. I dunno if he even knew what the fuck was going on any more."

"You shot him?"

"Uh-huh. You'd think it should have felt like closure or somehin', but it didn't. Not really. This guy was so out of it; it didn't even feel like I was killing the same bastard who'd done all of that shit to me. I felt like I was putting down an old, sick animal. After I blew that fucker's brains out, it occurred to me that I had maybe done him a favour. But…"

"But what?"

"Nuthin'. It was just a weird feeling, you know?"

Lupita stopped herself from saying more. If she followed this line of self-examination any further she might inadvertently reveal of herself to Genesis that she'd prefer to keep hidden. What she couldn't say, maybe couldn't even articulate if she tried, was the curious sensation that killing El Cortador had given her. As the contents of his head sprayed across the concrete floor she experienced an adrenaline rush that she recognized later – when she first injected crank – as being comparable to a narcotic rush, although more nuanced, with more *depth* than any drug high. Even though this man had been already half-gone, the sensation of having the power of life and death over another human being, the idea that a subtle application of pressure of her finger on the trigger had wiped a human being – all of his memories, experiences, wants and desires – clean off the face of the earth was a profoundly *moving* experience.

Although she tried not to think about it in the months that followed, some unspoken part of her knew that one day she would be invariably drawn to exercising that power again. With each successive life that Lupita snuffed out, the notion of abstaining from exercising this incredible power became increasingly hard to swallow.

Instead of saying any of this, Lupita gathered herself quickly and carried on, "The next thing I did, the very next thing, was I told Adolfo that I loved him and I wanted to be with him."

Genesis raised an eyebrow. "Really? You really liked this guy?"

Lupita shrugged. "I dunno. I needed an out, and I got the feeling that he did too. I'd noticed the way that Adolfo had been looking at me, fawning over me, the weeks he'd been waiting by my bedside. I mean, the guy was a professional fucking killer. I don't think he made a habit of volunteering to play nursemaid, you know? I mean… I *liked* him, don't get me wrong. He was kind to me. At that point in my life… I mean, that *was* love, or at least it was close enough, you know?"

"What did *he* say?"

"He told me that I was crazy. He gave me the whole speech about how I was fifteen and he was fifty-three. He told me I was delirious. But I could tell that his heart wasn't in it."

"So what did you do?"

An uncomfortable look came over Lupita's face.

"Look Genesis, I knew that one way or another I wasn't going home. I did the only thing I could think of. I made him feel guilty. I looked down at that bandaged stump and I asked him he didn't like me because I wasn't a *complete woman* no more."

"And that worked?"

"Uh-huh. He called his boss from a payphone, told him that El Cortador was dead and that he was going to take some time away. Then he and I split town. That was the end of that. Adolfo knew that he could never go back after pulling that shit with his boss. You know, I really *did* fall for Adolfo as time went on. We could relate to each other. When he was in his early twenties he got shot, right in the groin. They had to amputate a ball, and part of the penis. So he knew what it felt like to be incomplete. He couldn't have sex without using a prosthetic dick. In a weird way I think the fact that he didn't have a penis of his own *helped*. I'll tell you one thing, Genesis hun. He ate pussy better than any other man on God's earth, I swear. And he was the man who taught me how to shoot. It was Adolfo who turned me on to good music. I dunno… I dunno how I ever would have gotten over what happened if it hadn't been for Adolfo."

"So you *did* love him?"

Lupita shrugged. "I was fifteen. At the time I felt that I did. Looking back, I think I needed him more than anything else."

Genesis nodded, "What happened to him?"

"Brain haemorrhage. Two years after we made it to LA I found him on the kitchen floor, laying in a pool of Jack Daniels. I guess he was about to fix himself a cocktail when it happened. Jack and RC Cola was his drink. Mama Z, the lady we're going to see right now, she spoke to him. You know, *after* he passed. She told me that Adolfo didn't feel anything. That he didn't even know something was up until he'd already crossed over. It happened in seconds.

"Later, when I heard my pop died and I made it back to Houston for the funeral, Angel pulled me aside in the church and told me that Adolfo had been one of his finest men. Said he killed at least seventy men for him, and never fucked up. He said that when Adolfo left with me, he'd considered sending some of his guys out to bump me off because I'd poached one of his top guys. Can you believe that shit? The only reason he didn't was because he couldn't be sure that Adolfo wouldn't end up coming after *him* one day for revenge. Even big, bad Angel Caribe was scared of the idea of being on Adolfo Alarcon's shit list. Still, I kinda felt that maybe he was warning me that I wasn't welcome in Houston no more now that I wouldn't have Adolfo to protect me. After the funeral I left Texas, and I've never been back."

"That's a sad story," Genesis said. "This world is a fucked up place, Lupe..."

"It's not so bad, Genesis. You just realize eventually that in the great scheme of things nothing you do really means *shit*. The world just carries on, regardless of how you feel or what you do. When you accept that, it's a kind of freedom, you know?"

They lapsed into silence as they drove on. After a few more miles, Lupita saw that Genesis had finally passed out, her head resting against the passenger window, mouth hanging slightly open. She let her lover sleep. She thought about Adolfo, and about Mama Z who she hadn't seen in years. All of a sudden, it seemed, her past – which had long since been consigned to some dusty locked room – was flooding back; the incidents, the tastes, and the smells from back then as strong and potent as if they had just occurred. She reached over and turned the tape deck up a hair, not so loud as to risk waking Genesis. It was one of her favourite tracks, a slow, sultry swamp-blues number by Slim Harpo called *Lover's Confession*. As the Eldorado screamed toward Los Angeles, Lupita envisioned herself and Genesis as avenging angels, battered and bloodied for sure, minus a finger and having somehow left a trail of four corpses in their wake... She was not crying anymore; her face was stoic with silent determination. She was feeling high and holy, her mind engorged with blood and methamphetamine. Lupita and Genesis roared on, a pair of outlaw lovers out for whatever kind of redemption they could get.

TWENTY-SIX

James Stein's fingers *rat-at-atted* furiously against the keys of his MacBook. Depending on who you talked to, he was either a famous novelist or an infamous hack. Stein had been heralded on the covers of Esquire, Vanity Fair, and The New York Times Book Review as the Next Big Thing, Spokesperson of his Generation, the *enfant terrible* of American letters, all before he was 27. Two decades later he was stooped over a desk in his suite at the historic Biltmore Hotel – which had once hosted glittering parties for the likes of Mickey Rooney and Shirley Temple – tall and cocaine-gaunt, wearing acid-wash Levis and an ill-fitting white silk shirt. His face was slack and eyes glazed over thoughtfully, the pose of a man who was Creating. Under the desk, an aging crack-whore called Missy slurped loudly and enthusiastically on the head of his penis. Also in Stein's suite was Jacques Seltzer – who had been without sleep now for almost forty-eight hours – and a gaggle of filthy, naked homeless girls fixing dope on the enormous, king size bed. The combined smell from their bodies added an eye-watering element to the atmosphere in the room, which was already infused with the stench of illegal chemicals and drug-induced paranoia.

The TV blared out a constantly shifting soundtrack of daytime soap operas, music videos, braying game show audiences, offers of rush delivery from home shopping channels, sober sounding newsreaders, stern TV judges and ranting televangelists. One of the girls, a pasty, overweight white girl from the Pacific Northwest who went by the name "Snoopy" was helping a young Chinese girl called Suzy to find a vein in the back of her knees.

"Man," Snoopy said, "You got all those fuckin little veins that roll whenever you try to get the needle in. Shit. Sorry Suzy, I don't wanna make a mess of you..."

"Nah, nah is cool honey, is cool. I'm so sick of muscling this shit. My ass feels like a fuckin pincushion, ya know? Take your time..."

"Wait!" Stein called out, "What did you just say there?"

Missy pulled his dick out of her mouth and looked up. "Wassat? I didn't say nuthin!"

Stein peered down below the desk. "Not you. You're doing great. Carry on..." then, looking over to Suzy who was lying there on her belly, still absently flicking through the channels while Snoopy probed the backs of her legs with the syringe, "I'm talking to *you*. Somethin about muscles?"

"Muscle-*ing*! Like when you shoot the dope into your ass cheek. When you can't find a vein? It comes on slower, but it's better than smoking it. Just look at my ass, though!"

Stein peered cautiously at her pale, flat ass. It was covered in purple and yellow patches, craters of abscessed flesh, and angry, weeping sores.

"Ah yes, I see," he said. "Carry on..."

As the girls continued to chatter absently while they got high, Stein typed furiously, recording it all as it went down in a garbled, free-form rush.

Jacques, meanwhile, was standing in his sagging underwear with his ear pressed against the wall. Another street kid, a tall, gawky teenage punk with milky white skin who called herself Vio-Lette crept toward him, wired and antsy from the effect of a speedball. She smiled at Jacques, the many piercings on her face moving upwards in perfect synchronization.

"Hey, man. Whaddya doin'?"

"*Shhh!*"

When Jacques turned to her with his finger to his lips, the look in his eyes was so crazed that Vio-Lette froze in her tracks with a startled look on her face.

"They are *taping* us," he hissed, "I can hear it!"

He still had a crack pipe clenched in his trembling fist, and his jowly face was unshaven and flushed red. "I can hear everything! Whatever we say in here they... they *record* it somehow... then play it back... Listen, I can hear them talking about... her ass!" Jacques pointed accusingly at Suzy, "*'When you shoot the dope into your ass cheek...'* I can hear her saying it again, as plain as day!"

"Um, okay dude..." Vio-Lette muttered, backing away from the cracked-out Frenchman slowly, "Whatever you say..."

"Got it!" yelled Snoopy, "Okay, don't move! This vein is fuckin tiny, I don't wanna blow it out. I gotta feed the shit in nice and slow..."

"Take your time, girl. I haven't had a decent hit in a week and a half..."

Stein stopped typing suddenly and cocked his head to one side.

"Wait... *what* was that? Did you say, *'Feed the shit in nice and slow'*?"

"Um," Snoopy muttered, brow furrowed in concentration as she worked on Suzy's hit, "I guess."

"Hm. That's not working for me. I wanna try something... different. Say, *'I gotta feed the shit in... smooth as silk.'* Okay? Just try saying *that* to her."

Snoopy slid the needle out of Suzy's leg, and Suzy felt the heroin hit. A rushing surge of negative pleasure washed over her. She murmured her thanks as a tiny red-black bubble of blood formed over the puncture wound.

"Uh, okay man, whatever," Snoopy said. In an inflectionless monotone, she repeated, "*I gotta feed this shit in... smooth as silk.*"

Stein gestured to Suzy whose eyes were rolling back in pleasure. "And then she says, *'Go for it'*."

The writer snapped his fingers and resumed typing furiously. "Better!" he said to no one in particular, "Smooth as *silk*. That has a nicer ring to it."

Vio-Lette perched on the end of the bed next to Snoopy. "These dudes are hella bugged out," she whispered.

"No fuckin shit. But they got some great blow. I shot some coke like twenty minutes ago? I'm *still* jangling."

"The fat one is listening to shit through the walls. He thinks we've been bugged or somethin."

Snoopy shrugged. "They're harmless, I guess. This one over here just sits around smoking freebase and typing bullshit. I think he's just... writin' down everything that we say. Told me he's some kinda famous novelist. Yeah *right*. He keeps making me re-*say* things. Says I don't sound *authentic* enough."

"What I don't get is we've been here for an hour already. I mean, they told us to get naked, but have any of these guys *tried* to make a move on you? Every time I try to go over to fatso he starts rambling on about listening devices an' shit."

Snoopy nodded her head toward Missy who was still slurping on Stein's cock. "Nope. Weird isn't it? He didn't even ask her for head. This bitch just crawled under the desk and started sucking; I don't even think the writer dude *noticed* at first. You know how *that* ho gets when she's high."

"Shhh!" Jacques hissed, "I can *hear* something!"

The girls groaned. Snoopy decided to help herself to some more of the coke, careful to put Suzy's syringe out of the way. The last thing she needed was a HIV chaser to go with her already virulent case of Hep C. She eyed the pile of cocaine, heroin and downers on the desk.

Jacques froze again. This time everybody heard it. A hard, insistent knocking was cutting through the room.

Immediately jerking out of her nod, Suzy barked, "Who the fuck is *that*?" Even Missy heard this time, pulling Stein's cock out of her mouth in surprise.

"I dunno," James said, shooting an uneasy glance towards Jacques. The Frenchman's eyes glistened with rampant paranoia.

"It is the fucking *police*, James! Someone has *informed* on us!"

At the mention of the word "police" the girls all jumped to their feet, and started desperately pulling on their filthy clothes. Missy nearly cracked her skull on the heavy oak writing desk in her rush to get out from under there. James leapt to his feet, trying to pacify them. "Relax! Cool down, it isn't the fucking cops, okay? Chill..."

Stein fanned the air futilely with his hand, doing little to dissipate the fog of crack, heroin and marijuana smoke that hung in the air, thick as molasses. He crept toward the door, and put his eye to the peephole. He started laughing.

"It's that bald asshole who works for you!" he announced.

Jacques cursed furiously in French and then stormed toward the door. Leaving the chain on, he opened it a crack.

Standing in the corridor with a bunch of legal papers under his arm, Gibby saw Jacques' bloodshot eye bulging out from the crack in the door.

"What IS it Gibby? We're *working*!"

"I called you..." Gibby said, "This morning, remember? You said to come over here. It's about this whole Randal situation, and the new guy he wants to introduce you to."

"Yes, yes. So? Spit it out, man."

"Well as I mentioned on the phone there are some... conditions... that he is insisting on being met in regards to..."

"Yes! Okay. Tell him yes to everything. I don't care, Gibby. It's not as if it is *my* fucking money. Tell him *yes*. Is that all?"

Gibby crept a little closer to the door.

"Well if you're sure... I mean I took the liberty of having the relevant papers drawn up by Gilles back at the Paris office... if you wanna sign... I can send it back to him by the close of business today."

Jacques' meaty hand reached out and grabbed the papers. The door closed. Gibby heard furious scribbling on the other side. A moment later the door opened a crack and the papers were roughly shoved back into his hand. Gibby glanced at the pages. Despite the fact that he had taken the time to place red stickers on each sheet at the places where Jacques was required to sign, his client had simply scrawled his initials in a childlike hand across a third of the necessary pages. Rather than ask Jacques to try again, Gibby decided to say nothing. It seemed easier that way.

"Thanks, Jacques. So, uh, before I go.... I wanted to ask... how's the, uh, *script* coming along?"

The door slammed shut again. Gibby heard the lock being scraped back moments before the door was flung wide. He was suddenly confronted by the sight of Jacques standing there in his white silk boxer shorts, holding a burnt-black crack pipe in his hand. He was red faced and shiny with chemical sweat. Behind him was a gaggle of semi-naked, filthy-looking street kids, passing around a square of tin foil that they were apparently smoking drugs on. Next to them, with a champagne flute in his hand and his semi-hard pecker hanging out of his unbuttoned Levis was the bestselling author James Stein. Gibby looked back at Jacques. The director's eyes burned with a terrifying over-intensity.

"The SCRIPT?" he said, white flecks forming around the corner of his mouth. "The fucking SCRIPT? WE ARE WRITING

THE SCRIPT RIGHT NOW, GIBBY! How are we supposed to CREATE with these constant DISTRACTIONS?"

"Yeah, Gibby," Stein chipped in, "No offence man, but you're totally interrupting my flow... I mean we thought you were the hotel security or something."

He emptied the glass down his throat. "I can't write now, my nerves are fucking shot," he added, ruefully.

The grimy-looking girls tore their attention away from the drugs on the foil long enough to stare disapprovingly at Gibby. In the ghostly half-light of Stein's suite they seemed particularly ominous to him; their pale, hungry faces reminded him of some hideous cross between the Brides of Dracula and Macbeth's witches. He backed away from the door. There was a choking air of 3am desperation in that room, repellent and overpowering, despite the civil hour. The blinds were drawn and to Gibby it looked as though the sunlight had not penetrated that grim cavern for years. He opened his mouth, but the door slammed in his face just as he was about to stammer out an apology for interrupting.

He gathered the paperwork, and thought about Kenny Azura again. What the fuck could he show Kenny? Getting close enough to even see what Jacques was working on was out of the question. The man was in the midst of a fully-fledged bout of drug-induced paranoia. He would have to be treated with kid gloves. Besides, there was obviously no script to speak of. As for the papers, the signatures were useless. This was a minor worry, because on many occasions Jacques had often been so drug addled that Gibby had resorted to signing papers on his behalf, so replicating his client's signature was almost second nature by now.

As he pondered this, an idea came to him that seemed to offer a way out of the Kenny situation regarding the script. But it was risky... very risky. Putting the thought out of his mind for the time being, Gibby reluctantly made his way toward the elevator.

TWENTY-SEVEN

Mama Z's place was a run-down bungalow with a weed-choked front yard on Electric Avenue and Hampton Drive in the Oakwood section of Venice – an area so desolate after sundown it was referred to locally as Ghost Town. It was a tough, crime-ridden part of the city, an economically deprived enclave surrounded by million-dollar homes. Although it was only seven blocks from the beach it exuded the grit and the dust of the inner-city. After dark – if you had the right kind of face – you would be practically berated into buying low-grade ghetto crack from the ever-shifting population of users and dealers who simultaneously fed and controlled the local drug trade.

The two main street gangs that dominated the neighbourhood, The Venice 13 and the Venice Shoreline Crips, had negotiated an uneasy truce in the 1990s after a particularly bloody gang war left dozens dead. In those wild frontier days, bullet-ridden cars and bloody corpses splayed in basketball courts were a common sight. While the ceasefire held the crack trade flourished, despite the ever-encroaching threat of gentrification to the area.

Stinking of booze and old blood, Lupita's Eldorado crept down the unlit streets while she peered out, looking for the correct house. Genesis was dizzy, her hallucinatory state brought on by a combination of blood loss and intoxication. As they crept toward this maze of projects and tumbledown wooden shacks, she'd noted the sinister change in the streets. Heading down Lincoln, shadowy figures lurked in the alleyways watching their car crawl by with steady, suspicious eyes. Glass crunched underneath their tires as they drove over a discarded bottle of Cisco. "Here we are..." As they pulled outside the house, an old crackhead in a filthy, shit-stained suit staggered down the street spitting up foul yellow bile and cursing incoherently to himself.

They hurried up to Mama Z's door and rang the buzzer. The porch light flicked on. Behind the door a deep voice barked, "Whozat?"

"Lupita. I'm here to see Mama Z."

"You say *Lupita*?"

"Yeah."

They could sense someone moving about behind the door, checking them out through the peephole. Then the heavy sound of four deadbolts being scraped back. The door opened and a mountain of a man stood on the other side. He was about six-two, with a face prematurely hardened by correctional institutes and hard living. There was a crude crucifix tattoo on his neck. His eyes darted between the two women. A huge grin slowly spread across his face, revealing a row of gold teeth.

"Fuckin' God-DAMN. Momma *said* you wuz comin'. You know Momma – she wuz talking with the spirits and they *tole* her you wuz in trouble, girl. Come on in..."

"Jesus *Christ*, Sonny!" Lupita said, "You're all grown up."

Sonny leaned in and kissed her on the cheek. "Good to see you, Lupita."

"How old are you now?"

"Twenty-two."

Lupita shook her head. "You was, like, fifteen years old the last time I saw you. You look good, Sonny. This here is my girl, Genesis."

Sonny looked over to Genesis, his brow knotting as he took in her pale skin and the hand wrapped in bloody bandages. "I know all about this one, too," he said darkly. "You better come in. Mama's entertaining in the main room."

Mama Z's place was small and the smell of garlic, cumin and incense permeated the air. Genesis followed Lupita inside. They found themselves in a sitting room that was as cramped and dimly lit as the rest of the house. There were two couches, and an ancient TV/VHS combo tucked away in a corner. Genesis looked around the room. Images of Death were everywhere: grinning skeletons glared at her from all corners, draped in white or red robes, large and small, scythes in hand. Some of them stood on globes, and others held hourglasses or owls in their hands. Some had dollar bills and cigarettes crammed in between their fingers and toes, forming the centrepieces of ramshackle altars where offerings and petitions were made to these strange deities. The statues, flickering votive candles, and framed pictures that filled this tiny living room all carried this same foreboding image.

Sitting on one of the couches was an old white man, skeletal and deathly pale. In the flickering candlelight he looked like a corpse – his cheeks sucked in so that there were just hollows underneath his slit eyes. His toothless mouth was shriveled up underneath a hooknose. He was slowly lurching forward, deep into a smack nod. When his head almost touched his knees he jerked up again, muttering sleepily to himself. After a few seconds he began the slow process of collapsing in on himself again. On the other couch was a man who was so badly disfigured that at first glance you couldn't even tell his race. Underneath the scars his skin may have been black, white or anything in between. The flesh of his face had been pulped so badly by some terrible accident that the skin was the colour and texture of raw chuck steak. Next to him was a little old lady. Her thick white dreadlocks stuck out from her skull at crazy angles, making her head seem too big for her tiny body. Her back was turned to them, revealing a hopelessly curved spine. She was bending over the disfigured man, fixing a shot into his arm, muttering to herself in Spanish.

Nobody said a word to interrupt this grim ritual. They just stood there observing, until the old lady slowly reached over to deposit the spent syringe into a mason jar full of pink, bloody bleach-water that sat on top of the TV set. Several other needles were in there, bobbing around in the solution. The disfigured man's eyes glazed over and he smiled – or at least it looked as it he were *trying* to smile, but his facial wounds made it hard to tell. His lips looked like two hamburger patties trying to curl upwards in synchronization. Without turning around, the old lady croaked, "Lupita. It's been a long time. I wondered when you'd get here."

Slowly, painfully the little woman got to her feet. She turned, and walked over to Lupita. Mama Z's skin was dark and wrinkled. Her left eye was green and the right a milky-white, like there was a thin, translucent veil over it. She wore large hoop earrings, a gold crucifix around her neck and a loud, printed blouse with a multi-coloured leaf pattern all over it. She had several gold teeth that flashed when she spoke. She reached her hand out to Lupita. Genesis watched as Mama Z clasped her small claw-like fingers over Lupita's hand. On each of the tiny fingers was a gold ring. The skin of the hands was parchment thin and scarred with ancient needle tracks, stretched tight over a delicate frame of bone and tendon.

"It's good to see you, Mama Z. This is my girl, Genesis."

Still light-headed from blood loss, Genesis stared at this strange old woman. Her wild, untamed hair, mismatched eyes and claw-like hands reminded Genesis of something Jim Henson might have created in one of his wilder moments. Dazed, she managed to mutter a hello. The old lady looked at her and smiled coldly.

"Looks like you got yourself a little boo-boo, young lady. My granddaughter Duchess is a nurse. She can take a look at that for you."

Mama Z turned her attention back to Lupita. "You look hungry, child. Come on through to the kitchen."

*

At the kitchen table, Lupita was eating a bowl of mondongo – tripe stew – that Sonny had heated up for her. Mama Z was telling Lupita about the disfigured man in the other room. It turned out that his name was Raphael, and that Lupita had known him years ago.

"Poor Raphael," Mama Z cooed. "He used to be such a *pretty* junkie. All the girls useta go crazy for him, don't you remember, Lupe? He had that pencil moustache and those pretty eyes, almost like a girl's. Used to have the most gorgeous caramel skin, too. Looked like Clarke Gable. But now, boy... he just a *mess*."

Lupita ate a forkful of food and nodded. Mama Z's granddaughter, Duchess, knelt at Genesis's feet. She was a stern young woman with an inked tear on one cheek. After fixing Genesis up with a shot of morphine Duchess wordlessly cleaned the wound out with iodine, and proceeded to sew it up expertly.

"I can't believe that's the same guy. He looks... so *different*. I'd never have *recognized* him."

Mama Z's face stiffened. In the half-light it created a disturbing effect, like the old woman was turning to stone in front of Genesis's eyes. "That's what happens when you start to leave your debts unpaid... *bad luck* and *trouble*. Poor Raphael was running up debts all over the damn neighbourhood, ever since he started hitting that pipe. Took a few beatings over it from some of the Shoreline Crips boys, but they didn't knock no *sense* into him. See, until recently he'd always had enough sense to play straight with Mama Z. Then that stupid boy started gettin' lazy. Got to the point that boy owed me almost six hundred dollars. Can you *believe*? The story I heard, he was holed up in some damn crack house, hitting on that crack pipe, and suddenly *boom!* That motherfucking pipe exploded. Just like

224

that. Showered his face with hot glass, fucked him up *good*. His lighter hit the carpet, and the shit just went *up*. When the firefighters drag his ass out of there his face was burned *up*. Soon as he got out of that hospital, the first place he stops – the very first place – is Mama Z's house to pay what he owes. He tells me he don't want that bad luck and trouble following him no more." Mama Z closed her eyes for a moment, and rocked back on her seat. When she opened them, the flickering votive candle on the table cast a sinister aspect on her face. Genesis could not take her eyes off of her, and forgot momentarily about Duchess's needle as it closed up the hole in her flesh.

"Someone like Raphael should know damn well that the dope game is controlled by spells and incantations," Mama Z whispered. "There's ain't no such thing as *luck*. Not in a magical universe."

"Amen," Lupita muttered.

Genesis glanced over at Lupita. Her lover's eyes were gleaming with the fanatical zeal of a true believer. The ominous feeling in her gut deepened further. A sudden, sickly thought occurred to Genesis – the old woman was mad. She was totally fucking insane. Suddenly, she sensed Mama Z's steely gaze upon her. She made eye contact with the old woman for a fraction of a second and then felt a sudden burst of pain, as Duchess' needle caused a jolt of electricity to race up her arm. Genesis yelped and Duchess muttered an apology before continuing to sew up the wound. Mama Z laughed a little. She rested her elbow on the table, and touched Lupita's face with her tiny curled hand. "But enough about that *foolishness*. Tell me, child… what kind of trouble you two in?"

Genesis moaned softly as Duchess finished off the stitching job. "You're all done honey," Duchess said. "Lemmie wrap that bad boy up for you…"

Lupita took a deep breath. "We had a run in with someone down in Laughlin. A *bruja*. She took a real dislike to us, I mean we tried to keep things cool, but the night before we left she put some kinda hex on us. I saw the evidence with my own eyes. Ever since we ran across her our luck has been running cold. Genesis got herself shot. We killed some lady. By accident... "

Mama Z nodded.

"I see. Duchess hon, you mind getting me my things?"

Without a word, Duchess left the kitchen and returned moments later with a heavy, leather-bound King James Bible. She placed it in front of Mama Z then resumed kneeling silently at her grandmother's feet. Genesis watched in silence as the old lady opened the book, and for a moment she thought Mama Z was about to lead them in prayer or some other hokey shit.

What came next threw Genesis off completely.

The pages of the bible had been glued together, and sections had been cut out of them, to form a stash box. Inside was a carbon-scarred dessert spoon, a leather tourniquet, an ancient looking glass and steel syringe, and a baggie of white powder. Mama Z handed Duchess the syringe. Without saying a word she took it over to the wall, where a holy water dispenser with an image of the sacred heart of Jesus was affixed. She drew a measure of the holy water into the syringe and returned to the table. Meanwhile Mama Z dumped a generous amount of the white powder into the spoon. She took the syringe, squirted out the holy water, and used the long nail of her pinkie finger to stir the solution until the powder had completely dissolved. As she did this she muttered a prayer in Spanish.

"Lupe, what is she–?"

Lupita elbowed Genesis hard in the ribs. Genesis quieted down, and looked balefully at Lupita. Lupita was oblivious to her, staring at Mama Z with an intensity that unnerved Genesis greatly. She reluctantly turned her attention back to the old woman who was now drawing the solution up into the syringe.

The old woman turned her eyes up to the ceiling and tilted her head back, exposing her leathery, wrinkled neck.

"*Dios te salve, Maria....*" The old woman muttered as she slid the needle into her neck, "*Llena eres de gracia: El Señor es contigo....*"

Here she paused, drawing the plunger back a little with her weird, claw-like fingers. In the half-light, Genesis saw the clear solution turn crimson as blood flooded the barrel. "*Bendita tú eres entre todas las mujeres.... Y bendito es el fruto de tu vientre...*" The old woman slowly pushed the solution home and hissed, "*Jesús!*"

She stiffened. Duchess reached up and gently removed the syringe from the old woman's neck. She quickly mopped up the dark blood that trickled from the puncture wound with a paper towel. Genesis watched in silent horror as the old woman's eyes turned up in her skull and her whole body began to twitch and convulse. Genesis tried to stand but both Duchess and Lupita reached out at once, placing their hands on her shoulders, holding her in place.

"Shhh... it's okay," Lupita whispered, "Just be *quiet*."

They stayed like that for what felt like an eternity, watching the old woman tremble and twitch at the table, drool hanging from her puckered asshole of a mouth, until the convusions slowed, her shrivelled-up old body giving the occasional jolt and shudder before finally relaxing into stillness. When it was over, Mama Z was slumped over in her seat. Genesis was convinced the old woman was dead.

Duchess cooed, and gently ran her fingers through the old woman's hair. She turned to Lupita and said, "It's good. I can take care of Mama now. Sonny has a room fixed up for you."

The old woman just slumped there; chin lying on her chest, not moving at all. "Mama left some stuff for you on the bedside cabinet. There's some clean works, too..."

Once they were safely squared away in Sonny's room, they fixed the dope Mama Z had left for them and lay back on the bed.

"Howzat hand feeling?"

"The hand? Fuck the hand. You wanna tell me exactly what the fuck that whole performance was about? I just watched a ninety-year-old woman shoot a bunch of fucking coke, have a seizure, and everybody just sat around staring at her like she was doing a fucking magic trick. What the fuck *was* that?"

Lupita smiled dreamily. "You make it sound so... *seedy*. She wasn't shooting coke. Mama Z ain't no *junkie*. She's has a gift. That's how she communicates with the spirit world. She's gotta put herself in a trance. It's the only way she can help us, hun."

"And you believe that?"

"Yeah. I do." Anger had started to creep into Lupita's voice so Genesis changed tack.

"But, I mean... are you *sure* she's okay? She looked like she might need help. Like a doctor or something?"

"Mama Z's fine. I seen her do this a million times. Don't worry." Lupita leaned over and kissed Genesis' neck, lightly.

"Lupe, you gotta see it from my point of view. This is some pretty weird shit."

"I guess. I don't see how it's any weirder than people turning water into wine, or lining up in church to eat the blood and flesh of Jesus, though."

"I find *that* shit weird too. But at least nobody's having convulsions."

"I told you. It wasn't a convulsion. Think of it like... meditating, okay?"

Genesis nodded sourly, but decided to keep her mouth shut. All she really wanted to do, now that her hand was sewn up, was get the hell out of this nuthouse as quickly as possible.

Looking again at the grinning skulls all around her, Genesis sat up gingerly and said, "And another thing... what's with all these fuckin' *skeletons* everywhere? This place looks like a spook house."

"Keep your voice down, the walls are thin in here." Lupita whispered, "Mama Z belongs to the church of Santa Muerte, *La Señora de las Sombras*. She's a very powerful Saint, patron saint of night people... musicians, prostitutes, bar workers, drug dealers..."

"You said *she*?"

"Uh-huh."

"So Death is a woman?"

"Of course. She can protect against violent death, she can also intercede in matters of the heart... and she can even *bring about* death so long as it's in the name of righteousness. She's worshipped mostly by the powerless. The poor." Lupita smiled cynically. "Of course she's not recognized by the Church. Not officially. But Santa Muerte is real... she's kind of an outlaw Saint."

Genesis examined the professional bandage job on her hand. Sleepy from the effect of the shot, she nuzzled into Lupita's neck and muttered faintly: "A female, outlaw Saint. I guess that's appropriate, at least."

TWENTY-EIGHT

A s he turned down Wilcox toward the Gilbert Hotel Randal felt a twinge of apprehension. It had been a long time since he had been face-to-face with his old friend, Jeffrey. He felt edgy and irritable and – although he refused to admit it to himself – Randal knew damn well that mild amphetamine withdrawal was partly to blame for his raw nerves. He had resolved to cut down on his Adderall intake, following his discovery that he had burned through almost sixty pills in the last couple of weeks. If he couldn't control his intake of prescription stimulants then he realized that that whole AA philosophy of having to admit powerlessness over your addiction had more merit than he had previously allowed. This was a possibility that Randal truly could not tolerate. Better to suffer through his cold turkey, refusing all the while to admit what it was, than to submit to that most dangerous concept of all: powerlessness.

He took a gulp of his diet Dr Pepper as he drifted past the Mark Twain Hotel, a hangover gnawing at the base of his skull. He'd tried to compensate for the lack of pills by drinking a half-litre of cheap vodka last night, and now he felt shaky and ill. The flat soda rested uneasily in his gurgling stomach. Craning his neck for an empty meter, he silently reflected on just how far – or not – he and his old partner in crime had come in the past twelve months. For Jeffrey, the distance could be visualized as less than a city block. He had moved out from the dump with the deceptively literary name and straight into the no-more-palatial environment of the Gilbert. This virtually identical fleabag hotel was within crawling distance of the first. Although Randal had never set foot inside the Gilbert, from the outside at least it looked like a sister to the Mark Twain: a sun-bleached slab of ugly concrete with crumbling signage. A den for drug addicts on the skids, trick-turning whores, and lost souls near the bottom of society's ladder.

To go along with his geographic stasis, it seemed that the rest of Jeffrey's life was in a similar state of limbo. He was obviously still strung out. Judging from the condition of the spectre that Randal had spotted shuffling down Hollywood Boulevard a few months ago, he was in worse physical shape than ever.

Pulling up behind an idling pick-up truck, Randal reluctantly allowed himself to ponder his own journey these past twelve months. It was an uncomfortable thought. Another stint in rehab, pitiful finances, miserable months of boredom and sobriety, an expanding waistline and a receding hairline... night after night spent gorging on take-out Mexican in his shitty apartment, his only respite jerking off like a crazed baboon to internet porn. When he wasn't eating or masturbating he was working a soul-destroying day gig, attending AA meetings and hating his own guts for what he had become. He was drinking out of necessity, depending on booze as a crutch to support him through the mind-numbing tedium of his day-to-day routine. It was perfectly obvious to Randal that he had morphed into One Of Them: a schmo. A regular Joe. A real *asshole*. Even his drugs of choice these days hammered home the extent of his downward spiral. He here was, Randal P. Earnest, a man who thought of himself as the outlaw black sheep of the Earnest clan, abusing prescription pills and alcohol like every other dull, lifeless, unimaginative Hollywood asshole out there.

In treatment he had always held a special kind of distain for those who found themselves strung out on doctors' prescriptions. He felt it showed a lack of moxie. When he was in treatment he'd noticed that the people who'd found themselves taking dozens of Oxycontin a day usually looked down upon the heroin addicts and the speedfreaks as being junkie scum. It was a baffling and disgusting example of drug-snobbery. Randal disparagingly thought of the pill freaks as the kind of weak, coddled junkies who were just too *soft* to make it out on the street. He didn't even want to dwell on how he'd once looked down on the drinkers, a group he could never relate to in all his years of ping-ponging in and out of rehab. Although Randal came from the kind of privilege that could have easily ensured he'd never once have to leave Beverly Hills, it gave him a special feeling of pride to know that he could make it among the whores, gang bangers and street-crazies that populated the city's underbelly.

These days Dr Titov was his main drug connection. Randal shook his head in disgust.

After a few good blasts on the horn, Randal saw Jeffrey come out of the front entrance, looking like some bedraggled ghost of Christmas past. He looked to be rendered in black and white against the stark brightness of the early afternoon sun: tall and skinny, thick greasy hair sticking out from his skull at all angles, eyes hidden behind a pair of plastic sunglasses, skin so translucent that it looked almost blue. He was wearing a pair of bone-hugging black jeans and a filthy T Rex T-shirt, possibly the same T-shirt he remembered Jeffrey wearing back when they'd been roommates at the Clean and Serene treatment centre.

Jeffrey pulled open the door and slid into the air-conditioned cool of Randal's car. He slammed the door closed and then coughed violently, letting loose a series of chest-rattling blasts. When he was done he stuck his head out the window and spat up what looked like a sizeable portion of his lung onto the street. The smell of unwashed clothes and stale cigarette smoke filled the car. Jeffrey's dry, cracked lips formed a crooked smile and he said, "*Randal...* Long time no see. What's going down?"

"Very little, man. It's good to see you. You doing okay?"

A pained look came over Jeffrey's face. "Don't gimmie the fake concerned shit, man. You can see I'm doing lousy. But it's okay. I'm still breathing, that's all that matters."

"I guess."

Randal stuck the car into drive and they took off, heading towards Sunset.

"Six months clean," Jeffrey was saying as they headed toward Chinatown, where Gibby had set up a noon meeting with Jacques. "That's really great man. I'm happy for you. How does it feel?"

"Honestly?"

"Yeah, honestly."

Randal was silent for a long while. Finally he said, "Tell you the truth it feels shit. I don't feel any different. In fact, in a lotta ways, I feel worse. When I was in rehab they told me that a lot of my hatred for the world was a kinda... you know, a self-fulfilling prophecy. They told me I was miserable because I was taking meth, and I used that self-inflicted misery to justify taking more meth. They said that a lot of my hatred and my unhappiness was generated by my addiction. That my addiction had... uh... twisted my worldview to make the drugs seem like a necessity, you know?"

"You gotta love that about AA."

"What?"

"*Your addiction.*" Jeffrey snorted. "The way they talk about it you would think it was a fuckin' sentient being that you gotta outsmart, or something. I guess I take a less complicated view. It's just about getting *high*, isn't it?"

"Oh yeah, I hear ya. Still, I've been *trying* Jeffrey. I really decided this time that I was gonna surrender and I was gonna listen. Do it their way."

233

"You let go and let God, huh? I'm sure Dr. Mike would be very proud."

"Maybe. But it worked. I haven't used meth since my last trip to rehab. The problem is, when I quit, nothin' really changed. I still turn on CNN and I feel fucking murderous. I still drive down the street and when I look around at the cars filled with assholes it just gives me the creeps. I get out of bed in the morning, and I change my underwear every day, and I show up at my brother's office, and I wear clean clothes, and buy the fucking LA Times every morning... I eat breakfast, give Christmas presents, take vitamins, go on dates for fucking *coffee* and *conversation*, I don't fuck whores, I don't get high, none of that all shit."

Randal gripped the steering wheel, his knuckles turning white. "*Nothing* seems any more bearable. I do everything that *they* do, I do everything they *tell* me to do, and the only difference between now and back then is that I don't even have *crank* to make me forget how dull and dismal and shitty it all is. I tell my therapist this, and my therapist wants to give me Xanax, and Wellbutrin, and fucking Zoloft or whatever. So I take those and then it feels like I'm sleepwalking through my fucking life. I can't get a hard-on and I can't take a shit, and my mouth feels like it's wadded fulla cotton the whole time. On the antidepressents it's not that I don't hate my life any more, it's just that the pills have zonked me out so much that I don't have the fuckin' *energy* to feel that strong about anything. And when I take that shit all the guys in AA are cool with it, it's fine and dandy because my fuckin' doctor gave it to me so I must *need* it, right? But now I'm a fucking zombie with a limp dick who just wants to sleep all fucking day! So I come off of all that shit, I feel like I'm going insane for a few weeks, and I'm back to square one. I know that with one fucking phone call I can get some shit that will straighten me right out. One fucking hit on the pipe and suddenly life is gonna seem like it's worth living again, and I'm gonna be able to fuck like a normal human being, I'm gonna feel like *me* again instead of some half-insane spastic-freak. But if I smoke some meth that would be *bad*, because I'm an *addict* and I can't get high any more." Randal wiped his sweaty brow. "I started drinking. You know, to ease the pressure a little. It only works when I'm *drunk* though. The rest of the time I still feel like shit."

Jeffrey raised an eyebrow. "So what you *saying*?"

"I dunno, Jeffrey. All I know for sure is that this fucking stinks."

"It sounds like you're already made your decision. You wanna go back on."

"Maybe I should. I don't know if could be any worse than *this*."

Jeffrey's heavy eyelids drooped and he stretched contentedly. He looked like a cat that had been thoroughly sated by a bowl of warm milk, and was about to curl up and take a solid four-hour nap.

"Well," Jeffrey said in a sleepy voice, "all I'm sayin' is that things ain't so much better where I'm sitting. And you got a hell of a lot more to lose than I do."

"It can't be all bad. You look liked you're feeling pretty good right now."

A wan smile crossed Jeffrey's lips. "Give it few hours, man. Then I gotta figure out how the fuck I'm gonna get high again. I'm broke and unless something changes I'm gonna be dope-sick and homeless soon."

"Yeah, well maybe this whole Jacques deal can help you out with that."

"I hope so. Look Randal, all I'm saying is that it's real easy for you to start over-romanticizing this shit now you're not doing it. I remember the day you showed up for Stevie's funeral. You didn't look like you were having such a great time then, you know?"

"Yeah, I remember."

"Look man, I'm not here to give you fucking life advice. I made my choice, you know, you gotta make yours. The way I see it is this. Life's a bitch any way you slice it. For me, I'll take the trade-off of knowing that I'm gonna feel incredible when I put a needle in my arm, over the uncertainty of having to wait and see if fate is gonna throw me a bone today. I know I'm never gonna be a CEO or whatever, but fuck man, I never had those kinda ambitions in the first place. Me? At this point, my view on life is this: I just wanna pay for my groceries and get out of the supermarket without incident, you know?"

Randal laughed and nodded. "That's pretty profound, man."

Jeffrey shrugged, rested his head against the glass, and a couple of red lights later he had drifted into a peaceful nod.

TWENTY-NINE

Genesis and Lupita were in Gold Diggers, a skuzzy little strip club on Santa Monica Boulevard, watching a heavily pregnant Thai girl preparing to perform. The tiny stage was little more than a raised portion on the floor furnished with a rusty brass pole. An uncomfortable silence descended upon the room as she fiddled for a few clumsy minutes with a boom box CD player to line up her music. It was early afternoon, and the place was all but deserted: a few tired-looking Latin men in stained overalls drinking beers with a couple of skinny junkie whores, and a fat transvestite sitting alone at a table drinking shots of tequila.

"Reminds me of some of the crummy places I used to strip at," Genesis remarked as the music – *"Love in an Elevator"* by Aerosmith – finally started up, "'cept we used to at least have a DJ."

"You know somethin' hun," Lupita said, "I think I'd have liked to have seen you dance. I bet you were pretty good at it."

"Well I'd have maybe got up to show you after this chick gets off the stage, but I doubt there's many tips to be made in this fucking dump. Shit, look at that waterbug."

Lupita swept the bug off the table and said, "True that."

The girl started dancing, if you could call it that. As the music played she just bent over and wiggled her acne-ridden ass in time with the beat, pulling her thong up into her pussy so the lips peeked out of either side. The lighting was unpleasantly bright, and made every blemish and imperfection on the girl's skin stand out. Genesis supposed that if this chick pulled that thong any further into her cooch then the baby might wind up throttled before it even made it out of the womb. As she considered this, one of the men wearing overalls ran up to the stage and dropped a couple of bucks by her feet, earning a smile and a seductive lick of the lips from the mother-to-be.

"Okay focus, hun," Lupita said, 'Cause we need to figure out our next move."

That morning, Mama Z and her granddaughter Patty had performed a cleansing ritual on Lupita and Genesis. It was one of the strangest things that Genesis had ever experienced. Since Genesis had been a sex worker and a habitual user of crystal meth for many years this was really saying something. Patty was grotesquely overweight, and had a seemingly self-administered bowl haircut. She wore an Elton John and Billy Joel Face 2 Face tour T-shirt from 1994. She looked to be maybe twenty, but her eyes were those of a child's still. When she spoke she refused to make eye contact with anybody but Mama Z, and her voice had the precise, clipped cadence of a computer. They'd both been instructed to strip and to lay face down on Mama Z's bed. Feeling ridiculous, Genesis did as she was told. Patty positioned them head to toes, while Mama Z lit some frankincense, filling the room with a thick, pungent smoke. Then for twenty minutes or so Patty passed an egg – the regular kind, straight out of the carton – over their bodies, while Mama Z prayed and chanted in Spanish. At one point the old lady smoked a cigarette down to the filter, blowing the grey smoke all over them, chanting furiously in between each drag.

At first Genesis felt self-conscious lying there naked in the room in front of Mama Z and Patty, but pretty soon her embarrassment gave way to a kind of amusement and, eventually, boredom. In fact, she had just started drifting off into a light sleep when she felt Mama Z's bony hand touching her back, and her raspy voice instructing her to "Wake up, girl, and put some clothes on..."

Genesis flicked on the TV and watched The Three Stooges in the next room while Patty, Mama Z and Lupita stayed in the bedroom. Mama Z cracked the egg and poured it out into a glass of water. They studied the form the yolk took in the water, talking in hushed Spanish among themselves. When Lupita eventually emerged she had a worried look on her face. Like something had upset her but she didn't want Genesis to know. Genesis looked up from the TV. "Hey."

"Hey yourself."

"You wanna watch the Stooges?"

Lupita shook her head and peered at the TV. "Whozat? Shemp?"

"Nah, even worse. It's fuckin' Joe what's-his-face. The guy who *replaced* Shemp."

"Oh. Well look, we gotta go Genesis hun..."

"Go? Go where?"

Lupita shrugged. "Anywhere."

"So it's all fixed? Are we still, uh, cursed, or what?"

"We can talk about it later. For now... it's time to move on. I think we've imposed on Mama Z's hospitality enough, don't you? Anyway, we're almost broke. We'd better go find a cheap room and figure out our next move..."

Genesis sensed a change in Mama Z as they grabbed their stuff and prepared to leave. She seemed suddenly serious, anxiously lurking around them as they packed up their meagre belongings. She gave them a weak smile as Lupita thanked her for her hospitality and they headed out to the car. It didn't matter too much to Genesis. She was so relieved that they were finally getting out of this weird old woman's house that she didn't dwell on the uncomfortable atmosphere too much. They said their goodbyes and headed toward Hollywood. Lupita was quiet and preoccupied. She didn't even turn the radio on.

"So come on then," Genesis asked, "What's the deal?"

"Huh?"

"With this curse you've been obsessed with. The curse the old lady put on us."

"The old lady didn't curse us."

"Really? So that's good, then? We're cool?"

"No. Not at all. I think this goes way deeper than that old bitch at the motel."

"Goes *deeper*? What the fuck are you talkin' about, Lupe?"

Lupita sighed. "Mama Z seems to think that we crossed paths with a Palero – someone who practices Palo Mayambe."

"And what the fuck is that?"

"It's a form of black magic. Some people call it the dark side of Santeria. It was brought over to the Americas via Congolese slaves, you know, back in the day. Look, Genesis, I'm sorry. I'm just kinda disturbed by the whole thing because when Mama Z cracked that egg..." Lupita drifted off. Her face looked ashen. "When she cracked that egg... there was *blood* inside, Genesis. The fuckin' yolk was blood red."

Genesis snorted. "Oh Jesus *Christ*, Lupe! Blood in the egg? That's retarded. Save the ghost stories for someone who believes in that stuff."

"I'm not kidding. There was *blood* in the egg."

Genesis rolled her eyes. "*Okay*, so there was blood in the egg. So what does that mean? The fuckin' chicken was on the rag?"

"That mean's we got heavy spiritual shit to deal with, hun. When Mama Z and Patty saw that, they knew it was Palo Mayambe right away. The weird thing is, Mama Z said that as far as she could tell this thing had been brewing since the moment we got together."

"Oh come on! The old lady says we're cursed because we're *together*? You know somethin', I'm beginning to think that Mama

240

Z told you this stuff because she doesn't *like* me. I saw the looks she was throwing me when we were getting ready to leave. Is it because I laughed when she was doin' that ridiculous performance with the egg? I was trying to keep a straight face, Lupe, I swear! I know you like that old lady, Lupe, but if you ask me she's batshit crazy."

Lupita's nostrils flared in anger. "Don't talk about Mama Z like that, Genesis! You can't even begin to understand the kind of knowledge that Mama Z has. You can be all flippant and ignorant if you want, Genesis hun, but don't you *ever* disrespect Mama Z to me."

"Okay, Jesus Lupe I was kidding!" Genesis backed off immediately, suddenly terrified by the anger this comment had provoked in Lupita. "Why you so serious all of a sudden? It's just when you tell me that this shit has something to do with us being together..."

"It's not *because* we're together. Nobody said that. All she said was that this luck has been following us ever *since* we got together. When she said that, it got me thinking about what happened the night we met. You know, what went down with Paco. You knew that motherfucker better that me – he was Puerto Rican, right? Did he have a basement in his place?"

"A basement? Sure, I guess. There was a door at least, but I never went down there. It was always locked. He told me it was fulla chemicals he needed to cook meth with, and if anything happened it could blow the whole place sky high. Why?"

"That makes sense... Palo Mayambe is big in Puerto Rico, for sure. And all Paleros keep a special room that they keep locked up good. It's a "house of the dead" where they can go communicate with the spirits. I'm pretty fucking sure that Paco was Palo Mayambe. My guess is that when I killed Paco we unleashed some kind of unholy fucking vengeance against us."

"Great, well this just keeps getting better and better. So Paco was a fucking meth-dealing wizard who's out to get us from beyond the grave. That's just... *perfect*."

Genesis decided that so long as there was no way of talking sense into Lupita, it was probably prudent to play along for the time being. "So what do we do?"

"We got a ritual to perform. Mama Z gave me the all materials we need with instructions. She says it should do the trick. But first... I need a fucking drink. Let's find a place..."

So they found themselves in Gold Diggers, contemplating their next move. Genesis had the feeling that there was something else on Lupita's mind, but she'd already denied it enough times this morning that Genesis was compelled to drop the issue altogether. Maybe she was just paranoid, disturbed by all of this crazy talk about black magic, curses and rituals. Lupita's eyes seemed far away, focused on something that was beyond Genesis's comprehension. She took a gulp of her whisky and coke.

"You know," said Lupita, "We need to make some money fast. We're almost out of drugs, and we're gonna need some funds in the short term. If you're up for it, I think I got a plan to make some bread."

Happy that they were at least no longer talking about black magic, Genesis said, "What you got in mind?"

Lupita nodded to their empty glasses. "I was thinking of pulling a little bait and switch. But let's get a refill first. I think maybe we're gonna need it, you know? To steady our nerves..."

THIRTY

When they arrived at *Phillipe The Original Restaurant,* it was unusually quiet for a weekday lunchtime. They crossed the sawdust-covered floor to the booth where Gibby was nervously checking his Blackberry, awaiting word from Jacques. Gibby looked up at Randal and Jeffrey with a pained expression on his face.

"*Please* tell me you've heard from Jacques."

Randal turned his palms up. Gibby took a gulp of his coffee and mopped up the ring of condensation with his napkin. "Shit," he muttered to no one in particular.

"Gibby, this is Jeffrey. He's the guy I told you about..."

"Siddown, siddown. You guys hungry? They got great French-dipped sandwiches here."

"Not me, man. I'm on a diet." Jeffrey said, patting his tight belly. "The H plan."

Still sick and disorientated from lack of amphetamines Randal shook his head. As they took their seats Gibby looked at them, his eyes darting rapidly between the two men. Randal looked ill and shaky but somehow Jeffrey looked even worse. Gibby had never in his life seen skin so pale on a living creature before.

"So," Randal said, "no sign of Jacques, huh?"

Gibby shook his head. "He called me screaming blue murder the other night, telling me that Stein had disappeared. Apparently he made off with most of Jacques' cocaine. Jacques woke up on the floor of Stein's room at the Biltmore and James, the coke *and* the script were gone. The bastard grabbed his cases, clothes, all of his shit and just... cleared out. Jacques was throwing a goddamned shit-fit last time I spoke to him. I told him we were meeting here at noon, but I ain't been able to get hold of him all morning. I called by the motel. No sign of him."

Gibby sighed and massaged the bridge of his nose dejectedly. These past few weeks, it seemed to Randal that the poor man had aged at least ten years.

"So Stein took the script? Man, Jacques must be fucking freaking out."

Gibby stared at Randal like he had lost his mind. "He doesn't give a shit about the *script*, Randal. He's pissed off about the cocaine. Apparently it was some top-notch shit he'd had Fed-Ex'd over from Paris. Anyway James hasn't vanished exactly. I managed to get a lead on him."

"Where?"

"On TMZ. This morning there was a picture of him leaving some fucking party in Malibu with Kate Moss. Taken last night. Who knows when the fuck we'll hear from *him* again."

"So what's happening with Kenny and the script? Doesn't this, like, sink the whole project?"

Drawn out of his sleepy silence by this comment, Jeffrey leaned in and drawled, "Wait... Am I still gonna get paid?"

"Oh, *now* he's awake!" Gibby sneered, "Don't worry your little head, princess. It's fine."

He shot Randal a *what-the-fuck-is-up-with-this-guy* look, before leaning in and continuing, "That's actually the one bit of good news I've gotten this week. Kenny's all signed off on the script. In fact, I'd go as far as saying that he's pretty gung-fuckin'-ho about *Black Neon* again."

Now it was Randal's turn to look confused.

"What – so there *is* a script? I thought you said..."

"Sure there's a script. I found it on the Internet. You ever hear of a movie called *Panic in Needle Park*? Old Al Pacino flick from the 70s, about junkies in New York?"

Randal shrugged. "Dunno. Maybe. What's that got to do with anything?"

"Well... it's a pretty good movie. I was thinking about it the other day. Joan Didion wrote the script. You know her stuff?" Randal looked blank, but Gibby carried on regardless. "Thing is I always felt that when Stein was at his best – and let's face it, we're talking strictly about the first book here – that he stole a lot of his best moves from Didion. That got me thinking about the movie she wrote. I downloaded a copy of the script, changed the title, switched a few things around. I changed the locale from New York to LA, stuck James and Jacques' names at the top and sent twenty pages of it over to Kenny."

"And?"

"*And*... I get a call from Kenny that very evening coked out of his fucking mind, yapping on about how it's the greatest work of genius he's ever read and how I should count myself lucky that I'm in a position to... what was it that he said? Oh yeah. *To be able to suck at the teat of Jacques Seltzer's greatness.* I gotta admit, even by Kenny Azura's usual standards, that was a pretty good one. The upshot is that despite the fact that Kenny is an idiotic know-nothing asshole, the deal is now inked and checks are being cut. Now all I got to worry about... is Jacques."

Randal laughed. It felt like the first honest-to-god laugh he'd had in a long time. "That's beautiful, man... You just signed a movie deal on the basis of a plagiarized, thirty-year-old script and the insane promises of a drug-addled Frenchman? I gotta tell you Gibby, even by Hollywood's usually ridiculous standards, that's pretty wild."

Gibby shrugged. "It was an act of a desperate man, Randal. Honestly, I doubt Kenny will even notice that the finished film bears no resemblance to the spec script I showed him. But even if he does... I just tell him that the concept changed as they started shooting. Hell, he'll put up with any old shit so long as he thinks it fell outta the asshole of Jacques-the-genius."

Randal smiled, quietly impressed by Gibby's cunning. "There's something I've been meaning to ask you about the movie, actually."

"Oh yeah? What's that?"

"The title. *Black Neon*. What does it even *mean*?"

"Your guess is as good as mine." Gibby shrugged. "All I know is that ever since he finished *Dead Flowers*, he always referred to this mythical fucking follow up he's been planning as *Black Neon*. Might have some deep significance, for sure. Or it just could just be a bit of Jacques' usual faux-profound bullshit. If you're interested there are legions of fanatical Jacques fans who've been debating this very same question online for years. You ever go on movie blogs and listen to what people are saying about stuff like this?"

"No," Randal said dryly, "Mainly because I have a fucking life, Gibby."

"S'cuse me ladies," Jeffrey slurred, getting unsteadily to his feet. "Nature calls..."

They both watched as Jeffrey wandered unsteadily toward the bathroom, nearly knocking over a khaki-clad guy with a tray full of sandwiches and sodas. As the guy cursed at him Jeffrey obliviously staggered off, veering dangerously, his lanky frame somehow defying gravity and remaining upright.

"Well, you outdid yourself," Gibby said, turning his attention back to Randal when Jeffrey staggered into the bathroom, "Looks like you actually managed to find the one person on this planet who looks like he's an even bigger fuck-up than Jacques."

Randal shrugged. "Isn't that what you wanted? No point in me sending you a boy scout."

"I guess. Just sticks in my throat that I got this junkie loser insured up the wazoo. I mean, if Jacques even farts in his presence that fucking smackhead stands to make a bundle."

Randal leaned in and in a very serious voice said, "That fucking smackhead is a good friend of mine. I suggest you cool it with the insults, Gibby. I understand you're stressed and all, but don't talk shit about this guy. He's one of the few decent people I've met in this town. I'm actually more concerned about the effect it will have on *Jeffrey* when we hook him up with Jacques, not the other way around, you know?"

Gibby rolled his eyes. "Touching. Looks like you two got a regular fucking bromance going on. Look Randal, I don't wanna insult you or any of that horseshit. It just riles me to think that I've spent fifteen years wiping Jacques' ass, and I still gotta fight tooth and nail to secure my payday on this mess. I'm the asshole who's placating Kenny, blowing smoke up Jacques' ass in the hope that somehow he'll fluke his way into making another half-decent movie... I'm the one having to cut the deals, fabricate the fucking scripts... and yet it seems that every half-dead, fucked-up junkie screw-up in Hollywood is just *dying* to waltz into this deal and get points on the fucking gross. I don't even wanna tell you how much we paid Stein to show up for a couple of days, type up some drug-addled nonsense and then vanish with a suitcase full of Jacques' coke. When it comes to *Black Neon* everybody seems to be making money and having a grand old time except for Gibby-the-fucking-moron, who instead is running around like a prick making sure that all of the plates keep spinning. It's enough to make you feel kind of *bitter*, you know?"

Randal shrugged. Gibby checked his phone again and said, "Lemmie try Jacques again."

He hit redial and waited. It seemed as if Jacques phone was just going to keep ringing, as it had been doing since Gibby arrived at *Phillipes* a half hour ago. Then, miraculously, on the forth ring someone picked up.

"Jacques?"

A confused sounding voice on the other end answered, "Um... no. This is... um, Jeff."

"Jeff?"

"Yeah. Did you say you're looking for... *Jacques*?"

Suddenly Gibby recognized the Anglo-Irish accent on the other end of the line. It was Jeffrey! Confused, he looked toward the bathroom that Jeffrey had walked into a few moments ago.

"Jeffrey, it's Gibby! What the *fuck* is going on?"

"Gibby! Oh hey buddy... So wait – this Jacques guy we're waiting for... Is he a kind of fat dude, eye-patch, pony-tail, smells of puke?"

"Um... yeah that sounds about right."

""Cos I just found this guy in a stall... I mean, the door was wide open and his pants were around his ankles, and he's like... out *cold.*"

"And why the fuck do you have his phone?"

"Oh, well... uh, I was just, you know... checkin' for a wallet. In case he like, needed... help? Like an ID or something?"

"Uh-huh. Stay right there, okay?"

Gibby clicked the phone off.

"What the fuck is going on?" Randal asked.

"It seems that Jeffrey and Jacques have just met. In fact, it looks like your pal was just rifling through my client's pockets just now. Apparently Jacques is passed out in the bathroom."

"Oh shit. I guess that's what you'd call an auspicious beginning, huh?"

"I guess. Come on. I'm gonna go get Jacques. Here–" Gibby tossed down a couple of bucks, "Go get some black coffee, will you? And make sure it's strong..."

THIRTY-ONE

E ven before Rachel had gotten the spike out of her arm, the seizure hit.

Her eyes rolled back into her skull like a velvet curtain rising to reveal an empty stage. Her right hand violently twitched, causing her to jerk the needle out messily. It ripped a hole in her arm, and a fine mist of blood sprayed out. It was Rachel's blood that shook Jeffrey out of his nod, spraying against his slack face. His eyes opened to half-slits. He saw Rachel flopping around on the bed, her skinny arms flailing about, skull rat-a-tat-tatting against the wall.

At first he thought he was dreaming. The image seemed entirely disconnected from reality. But then his eyes widened as his heroin-fogged brain started to really process what he was looking at. It came through in a series of disturbing flashes.

Rachel's thick pink tongue, hanging out of her mouth.

Her crooked, yellow teeth biting down on it, hard.

The eyes: no pupil, all white.

"Ung – uhhh – uhnnnggghhh–"

"Rachel? Baby?"

Her hands were buried in her crotch, tearing at it. Her tiny cock shriveled up, the balls reduced to the size of cherries by a steady diet of cocaine and black-market female hormones. It was as if they were so disgusted by the horrors of the world that they were attempting to retreat inside of her guts. Her hands looked like claws digging between her legs, seemingly locked into some kind of bizarre auto-sexual frenzy.

"Rach? Whaddya doing?"

"Uhhhnnggggh – ug! Uggghhh!"

Her skin was rubbery, taut. It looked like the skeleton underneath was trying to squirm out. Her eyes bulged out of their sockets. Instinctively he went over to her. Up close, he saw that her teeth were sunk deeply into the soft flesh of her tongue. Blood and drool hung from her chin, and the tip of her tongue was purple and swollen. Without thinking, he stuck his fingers in her mouth, wrenching the jaws apart, screaming at her the whole time to wake up. He pushed the injured tongue back into the safety of her mouth. He wedged his fingers in between the clamping teeth in an attempt to stop her doing any more damage to herself.

"Uhhhnnnggghhh!

UUUUUUGGGGGGGGHHHHHHHNNNNNN!"

Too late, he realized that her jaw was too powerful for him, and the teeth started to rip into his flesh. "Shit!" The more he pulled away the harder she clamped down, like some adrenaline-crazed pit bull. He started screaming for Jacques, who was nodded out on the toilet, his fat face slack and pallid. Jacques' heavy eyes blinked once, twice, and tried to focus on the chaos happening in the next room.

As Jeffrey tried to pull his bloody hand free of Rachel's jaw, her head clattered violently against the wall. Finally, with a yelp of pain he managed to rip his shredded fingers out of her mouth. Rachel rolled off the bed hitting the ground with a thump. She continued flopping around on the floor, like a bloody 110lb St. Vitus.

"Jacques, get the fuck in here man! I need your help!"

Jacques had been holed up in the Gilbert Hotel with Jeffrey and Rachel for the past few days. Back at *Phillipe's* – after Randal and Gibby had slapped Jacques around for a while and poured some black coffee down his throat – the director had been coherent enough to make his pitch directly to Jeffrey: he would move into the Gilbert Hotel with him and document his life with Rachel as part of his research for *Black Neon*. Smelling money, Jeffrey had easily convinced Jacques that he was the right man for the job. The charm came thick and easy, especially after he had fixed a shot of dope in the bathroom and emerged feeling good enough to spin a few tales of his adventures on the street. Randal joined in and soon the pair of them were swapping war stories of drug deals and rehab adventures, much to the delight of Seltzer, who seemed to be totally enamored by Jeffrey by the end of the meeting. Jeffrey signed the papers, and the deal was set.

Rachel had been initially less than pleased, snapping, "Where the hell did you pick up this jerk-off?" when Jeffrey showed up at the hotel with Jacques in tow. When Jacques opened up his suitcase to reveal large amounts of high quality narcotics, she quickly came round to the idea. Once Jacques moved in the exact chronology of events became pretty fuzzy. Jacques had brought with him a massive influx of drugs. Time had ceased to become relevant to Jeffrey and Rachel's existence, while they gorged themselves on Jacques' dollar. It was, Rachel commented during a heroin and cocaine binge, like the honeymoon they'd never had.

Jeffrey's eyes were darting between his bloody hand and Rachel's trembling body when he sensed movement behind him. He turned and was confronted by the sight of Jacques Seltzer, his shirt unbuttoned and massive pale belly poking out of it, filming Rachel as she continued to have a violent seizure on the floor.

"What are you *doing*, motherfucker?"

"I am documenting, Jeffrey! What does it look like?"

"I need you to *help* her, man! HELP HER!"

Jacques looked away from the viewfinder for a moment.. His eyes narrowed to slits. "Do I look like a fucking *nurse* to you, Jeffrey? I am an artiste! My only loyalty is to the *muse...*"

He carried on filming.

Cursing, Jeffrey looked at the phone, and considered the kind of heat that calling in the paramedics could bring down on all of them. The room was strewn with needles, pipes, and narcotics. James Stein's only real lasting contribution to *Black Neon* was that he had hooked Jacques up with his LA drug connections. Instead of buying small amounts from shady street dealers Jacques had started having weight delivered straight to the Gilbert. He rented his own room there but spent most of his time holed up in Jeffrey's place, getting high and filming. Jacques encouraged Jeffrey to invite all of his dope-fiend buddies to come over and share the wealth, and he proceeded to shoot all the action as it went down. Now their room looked like some Mexican drug factory, with ripped-open bags of cocaine and powder heroin casually strewn about. In response to Jacques' generosity Rachel and Jeffrey had dramatically upped the amount of drugs they had been consuming, gorging like pigs on everything they could lay their hands on.

Before the seizure hit, Rachel had been injecting cocaine for almost twenty-four hours straight. Her skinny body was bloody and swollen with needle marks; a grim compulsion kept her reaching for the needle.

Fearing that Rachel would suffer irreparable brain damage or worse if he didn't act, Jeffrey cursed himself and picked up the phone. Jacques dropped the camera immediately.

"What are you *doing*?"

"I'm calling the fuckin paramedics, asshole!"

"No!" Jacques screeched, "Have you lost your mind? The fucking cops will have a field day!"

"She could *die*, Jacques!"

Jacques reached out and grabbed Jeffrey's arm. "No ambulance," he hissed, "She will be fine. I promise!"

Jeffrey shook his arm away. "You *promise?* How the fuck can you promise me that? You said it yourself, Jacques – you ain't a fucking nurse!"

"I swear to you Jeffrey, if you go to jail for the sake of this – this – this *chick with a dick* – then you will regret it! Let it run its course, Jeffrey, it will be cool, yes?"

Without another word, Jeffrey kicked Jacques in the balls as hard as he could. The big man collapsed to ground with a thunderous clatter. He cupped his injured balls and howled in agony.

"Why don't you put that in your fucking movie?" Jeffrey hissed, "You fat cocksucker!"

As Jeffrey started dialing 911 again, Jacques staggered to his feet and bleated, "We are OVER, Jeffrey. Have fun babysitting this junkie tranny in jail, you piece of shit! I will finish *Black Neon* without your fucking help!"

"Yeah hello? I need an ambulance..."

With a grunt of disgust, Jacques collected as much of the drugs as he could carry, and stormed out of the room.

Rachel stood in front of the television cameras, the studio lights blinding her. She could see indistinct silhouettes in front of her, holding clipboards, and watching her eagerly. Before anybody spoke, Rachel knew instinctively what was going down. The cameras were pointed at her because she was the star of her own television show. Imagine! A show all about the life of *Rachel*. She could hear far-away applause. At first when the voice spoke to her, the voice of the Director, it seemed to echo as if it were coming from some cavernous place inside of her skull. As he walked toward her the words came into sharp focus. He was congratulating her on a job well done.

"I'm so happy," Rachel beamed. It was true. She felt like an Oscar winner. As if she were about to burst into tears of pure joy.

The director was standing in front of her. He placed his hands on her shoulders. Although she was right next to him, his face still looked strangely out of focus. As if she were seeing it from far away, without her glasses. "You're doing be great, baby," the Director said, "We all love you. The *camera* loves you."

The Director waved his arm around the bright, vast studio.

"These people are all here for *you*. They're all here to see *Rachel*. This is your big moment."

She leaned in and embraced him. He radiated warmth, a special kind of warmth, a feeling she hadn't known since she was six years old, falling asleep in front of the television curled up on Nay Nay's lap like a kitten. The smell of her Jean Nate and her menthol cigarettes. Her asthmatic old beagle Mickie, curled up asleep at Nay Nay's feet. She felt the sudden lurch of nostalgia, of almost unbearable longing.

"Are you God?" Rachel asked.

Instead of answering, the Director merely said, "Look who's here..."

Looking around, squinting because of the lights still beaming in her eyes, Rachel could see familiar faces amidst the blinding white that surrounded her. Nay Nay was there. Her parents too. Other faces, faces she hadn't seen or thought about in a long, long time. Calvin Dodson, the leader of a gang of kids at school who had once tortured her, called her a faggot, beat her up regularly. Here Calvin was, in fact here they all were, unchanged by the intervening years, except now they smiled at her, applauding her eagerly. Everybody was cheering her, *approving* of her. She felt like a prom queen. She was the star, and now every rotten motherfucker on this earth was here to tell her how gorgeous she was, how *amazing* she was. This whole shitty fucking world was here to kiss her goddamned ass. That's when Rachel knew for sure that she was in Heaven.

Rachel had truly no idea that joy of this magnitude even existed. She wanted to go over to them, to thank them all for being here for her crowning moment, but the Director stopped her. For the first time she looked in his eyes, and his features shifted into sharp focus. He was familiar, handsome in a chiseled, All-American kind of a way. Dark, neat hair and movie star eyes. He had a mean mouth though, a smile that suggested cruelty. Rachel recognized him immediately as the star of the very first porno movie she had ever seen, an Eighties straight-to-video number set in prison called *Powertool*.

"Jeff *Stryker*?" she breathed, "You're *God*?"

The Director merely smiled that ambiguous smile and his face shifted out of focus again. His grip on her shoulders became firmer.

"But... but I want to see them...my family... my *fans*..."

The Director shook his head.

"Not yet," he said, "It isn't your time... not yet."

Rachel started to protest but her voice was carried away, as if by a strong wind. The lights became brighter, brighter, until there was nothing but dazzling white all around her. She closed her eyes, then opened them again. She could see nothing, but she could hear someone far away yelling, "Sir! Put that damn cigarette out! If you two have been freebasing in here you could blow this whole room sky high!"

Rachel blinked again. An unfamiliar face was peering down at her. He was shining a torch in her eyes.

"Pupils are dilating. She seems responsive."

She tried to move, but quickly realized that she was strapped down to a gurney.

Another face peered at her. A familiar face this time. Jeffrey, with an unlit cigarette in his mouth. "Baby? You see me?"

Panic gripped her. She started to thrash against the restraints. Jeffrey shushed her and told her to relax. "It's okay.... Calm down, baby... I had to call the ambulance. It's gonna be okay..."

As they carried her out of the room and Rachel became more and more aware of where she was, she started screaming. A ragged, pitiful sound rose up from deep inside her guts. As Jeffrey followed them timidly out to the ambulance, he heard her scream: "Jeffrey! You motherfucker! Why did you wake me up? Why did you wake me UP???"

THIRTY-TWO

Genesis led Xavier Romero, a twenty-two year old construction worker from Peru, back to her room at East West Hotel in Koreatown. The East West was a by-the-hour dump on 8th Street, whose 40-dollar-per-night rooms were furnished with rickety lawn furniture and lumpy beds that had seen their fair share of action over the years. The kid was a little unsteady on his feet, weaving like a battered prizefighter as he followed behind. He stank of stale booze, and had picked up another bottle at the liquor store next door to the hotel. Genesis watched hungrily as he'd pulled out a wad of crumpled twenty-dollar bills, clumsily dumping them on the counter for a bottle of Old Crow Reserve. The old Korean, noting his condition, had tried to short-change him. Mindful that Xavier shouldn't give away all of his cash before she'd gotten him to the room, Genesis intervened and tucked the correct change into the pockets of Xavier's Dickies.

Genesis had originally found him staggering out of some murky Korean dive bar, drunkenly trying to light a cigarette, work clothes splattered with paint and pockets fat with crumpled notes. She asked him for a light, her tight, short dress showing off her body in all the right places. Xavier did not go in for small talk. After he lit her cigarette he looked her up and down and asked, "What does a hundred get me?" in clumsy English.

Genesis smiled, her eyes widening in faux surprise. "Anything you want, hun. Why don't you come with me, I got a room over here..."

Once they'd gotten inside the shabby hotel he'd looked a little unnerved by his surroundings: the old Bangladeshi man who sat picking his nose behind the reinforced glass at the reception desk, the threadbare carpeting, the *"NO GUESTS NO EXCEPTIONS!"* sign, and the smell of stale cigarettes and damp. She rushed him through the lobby before he got cold feet. Now Genesis was sliding the key into room 409 and shoving Xavier – who was babbling drunkenly about his wife and three kids back in Lima – into the room. She clicked on the light, and pointed him toward the bed.

"I'm gonna go freshen up honey," she said, "Why don't you get comfortable?"

Xavier staggered toward the disheveled twin bed. Genesis closed the bathroom door behind her. She pulled back the shower curtain quietly. Lupita was standing in the bathtub with the Heckler and Koch in her hand. Noticing the weapon Genesis frowned. Lupita put the gun to her lips in a *shushing* motion.

You found someone? Lupita mouthed.

Genesis nodded. *He's on the bed. What's with the gun?*

It's a robbery, Genesis. I don't want him to get stupid with me.

It's not loaded though?

Lupita shrugged. *What use is an unloaded gun? Is this guy okay?*

Harmless. Drunk. He's got money, too. Just got paid.

Good. C'mon.

In the other room Xavier was on the bed, his pants pulled around his ankles, grimly trying to massage his bourbon-numbed pecker into some semblance of life. He took another hit from the bottle. He didn't want a repeat of what happened with the black whore he'd picked up two weekends ago. She'd demanded full payment even though he couldn't get hard. *Lousy black bitch* he fumed, still working his cock, *I should have kicked her ass.* He'd paid her because she started screaming for her pimp. Besides, he imagined the disgrace he would have caused his family if he had been arrested for beating a *prostitute*. He thought about what his wife Fermina would say if she could see him now in this scummy room waiting for a white whore to fuck him. Xavier Romero lay back, still thinking absently about his wife, still kneading his prick furiously when the door to the bathroom opened.

He found himself staring down the barrel of a gun.

A different girl, not the white whore that had brought him here, was yelling at him in Spanish.

"Don't move motherfucker, don't move!"
    Xavier froze. *"What's the problem?"*
    "This is a fucking stick up. Stop touching that little dick of your, or I'll blow it clean off!"
    Xavier raised his hands, and felt his penis go flaccid in an instant. "Don' shoot," he said, in English.

Genesis crept out of the bathroom behind Lupita. An apologetic smile on her lips. Xavier spat, "Fucking... white... *BITCH!*"
    Lupita pressed the gun against Xavier's face. "That white bitch is the love of my fucking life. One more word out of you, asshole, and I'll kill you right now."
    Xavier decided to keep his goddamned mouth shut.
    "Sorry man," Genesis said, shrugging. "It's a dog eat dog world out there. We're just surviving, you know?"
    Xavier scowled, but said nothing. He turned his head away, unwilling to look at the gun that pointed at his face a moment longer. A pained expression came over him. Almost feeling a sorry for the poor bastard Genesis crept forward and said, "You know... maybe you should stop picking up whores, you know? When you're *drunk*, at least. Or maybe you could go to a cathouse or something? There's tons of 'em in Hollywood if

259

you ask around. Doing shit like this, picking up girls from the street, you're kinda leaving yourself wide open..."

Xavier shrugged, sulkily. Lupita cocked the gun and rolled her eyes at Genesis. "What are you, his fucking life coach?"

"I'm just *sayin'*. He's got a wife and three kids back in... uh, where are you from?"

"Peru," Xavier said.

"Right. A family back in Pay-Roo that he's supposed to be supporting, and now he's getting ripped off because he doesn't use his head. I'm just tryin' to *help*."

"Well *don't*, okay? Let's just get this shit over with. Toss the wallet over, cocksucker. No tricks."

Reluctantly, Xavier did as he was told. He carefully reached into the pockets of his Dickies and pulled out a fake leather wallet. As he pulled it out some loose notes came vomiting out on the bed. "Get that for me, will you, Genesis hun?"

Genesis approached the bed cautiously and scooped the money toward her. She rifled through the wallet expertly. "Here." She tossed his phony-looking state ID back to him.

"What are you doing?" Lupita asked.

"We don't need his ID."

"So?"

"We're already taking his bread! No point in ruining his night completely..."

Genesis started counting the money.

"So you got a family, huh?" Lupita growled.

"Yes."

"Bet they're counting on that money each month, huh?"

Xavier nodded moodily.

"But you think it's okay to blow your money on pussy, huh?"

Xavier said nothing.

"You wanted to fuck her, huh?" Lupita carried on, her voice rising in indignation. "You wanted to fuck my girlfriend? I'll bet she have given you something you couldn't get at home, huh? You fucking piece of *shit*. You wanted to *fuck* my *girlfriend?*"

"Shit, Lupe, calm down!" Genesis put her hand on Lupita's shoulder. She was trembling. "It's cool. We made out good, three hundred. Let's get out of here."

"Not yet. I got something I gotta do first. Reach into my bag over there. There should be a package, wrapped in plain brown paper. Right on top. You got it?"

"Yeah. I found it."

The package was about a foot long, heavy and round. Genesis unwrapped it. Inside was a red, votive candle. It bore an image of the strange, skeletal saint whose grinning visage had been plastered all over Mama Z's place.

"Oh what the fuck is *this*, Lupe?"

"Just light it, okay?" Then, focusing on Xavier again, "Strip." Xavier looked confused.

"*Quitar la ropa!*"

Xavier began undressing. Genesis pulled Lupita aside. While Xavier dropped his shorts Genesis whispered, "*What the fuck are you doing?*"

"Look Genesis, I gotta be straight with you. There *was* something I wasn't telling you back at Mama Z's place. The thing is… we gotta kill this guy."

"*What?*"

"It's the only way to lift the curse. We're gonna be dodging bad luck the rest of our lives unless we get this death sentence of Paco's from over our heads. That's the ritual I was talking about. The prayer that Mama Z gave me… it has to be conducted in the presence of someone who died. Who *just* died. You have to do it before the spirit leaves the body. They carry the petition up with them… from my lips to the spirit's ears."

There was a frozen moment in the room as Genesis tried to process this information. Then her face contorted in fury.

"You fucking *liar!* You were planning this all along? I fucking *KNEW* something was up. Why couldn't you be *straight* with me?"

"Because I knew you'd be upset."

"UPSET?" Genesis was yelling now, "You made me a *promise,* Lupe! You swore..."

"Enough! Calm down!"

Genesis burst into tears. Lupita kept the gun on Xavier, but glanced over to Genesis. "Shit," Lupita hissed, "this isn't the time for a fucking lover's quarrel, okay? We can talk about this *later!*"

"Later? You mean AFTER you KILL him?"

Genesis said it loud enough this time for Xavier to hear.

Lupita cocked the gun at Xavier. Genesis turned away and started sobbing bitterly behind her. At the mention of killing him, a now naked Xavier had leapt to his feet and put both of his hands in the air.

"Please don't kill me, lady!" he begged in Spanish, *"I have a family. You have my money! Please don't kill me."*

Lupita's finger tightened around the trigger... but something made her hesitate. Something buried in his chest hair that caught her eye, glittering in the hotel room's dim light. She frowned, and peered at him closely. Motioning to his chest with the gun, she asked, "What the fuck is that?"

Xavier looked down at the gold pendent around his neck. It was an image of Death, framed in gold.

"This?" he said softly, holding up the pendent so she could see, *"Santa Muerte."*

Lupita immediately loosened her trigger finger and dropped the gun a little. She shook her head, a sick smile on her lips. "Jesus fucking *Christ.* You gotta be kidding me! Siddown, asshole!"

"Please don't kill me..."

"Sit down and shut the fuck up, okay? I gotta think. Genesis, get over here."

Genesis stopped sobbing a little, and sniffed. "What do you *want*?"

"Grab our stuff. We're getting out of here."

Genesis wiped her snotty face with the back of her hand. "Right now?"

"Yeah. Right now."

Lupita walked over to the bed, and brutally smashed Xavier across the back of the skull with the butt of the gun. His brain smashed violently against the inside of his cranium. Coupled with the effect of the booze, the blow put him out cold. He fell back onto the bed. She cracked him on the skull one more time to make sure that he wouldn't get up for a while.

"Thank you," Genesis said, as she gathered up their stuff. "Thank you for not killing him. That means a lot to me."

Lupita shrugged, silently fuming. She had just about enough of Genesis's fucking nagging. She didn't mention that she *couldn't* kill him after seeing that he was under the protection of Santa Muerte. If she did that she'd have simply been swapping one kind of bad luck for another.

Taking Lupita's silence as a prompt to carry on Genesis softened her voice and said, "I mean it sweetie. That's a great first step. You've got to *stop*. It's becoming a real... problem for you."

"This is not a *problem*," Lupita said through gritted teeth, "We gotta perform this ritual, otherwise bad luck is gonna follow us for the rest of our fuckin days."

"But there's *always* an excuse! Can't you see that? You had to kill this one in self-defense. You gotta kill this one to cure our bad luck. This is all just... it's too *convenient*. You're just making excuses! You got to quit killing people, Lupe. You've got to do it *cold turkey*."

"We gotta perform the ritual, and we gotta do it soon."

Genesis sighed, exasperated. "I don't believe that we *do*, Lupe. What kind of a religion can condone cold blooded murder?"

Lupita laughed sourly and asked, "And you say you *grew up* in this country?"

Lupita tucked the gun away, and stomped around the room looking for any trace of evidence that they might have left behind. "Look, what if I promise to find someone... someone who's a real *asshole*. Someone with no fuckin' wife and kids back home. Like a – a child molester, or something?"

Genesis shook her head. "I got a better idea. Just don't kill *anybody*. It's that easy."

"It's *not* that easy. Fuck, you don't *understand*, baby. It's *not* that easy..."

"It can be," Genesis said. She came over to Lupita and wrapped her arms around her. Lupita froze but Genesis pulled her closer, nestling her face between her breasts. "Just let me help you," she said running a comforting hand through her lover's hair, "You've got a problem, Lupe, honest-to-god you *do*. We need to fix it right now... if we can't work this out then how can we have a future? I'm asking *one thing* from you. No more killing. Can't you make me that promise?"

Lupita muttered something non-committal.

"What you say?"

"I said, we'd better get out of here before this bastard wakes up and I'm *forced* to kill him. Alright?"

Content to take whatever small victory she could get, Genesis nodded and said, "Okay." She kissed Lupita lightly on the forehead. She went over to the nightstand, and grabbed the half-full bottle of bourbon before they split. The room had been rented using cash and one of Lupita's many fake IDs. By the time Xavier woke up, Genesis and Lupita would be gone without a trace.

They headed out of the hotel and onto 8th street with the gun stashed in the bag. Their next stop was to meet Lupita's LA heroin connection, Macho. As they walked toward the car

264

Lupita said, "I haven't made any promises, Genesis hun. Don't go thinking just because I let that bozo live that I'm making *promises*."

"I know," Genesis said sadly. "Let's just take it... one day at a time, okay? Not killing that guy was a great start. You say you can't promise anything. But can't you at least promise me that you'll *try*?"

"That's just it, Genesis hun. You seem to be under the impression that I can't help myself. That I'm some kinda... psychopath. That's not the way it is! Each time I did it... I did it out of *necessity*."

Genesis laughed sadly. "You sound just like my pop."

"How d'you mean?"

"Every time he'd take a drink. Once he started he just couldn't stop till it was all gone and he was passed out in some whore's bed, stinking and shaking. But he swore up and down that he didn't have a problem with the booze. That's what he'd yell at my mom: *I HAVE stopped drinking! This time was an EXCEPTION!*"

"That's a whole different thing, hun. If I don't perform the ritual then we're fucked. We got some bad vibes hanging over us after what went down with Paco. Ain't nothing gonna go our way again unless we fix it."

"Come on. Paco was a meth dealer, not a fuckin' tater tot, or whatever you called it..."

"Tata Nganga, Genesis. He was a Tata Nganga. It's, like, a high priest."

"Well, whatever. If we're so fuckin' cursed, how come it all went okay with old Xavier up there? If this curse was so fucking strong, how come we was able to rob his ass and get away with it?"

"It *didn't* go okay. Far from it! Remember, I wasn't just there to rob his ass. I was there to lift this damn curse, so it *definitely* didn't go according to plan."

Genesis threw her arms up in exasperation. "I'm sick of all this voodoo talk!"

"Look sharp," Lupita said, "We're bein' tailed."

Glancing to her left, Genesis saw a black BMW crawling up the street beside them. Through the tinted glass she could make out the driver was gesturing wildly at them.

"Well look at this prick," Genesis smirked as she proudly strutted down the street in her heels, "He's seen me all dressed up in my fuck-me clothes, and he's just about goin' crazy."

"Looks like he might have got some bread. Come on."

"What? Oh shit, Lupe *wait*..."

But it was too late. Lupita was already over by the car as the automatic window rolled down. Cursing to herself, Genesis clip-copped over to the window. A large man in a stained, wrinkled suit leaned out to them.

"You lookin' for something, mister?" Lupita asked, smiling at him.

"I'm looking to have some fun. I have drugs! Enough for all of us. How much for the both of you to get in the car, get a little high with me... and then maybe we can all get naked?"

"Five hundred," Lupita said without hesitating. "Each." A cold smile formed on her lips.

Oblivious, the man nodded his head. "Get in."

The door unlocked. Genesis grabbed Lupita and hissed, "What are you doing? We already made our money, let's go!"

"You heard him, Genesis hun. He's got drugs, and he's got money. We don't wanna look a gift horse in the mouth."

Reluctantly Genesis nodded. She pulled Lupita in close and whispered, "Remember what you said. You said that you'd *try*, Lupe."

Lupita nodded the faintest of nods before she clambered into Jacques Seltzer's rental car. Genesis followed reluctantly behind.

"Ladies!" Jacques grinned lasciviously, and then they peeled out with a squeal of rubber.

THIRTY-THREE

i

Randal was stepping out of another identikit AA meeting, this one at a café on Fountain and Vine, when his phone rang. It looked at it: Gibby.

"Gibby. What's happening?"

Gibby sounded even more harassed than usual.

"What's *happening* is that that shit has hit the fan, big time. Have you heard from Jacques?"

"Me? Nah, why would I? Last time I saw him he was passed out in the crapper at *Phillipe's*. He's with Jeffrey, isn't he?"

"I wouln't know. I haven't heard from him in days. His phone's switched off."

"He's probably passed out in a gutter somewhere."

"Yeah, I guess, maybe." Gibby sounded unconvinced. "If that's all it is, then his timing is *fucked*. I need to speak to him right now or we're all up shit creek. Kenny got hip to my little trick with the *Black Neon* script. He knows it's a fake and he's threatening to pull the plug."

Randal stifled a laugh. "Oh shit! How did he find out?"

"Christ knows. My money is on that bitch Sharon Lindenbaum. She hated Jacques from day one, and I'm guessing she demanded to see what Jacques had come up with. She's a hell of a lot smarter than Kenny is. She'd have spotted that it was a phony straight away. *Fuck!* I had Kenny on the phone screaming at me for an hour and a half. He says if Jacques doesn't sit down with him for an emergency meeting *today* he's gonna have Dreamscape's lawyers bury *Black Neon*, and they're gonna throw me in the pit before they start filling it in. Oh God," Gibby sounded like he was on the verge of tears, "If I don't get hold of Jacques today, I'm fucking *ruined*."

"Shh, it'll be cool Gibby." Randal did his best to placate the hysterical agent. "It's probably nothing. His phone's just off. Maybe he's sleeping off a heavy night or something. He'll be back sooner or later. Once you get Jacques in a room with Kenny it'll all be fine again. Seems like Jacques knows how to butter Kenny up. He'll just sprinkle a bit of that Jacques Selzter magic on the situation and Kenny'll cool out. You know how dramatic the little fuck can be..."

"It's not just Kenny!" Gibby whined, "I'm really *worried* about Jacques! Up until a few days ago he'd been uploading pictures and video to a server, you know, gathering material for the movie. Hundreds and hundreds of images, hours of film footage too..."

"You're *kidding* me. I'm impressed, to tell you the truth... I'm pretty shocked old Jacques has been doing anything, besides get high..."

"That's just it, Randal. The amount of shit he's been uploading.... With Kenny crawling up my ass over the script, it'd just been too overwhelming to deal with. Last night I finally got a chance to start going through the material.... And to tell them truth, I'm pretty fucking *disturbed* by it."

Randal found his car, pulled an orange parking ticket off the windshield and dropped it in the gutter. He slid into the driver's seat. "Disturbed? Howdya mean?"

"It's just.... well look, you know the kinds of images that are Jacques' stock in trade. Extreme shit. But *this* stuff... it's different. These images are.... Repellent. Twisted."

"Gibby, you told me Jacques exhibited pictures of a guy getting meth injected into his pecker before now. What makes these pictures so awful?"

"I guess the main thing is that Jacques is *in* most of them. The whole line between observer and the observed.... It's just *gone.* I got tons of footage on my hard-drive of these emaciated, dead-eyed crackhead whores fixing dope and turning tricks on filthy looking mattresses... and if you look closely, there's fucking Jacques like some junkie Alfred Hitchcock making a cameo in his own film! I don't even know who *shot* half of this stuff. It sure as hell wasn't Jacques. I mean, there he is, all flushed and tweaked out, sucking on the tit of some bugged-out, toothless transsexual meth freak, or fixing a shot while some underage hooker turns a trick in the bed next to him... it's really sick shit, man!

"And that's not all of it. I've got hours of Jacques interviewing junkies, street freaks, prostitutes. He's getting high with them on camera, screwing them, all of this interposed with footage of him checking motel rooms for bugs and ranting about how David Lynch is using his connections with the FBI to steal Jacques' ideas. Jacques seems *crazy*. Like he went over the edge, totally."

"Gibby, I kinda got the impression he'd gone over the edge a long time ago..."

"Shit! You don't *know* him like I do, Randal. Sure, Jacques is an animal. Sure he loves this stuff, the sleaze, the grittiness, the underbelly.... But there was always a *line*. He'd go right up to it so he could record everything he saw, but up until now..." Gibby trailed off, a despondent sound in his voice.

"Look, I'm serious Randal. I'm worried about him. I never saw Jacques this fucked up before. This is a whole new depth he's sunk to. He looks like a bum in these pictures. Some of these final shots I received... the *people* he's with... there's something really unsettling abut them, it's beyond deviant. Jacques isn't observing the scene anymore, Randal, he's up to his fucking neck in it. I'm worried Jacques has gone *native* on me, man. This is some real Colonel Kurtz type shit..."

"When was the last time you heard from him?"

"Right after he disappeared off with Jeffrey. There's been no new photos, no calls, zero. I'm warning you Randal, if that fucking asshole you hooked him up with has let anything happen to Jacques I'll kill that junkie bastard myself."

"Jacques is a big boy. I'm sure he's fine. Maybe you just need to get him out of LA for while, cool him out."

"My thoughts exactly. But unless I get Jacques in a room with Kenny today it's all gonna be a moot fucking point, because the film is *dead*. That's why I need you to speak to Jeffrey and find out what the fuck is going on."

Randal winced at the suggestion. "Look Gibby, part of the reason I even put you in touch with Jeffrey is that I needed to get away from this whole mess. I'm already too involved for my liking."

"Randal, *please*. Jeffrey's your friend. Just call him, find out where Jacques is. Pass on the message that I really, really need to speak to him. This is life or death we're talking about here!"

"Shit. Okay, Gibby. Okay."

"Good. Good, thanks Randal. Call me back, I'll be waiting."

Randal clicked the phone shut. He was suddenly ravenously hungry. He decided he would drive over to *El Siete Mares* and pick up some fish tacos. His stomach growled psychosomatically.

ii

"Jeffrey!"

"Randal... hey buddy."

"What you doing?"

Jeffrey looked around his heroin dealer Peewee's chaotic apartment. Peewee was cross-legged on the floor watching a Mexican wrestling flick, *Santo vs The Mummies Of Guanajuato*, on cable. His sister, Patricia, was smoking a primo and staring vacantly at a series of cigarette burns that ran the length of her arm. In front of Jeffrey were his spoon, needle, cotton and lighter laid out before him like the components of a Japanese tea ceremony.

"Uh, nothing..." he said.

"You know, I just got a call from Gibby. He's freaking out big time. Worried about Jacques."

"That piece of shit? " Jeffrey scowled, "What's he worried about *him* for?"

"Because he hasn't heard from him in days. Is he still with you?"

"Nah. I haven't seen that bastard in a while. We had a bit of trouble... a disagreement I guess you'd call it."

"What kinda disagreement?"

"I, uh... it was the kind of disagreement where I kicked him in the balls and he stormed off. Ain't seen him since."

"Shit. Maybe he's just hiding out in his room?"

"I dunno. I had to take Rachel to the ER, she fuckin' OD'd on coke. Instead of helping, that fat shithead started filming her while she was having a fucking seizure, and then tried to talk me out of calling an ambulance. Can you believe that shit? Then to top it all off, when I was waiting around in the hospital to see how she was, the fucking pigs showed up looking for us. Fucking paramedics told them about the drugs in our room. I had to slip out before they clocked me. I just left her there, bro. I went back to the hotel, grabbed some shit, and split. I've been hanging out with a buddy of mine, waiting for this whole mess to blow over. Last fuckin' thing I need is the heat showing up at my room asking all kinds of questions. I ain't heard shit from Rachel either, so I'm figuring they probably busted her. When you called I was kinda hoping it might have been her calling me from downtown..."

"Look – where are you? I'm gonna come by, pick you up. We gotta go check on Jacques, make sure he's alright."

"Fuck that guy!" Jeffrey said, then looking at his works laid out in front of him, "And anyway, I'm busy. That guy's a real asshole. If you ask me, he probably got himself killed already. As soon as that prick moved into the Gilbert he had every fucking junkie creep in Hollywood passing in and out, getting high on his dollar. Motherfucker was acting like Daddy fuckin' Warbucks. I'm talking *ounces* of shit just laying around. I told him, you keep waving that stack around like that and someone is gonna take it from you. In this scene a man could get his throat cut for a ten-dollar bill, you know? Silly cunt wouldn't listen to me. If you ask me, it's a miracle he made it this long. Motherfucker had no street smarts. None whatsoever."

"I hear you, Jeffrey, but unless I can get hold of Jacques today Gibby is gonna shit a brick. Let's just take a quick look for him, just to see if he's at the Gilbert or hanging out at any of his usual spots. At least that way I can get Gibby off my damn back, you know? Where are you exactly? I'm over in Silverlake right now, grabbing some food."

"I'm close to you then. Grab a pen, there's a *Jack in the Box* near here, I'll meet you over there..."

iii

"I don't believe one motherfucking thing that fat doofus says, Genesis hun. He stinks of puke, that ratty suit he's wearin' looks like it was stolen off a sleeping bum. If you ask me even that fuckin' eye-patch of his is a put on."

Lupita took a long sip of her Wild Turkey and ginger. Genesis looked confused.

"He told me he's an artist," he said slowly, "From Paris. That's in France, isn't it?"

"Paris my *ass*. And if that motherfucker is an *artist*, then I'm Mother-fucking-Theresa."

"Motherfucking Theresa," Genesis mused, "Good name for a band."

Lupita laughed. "True that."

They were in a Mexican bar in Echo Park. The jukebox was blasting a particularly ferocious slice of merengue called "Qué será lo que quiere el negro" by Miriam Cruz. The barmaids wore tight, white shirts that left folds of their soft, brown flesh hanging out at the tits and the belly, along with short, pleated black skirts and knee socks. When they served drinks to the smattering of washed-out old Mexican men frequenting the place, they leaned across the bar in such a way that the drink orders had to be delivered directly into the shadowy folds of their cleavage.

Jacques was here to meet his connection. He brought them inside and ordered drinks while ostentatiously flashing the wads of cash he had in his wallet. After a few minutes his cell rang to the tune of the Rolling Stones' "Brown Sugar". Jacques excused himself and had a whispered conversation by the soft glow of an ancient cigarette machine.

"He is very close," Jacques told them after he returned, "If you will excuse me for a moment, ladies, I shall return… in ten."

Lupita had shrugged, cool and non-committal. Genesis – who even didn't want to be in here in the first place – barely grunted. Jacques bowed. "Excusez moi…"

"He seems *harmless*, I suppose," Genesis offered as they waited for him to return. "I just don't know why we're doing this. If you ain't feeling it either, then let's just drink up and get the hell out of here. We made some decent bread already."

"Hell no!" Lupita snapped. "You saw the stack that mother-fucker was flashing? Besides, he's out picking up *drugs* right now. Why quit before the main event? I ain't leaving without the drugs *or* the money hun."

Genesis sniffed. "So long as that's all you're after."

"Huh?"

"You heard."

Lupita scowled. "Don't be getting all *cryptic* an' shit on me, Genesis hun. If you got something to say to me girl, then spit it out."

Genesis shrugged, half turned away from Lupita and sipped her drink.

"Out with it," Lupita hissed.

"I'm just *sayin'*. I'm hoping you ain't planning on breaking your promise to me, is all." Genesis turned and put her mouth close to Lupita's ear. "I hope you ain't planning on trying to pull some of that crazy voodoo shit with this bastard once we're alone with him."

"It ain't voodoo. It's Santeria."

"Whatever the fuck it is. That ain't the issue. I'm more concerned with whether or not you're planning on killing this idiot."

Lupita glowered at Genesis. Genesis held her gaze.

"Well?"

Lupita sniffed and turned back to her drink. "You worry too much, that's your problem."

"*My problem*?" An anguished look came over Genesis's face. "My *problem* is that the woman I love, who *says* she loves me, can't even be straight with me. You're the one who insisted on picking up this guy. I sure as hell ain't planning on fucking him, and to be honest I'm not even all that keen on the idea of getting high with him. All I wanted to do was stick to the plan, and head up to San Francisco like we'd *agreed*. You're the one who insisted on another fuckin' detour! The very least you can do is tell me if you're just planning on robbing this fucking asshole, or if you're planning on killing him. Why can't you be *straight* with me, Lupe? What's your *damage*?"

Lupita took a sip of her drink and looked at Genesis. "I ain't decided yet," she said finally, "Okay?"

"Not good enough. You promised me, Lupe. No more..." she dropped her voice again, "no more killing. You *swore*."

Lupita slammed her fist down on the bar. All around the bar, eyes darted in their direction. Lupita looked round the room with a murderous glint in her eye, and one by one the population of this dark, lonely place looked away again.

"This is about my religious freedoms!" Lupita whispered. "How dare you try and interfere with my cultural practices!"

"This ain't about your *culture*, Lupe, don't gimmie that. It's about whether or not you plan on killing someone else. You're hiding behind this whole black magic thing as a fucking excuse. Ah, what's the *point*?"

Genesis turned away, raising her shaking hands to her face.

"All right, fuck it!" Lupita hissed, grabbing Genesis by the shoulder. "You wanna break my fucking balls over this, fine! We can leave *right now* if you want. Take our fucking chances. But I'm telling you, Genesis hun, I dunno if we'll even *make* it as far as San Francisco with this bad mojo hanging over us. I don't wanna hear it from you when that fuckin' tsunami of bad luck comes crashing down on us all sudden-like, because I *warned* you girl. I told you what we gotta do, but if you don't *trust me*, then what the hell..."

"It's not about trust," Genesis said. "That's not fair."

"Of *course* it's about trust. Well fuck it, anyway. Finish up your drink. You wanna get out of here, let's do it before fatso gets back. Here I am with the woman I love, and she don't even *trust* me."

Genesis's eyes were brimming over. "Forget it," she croaked.

"Forget what?"

"Forget leaving. If you wanna see what we can get out of this guy, then fine. I *trust* you, Lupe. Okay?"

Sensing she had an advantage, Lupita pressed on. "No, no.... it's fine Genesis. Drink up. Let's go."

"I don't wanna," Genesis offered weakly.

They both lapsed into silence for a moment.

"Okay, then let's do it this way. If he ain't back by the time we finish these drinks, then we split. Otherwise we go with him. Let fate decide."

Genesis nodded, ever so slightly. She looked at Lupita's drink, which was almost finished. She looked at her own, which was three-quarters full. She picked it up and started to gulp it down, greedily. By the time Genesis had finished, Lupita's glass was drained also. Genesis looked at her expectantly.

"Okay, you win," Lupita said with an exasperated sigh, "Let's go."

As they walked toward the door, it opened. Jacques Seltzer stumbled inside, glistening with sweat.

"Ladies!" He laughed, "Leaving so soon?"

Lupita shook her head. "No way, Jack. We was just looking to see where you were. Ain't that right, Genesis hun?"

"Yeah," Genesis said weakly.

"Good! Let us get out of here, I have the stuff, I have a room. The night is young..."

Jacques turned and headed out into the evening sunlight. It was the golden hour, and everything outside this cave-like bar glowed with the vague tint of unreality. Lupita looked at Genesis, who seemed lost in her own thoughts. She nudged her and said, "Come on, Genesis hun. Shake a tail feather. You can't argue with fate, and besides... this fucking mooch ain't gonna rip *himself* off..."

iv

Randal was outside of The Gilbert fiddling with the radio, finally settling on a classic rock station. He tapped the wheel with his fingers and whistled tunelessly along with Manfred Mann's Earth Band's version of *Blinded By The Light*. A cop car crawled past him and Randal reflexively checked his reflection in the rear view mirror. He patted his glistening forehead with a Jack in The Box napkin, and took a sip of his melted ice water. He jumped when Jeffrey opened the door unexpectedly and slid into the passenger seat.

"Calm down," Jeffrey laughed, "It's just me. Why so tense?"

"I'm fine. So no luck, huh?"

"Nope. They told me he cleared out. Packed up his shit, dropped off his key and split. They ain't seen him since."

"Shit. Any other ideas?"

Jeffrey shrugged. "He could be anywhere. He's got a fucking gorilla on his back and unlimited resources to feed it. I mean, I guess we could take a look around... But unless he *wants* to be found I dunno what good it's gonna do."

Randal ran his hand through his hair. "Makes sense. Fuck it. Let's find a parking space. I could murder a fucking drink. Let's get some booze and we can figure out our next move from there..."

"Sounds good...I think I got the perfect place for us. Pal of mine from the methadone clinic was hanging out with Jacques the night before he split. They were getting real buddy-buddy, I think he ended up going over to his place. Guy claims he's old Hollywood. He was telling stories about his famous uncle, and old Jacques was just eating that shit up. He's a drunk, has a place near here. Maybe he has an idea of where Jacques is. At the very least, he should have a bottle or some pills on him."

*

Pop Gun Eddie was halfway down on a bottle of Brass Monkey when they showed up to his place. Brass Monkey was a favourite pre-lunch cocktail of Eddie's – a bottle of Olde English drunk down to the label, and then topped off with orange juice. Eddie held a firm belief that his regular intake of vitamin C in this concoction was the secret to his health and longevity.

Eddie's place was a tiny, dark apartment in a rundown complex near Selma. The door that led to the street had been busted for more than a year, and the landlord – a senile old red-head who claimed to have starred in several 'Our Gang' shorts – didn't fix shit anymore as the building was in foreclosure anyway. As a result the hallway had become a favourite place for drug dealers to make sales and the homeless to congregate after dark. Eddie didn't mind this at all: it meant he often he didn't even have to leave his own building to cop dope.

After he and Randal had picked their way around two eye-watering bums passed out near the mailboxes, Jeffrey rapped on the door.

"Hey Eddie – you there?"

Eddie let them in. He was wearing a pair of dingy, once-white boxer shorts and a stained wife-beater. In the dim light of Eddie's apartment it looked like the old guy suffered from elephantiasis of the balls: the ratty looking underwear hung heavy down to just above the knees. Jeffrey had never seen the old man not wearing his pinstripe suit, and was taken aback by how pale and skinny his legs were. They peeked out of the saggy underpants, brittle and bony, the fluorescent white flesh dotted with oddly placed patches of dark hair. There was a pumpkin-shaped belly that – like the balls – seemed weirdly at odds with how skinny the rest of his frame was.

"Pull up a pew, boys..." Eddie gurgled, motioning to the couch. The couch was covered in a dusty collection of junk – ancient magazines with stickers on them bearing the address of various doctors' surgeries, shoplifted DVDs still in the shiny packaging, a few ratty looking paperback novels, and some funky-smelling socks and undershirts. "Just shove that stuff outta your way," Eddie said, "it's the cleaning lady's day off."

They sat. On the way over to Pop Gun's place, Randal had bought a bottle of Rebel Yell and a six-pack of coke. Brushing away a copy of Time magazine with Stephen King on the cover and a DVD of *Mighty Joe Young*, Jeffrey said, "You wanna drink, Pop Gun?"

"Why not? I'm just about done with breakfast. There's some clean glasses in the sink."

Randal picked his way through the piles of junk – old fax machines, 1980s IBMs, boxes of dusty dining sets, and bundles of yellowing newspapers – that piled up around Eddie's filthy apartment, to get to the kitchen. As well as dark – the dusty shades were still drawn – the apartment was hot. The heat, coupled with the stink of unwashed bodies and stale cigarette smoke, gave the apartment an almost unbearably oppressive atmosphere. Watching Randal go, Eddie said, "So what brings you boys around these parts?"

"Looking for someone. You remember that French guy who was hanging out with us the other night?"

Pop Gun Eddie laughed a long, wheezy laugh. "Do I? Motherfucker paid me three hundred dollars to come over and take some pictures of me..." Catching himself mid-sentence, he frowned at Jeffrey. "And *no*, not *those* kinda pictures thank you very much. The pecker stayed *in* the pants, you filthy-minded bastard. He just wanted pictures of me, y'know, hanging out here. Doing my usual shit. He shot some video of us fixing dope together and he asked me a bunch of bullshit questions. Then he nodded out and pissed in his pants, right where you're sitting. He's kind of a crank, right? Told me he was a filmmaker or some kinda shit."

"That's right," Jeffrey said, sliding over to the other side of the couch. "My friend here..." Jeffrey nodded at Randal as he returned with the cocktails, "He needs to get hold of him. Except nobody knows where he is. You seen him since then?"

Before he took his glass, Eddie polished off the Brass Monkey with a long pull. He burped, tossed the empty bottle aside and started in on the whisky. "Can't say I have. He did tell me that he was, uh, goin' somewhere. Wanted to pick up some whores, he said. Even asked me if I wanted to come along, which was nice of the fellar. I told that motherfucker that I ain't got any use outta my pecker since I had my accident, ya know. Fucked up the ol' equipment when I got a bad hit shooting a speedball in my groin, back in ninety-three."

Randal and Jeffrey winced in unison.

"What happened?"

"Fuckin' gangrene." Eddie placed a protective hand over his filthy underpants. "These puppies swelled up like a pair of fuckin' cantaloupes. Never really gone back to their proper dimensions. Doctors had to stick a big syringe in there – like something you'd see a vet use on a fuckin' horse – right in the old fun sack, ya know? And they musta drained two pints of the evilest smelling yellow goo I ever saw right outta them. Since then, nuthin's been right down there. The fuckers are three times the size they useta be, but I couldn't get hard if Farrah Fawcett herself stood right here in front of me, bent over and shoved a crucifix up her asshole. It even hurts to piss mosta the time. Still..." Eddie looked reflective for a moment, "S'pose it saved me a lot of trouble in the long run. The bitches were an even harder habit to keep up than the dope, truth be told. And a hell of a lot more expensive, too."

V

Jacques was driving like a madman, weaving in and out of traffic, one hand on the wheel and his face intermittently buried between Genesis's breasts. Genesis was pouring out the contents of a coke baggie between her tits and Jacques was snorting and sniffing wildly. He made a disgusting noise as he hoovered up the cocaine, somewhere between an asthmatic warthog and a broken vacuum cleaner. Once she had seen the size of Jacques' coke stash Genesis had loosened up a little about the whole deal.

As he buried his face in her cleavage, Genesis was squealing, "Oh shit! You are fucking crazy, Jack!"

On the car stereo Jacques had the Rolling Stones' *Miss You* blasting at an almost unbearable volume. In the backseat, Lupita watched all of this go down with an unreadable expression on her face. Her bag was next to her with their clothes, the guns, and the shit Mama Z had given her all tucked away for later. Every so often she would glance up to make sure that they weren't weaving into ongoing traffic, or to look around for cops. So far it seemed that Jacques' luck was holding. When he finally dislodged his head from Genesis's tits his face was red and sweaty, cocaine smeared around his mouth and nose. He looked like a fat kid who had just sneezed into a bag of powdered sugar.

"Watch the road, Jack," Lupita intoned.

"Real cocaine and fake tits!" Jacques screamed, "My favourite combination!"

"Honey, who said these titties were fake?" Genesis pouted, adjusting her top.

She flirted with the practiced efficiency of the seasoned whore. Jacques wiped his face with a sweaty hand and then licked the coke residue off his palm with a fat, pink tongue. "They are real?" he asked incredulously.

"Sure honey... I'm just working with what my momma gave me."

Jacques bellowed with laughter and stepped on the accelerator. Lupita fought to keep her face neutral, but the sight of this disgusting, red-faced pig slobbering all over her lover was almost more than she could bear. She could feel the rage rising in her chest, threatening to force her hand into the bag and onto the gun. She imagined drawing the gun, pressing it against the back of Jacques' head, and blowing a hole clean through his skull as they careened down the street. No doubt they would be all killed or at least maimed in the ensuing crash, but the more that Jacques pawed Genesis the less Lupita cared about the consequences. Jacques looked into the rear view mirror and caught Lupita's steely gaze on him.

"I think she is having fun with me, yes?"

"What – about the tits? Could be..." Lupita glanced coldly at her lover. "Genesis here's a real laugh riot. Ain't that right, hun?"

Genesis looked at Lupita uneasily. With a stiff smile Lupita quickly changed the subject. "Anyway, can I get some of that stuff or you just planning on pouring it all between my girlfriend's tits?"

"Oh, oui! There is enough for *everybody* my dear. Look under the passenger seat..."

Lupita reached down and pulled a leather briefcase with a combination lock from under the seat. The first thing she noticed about it was the weight. It felt as though it might have several encyclopedias tucked away inside. It clicked open when Lupita pressed the release. When she saw what was inside her eyes widened in astonishment.

"What the fuck *is* this?" she asked in a faltering voice, "I mean... this shit isn't what I *think* it is, is it?"

Inside the case were several large brick-shaped objects, wrapped tightly in wax paper, bound together with thick colour-coded rubber bands. Jacques grinned, his eyes darting between Lupita's astonished face and the road ahead. "Well my dear, that would depend on what you think it is. It is the drugs, oui? Four bricks – cocaine, freebase, heroin and methamphetamine. Two point two pounds apiece, and the finest quality around."

"No – fuckin' – *way*!" screamed Genesis, scrambling halfway into the backseat to gawp at the briefcase on Lupita's lap, "Lemmie see."

Jacques looked over to his right, and found himself face-to-face with Genesis's ass as she wiggled excitedly to get a better look at the drugs. He leaned into it and bit her lightly on the buttock. Genesis squealed.

A dark look crossed her face as Lupita snapped the case shut. "And you're just driving around with this kinda weight in your car? You could get us put away for *years* pulling a stunt like that. Not to mention *killed.*"

Jacques sniffed loudly again, sending a gooey mixture of snot and cocaine gushing into his esophagus. "I am an *artiste* my dear. I do not fear death any more than I fear the police. In fact, I *court* death – it seems to be the least awful thing that could happen to someone, oui? You say this beautiful girl... is you *girlfriend*?"

"That's right."

Jacques turned his attention back to Genesis, who was sitting in the passenger seat again. "Does she fuck you well, my love?"

Genesis leaned in and licked the white tip of Jacques' nose. "She's the best I ever had," she said.

"*Magnifique,*" Jacques breathed. "Young love... it is so ... beautiful. I was in love once. A long time ago." Jacques shook his head, and stared at Genesis again. "I want to watch the two of you... make love."

"Make love, fuck, whatever you say, Jack baby. It's your dollar. Now lemmie have some more of that coke, baby." Genesis pouted as she said it, shooting Jacques a little-girl-lost look that made his pants tighten.

"Of course!"

Without taking his foot off the accelerator, Jacques reached down to his ankle and pulled a hunting knife from his snakeskin Chelsea boot. He tossed it, still folded up, to Lupita. She caught it with a fluid movement. "Dig in," he laughed, "There is more than enough to go around..."

Lupita was beginning to realize just what a prize catch Jacques really was. He was clueless, almost idiotically trusting. Probably the asshole figured that there was no way he could ever be in danger dealing with a couple of chicks. He seemed to be the type – not a woman hater exactly, but at the very least a casual misogynist. No, Jacques would pose no problem at all.

She glared at Genesis as she ran her hands through Jacques' greasy hair. God*damn*, she knew they were meant to be lulling him into a false sense of security, but did the bitch have to flirt with him quite so *brazenly*? She knew the girl liked dick, but still the sight of her allowing this fat, sweaty monster paw her body made Lupita's flesh crawl. Shivering, she plunged the knife into one of the packages and ripped a hole in it, sending a small white cloud puffing up into the air. She had struck coke. She dug the blade around and slowly slid it out again with a heavy pile of white powder clumped on the tip. She held it to her nose and inhaled. She knew immediately that the stuff was high grade. It sent a frosty blast of pleasure tearing through her skull, numbing her palate as quickly as a shot of lidocaine. Jacques watched her as she did it, his eyes darting between her face, her lithe body, and the arm that ended at the elbow.

"My dear," he declared, "Your body is incredible. You are possessed of a rare beauty. If you don't mind me saying, I find your missing arm incredibly... *erotic*."

"Nah," Lupita said with a dry smile on her lips, "you ain't the first to tell me that."

"I am sure. I assure you that my photographs of you will soon be hanging on the walls of the most prestigious galleries in Europe!"

"Uh-huh. Seems more likely they're gonna end up on some fucking amputee porn website. Is that were you get make your money, pal? You, like, one of those Internet perverts or something?"

"Pornography?" Jacques spat the word out. "Is that what you think of me? Some kind of low-rent exploiter of women?"

Lupita fixed herself a blast for the other nostril, before handing the shit over to Genesis in the front seat.

"Sure, why not? I mean, it's either that or drugs, right? A guy like you, driving around in a fancy-ass car with enough coke to destabilize the economy of a small Central American country? That's what I figured. I mean... let's be honest. You don't seem to be the drug dealer type, ya know? Fellow like you looks like he wouldn't last two minutes in that game... No offence."

Taking a blast of the coke, Genesis cooed in her best Betty Boop voice, "Of *course* we don't think that, honey... Lupe's just teasing. You said you're an *artist*, right?"

Jacques laughed. "My dear, I not think that your beautiful girlfriend here shares your confidence in my honesty. For my sins I *am* an artiste. A low rent exploiter of my own talents, if you will. But enough bullshit. My dear, can you pour a little more of this nose candy between those beautiful breasts for me?"

"Sure thing, baby."

Genesis poured a monstrous amount of blow between her tits, which were still moist with Jacques slobber. Jacques looked into the rear view mirror and fixed Lupita in a maniacal gaze.

"I am an artist, my dear. An artiste and an explorer. I am here to find America's soul!"

With that he stuck his face between Genesis's tits again, snorting wildly. The car swerved, and around them drivers honked and screeched on their brakes.

"Well good luck with that my friend," Lupita said, a dangerous look on her face, "'Cos I really doubt you're gonna find what you're looking for down there, you know what I'm sayin'?"

vi

In Pop Gun Eddie's apartment, halfway down on the bottle of Rebel Yell, Randal felt a familiar despair gripping his insides. Still feeling hollow and jittery because of drug-lack, he knew that the booze could at least be counted on to coat his screaming nerves and help him forget his misery. It was a transient solution though. Unlike meth, booze burned its way through Randal's system quickly, requiring more and more to maintain the illusion of comfort. Instead of the clarity and focus that meth granted him, the more booze he poured into the gaping hole in his psyche, the slower and sloppier Randal felt himself becoming. He could feel the whisky doing its job as he drained his glass. Next to him, Jeffrey and Pop Gun Eddie crushed their methadone tablets for injection. Artificial goodwill bubbled up inside Randal, the notion that people were subtly becoming friendlier, stories more interesting, even the smells that permeated Pop Gun's squalid apartment seemed less gag-inducing the more he drank.

The rising despair stemmed from the fact that Randal remained stubbornly aware that this was an illusion, that after the next drink his current state would inevitably give way to something else. Randal would morph into a loud, sloppy cartoon of his normal self. The benevolent goodwill that Randal felt toward all men right now would become an embarrassing over-friend-liness, followed by the urge to confess all of the darkness that was inside of him, to confide in strangers, to laugh loudly at banal bullshit. Then there would be a sustained period of self-loathing. This ugly phase would end only when he slept. Tomorrow he knew he would wake with a burning head and a sour belly and begin the frantic recriminations: reliving every stupid word, every phony smile until he could take it no more. He would be forced to either drink again, get high, or punch himself repeatedly in the face.

For now he just drank and tried to drown out the nagging part of his brain that knew what was around the corner, losing himself in Jeffrey and Pop Gun's brow-furrowed murmurs as they probed their bloody arms with needles and absently talked shop like a pair of old businessmen swapping trade secrets.

"Well, you know, Rachel always tells me to soak 'em first.... Says it gets the blood up..."

"Nah, that's an old wive's tale. You gotta drink water. That's the key. If you're even a little bit dehydrated, the shit won't *flow*. You know, my Uncle John... he did a movie with Lucille Ball. *The Magic Carpet*. Now John, he never fucked with no dope, he was strictly a juicer. But he *swore* to me that Lucille was heavily strung out on this shit called bufotenine, which is a heavy hallucinogenic extracted from the venom of the Sonoran Desert Toad. Claims she used to inject the stuff into her ass on regular basis."

"No shit? What about Desi?"

"I dunno about Desi. But I did hear that Albert Most – fellar who founded the Church of the Toad of Light in Colorado – was a fanatical fan of I Love Lucy, and that's what hipped him to the whole toad-juice thing. Those guys collect the slime and smoke it. It's, like, a sacrament, ya know?"

Randal looked at his glass. Maybe this time, he thought, he would finish this drink and leave it alone. After all, it was the middle of the afternoon and they were supposed to be out finding Jacques. Pop Gun Eddie had given them a lead, albeit a slender one. He felt good now, good enough at least, and maybe if stopped while he was feeling good he could sidestep tomorrow's recriminations and regret. He drained his glass feeling determined, and cautiously upbeat.

After feeding his hit in slow and easy, pushing the chalky mixture into his calcifying veins, Jeffrey sat back and sighed. "Man, that shit is a hell of a lot more bearable if you shoot it."

"Yeah, the juice ain't worth a shit. These pills came from a place south of the border. Got a buddy who makes the trip to Juarez regular, got a family who run a little *farmacia* who know him pretty well down there. He always sells me a little excess to cover his travel expenses."

Jeffrey noted Randal's empty glass and said, "I'm gonna need a minute, man. Don't think I could walk right now. You wanna get another drink?"

Randal looked at Jeffrey, and then back at his empty glass. Sensing that he had no choice in the matter he said, "Sure. Why the hell not?"

After he'd poured the drink, Pop Gun looked Randal up and down. Next to him Jeffrey sank into a heavy nod.

"You're real worried about this French guy, huh?"

Randal looked up from his glass with a puzzled expression. "Me?"

"Yeah you. He a pal of yours?"

"A *friend*? Not exactly. I can't stand the fucking prick."

"Well if it ain't this French fellar, what is it? *Something's* bothering you. You've been starin' at your glass the last twenty minutes like a man with the weight of the fuckin' world on his shoulders."

Next to him, Jeffrey yawned and stretched. He contentedly picked at the bleeding spots on his hollowed out face. "Eddie's right, man. You've been a real downer today. You sure you don't want one of these pills? It'd take the edge right off..."

Randal shook his head. "I told you, man. I'm trying to stay off all of that shit. And it ain't Jacques, okay? I'm only looking for him because I feel bad for Gibby. Plus... I'm being nosey. If Jacques really does fuck up this movie thing then an asshole I know called Kenny Azura is gonna get some major egg all over his smug fucking face, and I can't wait to see that happen..."

"So what is it?" Eddie asked, with all the sweet con of a therapist dripping from his voice, "What's bugging you?"

"It's me, I guess."

"Howdja mean?"

Randal took a deep breath, considering whether or not to answer. He looked at his old friend Jeffrey, with rivulets of blood drying on his skinny arms and his dope-numbed eyes half hidden behind sleepy lids. Then over to Pop Gun Eddie with his monstrous swollen balls and useless pecker.

Shit, it wasn't as if *they* were gonna judge *him*.

"I'm going through a... well, I guess you'd call it a crisis of faith."

Jeffrey laughed. "Jesus Christ Randal, don't tell me you fucking converted or some shit when you got clean! If that was the case, I'd *know* the fuckin' world was comin' to an end..."

Randal shook his head. "Not that kinda faith. It's just that... fuck, man. I was so *sure* of everything before I went clean this time; you know I mean I was so sure about how it all *worked*. But now..." Randal drifted off, his eyes searching futilely around the crummy room for the right words.

"Gimmie an example," Jeffrey said.

"Well, the whole drinking thing, for a start."

"Drinking thing?"

"Before I checked into treatment, I never really liked booze, yeah? Wasn't my thing. I mean I liked a *drink*, who doesn't? But not the same way I liked to get high. Ever since the first time I went into treatment all of those asshole therapists would tell me that I couldn't drink no more, tell me I was an alcoholic. I'd just laugh at them. You remember the guys in *Clean and Serene*, right? All those fucking arguments we'd have with the counsellors?"

"Well, yeah." Jeffrey sneered, "It's a lotta horse shit."

"Right! Except... except this time when I came out of the treatment centre, I cut out *everything* for like six months. Booze too. My fuckin' brother had me on a real short leash and was giving me piss tests and all that kind of shit." Randal looked over to Eddie. "My brother's into the whole twelve-step thing in a big way. He got clean in the fuckin' Eighties. He's been hooked on those meetings almost as long as he'd been a cokehead, you know? But he follows that shit to the letter, never misses a meeting, sponsors like six guys, the whole bit. A real pillar of the fuckin' community."

Eddie nodded sagely.

"So I'd *never* been this clean for this long before. Harvey has control of our pop's estate, and he's been threatening to cut me out of my inheritance if I don't get my shit together. I had no choice. For six months, I was living like a fuckin' monk. After a while, Harvey gives me a bit of space, thank Christ. But I'm determined, you know, not to fuck up this time. I stay totally away from the speed, you know, that was really my thing. But I started drinking again. I needed *something* to ease the pressure, you know? This time though, it was kinda... different."

Pop Gun leaned forward, his brow furrowing. "Different how?"

"Well, just knowing that the booze was *all* I could do... it made me treat it different. I'd never drank every day before. Never felt the urge. But all of a sudden, that's what I'm doing. Four o'clock every day I'd have a cocktail. Just the one. And that first fucking sip... it was like... '*Ahhhh!*' Relief, you know? Then pretty soon it's not just the one cocktail, it's a bunch. And it ain't happening at four o'clock, it's three. And then two. The drinking was different, I guess 'cos I was drinking to try and fill the hole that was left by the meth, you know? And it wasn't just how much I was drinking – how the booze *worked* on me was different too."

"You mean you started getting hangovers and shit?"

"No, not that. But the next day I would feel... depressed, I guess is the word. Really down. I found myself watching the clock, just waiting for four o'clock to roll around. That's why I started drinking earlier and earlier. Because I'd get too fucking *impatient*. I just felt like..."

Randal drifted off, mortified by the words that were about to come out of his mouth. He fidgeted uncomfortably. Before he could force the words out, Pop Gun Eddie beat him to the punch.

"You felt like an alcoholic?"

Randal almost physically recoiled at this suggestion. "No," he said quickly, before quietly adding, "I guess. Not really, but... *yeah*."

All three of them sat there for a while saying nothing. Randal rubbed his hand over his face. He was suddenly bathed in sweat. Jeffrey looked like he may well have been sleeping, eyes closed to serene half slits. Pop Gun Eddie straightened up and cleared his throat.

"You know what I think?" he said.

"What?"

"I think that there's no way in hell you're an alcoholic."

"I agree," Jeffrey chipped in. "I've known you too long, Randal. And I've known *plenty* of alcoholics. You're a natural born speed freak. You ain't a juicer."

Even though it was a pair of bedraggled dope-fiends telling him this, Randal was ready to seize upon any suggestion that this deep, dark fear he harboured was unfounded. "You don't think?"

"Your problem," Pop Gun continued with an air of ragged authority, "is that you *think* too much. You still going to them meetings?"

"Yeah. Now and then."

"You see, *that's* the problem." Pop Gun waggled his finger at Randal in a gently chastising manner. "Those meetings got you pathologizing yourself. Analyzing yourself, defining yourself in those terms. *That's* why your drinking changed. Now you're *ashamed* to drink! You weren't before. Now you judge yourself, and you view everything through this prism of *addiction*. Every time you drink you get down on yourself. You're hiding it from those guys at the meetings, I'll bet. Your brother know you're juicing?"

"Of course not. He'd freak."

"Sure he would! Even though what you're doing is perfectly legal and socially accepted, you gotta hide it because those cats look *down* on that kinda behavior. They've got you *thinking* like an alcoholic, Randal. That's why you're *drinking* like an alcoholic."

Jeffrey laughed. "I like that Pop Gun. You could start a support group with a slogan like that."

Randal smiled at this, and Pop Gun sat back with a big stoned grin on his face.

"I guess you have a point." Randal conceded.

"A point?" Jeffrey said, "The man's speaking *gospel*, Randal. Look at me, man. I know I'm physically dependent on this shit, yeah? Of course I do. But I don't *care*. I'm a dope-fiend because that's what I *want* to be. It's all I *can* be, truth be told. The difference between what I do or what Eddie does and what *you* do is fucking simple. I ain't *ashamed* of how I live my life. That's why I stay away from those damn meetings. The way those fuckers operate... it's just like the church, and I had a gut-full of that shit when I was younger. Those fucking meetings, they *thrive* on shame, man."

Jeffrey bent over, picked up his glass, and finished his drink. Between the methadone and the booze he felt pretty fucking good right now. He sat back, crossed his legs, and stared at Randal like a skinny, stoned Buddha.

"It isn't the drugs that fuck you up, Randal," Jeffrey said. "It's the *shame*."

Randal looked at his feet for a moment, taking in the filthy, cigarette-scarred carpet. Then he looked up at Jeffrey. "But what about *you*? You're saying that this is *it*? You made your choice? When I roomed with you at Clean and Serene you were pretty determined to stay off dope, remember that? I mean, I know none of the shit we'd planned turned out like it was supposed to... but what the fuck has changed in a year that makes you feel so sure that what you're doing is *right*, now?"

"What changed is simple. It was nuthin' to do with what happened with the sex tape, or even with that cocksucker Damian ripping us off. It was just that after I got clean... it just made me remember why I used in the first place. You get complacent about it when you've been using a long time. The grass is always greener, yeah? Shit starts to *bug* you about your habit. All of the hassles and the bullshit... you get *tired*. Like those guys who marry these beautiful chicks, and eventually they end up cheating on them with some fucking pig. It ain't that their wives ain't beautiful any more, or that they even wanna fuck that pig. They just get too comfortable in their surroundings, and forget how good they got it.

"You get tired of the hassles, so you get clean, sort your life out, all of that shit, you know? But you end up switching your one big problem for a ton of other problems. They might be *different* problems, but they're problems all the same. Being clean is a *hassle*, man. It's the same shit that you're going through right now. You gotta fill your time with some other shit, otherwise you're gonna go batshit crazy. The big joke is that the stuff that's legal and available, like booze or god or whatever.... Most of it is a hell of a lot worse for you than smack.

"It took me a long time to make peace with it, but the truth is that I prefer just having one problem to deal with than a few dozen. My life might be in the fucking toilet right now..." Jeffrey stretched his arms, as if presenting the bloody, track-marked things to Randal to emphasize his point, "but I wouldn't swap places with *you* for a million bucks. No offence."

"None taken."

"You'll probably live longer than me. You got an apartment, and a car, and clean clothes, and all of that shit. I got a whole lot of problems, but it's nothing that more dope can't fix. At least I don't have to beat myself up about who I am. At least I don't have to do a bunch of shit I *hate* to compensate for the fact I *can't* do what I *wanna* do. That's a trade-off I'm prepared to make..."

"I guess you got it all figured out," Randal muttered sourly.

"Look man, I ain't trying to do a sales pitch here. If you stay clean, then good luck to you Randal. It'd make me happy to see you live to be ninety, so long as you were *happy*. For me, a preacher in favour of dope is just as hokey as a preacher against it. I'm just telling you where I'm at in *my* life. Barring some kinda message from God himself... and believe me, I ain't holding my breath on that count... this is the way I'm gonna live, and it's probably the way I'm gonna die."

Randal picked up his empty glass, and stared at it. "Doesn't that sound kinda fatalistic to you?"

"Fatalistic?" Jeffrey snorted, "I hate to break it to you Randal, but you're gonna die too. Whether you get high or not it doesn't make a shit load of difference as far as I can see. All you gotta decide is this: how do you wanna kill time in between?"

Jeffrey sat back and stretched on the couch with a beatific grin on his face. He looked over to Pop Gun Eddie who was as stoic and still as a religious statue.

"Guess it makes sense," Randal said.

"Hell, I got nuthin' but time these days to sit around and think about it. That's the thing. People put down dope-fiends as being these thoughtless, selfish, unthinking pleasure seekers when it ain't nothing like that. As far as I'm concerned, this is a *philosophical decision*, and I made it after a lot of careful fucking consideration."

"C'mon," Randal said, standing. "We'd better keep moving. Thanks for the hospitality Eddie."

"Anytime, baby. Hope you get this shit worked out to your satisfaction."

"Thanks. When Jacques told you he was gonna look for whores, he give you any specifics?"

Pop Gun nodded. "Said he wanted some young pussy, and I told him Koreatown has a lot of that kinda action. I couldn't give him any specifics though: as I said, the last time I got this pecker wet, Clinton was in office, ya know?"

vii

In the bathroom of room 23 of the Budget Inn on Sunset Boulevard – a faceless sleaze-pit sandwiched between an outpatient drug rehab and an auto shop – Genesis and Lupita were arguing in hushed voices about whether or not to kill Jacques Seltzer.

They were both naked and severely tweaked. For the past hour they had been smoking monstrous amounts of crack with Jacques, with the occasional bump of heroin to smooth off the edges. Genesis had never seen so much crack in her entire life. The brick, a solid two-pound lump of pure freebase, gave off a pungent stench of acetone so powerful that her guts had started churning and bubbling as soon as they had unwrapped it. The first hit from the pipe had made the blood rush in Genesis's ears so intensely that she nearly blacked out. A tidal wave of pure pleasure, something in between an orgasm and a heart attack washed over her. They smoked furiously while Jacques snapped pictures of them getting high and blowing the smoke into each other's mouths'. After a while their benefactor managed to turn his attention away from the drugs long enough to instruct the girls to strip. They did as they were asked, slowly peeling their clothes away and standing naked in front of him. Before he could lay a finger on either of them Lupita grabbed Jacques by the chin and – with a sardonic smile on her lips – raised his sweaty face to hers.

"You wanna see me *fuck* her, right?" she breathed.
"Yes!"
"You wanna take pictures, yeah? *Nasty* pictures..?"
"Oui!"
"Okay baby, that's cool. But first... first we gotta renegotiate."
Lupita let the words hang for a moment to gauge Jacques' reaction. She removed her hand from his face. He didn't flinch. In fact he was nodding so furiously he resembled one of those goofy toy dogs you see in the backs of some folks' cars. Spurred on by this Lupita continued, "We want two grand to stay the night. We know you can afford it, pal. If you need to hit the old ATM or something before we get down to business, then do it now. This rock is making me as horny as hell, and once I get to work on the little lady here..." Lupita shot a theatrically seductive look in Genesis's direction, "I ain't gonna want to stop what I'm doing to run errands, you know what I'm sayin'?"

"No need," Jacques gurgled, almost breathless with desire, "I have all the money we need... right here."

Following Lupita's cue Genesis stepped forward pushing her chest out. She shoved her breasts toward Jacques. She caressed them, squeezing them together, enjoying the power they exuded over the hypnotized Frenchman. "We wanna see the green first, baby. I mean, we're having a lot of fun spending time with you an' all, but we just gotta be sure that *everybody* is on the level. We got bills to pay, ya know?"

Jacques jumped to his feet, his pants bulging out obscenely at the crotch. He rummaged through the pockets of his crumpled suit and pulled out a Wells Fargo envelope. He started counting out one hundred dollar bills on the bed. Lupita and Genesis looked at each other as the money started to pile up. When he made it to a thousand he stopped. He placed the envelope back in his jacket and turned to them. "We have a deal, yes? Half now, half later?"

Genesis and Lupita nodded at each other. Lupita snatched up the bills and fanned through them. "Looks like we're in business. Why don't you make yourself comfortable? Me and Genesis here are gonna go get ourselves ready."

Noting the look of confusion on Jacques' face she clarified, "Honey, I never travel *anywhere* without my strap-on. And you ain't lived until you seen old Mandingo in action, ain't that right, Genesis hun?"

"Oh shit," Genesis said, "You in for a fucking *treat*, honey."

Lupita leaned in and placed her face inches from Jacques face. "I hope your heart can take it, Jack... 'cos we're about to blow your fucking *mind*."

Jacques just nodded dumbly licking his dry, cracked lips as he watched as the two girls walk away. Lupita casually stooped to pick up her bag on the way, and they both went into the bathroom to 'freshen up'.

"Lupe, baby," Genesis was begging now that they were locked away in the bathroom, "Don't do it!"

"Keep your fucking voice down," Lupita whispered as she checked the clip and attached the silencer. "I don't want that fat fuck storming in here before I'm ready. Could get messy."

"You *promised* me, Lupe. This guy's no threat. And he's a fucking goldmine. There's no need to hurt him! You *swore* to me that you weren't gonna kill nobody."

"Aw *Jesus*, this again? Okay you listen to me Genesis hun, and you listen good. I did not promise *shit* to you, okay? I got one fucking thing on my mind right now and that's lifting this fucking hex that has been dogging our asses all the way from Reno. For the first time in I can't remember how long we're finally running a little hot as far as our luck goes…. This goofy fucking bastard appears outta nowhere with an envelope stuffed full of cash and more fucking drugs than we can get through in a month, and you honestly think that the agreement we had is somehow still *valid*? Get real! Shit's *changed!*"

A triumphant look crossed Genesis's face. "So you admit we had an agreement."

"It was barely that! I just said what you wanted to hear because you were getting upset. I was trying to calm your ass down!"

"So you *lied* to me, Lupe!"

Her nostrils flaring, Lupita turned her back to Genesis. In a low, dangerous growl she said, "What is it Genesis? Huh? You seem real fond of this bastard. You wanna fuck this guy, or something?"

"What?"

"You fucking heard me. *Do you want to fuck this guy?*"

"No! Jesus Lupe, come *on…*"

"Only you could have fooled me."

Lupita spun around.

The gun was pointing at Genesis.

"I saw the way you was pawing at him back in the car. Yukking it up while he was sticking his face in your tits. I know you dug guys before I came along... I figure maybe now you see this fool with a stack of cash and a briefcase fulla drugs, and maybe you're starting to get a bit nostalgic for the old *dick*, huh? Is that it?"

"You've lost your fucking mind," Genesis murmured, "And for Chrissakes... Lupe.... *Please*... don't *point that thing* at me."

Lupita snarled, flecks of foamy white spit forming in the corners of her mouth. Her hand trembled.

"Maybe you figured you could convince me to put the fuckin' gun down long enough so that you could finish me yourself? Maybe you're planning on taking off with this fucking asshole! Maybe you're hoping he'll take you back to fucking *Paris*? Planning on running off so you can go be a kept woman, or some shit?"

The colour drained from Genesis's face.

"Lupe... Jesus Christ Lupe what are you *saying*? I fucking LOVE you." Big fat tears started forming in Genesis's eyes. She choked her sobs back as she spoke. "For the first.... time in my fucking rotten life... I love someone who... who loves me *b-b-back*! Who treats me nice... who *talks SWEET to m-m-me*...." She wiped her snotty nose with a trembling hand. "Who doesn't t-t-treat me like I'm some dumb bitch, some fucking *hole* they c-c-can use and toss aside.... Someone who's *guh-guh-good to me*... And you honestly think I'd *luh-luh-leave you* for that piece of shit out there? That I'd fucking *KILL* you? Oh... my... guh-guh-*God*, Lupe... you're breaking my *heart*..."

Genesis placed both her hands on her face and began to quietly cry. Collapsing back against the wall she slowly sank to the floor, crouching in the fetal position, her entire body wracked by brutal, silent sobs. Lupita watched her, her face stony at first. She was somehow shocked to realize that Genesis was actually *heartbroken* by the suggestion that she would double-cross her lover. Genesis was becoming a child in front of her. A challenge to her long-held belief that all human interactions were nothing more than an elaborate confidence trick, another obstacle to be scrambled over on the way to some larger goal. There was no leverage to be gained here, just a pitiful display of genuine despair and hurt. The kind of bewildered pain that can only be born out of love.

Lupita's anger drained from her. She placed the gun gently at her feet. An almost unbearable feeling of sorrow and regret enveloped her. She crouched down next to Genesis. She leaned in to her lover, placing her arm around her. She pulled her close and her own fat, hot tears smeared against Genesis's neck. When the words came they were halting and almost inaudible. Genesis could feel the hot breath brushing against her neck.

"Oh god... I'm so sorry Genesis hun... I'm so sorry.... I didn't mean that shit... I love you baby... I've just... I've just never KNOWN, you know... not since Adolfo died... nobody had ever really.... Loved me, you know? I've had to fight... I've had to kill...steal... do all of that shit... just to get by in this fucked up... lousy... world, you know? It's not that I didn't believe you.... It's just that it's so hard for me to believe... even for a second... that something so ... so beautiful could be happening to me.... Because deep down some part of myself... some fucked up... self-hating part of myself... doesn't believe that I deserve it! That I deserve... YOU!"

For a moment they just held each other like that, trembling and sighing. Genesis looked into Lupita's eyes. Both of their faces were slick with tears. Genesis realized that she had never seen Lupita cry before. In that frozen moment, in the bathroom of the Budget Inn on Sunset Boulevard, Lupita looked more beautiful to Genesis than ever before. When they kissed it happened in a perfect, unspoken synchronization. Their hot, mushy lips pressed together and they could taste each other's tears intermingling in their cocaine-numbed mouths. It was a kiss that each of them felt resonate deep down within themselves. When it was over they broke apart, breathless and trembling. Some subtle tremor had happened in the universe, sending shockwaves spreading outward like the splash of a rock on the surface of a still lake. It was unstoppable now, reaching ever outwards and subtly altering everything in its wake. Lupita fixed Genesis in a very serious stare.

"You're right, Genesis hun. About everything. I won't kill him. This has to stop now. If you want, we can just walk right out. Leave him to it. I'm sure old Jack'll manage just fine without us. Hell, if we just sneak out... he's so fucked up he probably wouldn't even notice we were gone."

Genesis seemed to consider this for a moment. Then she shook her head. "I love you Lupita, but I ain't asking you to be no *saint*. I don't want you changing a goddamn thing about how you *are*. So long as you promise not to *shoot* the bastard, then I say we go out there, beat the living shit out of him, and take everything he's got. In fact I think we'd be insane *not* to rob him, you know?"

Lupita ruffled Genesis's hair, playfully. "That's exactly what I love about you," she said wiping the tears from her face. "You're not just beautiful, Genesis. You got your head screwed on, girl."

There was a sudden, loud crash from the next room. They froze.

"What the fuck was that?" Genesis hissed.

"No fucking clue."

"Sounded like the door just got kicked in. You don't think it's the cops?"

"Oh *Jesus*! No. Just calm down... wait here, okay?"

Lupita picked up the gun. She crept toward the bathroom door and unlocked it. She opened it a crack and peered through.

Looking back at Genesis she gave a shrug. Cocked the gun, opened the door slowly, and crept out.

Genesis picked her way to her feet, and wiped the tears from her face. Hearing nothing she cautiously followed Lupita into the next room. What she saw made no sense. Jacques was naked, sprawled out on the floor. The crack pipe was still in his hand. His face was frozen in a rictus of disbelief. His other hand was curled into a fist. It looked as though he was clawing at his hairy chest.

"What the fuck is going on?"

Lupita was kneeling next to him. She looked up. "Well, you ain't gonna believe this," Lupita said carefully, "But ol' Jack here is dead as a fucking dodo. Looks like a heart attack." She put her ear to Jacques' chest again and stayed like that for a few moments. "Nuthin'," she said finally. "Nuthin' at all."

Genesis covered her mouth with her hands and stared and the corpse. His corpulent flesh had a bluish-grey tint. She could not help but look at his pecker. Her eyes traveled down to the hairy folds where his belly hung over his crotch. She saw something small and red poking out of there. It reminded her of how her Aunt's dog – a horny Pomeranian called Funky – used to get a weird little hard-on every time Genesis rubbed its fur. Every time Genesis had seen death up close, it never failed to amaze her with its banality. She looked away.

"What the fuck do we do now?"

Lupita looked around the tiny motel room. "We don't have much time," she said. "Hun, why don't you pack up the suitcase and check his pockets for valuables? I'm gonna go get the candle and the prayer sheet. We got a fucking ritual perform, and then I think we'd be better get the fuck outta here. Don't you?"

vii

After driving around Koreatown fruitlessly for a while, pulling over here and there so Jeffrey could hop out of the car and talk to the occasional pissed off looking whore, Randal was ready to call it a day. After Pop Gun Eddie's place the trail had gone dead. Randal felt tired and irritable, the buzz from the alcohol long gone and replaced with the sick, throbbing precursor to a same-day-hangover. As he watched Jeffrey gesturing wildly to a disinterested-looking Korean hooker lingering outside a run-down deli, Randal decided that enough was enough. He gave a couple of loud blasts on the horn and waved for Jeffrey to come back. Jeffrey hopped back into the car.

"No luck, huh?"

"Nah. But she did offer to blow me for fifteen dollars. When I told her no, she got real pissy with me. So I told her, *I'm gay, baby. It's nuthin' personal.* You know what she says to me? She tells me that she don't mind, and that she'll play with my ass, no extra charge."

"Nice."

Randal was about to pull away.

"Where we heading now?" Jeffrey demanded.

"Back to Hollywood, I guess. There's no sense in carrying this on. I clocked up six missed calls from Gibby already, so I guess I'm just gonna get back and give him the bad news."

"You got a twenty I could borrow?"

"Sure, Jeffrey. Come on, I'll drop you off wherever you need to go."

Jeffrey shook his head. "It's fine, man. I'll get out here. I feel like walking."

Randal looked at his old friend. It was the early evening, and as the shadows lengthened so Jeffrey seemed to age dramatically. His bluish-white skin seemed even unhealthier now – the only patches of colour were the bloody scabs where he had scratched and picked at his own face, giving him the effect of an acne-scarred concentration camp survivor. There was no spare flesh on him any more. The eyes seemed too big for the face, a face that was all cheekbones and sores. The mouth was that of a little old man, his full lips absurdly big on a maw that was sucked in and almost toothless. His black hair was lank and greasy. An unpleasant thought occurred to Randal. He knew that there was a very good chance that this would be the last time he'd see his friend alive.

He thought back to the day they'd both attended Stevie Rox's funeral. He had been convinced that Jeffrey was dying back then. However after another solid year's chronic drug use it was clear that Jeffrey had actually been comparatively healthy that day. There was still so much flesh on Jeffrey's body yet to be hewn down to the bone. Today there was no place where Jeffrey's skeleton could not be clearly seen poking through rubbery skin. He had been handsome in a fucked-up kind of way when Randal had first encountered him back in *Clean and Serene*, but now his look had moved beyond heroin-chic. He had drifted into the murky realm of death porn.

"Did you say you wanna *walk*?" Randal asked incredulously, reaching into his wallet and pulling out his last bill.

"Yeah. Seems like a nice night for it."

"Walk *where*?"

Jeffrey pocketed the money and looked at Randal with eyes that projected a lifetime of pain and disappointment. He gave an almost imperceptible shrug and muttered, "*Anywhere*, man. It doesn't really matter, does it?"

They sat like that for a moment, just staring out of the car together, dreamily watching the action on the street. Suddenly tired beyond belief, Randal reached a hand across and rested it lightly on Jeffrey's knee. It felt like touching a jagged rock, wrapped in a thin layer of old denim.

"Well you take care of yourself Jeffrey," he said. "Be careful, you know?"

Jeffrey sniffed and shot Randal a wry grin. "Okay, Randal. And you man... Don't let the fuckers grind you down, okay?"

"Yeah."

Jeffrey opened the door, and slowly – his brittle body full of stiffness and pre-withdrawal aches – made his way out of the car. He slammed the door and then poked his head in through the open window.

"As one judge said to the other, be just. And if you can't be just... be arbitrary."

With that, Jeffrey was gone. Randal watched him for a while ambling up the road, another broken ghost on a sidewalk full of such spectres. He seemed at one with his dilapidated surroundings, fading in to a panorama of check cash joints, broken neon signs, shady doorways advertising palm readers and fortunetellers, idling bums, street drinkers, whores and other assorted lunatics. Jeffrey was not alone anymore. Like a salmon tossed back into the stream, he had returned to his own kind and it was only a matter of seconds before he was swallowed up altogether. Before he left, Randal caught something out of the corner of his eye, lying in the seat where Jeffrey had been only moments earlier. Something small, round, and black. Reaching over, Randal found himself holding a small package about the size of a ball bearing. Picking it up and looking closer, he knew immediately what it was. It was a balloon of heroin. It had no doubt fallen out of Jeffrey's pocket when he had been stuffing the twenty-dollar bill into his jeans. It seemed inconceivable to him that Jeffrey would ever be careless enough with his dope to just drop it in Randal's car, but here it was.

He considered getting out of the car to chase Jeffrey down. After all – assuming it *was* an accident – then Jeffrey would certainly be devastated by the loss of the drugs. But he hesitated. He turned the radio back on and found himself listening to America's *Horse With No Name*. He laughed a little to himself, remembering a crackhead pilot he had once spent time with in Cirque Lodge out in Utah who had been obsessed with the song and would delight in explaining the many convoluted drug references he believed to be hidden in the lyrics. That had been years ago, and who knew if the pilot was clean or not today, or even alive? The thought gave him pause. He had been in and out of drug rehabs, hospitals, treatment centres and the rest for most of his adult life. When he was younger he'd always assumed that he would somehow just grow out of this self-destructive need to construct his own version of reality with drugs and sex. But life as a straight, as a citizen, still seemed as alien and far away to him today as it had when he was eighteen years old. What a joke. What a horrible, unfunny, awful joke.

Randal pulled away and headed toward home.

viii

When the phone started ringing, Gibby ran frantically around his apartment trying to locate it. On the third ring he found it, almost buried by a partially collapsed pile of unpaid bills next to his laptop. When he saw who it was, relief flooded his every fibre. He took a long, deep breath to compose himself and then assuming his most professional veneer, answered.

"Jacques! What's happening baby?"

"This ain't Jacques," said an unfamiliar voice. "Your name Gibby?"

"Yes." A note of alarm crept into Gibby's voice. "Who is this, please?"

"It don't matter who this is. Let's just say I'm an acquaintance of Jacques', okay? You a pal of his? I found your card in his wallet. Fat dude, takes dirty pictures for living?"

"Yes, yes...I – I'm his agent." Gibby was gripping the cell phone so hard his knuckles were turning white. "Where is he? Is everything okay?"

"I think," the unfamiliar voice said, "You'd better sit down."

*

In room 23 of the Budget Inn, next to the corpse of Jacques Seltzer, a red votive candle was still burning. Jacques' naked body was shiny and slick, having been vigorously rubbed down with Florida Water. The whole room stank of a mixture of sweat, death, citrus and cloves. As she talked on Jacques' phone, Lupita was packing away any evidence that they had been here at all.

"Here's the deal, Gibby. Jacques is dead. Dude was getting mad high with me, and he just conked out. Fuckin' heart gave out, or some shit. One minute he was fine and the next he was on the floor, not breathing.... Ambulance? Nah, this poor bastard needs a hearse, not a fucking ambulance. Now, you got a pen? I'm gonna tell you where he is. My advice to you is that you come over here first and do a bit of housecleaning... 'cos let's just say if this guy was as much of a big shot as he *thought* he was, then the pigs are gonna have a field day dragging his name through the mud with all of the paraphernalia they're gonna find in here."

"Are... are you *sure*? I mean – are you sure he's *dead*?" Gibby asked in a small, strangulated voice.

"They don't come any deader than this. Now listen. He's in room twenty-three of the Budget Inn. That's on Sunset between Highland and Mansfield. You got that?"

"Yeah, I got it. Okay, fuck... listen, what's your name?"

There was a cold laugh on the other end of the line. "You don't *need* my fuckin' name 'cos you ain't ever gonna hear from me again. Take it easy, and you know, uh… sorry about your friend and all."

With that, Lupita clicked the phone shut. She turned it off again and tossed it on the bed. Genesis was standing by the door with the briefcase full of drugs in her hand. "Ready to split?"

"Sure. One second."

Lupita picked up the digital camera that Jacques had been snapping them with. She flicked through the images on there – there were hundreds – and deleted any that featured her and Genesis. Then as a final thought she pointed the camera at Jacques' nude corpse.

"Say cheese." She snapped a picture, turned the camera off, and tossed it on the bed next to the phone.

"You don't wanna take the camera?"

"Nah. What the fuck do I need a camera for? And anyway… now we done the ritual our luck should be back to normal. I don't need any fuckin talismen from this motherfucker bringing weird vibes into our life, ya know?"

"But we're taking the drugs. And the money."

"That's different. None of that is *permanent*. Give it a month, and all of this shit is gonna be gone. I don't want anything in our lives lingering around that might invite any *spiritual trouble*, you know what I mean?"

Genesis shook her head and smiled. "Tell you the truth, Lupe, I don't have a fuckin' *clue* about what you're talking about. But it's cool. If you say we're in the clear, then I'll take your word for it."

On a whim Lupita crouched over Jacques' corpse and flipped up the eye-patch. Underneath a perfectly normal eye stared vacantly back at her.

"Told you it was a put-on," she muttered to herself.

"What's that, Lupe?"

"Oh… nothin."

She put the patch back in place. Taking one last look around the dismal hotel room Lupita said "Looks like we're all done here." She stood and flexed her neck muscles, eliciting a series of pops and crunches, before heading for the door. "C'mon, Genesis hun. Let's shake a tail feather, I wanna grab some food. It's been a long fuckin' day..."

She kissed Genesis on the forehead and they headed out, leaving Jacque Selzter's corpse alone, cooling on the floor.

X

Randal had just made it back to his place and flicked on the TV when the cell rang again. They were showing *Night of the Living Dead* on cable. On screen a guy was teasing his sister: "*They're coming to get you Barbara...*" He checked the phone and answered.

"Hey Gibby. Look, before you ask... I spent all day out there looking for him. Nobody's seen nothing. If you ask me, he's probably holed up somewhere with a couple of hookers and an 8-ball of coke, and you need to stop worrying. When he's ready he'll give you a call. And anyway, I'm tired man. It's been a shitty day."

There was silence on the other end.

"Gibby? You there?"

"Yeah." Gibby's voice sounded small and weak. "I heard from Jacques. Well, I heard from someone who knows where he is at least."

"Told you. Look man, if you're gonna rep someone as fucked up and irresponsible as this bastard, you gotta stop worrying about him. You're gonna give yourself an ulcer. Fuckers like Jacques will probably outlive us all. People like him... Keith Richards... They're like fuckin roaches, ya know?"

"Jacques is *dead*, Randal. I'm on my way over there now. He's fucking dead. I'm in the shit, big time."

"Oh."

Randal kicked off his shoes, and tossed his keys on the coffee table with a clatter. He fell back into the couch still holding a paper sack from his local bodega and said, "Jesus man, I'm sorry to hear that. I really am."

"Yeah." Gibby sounded like all the life had leaked out of him. "Well look... I, uh, I just wanted to let you know. I appreciate you looking for him. Once I get a proper look at the situation I can let you know the details. I'll call you later, okay?"

"Okay. Take care, man."

Randal closed the phone. He looked into the paper sack next to him, which contained a roll of Reynolds Wrap and a disposable lighter. He'd purchased the stuff on a strange kind of autopilot on his way back to the apartment. He thought of the heroin in his pocket. He closed his eyes, and sighed. Although heroin had not been his drug of choice, not really, Randal knew that this wouldn't have any bearing on whether or not he would smoke it. After all, now that it was here in his possession, was there any other option? What it offered was irresistible in its promise. It offered the chance to feel *different*. That was something Randal had spent his whole life chasing after.

The big lie, Randal knew, was the idea that by smoking this heroin he would somehow fail. Relapse. Fuck it all up. Life wasn't like that. Life was a series of seemingly small decisions that led to other seemingly small decisions. Life was the moment you stopped and looked at the twisting, convoluted path all of those small decisions had led you down. Here and now this small bag of heroin did not represent success or failure. It simply represented a choice: how do you want to feel right now? Where do you want to go tonight?

He looked at the TV again. He watched a gaunt-faced zombie pick up a brick, and smash its way into a car while the woman inside screamed hysterically.

310

He looked back down at the heroin in his hand.

Where do you want to go tonight?

xi

"John Bonham." Lupita said.

"Anna Nicole Smith," Genesis countered.

"Good one. Bon Scott."

"Who?"

"Singer from AC/DC."

"Oh." Genesis looked thoughtful for a moment. "What about Elvis?"

"No. Elvis died taking a shit."

"Oh yeah. What about Janis Joplin?"

"Nah." Lupita took a long sip of her chocolate malt, "She OD'd on heroin for sure, but she didn't choke on her own puke as far as I know."

Genesis and Lupita were finishing up their drinks at Mel's Diner on Highland. They were trying to name all the celebrities they could think of who had choked on their own vomit.

"Lousy way to go," Genesis said thoughtfully, "I mean choking on your puke like that. I mean, the last thing you'd taste'd be your own barf? Jesus fuck, that's *awful.*"

At a table across from them was a family of four with two young kids. As Genesis and Lupita's conversation had grown louder and cruder, Lupita had caught the mother throwing some disgusted looks their way. After the waitress brought the check and Lupita dropped a twenty on the table, she finally made eye contact with the woman and smiled. The woman's cheeks reddened and she looked away quickly.

Lupita got up out of her seat. She walked over to their table. The husband, a perfectly bland looking guy with a powder blue shirt and a wispy moustache, looked like he was about to say something, and then looked determinedly down at his plate. Genesis grabbed Lupita quickly and said, "C'mon, let's get out of here. No point in causing a scene."

Lupita shrugged Genesis away. "Excuse me."

They continued to pretend she wasn't there.

"*Excuse me.*" The husband finally looked up at her. "I saw you looking at us. I just wanted to say... Well, I just wanted to say *I'm sorry* if our conversation offended you. Sometimes I get a bit carried away, you know? You know how it is when you're with the person you love... it's like other people just don't *exist.*"

She turned and planted a long lingering kiss on Genesis's lips. The father and mother sputtered with horror as their two children ogled Genesis and Lupita with open mouths. Their tongues intertwined, wrapped around one another furiously. They finally broke off. Lupita turned her attention back to the family, casually wiping her wet mouth with the back of her hand.

"Here." She dropped three twenties on their table. "Have dinner on us."

"That's... that's really not necessary..." the father stammered.

"Sure it is," Lupita said, taking Genesis by the arm, "I insist. Really."

When they got out to the street, Genesis burst out laughing. "Jesus Christ, Lupe! They looked like they were about to shit their pants."

"Hell, what's the point in good fortune if you can't spread the wealth around a little?"

Genesis kissed Lupita on the neck. As they headed back to the car Genesis said, "Okay, I got a good one. What about famous people who died in plane crashes?"

Lupita shrugged. "Buddy Holly."

"That's obvious. How about Ronnie Van Zant from Lynyrd Skynyrd."

"Big Bopper."

"Rich Snyder."

"Who?"

"Guy who founded *In and Out Burger*. Who you *been*, girl?"

They laughed as they got into the car. They started the engine, and Lupita turned up the volume on the stereo. *"Don't Jump"* by Billy Fury filled the car.

"This is undoubtedly the best rock'n'roll song about someone thinking about throwing themselves off a cliff ever recorded," Lupita said.

"No doubt," Genesis said.

Later they pulled up outside the place they were staying at, a nice little hotel called *The Sunset* in West Hollywood. This was their last night in Los Angeles before they split in the morning for San Francisco and Lupita had insisted that they stay somewhere decent. Genesis had been bugging Lupita to go to the Bay Area for the longest time. Anyway Lupita had some old friends she'd been meaning to look up. With the money and the drugs Jacques had been carrying around with him they wouldn't have to worry about making a dollar for quite a while. It was a rare feeling, to feel free, to feel that you didn't owe anybody anything. It was always fleeting, but sweet while it lasted.

They got out of the car. The night was cool and the air around them was alive with the steady rumble of traffic and the rhythmic chirp of crickets.

"It's a beautiful night, isn't it?"

"Sure is."

"I got a good feeling about us, Genesis hun..." Lupita said dreamily. "I got this weird feeling that everything is gonna be alright..."

She reached down and clasped Genesis' hand in hers, giving it a reassuring squeeze.

Hand in hand, Genesis and Lupita walked off into *The Sunset* together.

EPILOGUE

(From The LA Weekly)

FRENCH DISS

A year after it took the Cannes film festival by storm, RICK KENT ruminates on the international smash hit Black Neon, and the myth and bullshit surrounding the story of the "imploding dimwit", Jacques Seltzer.

Given his virtual canonization since his untimely death a year ago this month, taking a swipe at the controversial movie director / photographer / auteur / over-hyped fraud (take your pick) Jacques Seltzer is not a move destined to win you many fans. In fact my original obituary for Seltzer, published in these very pages ("The Legend of the Imploding Dimwit") earned me more hate mail in one fell swoop than I had previously managed in my twenty year career in cultural criticism. The (admittedly less plentiful) letters of encouragement I also received at least convinced me that I was not the only one who was totally sickened to see the posthumous blowjob being awarded to this guy ever since his much anticipated BLACK NEON finally hit the screen, after fifteen years of intrigue, rumor and delay.

Instead of a coherent follow up to the much loved (by some people) DEAD FLOWERS, what we got instead was the retarded, drug-addled cousin of the wonderful HEARTS OF DARKNESS: A FILMMAKER'S APOCALYPSE (which documented the quagmire that was the making Francis Ford Coppola's APOCALYPSE NOW). The audience is served up a self-indulgent mess cobbled together by Chainsaw Pictures from the raw footage of the unfinished movie that ultimately killed Seltzer. Instead of any kind of overarching narrative, the viewer was subjected to endless shots of Seltzer getting high, copping drugs, having sex with prostitutes, and rambling at great length about art and destruction in his usual pretentious, faux-intellectual manner. This dull mess was strung together with a series of talking heads. The usual suspects – Bono, Henry Rollins, Kenny Azura, Thurston Moore, James Stein, Sean Penn, Charlie Sheen – pontificate at length about Seltzer's supposed brilliance, often offering little more than well-worn platitudes and clichés about the link between genius and self-destruction. This cinematic travesty was soon followed by a tie-in coffee table book of photographs that has spent the past twelve months hovering around the New York Times non-fiction list's top twenty, and the kind of media fanfare that is usually reserved for movies with some... oh, what's the phrase? Artistic *merit*?

For years, people debated what BLACK NEON meant. That deliberately mysterious title was dangled in front of the unfortunate aficionados of Seltzer's work for well over a decade, causing all kind of ridiculous speculation as to what it might actually *mean*. It seems the kind of fan boys who worship Jacques Seltzer's particular brand of faux-artsy hokum are especially susceptible to this kind of manufactured speculation. Blinded by their notion that Seltzer was producing Great Art, they drove themselves into paroxysms of intellectual gymnastics, inventing and superimposing all kinds of profundities into his work when the simple truth was that this stuff was no more profound than the latest piece of shit by Michael Bay. Back when *Dead Flowers* was out, we remember the spectacle of Jacques Seltzer pissing on a Playboy journalist, showing up for an interview – drunk of course – on French national television in blackface, the drunk-driving crash that killed the beautiful and talented Isabella Simonelli, the declarations that he was the messiah, and all the rest of his tacky, shlocky nonsense. Instead of condemning this overweight joker for what he was – a spoiled, talentless moron who had mistaken obnoxiousness for wit, and drug addled stupidity for some kind of Blakean profundity – the public gobbled up this unseemly spectacle, egging him on to ever greater heights of ridiculousness and self-parody.

If we can bring ourselves to flick to the last image contained in the aforementioned bestselling photo-essay "SICK CITY: THE LAST TESTAMENT OF JACQUES SELTZER" (*Fantasmagraphique*) we find an image of Seltzer laying there dead as a dodo, as naked as the day he came into this world except for that iconic eye-patch. The emperor truly has no clothes. Jacques Seltzer, a man who had once been compared to both Andy Warhol and Federico Fellini in the space of a single New York Times review (which says more about the idiocy of the critic making the statement than it does about any alleged talent that Seltzer actually possessed) is finally exposed for what he really is: a fat, dead moron whose heart conked out in a sleazy Hollywood motel room. Not a martyr, not a genius, nor any of the other ridiculous labels that have been thrust upon him since his squalid little death. He's just another dead junkie, and not even a particularly talented one.

What *is* BLACK NEON?

A year after its release I think we can finally answer the fan boys' question.

First and foremost BLACK NEON is an unholy mess. It's a collection of snapshots of drug addicts, transvestites, whores and drug dealers. Unlike, say, Diane Arbus who managed to infuse her subjects with a peculiar kind of beauty and pathos, here street life is presented as a spectacle to be gawked at, even as the line between the subject and the artist becomes blurred.

Does BLACK NEON really mean – as Bono speculates in one monologue – "That twilight place where the darkness inside of Jacques Seltzer finally ignited with the eerie combustion of Creation"? After viewing this sleazy, disjointed mess most people are still none the wiser. In their naivety, they seize upon this lack of narrative coherence as a sign that the movie is somehow intellectually daring and simply operating on a level that our small minds cannot yet comprehend. My friends, the truth is hiding in plain sight. BLACK NEON is a suicide note, the last gasp of a man who knew he had been wildly overrated, a man who could never – with his meager abilities as a filmmaker – live up to the hype he had himself created. Instead of even *trying* he chose the easy route – an OD, an unfinished movie, and let the public fill in the blanks with their own fevered imaginations. "It's better to burn out than fade away," claimed Neil Young, and for Seltzer it was not just better, it was actually a *necessity*. If Seltzer hadn't died trying to deliver this movie then there is no doubt that BLACK NEON would have been the cross his reputation was ultimately nailed to. Instead BLACK NEON remains the shadowy, elusive beast it has always been despite a successful theatrical run and huge sales on DVD and Blu-Ray. One critic has called it the cinematic equivalent of the legendary lost Beach Boys album, *Smile*. I call it bullshit. It's this critic's opinion that if Jacques had have delivered a finished movie, the best he could have been expected to come up with would have been *Kokomo*. And that's being generous.

No, BLACK NEON, despite the puzzling success it has achieved in these last twelve months, is a stinker. It is as vague and non-committal as its title, profoundly un-profound, about as deep and meaningful as a puddle of skid row piss. In other words, it's the perfect homage to the dubious talent of Mr. Jacques Seltzer, one of the most overrated hacks in all the annals of cinema...

*

Randal shuffled slowly forward, moving inch-by-inch toward the customs desk. Weak and shaky, he had downed several whiskies on the plane in an effort to smooth over the insanity of his current situation. Now the combination of the tropical heat and all that booze made him feel unsteady. Sweat poured down his pallid face. Around him was a sea of pale, white flesh in Hawaiian shirts, flip-flops, khaki shorts and sun hats. Just ahead of him a group of blonde, corn-fed girls from somewhere in the Midwest squealed as a tiny crab scuttled past their feet, eventually disappearing underneath a vending machine. The line moved forwards. Randal wondered one more time exactly what in the hell had possessed him to get on that plane. His shirt was soaked through as the last of the meth worked its way out of his system. In his bag he had enough clothes to last him a couple of days at the most. He looked once more at the hastily scribbled address on the scrap of paper in his hand.

Jesus Christ, he was out of his mind.

He was supposed to have checked into a North Hollywood treatment centre called Cri Help this morning. Instead he allowed himself to be talked into this insane rendezvous. From the moment he ordered the cab driver to head to LAX instead of the rehab, Randal's recollections of the day took on the woozy logic of a fever dream. Smiling at the girl at the booking desk as he handed over his credit card. Shooting the last of his 8-ball in an *Applebee's* bathroom, dumping the syringe down the toilet bowl. Talking to a pretty brunette in some faceless airport bar, telling her his name was Tommy and that he was on his way to his brother's funeral. Filing on the plane. The cold bolt of dread as he watched Los Angeles – splayed out before him, glittering and empty as a just-paid whore – submerging further and further beneath a sea of smog. It seemed it was only then that he fully comprehended the enormity of what he had done.

Now, as he edged closer to the customs desk, he considered the possibility of turning around and begging someone from the airline to put him on the next plane back home. Maybe he could tell them that his mother was dying. Who in the hell could say no to a dying mother, for Chrissakes?

"Next!"

Randal looked up. While he had been standing there debating whether or not to turn around, he had somehow worked his way up to the head of the line. He walked up to the customs agent – a pretty but stern-looking young woman – and handed over his passport.

He smiled nervously as the agent swiped the passport and then proceeded to tap disinterestedly on her computer for a while. An insane notion gripped him. The computer would tell her that he was on the lam – from his family, from drug treatment, from life itself – and he would be carried out of here in chains. He was about to break down and beg her not to have him arrested when she looked up to Randal and asked, "Where will you be staying while you are in the country?"

"Uh... I'm staying with a friend of mine. In..." he peered at the scrap of paper again, "Montpelier?"

The girl looked him up and down and then nodded. She smiled, revealing a row of bright, white teeth with a prominent gap in the middle. She stamped his passport, and then handed it back to Randal.

"Welcome to Jamaica," she said.

*

The cab ride took around twenty minutes. He had followed Jeffrey's advice, and avoided the van drivers who congregated around the main entrance of Sangster International airport eager to hustle the tourists over to their all-inclusive enclosures for inflated prices. Instead he walked out to the car park, where he found an idling taxi. The car was old, beaten up. The driver was skinny and weather-beaten, eyeing Randal up and down before gesturing for him to get in the backseat. The driver stopped along the way several times to pick up more passengers and by the time Randal had made it to his destination he was sandwiched in between an old Rastafarian who was singing along to the radio in a sweet, high voice and two teenage schoolgirls in their uniforms. In the front seat was their mother, an enormous woman with a braying laugh, and everybody talked among themselves in an impenetrable patois while Randal drifted in and out of consciousness.

"We're here, man! Wake up!"

Randal jerked awake. The car was empty now. Randal handed the guy a ten and stumbled out onto the roadside without waiting for change. He was on what looked like an unfinished two-lane highway. On the opposite side of the road were lush, green hills that rose up toward the sky until they were totally engulfed by a low ceiling of mist. On Randal's side was the Caribbean Sea, perfect, blue and sparkling. It was late afternoon, and the humid air was cooled slightly by a breeze that blew in from the water. He was standing outside a wooden shack with a hand-painted sign that read *Jerrell's Place*. Music drifted out from the bar, the clinking of glasses, laughter. Outside the shack a child who looked no more than ten or eleven years old was cutting up mangoes with a machete. He walked in.

It was easy to spot Jeffrey. For a start he was the only other white person in the place. He was dressed in head-to-foot black. All eyes turned to Randal as he walked into the shack. Jeffrey was sitting at the bar, tossing back a drink. When he noticed Randal he waved him over. The locals went back to their conversations.

Randal took the seat next to Jeffrey. The far side of the bar was completely open, so you could step out onto the white sand if you wanted. Beyond that was the pure blue of the Caribbean sea.

"So you made it, man..." Jeffrey grinned, "I thought maybe you mighta changed your mind."

"Me too."

The barman, a tall, old guy wearing a neon green vest with a head full of grey dreadlocks came over and filled Jeffrey's glass again. "Same for my friend," Jeffrey said, and the barkeep lined up another shot glass full to the brim with a clear liquid.

"How you feeling?"

"Edgy as hell. Did my last hit right before I got on the plane."

Jeffrey nodded. "You'll be fine. Have a drink, this shit'll blow the cobwebs out."

"What is it?"

"*John Crow batty*. It's a kind of local moonshine. Come on. We're celebrating."

They clanked their glasses, and tossed back the shots. Randal nearly choked. The burning, fuel-like substance made him break out into a cold sweat. "Holy fuck," he croaked, "That shit is disgusting!"

Jeffrey grinned. "You get used it. You know I kicked my dope habit with nothing but a bottle of this shit and an ounce of weed? It was weird. I was expecting the worst cold turkey of my fucking life, but being out here... knowing that I *couldn't* get it, even if I wanted it... it made it seem more manageable, you know? After the third day, I was on my feet. Stayed drunk for about two weeks after that. Now..." Jeffrey looked out to the sea. The surface of the water was still except for the shimmering reflection of the sun. "Now, the very idea of going back on it just seems *alien*."

"You're telling me you're clean? *Really* clean?"

"Clean as I've ever been. I haven't touched dope in six months. Nothing stronger than rum or weed for me, and I gotta tell you.... I never felt better."

Randal looked his old friend up and down. It was true; he looked almost like a different person from the ghoul he had last seen shambling away from him in Koreatown. He was still pale – positively ghostly for someone who had spent the past six months in the Caribbean – but nothing like the translucent white of the old Jeffrey. His face had filled out a little, his hair was clean, and his cheeks were no longer covered in angry-looking sores. The biggest change of all, however, was in his eyes. Randal noticed, for what felt like the first time, that Jeffrey's eyes were green. They'd always seemed a lifeless, jaundiced yellow before. Now they sparkled as he spoke, burning with the intensity of the newly born.

"You're singing a different tune. Last time I saw you, you told me that you'd made your decision. You were gonna stay on using until you croaked."

"That's not what I said. I seem to remember saying something about... *barring a message from God himself* this was my life. Well, surprise sur-fuckin-prise; old God came through for me. I got a message from him all right, clear as day."

"Oh yeah? Go on..."

"It started off with Rachel. You remember this from the last time we spoke, right? Rachel had OD'd and I'd split? I left her there at the hospital when the pigs showed up?"

"Yeah, I remember."

"Well, I told you I had a feeling that Rachel was in trouble. After I saw you the last time, she dropped off the face of the earth altogether. I didn't hear boo from her for months. All of a sudden I get a call from a number I don't recognize. It's her. Turns out she's still alive and I was right – the cops busted her that night. Right there on an emergency room stretcher."

"You gotta love the LAPD..." Randal shook his head. "What they pinch her for?"

"Possession. She told me they planted a balloon of dope on her, the fuckin' assholes. It was the end of the month, you know? I guess they were trying to make their quotas. Anyway, it gets better. When she got downtown, they put her in isolation... away from the general population. I guess they were worried about some asshole queer-bashing her, you know? She was locked up in a cell with this other crazy transsexual chick that was being held over an outstanding warrant. Turns out this chick was a member of this fuckin' church, *The United Church of the Forbidden Gospels of Our Lord Christ."*

"No shit? I heard of that outfit! They're, um, a breakaway evangelical sect who minister to transsexuals, right? They're run by that fruitcake... shit.... Sister Ruth, right?"

"Yeah, Sister Ruth Magdalene! That's them. You actually *heard* of them?"

"Only bits and pieces. I read an article on them in the *Weekly."*

"Well, apparently Sister Ruth usedta be a big hit on the drag circuit, performed under the name Miss Kunty Kinte for years. Then, so the story goes, Jesus came to her in a vision and had her transcribe some gospels that she claims were written out of the bible over the years by unbelievers and bigots. When she came to there were all these new gospels all written out while she was in a trace, or whatever. She's been running that church ever since. Supposedly she believes that Mary Magdalene was actually a tranny, and that transsexuals and cross dressers are especially blessed in the eyes of the lord, and blah blah blah. The regular church has denounced them as quacks, but apparently they're one of the fastest growing evangelical sects in California, ya know?"

The barman came and re-filled their glasses. Randal tossed back another. "You know something, you're right. This shit does get better the more you drink..."

"Told you. Anyway, fuckin' Rachel swallowed that bullshit hook line and sinker. The chick she was locked up with hooked her up with a lawyer on church funds, she made bail, and the next thing you know she's out in Reseda running around in some damn commune with this bunch of nut jobs, calling herself Sister Naomi and telling me that she can't see me unless I quit dope and accept Jesus Christ as my savior."

"So she got clean, huh?"

"Uh-huh. Kicked cold turkey in the cell. This fucking cellmate supposedly *laid hands* on her or some fuckin' mumbo-jumbo, and Rachel claims that the withdrawals just faded away like magic. A *miracle*, she says." Jeffrey laughed, sadly. "That's the fucking thing man, I loved the shit outta Rachel but she was always as gullible as hell. I had to keep her from joining the fuckin' Scientologists after she did a personality test with them one time. So now this bunch of drag queen evangelists got her head all twisted. She was quoting the fucking gospels to me over the phone, man! The only thing I ever saw Rachel read in the whole time we were together was that fucking O Magazine. She useta steal it from the all night newsstand on Cahuenga. All of a sudden the bitch sounded like fuckin' Joyce Meyer on crack."

"So wait. You're gonna tell me that she converted you or something? Where does God come into this?"

"I'm getting to that part. Obviously I wasn't gonna start praising Jesus with the rest of the nutcases so Rachel and I had to go our separate ways. Now Rachel was gone, and I was broke. Things got right down to the wire around seven months ago. I was at the methadone clinic. I'd spent my last ten bucks on my dose and I'm figuring out what the hell I'm gonna do now. I had, like, a day left paid up on my room. I go back there and the guy at the front desk tells me I got mail. Now this was weird. I'd been at the Gilbert for the best part of a year and I *never* got mail there. Figure maybe it's a mistake, but there's my name on the fucking envelope. I almost threw it away, figured it had to be a court summons or some shit. I open it anyway, you know what's inside?"

"What?"

"A check. For thirty *thousand* dollars. You wanna talk about *miracles*? That was God, right there."

They sat in silence for a moment. "*God* sent you a check?" Randal asked, incredulously.

"Nah. *Gibby* sent the check. It was all about that contract you had written up to protect me. Apparently they used a ton of footage of me in some dopey documentary that came out, and I was featured on the cover of this photo book they did. That shit's been selling like hot cakes, and ever since then I've been getting paid to do nothing. You ain't been in touch with Gibby recently? You really didn't know any of this?"

Randal shook his head. "I relapsed. Went out *big time*. He might have tried to call me once or twice the past few months, but you know how it is when you're using. I didn't wanna deal with the outside world, you know?"

Jeffrey nodded. "Well, when the money started coming in, that's when I decided that I needed to change things around. I mean, I could have stayed in LA for sure and put every dollar into my arm. But... I dunno. Something... some voice inside of me told me 'no'. I looked at the map, picked out a place, and just.... went. Before I split I hired an accountant Gibby put me in touch with, and he takes care of shit for me. Every quarter he sends me a statement. It's unbelievable."

"What's unbelievable is the fact that *I'm* here. I must be out of my fucking mind."

"That was God again. Or fate. Or whatever you wanna call it. I had a dream about you last night, that's why I called. And there you were, all ready to check into rehab again, start up with all of that bullshit again. I got to you just in time, Randal. Saved you from yourself. Look around you, man. You're in fucking paradise."

Randal looked around the little bar. A cool breeze blew in from the ocean. The smell of marijuana smoke hung in the air. Glasses clinked, laughter echoed around the cool, wooden shack. "I'm gonna be cut out, you know. This is it. I couldn't stay clean; I just skipped out on rehab and got on a plane to fucking Jamaica. I'm done. I'll never see a penny of my inheritance after this. I bet Harvey's down at the lawyer's office right now, thinking of new and exotic ways to fuck me over."

Jeffrey shook his head, and smiled indulgently. "What you mean is – you're *free*. That money was just a *trap*, man. That's what they used to control you. If you weren't the guy *they* wanted you to be, they'd threaten take your money away. Look at you. You were unhappy when you were clean, you were unhappy when you were sober. You needed to get away from all of that bullshit, Randal. That shit was either gonna kill you or drive you crazy in the end."

Randal shrugged. "You could have a point. I managed to get a bit of money squirreled away. Enough to last me a little while."

"I got a place, the next town over. It ain't a mansion, but it's home. I owe you, big time. If you hadn't set that shit up with Gibby I'd still be scuffling in Hollywood, man. There's no need to work. So long as those checks keep coming, the cost of living here is low..." Jeffrey shrugged. "There's nothing to do, and all the time in the world to do it."

Randal nodded. He looked around the beachfront shack. "So what do we do *now*?"

Jeffrey smiled, and motioned for the bartender to fill their glasses. "We get drunk."

"And after that?"

"You're *free* Randal. I'll help you get over your speed jonze, and then you can do whatever the hell you wanna do."

Randal picked up the glass and held it to his lips. The strong, pungent smell of the alcohol stung his nostrils.

"To new beginnings," he said.

Jeffrey clinked his glass to Randal's. The warm breeze that blew through this place cooled the damp shirt against Randal's skin, and he shivered slightly. They tossed back their drinks, wincing, and then Randal threw his arms back, stretching, beginning to feel relaxed for the first time in as long as he could remember.

"So come on," Jeffrey said. "You're in Jamaica. Nobody knows where you are. Just think... you could be in some crummy rehab right now, eating stale hot dogs and writing some fucking essay about your higher power. Well fuck that... the world's your fucking oyster. What *do* you wanna do, Randal?"

Randal rubbed his face, and yawned. All around him were the strange and foreign sounds of the Caribbean – alien-sounding words rising and falling in a musical synchronization, speaking all at once, voices thick with the mish-mash rush of patois. The soft undertow of song was carried all around the island; booming out from passing cars, the melodic implorations of an old man as he sold plantains by the roadside, the languid, rhythmic pulse of a reggae number crackling from a transistor radio behind the bar. Suddenly there was the rasping, mosquito-like buzz of a moped as it tore past them, the sound rising then falling until there was nothing left but the echo that bounced off the green hills inland, ricocheting out to the warm, still sea. Jeffrey was no longer on junk time, Randal mused, he was on a different clock altogether now. Still, it was a clock that was divorced completely from the rigorous demands of American Time. Maybe that was why withdrawing over here had seemed so easy to him. Maybe the pain originates not in leaving junk time behind, but in being dragged kicking and screaming back into the nine to five constraints of Their Time. Maybe his own withdrawal from Meth Time and into some other time would be as easy as stepping out of his clothes and into the warm blue waters a few feet to his left. Maybe this was what he had needed all along – to be divorced from Time completely. Maybe the drugs had just been a means to an end. Maybe his problem was time itself, and all of this, all of this madness was just a simple attempt to disentangle himself from its all-consuming constraints.

"You still with me?" Jeffrey said waving a hand in front of Randal's thoughtful face. "I told you that stuff is powerful."

"I'm good." Randal said with a contented smile. "Thanks Jeffrey. I got a weird feeling you could be right about everything. I think I finally *know* what I want to do."

Randal sat back and smiled dreamily.

"Oh yeah? And what's that?"

"I wanna do nothing." Randal watched as the barkeep refilled their glasses. He picked it up and held it to his lips. "I wanna do absolutely fuckin' *nothing*."